MONSTER OF THE DAGGER MOUNTAINS

MEREDITH HART

For the monsters

MONSTER OF THE DAGGER MOUNTAINS

He stole magic from a god. She's going to steal from him.

Three years of failed magical studies at the Towers of Silver City have left Kira's future hanging by a thread. She has one last chance to prove herself - a covert mission to capture the former student who murdered a god. All Kira has to do is gain the Godkiller's trust.

Without losing her heart.

Reznyk is a monster. Haunted by the price he paid for the magic he controls, he fled to the Dagger Mountains. When a group of mercenaries discovers him, Reznyk infiltrates their camp, ready to fight or run. Until he meets Kira.

Reznyk's plan to seduce Kira for information turns into a fiery connection neither can resist. Trusting her is impossible. Revealing the truth would uncover painful secrets he tried to bury. But sending her away leaves Kira at the mercy of the Towers, who will stop at nothing to capture his magic.

Reznyk fought a god. But can he fight his heart?

FAIR WARNING

WELCOME, READER!

I'm so glad you've chosen to join Kira and Reznyk on their adventures.

Before we begin, however, a word of warning. This book contains explicit language, sexual content, alcohol consumption, and violence. If this type of material offends you, please choose another book to enjoy.

Also, while this story stands alone quite nicely, *Monster of the Dagger Mountains* takes place in the same world as two previous series: *Fallen Hearts* and *Deceptions and Dragons*. You can find them all at writermeredithhart.com.

Still interested?

Excellent. Move a little closer to the fire, because the nights are cold in the Dagger Mountains, and let's begin.

CHAPTER 1
KIRA
THE MISSION

"We found him."

The room falls silent, all of the small side conversations swept away. Even I lean forward from my place along the back wall, although I know this has nothing to do with me. Nothing interesting ever does.

Fyrris, the Exemplar in the front of the room, allows himself a moment to bask in the sudden silence. His white robes gleam under the torchlight, and the expression on his face suggests he never had any doubt the fugitive Godkiller would be located. He probably looks like that when he's correcting an inferior, but I wouldn't know. I haven't yet had the privilege of receiving instruction from him.

Honestly, I haven't had any privileges. Because, despite all the promises those white-robed Exemplars made when they met me at the orphanage three years ago, I still have yet to show any spark of magical potential whatsoever. I grind my teeth together as the white-clad Exemplar clears his throat.

"Our ravens located him in the northern Knife's Edge

Mountains," Fyrris continues. "In a remote range known as the Daggers."

"Has that been confirmed?" Tholious asks.

If anyone but Tholious dared interrupt Fyrris, they'd be yanked out of the room before they could draw their next breath. But Fyrris just gives his shining star an indulgent smile.

"No," Fyrris replies. "That's why I'm here."

Just like I thought. No one can stay mad at Tholious. A murmur sweeps through the room, and I take advantage of the commotion to run my eyes across him. He's standing, along with the other three gray-robed Disciples who are expected to earn their white robes any day now, with his arms crossed over his massive chest and a stern expression that could be carved onto a marble god. His thick blond hair is swept back, all but one tiny strand that's just begging to be tucked behind his ear.

Fyrris clears his throat. I drag my attention back to something that will in no way affect my life. I'll be peeling potatoes and whacking straw dummies with wooden swords for all eternity at the rate I'm progressing through my apprenticeship in the Towers.

But I am getting closer to what I really want in this place. As long as I bite my tongue, smile, and nod, I can go anywhere I want in the Towers. No one questions a Guard's presence, after all.

"No doubt the Godkiller has placed wards," Fyrris continues. "With the magic he's stolen, he'll be able to detect the presence of an Exemplar in those mountains. However. Perhaps someone with less magical capacity could pass through his wards. He'll be aware of you, certainly, but it's unlikely he'll kill you."

Another murmur riffles through the room. I shift

against the far wall. Seats at the tables are earned, of course, and I haven't even passed the most basic of tests. After three damned years. I watch the men and women sitting in front of me and wonder which ones Fyrris is going to pick to go after the Godkiller. It sounds like a suicide mission.

"Does he have the amulet?" Tholious asks.

His voice is soft, but it still carries through the room, dragging a ripple of conversation behind it. I glance down at my feet; they're starting to ache, standing against the wall like this. Normally I'd be eating with the Guards right now, a position that suits me just fine. For now, at least.

But Benja, my friend and fellow Guard, told me I needed to be here tonight, in the room with all the apprentices and their colored robes signifying the levels of mastery they've achieved over the magic of the Towers. My own faded brown pants hang low over my boots, the cuffs coated with mud from the courtyard, their color advertising to anyone who knows anything about the Towers that I'm not even an apprentice.

"We don't know," Fyrris says. He shakes his head as he speaks, and the blinding white cloth of his robe shivers. I swear, he must use magic to get it that clean. "The ravens could only verify his presence. But we suspect that, yes, he does still have the amulet."

I run my fingers along the back of my arm, interested despite myself. If the Godkiller still has the amulet with him, he's an idiot. You don't run from a crime carrying the weapon that murdered the last old god. Especially if that weapon was stolen from the Towers of Silver City.

"That's why we need you," Fyrris announces.

His sharp eyes run across the tables, and the crowd of yellow, blue, green, and gray robes sway under his gaze. For

3

a heartbeat, Fyrris looks like he's staring right at me. A chill runs up the back of my neck.

But he can't be looking at me. No one ever looks at me, now that the novelty of my arrival's worn off and I'm no longer the woman scooped up from the orphanage to fulfill her glorious destiny. No, now I'm just another idiot without a spark of magic being trained to swing a sword. No one ever looks twice at me, and thank the gods for that.

"We're sending a team," Fyrris continues, as his gaze mercifully moves back to the apprentices. "A very small team, the best of you, will travel to the Daggers, locate the Godkiller's encampment, and determine whether or not he still has the amulet. If he does have the amulet, you will retrieve it."

The room erupts with voices. Tholious shifts, his stern expression melting into something that looks almost resigned. The best of you clearly means Tholious, and everyone in this room knows it. But who's going with him?

"You have, at most, two months," Fyrris announces, once the voices subside. "Once the snow settles, the Daggers become impassable. Before that happens, the amulet and its magic must be returned to its rightful home. Here, in our Towers."

The voices rise once more, a furious storm of whispers following the word magic. It's the greatest injustice the gods ever served, humanity's lack of magic. Elves and dragons play with magical powers all damn day, but humans go without.

A few rare individuals are born with the ability to manipulate the magic the Towers collect and store. The amulet the Godkiller stole must hold the magic of the old god he slaughtered, which would make it more precious than all the gems in Silver City.

Not for the first time, I wonder which one of the four Elites stole the damn thing. They were supposed to be the next Exemplars, those four. They were the best at manipulating the magic the universe keeps away from humans. Until one of them snapped.

Tholious clears his throat.

"Will we kill him?" Tholious asks.

Another shiver runs up the back of my neck. Of course, the Godkiller deserves to die for what he did. Instead of embracing his glorious destiny, becoming an Exemplar, and using his gifts to benefit humanity, he stole the Towers's amulet and destroyed the last creature of pure magic left in this world. Asshole doesn't begin to cover it.

Still, Tholious's question surprises me. The Exemplars are the ones who make life-and-death decisions, not the Disciples. Maybe Tholious is close enough to becoming an Exemplar that it doesn't matter.

Fyrris nods to Tholious. "That will be at your discretion," he says, all but confirming what everyone in the room already knew.

Tholious is going to hunt the Godkiller. And, knowing Tholious, he'll catch the bastard too. That should be enough to vault Tholious into the ranks of the Exemplars. He'll be wearing white after he returns, I'd bet my own nonexistent magical spark on it.

I run my eyes across the room, wondering which of the other brilliant and beautiful apprentices will be joining him. Probably Veloria. She's also a Disciple, and she's almost as gorgeous as Tholious, with her full cheeks and thick, golden braid. Plus, the Guards' rumors claim she had relations with one of those mysterious four Elites who were supposed to become the next leaders of the Towers. Maybe it was even the Godkiller. Maybe he was great in bed.

Well, Veloria looks like she's doing fine now. She's sitting at attention, her gaze fixed on Fyrris with a look of concentration so intense it's almost aggressive.

Great. Veloria and Tholious, the two new heroes of the Towers. According to the rumors, Tholious is as pure as those damn white robes he so clearly wants to wear, but I bet Veloria could tempt him. Just wait until they're alone in the Dagger Mountains sharing all their secrets around a fire or some bullshit, and we'll see how well the Towers's celibacy pledge holds up.

And then they'll murder the Godkiller and recover the amulet so they can return to the Towers as heroes. I yawn.

No one stops me as I slip past Daoug, the Guard stationed at the door, and blink in the sudden gloom outside the apprentice's dining hall. After the heat and chatter inside, the cool of the autumn evening comes as a surprise.

No one even notices me as I walk across the courtyard and slip into a small, narrow hallway. The latch at the end lifts when I press on the handle; the Exemplar who works here isn't good at locking the door on her way out. Still, I press my ear to the door, hold my breath, and count to twenty before opening it.

Nothing. My heart flutters in my throat as I slip inside the darkened staircase, closing the door behind me. I take a deep breath and press my fingers against my vest, tracing the hard outline of my lockpick kit. There's another door at the top of the stairs with a lock I've picked so many times I could probably do it with my eyes closed. Beyond that is a room filled with dusty stacks of parchment. The Archives.

And somewhere in those scattered records is the truth about my heritage.

CHAPTER 2
REZNYK
BROKEN GLASS

I wake to the sound of breaking glass.

My eyes snap open. I gasp in the dark. My hands twist in the rough wool smothering me. Where am I? Who's threatening me?

There's a wave of sleepy annoyance from the far side of the bed, a prickly, disinterested presence. My heartbeat slows as I send a flicker of magic across the room to light the lamp on the far wall. A pool of light spreads across the floor, revealing the same rough floorboards and thick log walls I've woken up to for the past six months.

"Right," I whisper to the empty room. "I'm an idiot."

That prickle of awareness spikes again. I turn to the foot of my bed and meet the indolent gaze of a large, scruffy gray tomcat.

"Excuse me, Sir Xavier," I tell the cat, with a little bow. "I beg your pardon if I've interrupted your slumber."

Xavier flicks a battered ear at me and sinks his head onto his massive paws. Annoyance radiates off him like heat from a furnace. I tug my legs out of the tangle of blankets, trying not to further upset His Highness, and drop my bare feet onto the floor.

It's cold. I run my hands along my arms, trying to fight the chill that permeated the room overnight. Nights in the high mountains are always cold. Especially for someone who grew up in the swamps.

"Look on the bright side," I mutter out loud, continuing my conversation with the empty room. "It's about to get a lot colder."

It's a bad habit for a man living alone: talking to yourself. One of many I've picked up in the past two years. With a sigh, I drag myself across the room. One of these days, I promise myself for the thousandth time, I'll drag a moth-eaten rug out of the old keep, shake the century's worth of dust out of it, and spread it in here.

But, since I'm rather terrible at fulfilling the promises I make to myself, I shuffle across the cold floor, shove my feet into my boots, pull my cloak over my shoulders, and take the lantern off the wall.

The stone keep before me sits wrapped in shadows, the only remaining structure in the middle of what was once an elven fortress for some long-forgotten war. When I first discovered this place, the lone tower squatting beneath three sharp peaks reminded me of a middle finger raised at the world.

It fits me perfectly.

My footsteps echo off the stone walls as I climb the stairs, muttering under my breath about what I'd like to do to whoever broke my wards this time. Damn it, this is exactly why I live with a cat. Because it's not ranting to yourself if you're talking to someone else, and the battered smoke-colored tom I saved from an ignoble drowning counts as someone.

But Xavier has the common sense to stay inside during the coldest part of the night instead of venturing into the ruined keep. Hells, not even the owls want to live in this drafty tower.

I reach the top of the stairs, panting slightly, although whether that's from my climb or the remains of my latest nightmare, I'm not sure. Always the same godsdamned nightmare, every godsdamned night. The heavy crossbow, the silver bolt. The rising sun. The fire.

"Fuck," I mumble under my breath.

At the top of the stairs is the only locked door in the keep, or hells, in all of the Daggers, for all I know. I fumble with the key ring while the lantern's golden light dances wildly across the dusty stone stairs. The key rattles when I press it in the lock. I push the door open.

Moonlight fills the room, dancing across the dozens and dozens of mirrors I've hung on the walls. All of my traps, linked to all of my magical wards, just waiting for someone to trip them.

The lantern's light splashes across the shards of glass littering the floor, making them glow like diamonds. My gut clenches like a fist. I know what woke me, what it had to be, but damn it, that knowledge doesn't make this any easier to see.

Still, I force myself to walk the room, methodically checking every trap, making sure the magic humming through the mirrors is as vibrant as ever. Two of the northern traps have grown weaker, and I take the time to repair them before moving on. The western wall is fine, as is the eastern.

On the southern wall, the highest mirror hangs empty. Below it, glass shines on the floor like freshly fallen snow.

9

I sigh as I stare at the wreckage of magic and broken glass.

It's exactly what I expected. Someone or something has crossed into the Dagger Mountains from the south. And from the look of the broken glass scattered across the stone floor, it's a large group. I set these wards to warn me of any human presence or anything magical. The southern wards exploded a few weeks ago when two ravens from the Towers crossed into the valley.

I should have killed them. It's what I'm trained to do. Hells, it's probably what they expected. I stood on the top of the keep in the light of the rising sun, magic crystalizing into sharp blades in both my hands, and I waited for the messengers of my doom.

"But I couldn't do it," I mutter to the shards of broken glass. "I couldn't even kill the godsdamned ravens."

With a sigh, I grab the broom and start to clean the place up. Those were the last of the mirrors, which is a damn shame. I can tie magic to anything, of course, but reflective surfaces have always been the easiest for me. Now I'll have to make due with polished pot lids, I suppose.

Dawn swells through the windows by the time I finish resetting the wards. My body aches with the strange fatigue that comes from manipulating magic. It reminds me of my time in the Towers, when the magic I used came from silver pipes and chains instead of my own body.

I pull my cloak around my shoulders as I lock the door behind me and walk down the stairs. Two things could have broken my wards: humans or magic. It was magic last time, when the Towers sent their raven scouts.

It doesn't feel like magic this time.

I walk out of the tower and watch morning spill across the forest far below me. Golden leaves wink and shine in that carpet of green, a constant reminder that the nights are only going to get colder.

Somewhere down there, hidden under that cloak of green and gold, are the bastards who broke my wards. Magic flares against my palms, forming blades as sharp as broken glass.

They have no idea what's waiting for them in the Daggers.

CHAPTER 3

KIRA

DID HE SAY WHY?

"Excuse me?" I manage to stammer.

Benja clears his throat. He looks like this is about as awkward for him as it is for me, which is saying quite a bit.

"Fyrris wants to see you," Benja says, for the second time.

"Fyrris?" I blink. "Like, the Exemplar Fyrris?"

Benja nods.

"Did— Did he say why?" I manage to squeak.

"He never does," Benja replies.

Gods above. I haven't done anything to deserve punishment, have I? At least, I haven't gotten caught doing anything that deserves punishment. The Archives flash through my mind, but I always leave things exactly as I found them, down to every messy stack of parchment covering every desk.

No, I haven't left a trail, and I've never been caught. As far as the Exemplars know, the only thing I'm guilty of is failing to live up to their expectations.

My mind drags up the memory of the Exemplars

visiting the orphanage on my twenty-second birthday. When I aged out of Silver City's Home for Unfortunate Children, I had a depressingly narrow array of unpleasant options before me. I chose "no" to all of them and stayed on at the orphanage, helping Dame Serena wash clothes, wipe bottoms, and keep the storeroom stocked.

Until two white-robed Exemplars showed up, invited me to join them in the cramped drawing room, and told me something straight out of every fairy tale I'd ever recited to the unfortunate children of the orphanage.

I am not a nobody. I am special.

The man I now know as Fyrris explained the situation. The Towers do not allow their Exemplars to have romantic relationships, but sometimes, as anyone in an orphanage knows, mistakes happen.

I was the result of one of those mistakes. My parents were once white-robed Exemplars, the greatest citizens of the Towers of Silver City, those few, gifted humans who are able to manipulate magic as well as the elves and dragons.

And I, Fyrris suggested, have that ability as well. If I was willing to work, to really apply myself to the training the Towers provides, I could discover untold potential. He made no promises about wearing one of those white robes myself; my mind filled that part in all the same.

I jumped at the offer, leaving the orphanage that had been my home for my entire life in a matter of hours. I spent the night of my twenty-second birthday in a hard, narrow bunk in the Guards' dormitory, where I would temporarily live until my magical spark manifested.

Where I'd lived for three years now, turning that story over and again in my mind, wondering if I misheard something Fyrris said. Because my magical spark doesn't seem to exist. And the contraceptive tea everyone in the Towers drinks once a month doesn't seem to fail.

Those discrepancies drove me to embrace my role with the Guards. Now, as long as I smile and bite my tongue, I can move through the Towers like a ghost. I've picked every lock in this damn place and searched every room for some hint of the people who must have been my parents.

And then I found the Archives.

Before discovering the lonely rooms filled with parchment and dust, I'd only read invoices and lists of supplies. Poring over the stacks of records in the Archives makes my head ache, but I've kept at it. I've searched half the room by now. Given time, I'll find something about my parents. Who they are, or who they were. Why they had a child in the Towers. What happened to them—

Oh. Oh, no. Another possibility surfaces. I feel like I've just been dropped into freezing water.

Maybe Fyrris doesn't want to punish me. Maybe he wants to dismiss me.

I shiver as I meet Benja's eyes. I can't be dismissed. All this time, all these failed tests of my failed magical potential, I just assumed the Towers would keep me on as a Guard. That's where most of the Guards come from, although they aren't too keen to talk about it. Almost everyone in this dormitory started as an Entrant, failed, and learned how to swing a sword instead.

"Benja," I squeak.

Benja shakes his head, as if he's answering a question I haven't asked. "You don't want to keep him waiting," he says.

Numbly, I come to my feet and stumble after Benja. We leave the Guards' wing, cross the training courtyard with its wooden dummies, and then walk through the main courtyard, which is filled with people going about their morning business. I imagine every head follows my slow, sad progression, even though I know better. No one in the Towers cares about Kira Silver. Not now, and not ever. It's useful, after all, being a ghost.

Benja leads me through a gracefully arching doorway and into another courtyard, the realm of the apprentices, a place that makes my throat feel tight in a way I like to pretend is a reaction to the magic everyone says is in the air, but is probably just garden-variety anxiety.

Whatever it is, magic or anxiety, it's especially strong this morning. I'm breathing in quick little gasps when Benja pushes open the door to the dining area. I expect to see the place filled with robes again, yellow, green, blue, and gray, just like it was when Fyrris declared they'd found the Godkiller.

It's not. I suck in a breath and try not to let my heart explode out of my chest.

Fyrris sits at the head of a table that's been pulled into the middle of the room, his white robes gleaming. Tholious is seated to his right, looking grave and handsome in a stony, kingly way, as usual. And behind the two of them, four men dressed in black stand with their arms crossed over their chests, swords at their sides.

"Kira Silver," Fyrris says, with a smile that really does not fit his face. "You may enter."

I freeze in the doorway. The men standing around the table aren't Guards; I know all the Guards of the Towers. And these aren't thugs or dockside brawlers, even though two of them look big enough to flip the table over with one hand.

No, these four men, with their bland, impassive expressions and simple black tunics, are something else. Something everyone in Silver City knows to stay the hells away from.

Hired mercenaries from the Guild. Sweet, holy stars. Every alarm bell inside my skull starts tolling, even as some distant part of me is flattered.

Fyrris must know what I've been doing. He's discovered I've been reading through the Archives, searching for any reference to the Exemplars who were my parents. And Fyrris hired four mercenaries to dismiss me? What in the Towers is he expecting me to do?

"Please be seated," Fyrris says. There's an edge to his voice that makes a shiver crawl over my skin.

I stumble forward and sink into a chair on the other side of the table. It's a big table; Fyrris and Tholious seem very far away. The door slams behind me. A quick glance backward confirms that Benja left the room.

I'm alone. Alone with an Exemplar, a Disciple, and four mercenaries.

"Very good," Fyrris announces. "You'll leave this afternoon."

I blink. Tholious nods at Fyrris. He's wearing the sort of expression I imagine generals and kings make when they're considering very important plans, and I'm not at all sure how my impending dismissal from the Towers figures into this. I have the strange sensation that I've slipped into another reality.

"Remember, you're hunting direwolves," Fyrris mumbles, as a sort of afterthought before glancing in my direction. "Kira?" he snaps.

"Yes?" I stammer, still stunned to hear my name come out of his lips.Before today, Fyrris hadn't spoken to me since he came to the orphanage three years ago.

"Wear your hair down," Fyrris says.

With that, he comes to his feet. Tholious mimics him, nodding and bowing as Fyrris makes his way around the table. Fyrris is halfway to the door when I realize I should probably do the same, that an Exemplar of the Towers really should be greeted on your feet, but of course, Fyrris ignores me and my scrambling attempts to stand and bow as he walks past.

And then it's just me, four mercenaries, and Tholious.

Tholious turns to me with a sort of frown, like he's about to deliver bad news. My hands freeze halfway to my braid, and my heart sinks.

Is Tholious going to dismiss me? But then, why would Fyrris tell me to wear my hair down? Who in the nine hells cares about hairstyles when you're kicking someone out of the Towers?

"So," Tholious says, looking like he's trying desperately to smile. "It looks like we'll be traveling together."

The room is so silent I can hear my own heart thunk around inside my chest.

"What?" I finally say.

One of the mercenaries makes a strangled sound that's almost a laugh. Tholious runs his elegant fingers through his beautiful golden hair. Now that he's closer, I can see he looks like he hasn't slept well in at least a week.

"Hunting the Godkiller," Tholious continues, with the same amount of emotion people use when they say they're getting a cup of tea from the kitchen. His eyes flicker to the row of mercenaries, then fall back to my face. "And, well, I guess you heard the rest," he finishes.

"Let me explain it," one of the mercenaries says, interrupting Tholious. "You and Matius go...prepare the supplies."

There's that strangled laughing sound again, quickly

silenced when the mercenary who spoke scowls at the man who laughed. The shortest of the four Guild members, a man with hair so bright it's almost copper, joins Tholious at the door. The two of them exchange a glance. Tholious's cheeks flush. They leave together as the man who spoke walks slowly around the table to stand in front of me.

He's tall, this black-clad mercenary, and handsome in all the wrong ways. He's got dark hair, dark eyes, and high cheekbones, the kind of face that would be considered beautiful if he were an elf or a noblewoman. It's not a look I find particularly attractive; I've always been drawn to men who look like marble statues of gods, like Tholious. But this mercenary wears it well.

"I'm Zayne," he announces. He turns to the other two men and waves his hand. "Barrance, Girwin, go collect our shit."

The remaining two mercenaries, who must be Barrance and Girwin, walk through the door. It slams shut as they leave. Zayne grins, then turns back to me.

"Ah, it's cute how they try to hide it," he says.

"Who?" I stammer. "Hide what?"

Zayne tilts his head at me. "Tholious," he says. "Darling of the Towers. Your new hunting partner. He thinks what they've got going on is a secret."

"Excuse me?"

The ground feels like it's tilting beneath me. That sense of having slipped into some sort of dream world grows stronger. Zayne's grin widens, becoming something predatory.

"Don't get too excited, sweetheart," he says. "Tholious only has eyes for one."

I frown. I've been in the Towers for three years, and I haven't heard so much as a breath of a rumor about

Tholious's nighttime escapades. The Guards gossip about damn near everyone else, but not him. The only person in this room he even seemed to notice was that mercenary with the red hair—

"Oh!" I say, with a gasp.

Zayne laughs, a soft sort of sound.

"Like I said," Zayne drawls. "Don't get your hopes up. We're going to be traveling together, tracking this Godkiller, so I want to be straight with you. Tholious is a fine-looking specimen, it's true, but that man's only interest is what's between Matius's legs."

I sit back down before my legs can collapse beneath me. "We're what?"

"Tracking the Godkiller," Zayne repeats, with a hint of amusement. "That's our mission."

"I'm not being dismissed?"

Zayne raises a delicate eyebrow. "Not that I know of," he says. "Why? You got a guilty conscience?"

I narrow my eyes at Zayne and bite back some of the things I'd like to tell him. Fuck off being first on the list.

"That doesn't make any sense," I mumble instead.

The mercenary shrugs in a way that makes me think he expects very few things in his life to make sense.

"Fyrris requested you specifically," he says.

I glare at him. That's too absurd to be a lie, but it can't possibly be the truth. I've spent three years trying to be invisible. I'm not the best, or the worst, at anything. I keep my mouth shut, even when I have to bite my own lips to do so.

There is no reason why Fyrris would choose me for anything. I've gone out of my way to be sure of that.

Zayne grins at me. "Don't get your hopes up with me either, sweetheart," he says. "It's going to be a long trip, and you're cute enough, but I never mix business and pleasure."

I blink. I'm cute? Cute enough?

"Don't flatter yourself," I snap as I shove myself out of the chair. "I'd be more interested in scraping up the shit that's left on the floor of the Tattered Rose after a feast day."

I slam my mouth shut. I've tried so hard to shut up and play nice inside the Towers, hoping against hope that I can discover the truth hiding behind the wide smiles Fyrris and the other Exemplar gave me when they came for me at the orphanage. But it only took a few minutes for this mercenary to get under my skin. Damn it.

Zayne's grin widens. "I think we're going to get along just fine," he says.

Fuck you, I think as I force myself to smile politely.

CHAPTER 4

REZNYK

HUNTERS AND WOLVES

H unters.

My lips pull back in a snarl. I've been watching their encampment all afternoon as rage simmers inside my chest like a pot at the back of a low fire. Hunger, I could forgive, I suppose. Poor families with mouths to feed following deer this far into the wilderness, that I could at least understand.

But this? This is a godsdamned festival.

These mighty hunters have claimed a large, grassy plain that used to be a series of beaver ponds. Several well-groomed horses graze lazily in the twilight, their ears flicking at horseflies dancing around them. Behind them, multiple gaudy tents line the southern edge of the field, with pennants flying above them as if they were commanding armies. Servants bustled around the encampment all afternoon, cooking and cleaning. When the mighty hunters returned, led by a group of rugged guides who are probably charging more shills than I've seen in my life to drag these rich men into the mountains, the servants even cheered.

No, it's not hunger that brought this group to the Daggers. These are trophy hunters, searching for something only the Daggers hold. Rage spikes beneath my skin, making magic boil. A shiver of alarm travels through the horses in the pasture; several of them lift their muzzles to peer in my direction.

I take a deep breath, trying to calm myself. Ever since I trapped this magic inside my body, I've been able to feel the animals around me. And horses are always nervous, even strong, well-fed horses like these. Good. My plan depends on their fear.

The trophy hunters are here for the wolves.

My jaw clenches tight as I cross my arms over my chest. I'd thought direwolves were a myth, just another story to frighten children, until I saw them for myself, crossing the boulder field in the moonlight, followed by—

Enough. Magic simmers under my skin. I pull breath over my lips, then stare at the waning crescent moon as it hangs low on the horizon in its wreath of mist.

I should kill them all. It's what I do, rain death and destruction on the deserving and the undeserving alike. I think of flames, animals and humans screaming as magic destroys this little outpost of civilization within my mountains.

But what good would that be for me? Then I'd have a field of corpses on my doorstep, and sooner or later, even more people would come to clean up the mess.

No, I need to create a legend. A nightmare. I want the Daggers to be a cursed land, a place even the Towers would fear. I inhale slowly, feeling my chest expand. Magic flickers across my palms like the sun winking off a mountain stream. I raise my eyes to the hunters' camp. Firelight paints the canvas walls of the tents; laughter and cheers drift through the open flaps. They must be well into their dinner now, and probably well into a few bottles of wine.

It's time.

I close my eyes and focus on my magic. Somewhere in the shadows, the long, low wail of a direwolf fills the air. I grin in the darkness. I was never a master of illusions, not like Aveus, but I can manage.

One of the horses snorts. Alarm flickers through our connection. It's not enough to convince the horses, my one illusion of a wolf howl, so I send a burst of fear through the magic.

A horse rears and screams. The big tent falls silent. Two guides appear in the doorway. I send another pulse of fear through the magic. Several of the horses buck and snort, suddenly nervous in the growing darkness.

Another illusion wolf howls. This time, one of the hunters inside a tent screams too. Guides pour out of the tents, crossbows and knives in their hands.

I create illusion wolves. Two, then four, pacing in the darkness beneath the trees. One of the guides fires his crossbow. The snap splits the night; the bolt lands in a tree. My illusion wolves come closer.

The horses are panicking now. Servants rush forward, grabbing halter ropes. Guides yelp and bark commands as they pour into the meadow. Torches cast wild shadows over the grass, and I see two of the rich hunters standing in the doorway of a tent, their eyes as wide and white as dinner plates. When I make one of my illusions bolt across the meadow, half a dozen arrows land in the grass behind it.

I pull shadows around me and walk closer to their tents, sending fear through the horses, making my illusion wolves howl and scream from the darkness. There are a dozen illusions now, sleek bodies threading through the shadows, silver fangs glinting in the torchlight. I've made these illusions almost as big as the horses, with teeth like daggers. Nightmares. Monsters.

The twang of a crossbow cuts through the screaming. I stumble as something pulls me backward. My magic flickers; for a heartbeat, the wolves vanish and the night is only filled with smoke and fear.

I look down. A crossbow bolt pins my black cloak to the ground. Panic rattles in the back of my throat. Suddenly, the screams sound very close.

Magic surges forward, surrounding me in darkness. I make my wolves leap across the far side of the meadow, snarling at the torchlight. Arrows and crossbow bolts thud into grass and trees, shredding my illusions. I yank on my cloak. There's a low ripping sound, and I stumble backward.

Great. My last cloak.

One of the horses breaks free from its handler and spins into a tent. There's a great crashing, crunching sound as the poles collapse. The poor beast screams as canvas tangles its legs.

Hush, I tell it through my magic, even as I stumble toward the trees. I try to send a sense of calm across our connection, but it's like tossing a teacup full of water onto a burning house. Even as I make my illusions melt away, the night is full of rage and terror.

I wipe my face and stare at the encampment. One of the tents is burning. The guides have established a perimeter of torches, and servants are rushing between the river and the smoldering remains of the canvas tent. Several of the hunters stand in the grass, blinking at the forest as if they've just been pulled out of one world and thrust into another. And one of them is yelling at a man who I think might be the cook.

"Fuck," I mutter under my breath.

I wipe my hand across my mouth, then pull back further into the forest. Smoke and screams follow me as I melt into the shadows.

Was it enough? I ruined their night, sure. Hopefully I ruined their entire fucking trip. But will the story of monstrous direwolves make it back to Silver City?

Well, hells. Maybe I can nudge it along.

A hunting party that large and that well outfitted? There's only one place they could be heading: the Golden Peaks Hunting Lodge. And if a lone stranger wandered in, bought them a few beers, and acted enthralled by their tales of heroism against fierce direwolves? Surely that would help the legend grow.

I frown at the moon. Dawn is hours away, and rain will come on her tails. I'll want to arrive after the hunting party but before they're all so drunk they won't remember how much I loved their stories.

I sigh, then pull my cloak over my head and sink to the forest floor. I might as well try to sleep now. Tomorrow's going to be a long, nasty walk through the storm to reach the Golden Peaks Hunting Lodge.

CHAPTER 5

KIRA

THIS IS INTERESTING

"Your draw," I declare.

Zayne grins at me over the faded red pattern on the back of his cards. Normally, I'd say anyone with a grin like that would be terrible at cards, but I've played enough rounds with Zayne now to realize it's all part of an act. And the act seems to center on getting just enough coin out of Barrance to keep the dimmest member of their mercenary group playing.

Zayne taps his fist on the wooden table, then raises an eyebrow at Girwin, the third and least talkative mercenary in our merry little band. I can't tell if Zayne and Girwin are deliberately teaming up to fleece Barrance with methodical efficiency or if they're just so good it looks deliberate.

I glance through the open window of the Golden Peaks Hunting Lodge as Girwin studies his cards. It's a beautiful day out there, and it's almost enough to make me wish we were still roughing it. Almost. It took us a full week to get here, and then we spent another five days roaming around the lonely roads and trails that cut through the Daggers.

This is easily the most desolate, gods-forsaken place I've ever seen.

That's not saying much, I know; before this trip, I'd never left Silver City. Still, these mountains scare the nine hells out of me. The first time Zayne said we'd sleep under the stars, like freaking animals, I panicked. I spent the entire night clutching my dagger and flinching at every sound that came out of the looming darkness. Two nights later, we heard wolves screaming at the moon. I almost pissed myself.

But now we're here, in this lovely hunting lodge that's so fucking fancy I'm guessing one night here costs more than my entire life is worth. The tracker the Towers hired, a weasely little man whom Zayne seems to hate, argued that we're more likely to pick up the Godkiller's tracks in the woods, but Zayne pulled Tholious aside for a low, whispered exchange of ideas, and now here we are, settling in for our second night as the only late-season residents of the Golden Peaks.

It beats the hell out of sleeping on the ground, I'll say that. And I even have my own room. It's tiny, but the bed's all mine, and the door locks. Luxury of luxuries. At this rate, I'm starting to hope we never catch the Godkiller.

"What in the hells are we waiting for?" Barrance grumbles.

He takes another pull from his mug of ale. Barrance is the only one drinking. Zayne and Girwin raise their mugs to their lips occasionally, but the level of foamy beer in their mugs doesn't seem to be going down. And I know enough about playing cards to know not to put any money up against someone who's only pretending to drink, which is why the stack of shills in front of me has stayed pretty much the same for the past two hours.

"We're waiting for Girwin to make up his mind," Zayne purrs.

Girwin glances up, gives us a quick glimpse of his teeth, an expression that's more like a feral animal trapped in a corner than a smile, and then taps his fist against the wood.

"Fucking hells," Barrance replies. "Took you long enough."

Barrance shoves a stack of shills into the meager pile in the middle of the table.

"I call," he declares.

Barrance spreads his cards out on the table, revealing his run of tens. Zayne makes a noise in the back of his throat as he looks at his cards.

"And we're waiting for our esteemed tracker to return," Zayne says.

I glance through the window again. Wind ruffles the pine trees across the river, making the shadows beneath them dance. Behind them, patches of snow gleam on the flanks of the Daggers. It's a nice view. From inside.

"You think that little shit's gonna show his face again?" Barrance says.

"If he wants to get paid," Zayne replies. He lifts an eyebrow in my direction. "Ladies first."

I lay my cards on the table. It's not enough to win, but I'm not upset. I don't have much in the pot and I'm still nine shills up for the trip. Barrance whoops like he's already won the game.

"What'd I say?" Barrance declares. "The Towers's punks can't play for shit."

I smile politely as I flip my cards and pile them back on the stack. I'm beginning to think the only reason Zayne brought Barrance along was to beat him at cards. It's a hobby I'm finding increasingly entertaining.

Girwin shrugs, then places his cards face down on the table. Barrance looks like a direwolf who's scented blood when he turns to Zayne. Zayne's face is completely expressionless as he meets Barrance's gaze.

The main door creaks open, then slams shut. I glance up. If that's the tracker, one of us should go upstairs and knock on the door where Tholious and Matius are doing whatever essential work they claim to be doing.

But it's not the tracker. It's a young man with dark hair and a grave expression. His face looks like it's streaked with ash, and he walks across the room with the easy confidence of someone who knows he belongs here, heading straight for the innkeeper behind the bar.

Zayne comes to his feet silently, then grabs his mug of beer as he leaves the table. Barrance stares at him, blinking.

"But what was your hand?" Barrance blurts.

Girwin hushes him. Barrance pouts. I watch Zayne lean against the bar as the grimy stranger and the innkeeper speak to each other in sharp, hushed tones. A moment later, the innkeeper tears into the kitchens like he's being chased by demons. The man ambles over to one of the tables by the windows. Zayne leans back from the bar, grabs his beer, and returns to the table.

"Well," Zayne says in a low voice as he sits down and picks up his cards. "This is interesting."

"What?" I ask.

"Show your damn hand," Barrance snaps.

Zayne lays his cards on the table, face up. Kings and knaves, a hand that could have beaten Barrance twice over. Barrance sputters as Zayne pulls the shills from the middle of the table into his pile.

"That man's a guide for a private hunting party," Zayne says, nodding at the stranger who just burst in through the lodge's front doors. "They were due to stay in the Daggers another week, hunting direwolves near Desolation Peak, but they're coming back tonight."

Zayne hesitates. I take the bait.

"Why?" I whisper.

"Seems their base camp was attacked," Zayne replies. "Direwolves descended last night, spooked the hells out of the horses, and scared the hunters so badly they decided to end their trip early."

"Shit," I mutter as the howls I heard in the mountains echo around the inside of my skull. The room suddenly feels colder.

"Unusual," Girwin offers. It's the first word he's spoken since the game started.

"Indeed," Zayne says, as he collects our cards and shuffles the deck. "And the guide said the wolves weren't alone."

Zayne deals a fresh hand to all of us, which we all ignore.

"There was a man with them," Zayne continues, in a soft voice that's hardly more than a whisper. "A man with long, black hair and a cloak."

"Godsdamn it," Barrance says. "That's our man. That's the Godkiller."

"Perhaps," Zayne says, with a shrug.

"Perhaps?" Barrance snaps. "Who the hells else could it be? Runnin' with wolves sure sounds a lot like magic, and this fucker's got that."

"I suggest," Zayne says, fixing Barrance with a pointed look, "we save our drinking for tonight. The hunting party should be here by this afternoon, and a bit of ale and a few friendly card games could loosen their tongues significantly."

Barrance frowns like he's about to argue but stays silent.

"Find out everything you can," Zayne says, in a low voice, "but don't be too obvious, and don't push it. With the storm coming tomorrow, we'll have plenty of time."

"Storm?" I ask, with another glance out the window and into the clear blue sky.

"Trust me, sweetheart," Zayne says with a grin. "I've seen a thing or two."

With that, he grabs his cards, flicks a shill onto the center of the table, and gives me a smile that makes me think I'll pass on betting this round.

CHAPTER 6

REZNYK

GHOSTS

A full day later, long and nasty doesn't begin to cover it.

My boots are full of water, my shirt sticks to my spine, and rain traces a path down the back of my neck despite the hood covering my face. I've slipped and fallen more times than I'd like to count, leaving my recently patched-up cloak muddy and utterly beaten to all nine of the hells. Good gods above, what I wouldn't give for a decent tailor right now.

Beside me, the river grumbles in similar discontent. The water is brown and swollen, filled with sticks and branches torn loose from their homes and sent swirling down the Daggers. The few animals I've sensed on my trek through today's storm have the common sense to stay hidden. I'm the only idiot trying to travel in this.

And I could swear the Golden Peaks Lodge is further away than it used to be. This lodge bills itself as the last outpost in the wilderness, a place of luxury for serious sportsmen who also happen to be richer than the gods. I've never set foot in it, but I should have enough shills squirreled away to spend a night there. If I can pull off my rich asshole act, just pretend to be Syrus Maganti for the night, at least before he joined the Towers—

Magic screams through my body.

I flinch, pulling back like I've been burned. The river grumbles beside me. Rain beats down on the muddy road. I hold my breath as my heart trembles like a frightened animal in my chest.

That felt like a warning. It was the same spike of pain that yanked me from sleep when the Towers's ravens tripped my wards. I step off the road, pull my cloak tight, and close my eyes. Magic trembles out of my body, feeling carefully around the forest. I touch the low, icy hum of the river, the slow boredom of small, hidden creatures huddled in logs and under stones, waiting for the storm to pass.

And there's a prickle of magic down the road. Fear pulls my throat tight.

I know that magic.

It's the Towers. They're here.

My jaw clenches so tight it aches. I should be flattered, really. They've come for me so quickly? Fyrris must be more desperate than I'd imagined.

And I won't learn anything more standing here in the rain. I force myself to leave the safety of the shadows, to put one foot in front of the other, to breathe as I walk down the last stretch of muddy road to where it meets the more civilized stone of the main pass to Cairncliff.

The Golden Peaks Hunting Lodge shines like a beacon in the storm. Light pours from its crystal windows, carrying laughter and the scent of roasting meat, like a last hurrah before winter sets in. They can only operate for another month, I think, before snow closes down the pass and the lodge with it.

Laughter and light mean the hunting party is here, which means I can mingle with them. I'll see if my illusions worked, and I'll do what I can to spread the tale of the fearsome monsters of the Daggers.

But the air drifting out of the lodge also carries the faint metallic sting of magic trapped in silver. The Towers's magic. Try as I might, I can't imagine anyone from the Towers laughing like that. Is Fyrris here with the hunting party? Maybe tossing back a few pints and taking up a hand of cards?

Gods, that mental image is almost enough to make me smile. I stand in the rain for a moment longer, feeling that thread of magic in the air. It hasn't changed since I first sensed it. It's stable, whatever it is. Whoever is carrying it.

I take one step closer to the lodge, then another. The magic doesn't waver, not even when I'm standing on the front steps. If it's a ward, I'm not tripping it. The magic inside my body relaxes somewhat as I climb the stone steps.

The Golden Peaks's massive front doors are carved with woodland animals of all shapes and sizes, gorgeous depictions of all the beautiful things you can kill when you stay here. When they swing open, warm air washes over me, followed by a burst of laughter. I step into the lodge, my cloak dripping all over the polished stone floor, and scan the room.

There's a huge table near the window filled with older men who look like they've been drinking all day. They're roaring with laughter and smacking cards on the table. I think I recognize two of them from last night, although they sure as hells don't notice me. I probably could have walked in here stark naked, and they wouldn't have noticed.

No, I take that back. There is one man at the table watching me. He's much younger than the rest of them, wearing black clothes and an affable smile on his strangely delicate features. A guide, perhaps? But he's also holding a hand of cards, and he has a decent stack of shills before him. Guides would know better than to gamble with their clients. Or at least, they'd know better than to win.

He's from the Towers, then. Why else would he be here? I shiver under my cloak.

But he doesn't feel like magic. A hired mercenary, perhaps? The Towers contract with the Mercenary Guild when needed.

I turn away, toward the table's twin, which is set slightly further back in the room. This one looks like it belongs to the hunting guides, a younger and smaller crowd who've just started their serious drinking. There's no rush of magic there either, and nothing from the bar in the back.

Two men stand at that bar, both of them leaning in and talking. At first I imagine they're trying to order drinks, but then one of them shifts.

My heart drops like a stone. Every part of my body goes cold. The woman sitting at the bar turns toward me with wide, pale eyes. I almost stagger backward out of the doors that are swinging shut behind me.

Lenore.

It can't be. Lady Lenore Castinac would never—

Magic buzzes inside my skull and flickers beneath my skin, and it's only the dull sense of rising panic that allows me to pull myself together. I can't lose it here. If my magic explodes, then whoever is in here carrying silver chains from the Towers will know in an instant. And if they have the silver chains, I'd be willing to bet all the money in the nine hells they've got nightmare steel too.

The woman slides off her stool, smiles, and presses past the drunk men around her. She's short and curvaceous with long hair the color of fading embers.

And gods, no, she's not Lenore. Lenore would never wear something that plain. Hells, Lenore would never wear pants. Besides, this woman's face is too round, and she's a good head shorter than Lenore.

But, my gods. The resemblance is enough to make me feel like I'm about to be sick.

It can't be a coincidence she's here. The only woman in the Golden Peaks Hunting Lodge just happens to look almost identical to the only woman I've ever loved, the air around me thrums with the angry hiss of the Towers's trapped magical energy, and none of this happened by accident.

I clench my jaw and try to breathe. Gods help me, if I'm going to have any chance at all of protecting what I've found in the Daggers, I need to figure out what in the hells is going on.

And the woman who looks so much like Lady Lenore Castinac walks directly toward me.

CHAPTER 7
KIRA
THE PLAN

"You shoulda seen it!" Thaddyus bellows, for what has to be the tenth time. "My shot was this close!"

He leans in, his fingers a thimble-width apart and just in front of my face.

"And I hit the bastard," Niles says, pushing Thaddyus out of the way and pressing his face so close to mine I can see the back of his throat when he talks. "I know I hit 'im. Then, poof! Damn thing vanished like smoke!" Niles lowers his voice to a stage whisper and rocks back on his heels. "It was magic. A magic wolf!"

The two men crowded around me make another round of impressed noises. I smile politely. I've been doing so much polite smiling today that my cheeks ache. Zayne made it sound like it would be hard, getting information out of the hunting party. Well, that's hilarious. All these assholes have done since they arrived is give us all the information we wanted. And then some.

At this point, at least all of the men in the hunting party shot a dozen wolves each, and every single one of those wolves was magical, and most of the men also shot the mysterious tall man in the cloak.

I can't keep it all straight, and I'm bored out of my gods-damned mind talking to the hunters. I should be trying to get information out of the guides, but Girwin is playing cards with them, and it seems to be an intimidatingly serious game.

Plus, I've tried to ditch Thaddyus and Niles for the past hour and had no luck. I moved from the table to the bar, to the other end of the bar, to a smaller table, and then back to the bar. They followed me the whole time. If I sat down with the guides, Thaddyus and Niles would sit down too. At this point, I'm starting to worry they'll follow me up to my room and talk at me through the door.

This has been one of the most excruciating days of my life. And coming from someone who once cleaned the outhouses at the orphanage after an outbreak of food poisoning, that's saying quite a lot.

I turn toward the stairs and try to mentally summon Tholious. That's the kind of thing someone with magical ancestry would be able to do, right? Summon one of the Towers's own? *Tholious*, I whisper in my head. *You're supposed to be leading this stupid mission. It's your turn to smile at these drunk idiots.*

"You've never seen wolves so big!" Thaddyus declares. His breath is so strong I could probably get drunk off it. "Damn things were the size of horses! Big horses!"

I sigh, then smile politely. Tholious does not appear at the bottom of the stairs, of course. The Towers's precious Disciple has been in a private room with Matius since breakfast, going over supplies, or whatever thinly veiled euphemism for wild sex they used this morning. I frown at the nasty gray rain beating against the windows. It's nice weather to spend all day in bed with a lover, I suppose.

The front door of the lodge bangs open. I jump. Thaddyus and Niles don't seem to notice. A tall, hooded figure walks through the door, then scans the room from under the deep shadows shrouding their face. Whoever this is, they're completely soaked; puddles are already forming on the stones at their feet. Their back stiffens as they turn toward the bar. The door swings shut behind them. This person must be alone, then.

An idea flashes through my mind like a bolt of summer lightning.

It's a stupid idea, but come on. It's not like I'm going to get anything useful out of these mighty hunters. Hells, at this point I could prop up a painted gourd on a stick, and I don't even think they'd notice it wasn't me.

I slide off my stool. I'm doing it.

I'm going to escape their monologues by pretending I recognize whoever just walked through that door. If I have any luck at all, the stranger will go along with it long enough to let me slip up the stairs and into my room. Without being followed by drunk men who want to tell me about all the imaginary monsters they've killed.

I walk up to the soaking-wet stranger and smile.

"Please play along," I whisper under my breath.

I want to explain that if I have to listen to any more drunken hunting stories I'm going to chew my own arm off like an animal in a trap, but I don't have time to whisper all that. I cross my fingers against my arm and hope for the best.

The figure's dark hood bobs in silent agreement. Thank you, gods of hunting lodges.

"Oh, it's so good to see you!" I announce. Loudly.

I touch the stranger's mud-covered sleeve gently and smile up at the hood like whoever's in there is my long-lost cousin returned from the bottom of the sea.

"You as well," the stranger replies, in a deep voice.

He's a man, then. That's no surprise. He must be rich too, to come here. The innkeeper approaches and clears his throat.

"May I take your cloak?" the innkeeper asks.

The hood bobs again, and then the man pushes it back. My breath catches against my throat. Holy hells. I wasn't expecting someone this young, or this ridiculously attractive.

I swallow hard as the stranger pulls off his cloak. Water drips down the curve of his jaw. His long, dark hair is plastered to the back of his neck, and his deep green shirt sticks to his chest, leaving absolutely nothing to my imagination. The innkeeper takes the cloak and offers him a towel. I turn away as the man accepts; I'm not stupid enough to stare as he drags a towel across that face.

Godsdamn it. I thought this stranger would be an older gentleman, someone I could pretend was an uncle or a grandfather. Now I'm going to either embarrass myself in front of a gorgeous waterlogged traveler or have to listen to drunk idiots tell me about their slaughter of imaginary wolves.

I glance back at the bar, where Thaddyus is still talking about the shot he almost made and Niles is blinking at the stool I just abandoned like he's trying to figure out what happened to his audience.

Yeah, I'll choose to embarrass myself. No contest.

"Thank you," the man says in his thick, deep voice as he hands the towel back to the innkeeper.

"Of course," the innkeeper replies. "What can I bring you?"

"A change of clothes, if it's not too much trouble," the man replies as he pulls a pair of thick shills from his waistband. "With a bottle of red, please. And have you eaten?" he asks, turning to me.

"Huh?" I reply, then mentally kick myself in the ass. "I mean, uh. No. No, I haven't eaten. Since breakfast, that is. Which was great," I add, as the innkeeper stares at me.

"Two dinners, then," the stranger says, with a soft half smile that does wicked things to my insides. "Your house special, please, whatever it is. And do you have somewhere that's a bit more private? We have some catching up to do, right?" he adds, glancing at me.

I blink but manage not to say anything stupid as the innkeeper leads us past the bar. Zayne catches my eye and raises an eyebrow over his hand of cards. I ignore him. I've heard all that I can stomach out of the hunters, and by the gods, I've earned a little break.

There are several doors in the hallway that cuts beneath the stairs. The innkeeper opens the first, revealing an elegant private dining room with a table, four chairs, and a large window. Several paintings of forests and rivers hang on the walls; it's a nice change from all the stuffed dead animals in the main lodge. The innkeeper lights three candles on the table, then waves as though he's ushering us across a threshold.

The stranger enters. I follow.

The innkeeper leaves, closing the door behind him, and suddenly I'm in a very small room with a complete stranger. I try to breathe, but all the air seems to have evaporated. The stranger walks to the window, glances out of it like he's looking for something out there in the mist and rain, and then turns back to me.

"I assume you weren't enjoying your conversation at the bar?" he asks.

A drop of rainwater traces a path down the front of his neck and slides under the lacings of his shirt. My mind goes completely blank. I stand there, like an idiot, until the door behind me creaks open again. The older woman who served breakfast this morning steps into the room with a large towel in one hand and a neatly folded stack of clothes in the other.

"Thank you," the stranger says, as he accepts them both.

The woman nods, then leaves. The stranger gives me that little half smile again, and I realize that if he's going to get undressed in front of me I'm probably going to spontaneously combust.

"Pardon me for a moment," he says, with a nod.

He walks out the door. Somewhere in the distance, thunder rumbles across the peaks of the Daggers. Now is my chance to leave, some distant part of my brain realizes. I should slip out of the door, up the stairs, and lock myself in my room until tomorrow.

But my stomach makes a sad little rumble of protest, and my mind conjures up the highly unlikely image of the handsome stranger changing out of his wet clothes in the hallway just outside. Then I imagine the look on his face if I opened the door and found him naked in the hallway. Which is completely stupid, but still, it's enough to make me hesitate. And I am hungry.

I force myself to sit down at the table and run a hand through my tangled hair. I hate wearing it long, but I'm following Fyrris's orders. Even if they don't make any sense. I can't afford to have the Towers think of me as a problem.

The door opens again, and the stranger reappears. Now he's wearing a pale linen shirt that looks too tight around the shoulders and dark, baggy pants. His long black hair is still plastered to the back of his neck, but the rest of him looks reasonably dry. He offers me an apologetic smile.

Well, hells. If I play my cards right, maybe I'll be able to invite him up to my room for a few rounds of Questions and then dare him to take off those black pants. Why should Tholious and Matius be the only ones getting laid on this expedition?

I smile as the stranger sits down across from me.

"No," I declare. "I was not enjoying my conversation at the bar. Thank you for rescuing me."

The man's eyes flicker up. He gives me that same little smile.

"You don't have to stay," he says.

"Oh, I'm staying for the food," I reply.

His eyes widen, and then he laughs. It's a strange, rusty sound, almost like he's forgotten what a laugh is supposed to sound like.

"Well, then I won't be under any illusions about the pleasure of my company," he replies.

"Just don't start telling me about how many monsters you've shot and we'll get along fine," I reply.

He raises an eyebrow. The soft glow of the candles on the table between us throws strange, shifting shadows over his features.

"Monsters?" he asks.

"Apparently, the hunting party was attacked by wolves last night," I say, waving my hand toward the door and the group of men behind it. The candle flames gutter. "But, you know, not regular wolves. Huge wolves. Magic wolves."

He frowns like he's trying to picture a magic wolf. I grin.

"Okay, honestly," I say, "I think they're just really shitty hunters. Both of them kept swearing up and down they shot, like, a dozen wolves, but the wolves all vanished into mist as soon as they were hit."

The man's smile broadens. I feel like I'm seeing him for the first time. Because that's a real smile, I realize. Because the smiles he gave me before, and the one he gave the innkeeper, were the same sort of smiles I gave the hunters when they told me about their magical wolves.

"Magical wolves who vanish when they're shot," he says. "That is awfully convenient."

"Isn't it?" I agree.

The door opens once more, and the older woman walks in with a bottle of wine and two glasses. She fills our glasses, leaves, and then reappears a moment later with two plates piled high with bony ribs in a thick, sticky sauce. She places a basket of rolls between us, and then, almost as an afterthought, adds two small bowls of what looks like a shredded cabbage salad. Topped with bacon.

"Meat, meat, and more meat," I say, after the woman closes the door behind her.

"This is a hunting lodge," the man offers.

"Oh, I'm not complaining," I reply, with a grin.

I would have killed for a meal like this at the orphanage, but I know better than to say something like that in polite company. Or when I'm trying to be polite company.

The man smiles again, that real smile that seems to spread across his entire face, and then he lifts his wineglass.

"I'm Reznyk," he says.

What an odd name. It sounds vaguely familiar, like it's the answer to some important question I've forgotten.

And that's something I can worry about in the morning, when I'm not sharing a bottle of wine with a gorgeous man who's blessedly silent on the subject of magical animals he's shot.

"Kira," I reply, lifting my glass to his.

Our crystal rims kiss with a musical ping.

"To magical wolves," he declares.

"I'll drink to that," I reply.

And I do.

CHAPTER 8
REZNYK
QUESTIONS

S he's nothing like Lenore.

The resemblance fades more and more as she eats her dinner of meat, meat, and more meat and I push the sad cabbage around with a fork. Kira's cheeks are rounder than Lenore's, her body softer. She laughs louder, and longer, and more frequently. Hells, she's talking to me.

Lenore didn't speak to me the first handful of times I approached her. Even after we became lovers, she remained strangely distant, unapproachable, and mysterious, like the snow-covered summit of Victory Mountain that hangs like a mirage over the streets of Silver City.

Still, this physical resemblance is unsettling. Deeply so. There's no spark of magic about Kira, but I'm certain she's from the Towers, just like I'm certain the black-clad men at the tables outside are from Silver City, and probably from the Mercenary Guild. There's just no other explanation for their presence.

But where is the magic coming from? Is Fyrris here? Hiding? Biding his time?

So many questions, and such an easy way to find all

the answers I need. Something low in my gut shifts at the thought, but I can't afford to be squeamish now. There's a woman sitting across from me who laughs and smiles when I talk, and I know exactly how to play this particular game, don't I? Seduction is such an easy trick.

"So, Kira," I say, as I push my mostly untouched plate aside and lean over the table to refill her wineglass. "I assume you aren't part of the magic-wolf-hunting party. What brings you out here?"

She glances up at me, then away. It's a guilty gesture, like she has something to hide. Perhaps I've pushed her too much too early.

"Oh, you know," she replies, with a sudden grin. "Hunting."

I can't help smiling back at her.

"Hunting...?" I ask, letting my voice trail off.

"The usual," she continues, with a flirty lilt to her voice. "Magical wolves. Fencing cats. The fox who stole the moon."

I make a little murmur of appreciation and take a sip of my own wine. It burns on the way down, leaving my cheeks hot. Gods, I need to be careful. I haven't had wine in an age, and I need to stay in control here.

"And what brings you out here?" she asks.

"I'm just passing through."

She makes a soft noise in the back of her throat, like a purr, and looks at me over the rim of her wineglass. I have the strangest impression she's about to declare checkmate. The door swings open again.

The older woman clears our plates. I ask for another bottle of wine, because of course, and Kira nods in agreement when I raise an eyebrow at her. Good. This feels comfortable, and it can't just be because of the wine. No, I can still do this. It won't be—

"There you are!" a voice booms through the room.

I grind my teeth together as magic burns a path across my skin. Keep it inside, damn it. The last thing I need is magic exploding across the table, especially when someone from the Towers is here in this lodge.

Kira jumps to her feet like she's been pinched. I try to smile as the door opens wide behind her and the two drunk men from the bar walk in like they own the place. Great. Drunk, rich idiots. How I've missed that particular aspect of civilization.

"You come here to hunt?" the first man asks me as he helps himself to the seat Kira just vacated.

"Just passing through," I answer, through gritted teeth.

The other man slaps me on the back. Magic hisses and spits inside my body. I turn my hands into fists beneath the table as I wrestle it back down.

"Too bad," he says, as he takes the other chair next to me. "The hunting here's great, you know. Why, just last night, I took a shot at a wolf the size of a warhorse! He was black as the grave, all but the eyes, they were red as flame. And my arrow went straight through the chest—"

I try to smile. Kira skirts the table, all but pressing her back to the wall as she slides behind the first man. When she reaches me, she bends down. Her hair brushes against my neck, and suddenly I lose all interest in the men who've just entered the room.

"Third floor, fourth door on the left," she whispers. "Bring the wine."

I nod and swallow, realizing for the first time that the pants the innkeeper brought me are a little tight in the crotch region. I shift in the chair as Kira leaves the room. I don't mean to notice the way her pants hug her backside, but gods, I'd have to be dead to miss that.

"Damnedest thing I ever saw," the man says, leaning over the table to stab a finger at my chest. "Have you ever heard of anything like that? Anything ever?"

I blink. Both men are looking at me like they expect some sort of answer, and damn it, it's going to take a few minutes and some deep breaths before I'm able to stand up without embarrassing myself.

"Never," I say, trying to channel Syrus.

I never expected to admire him, Syrus Maganti, one of the four Elites who joined me in the Towers. He was the sixth son of the Maganti family, so he'd grown up with all of Silver City at his fingertips. I was ready to hate him when I met him. He was too much like the men who'd run Blackwater, men who thought they owned everything and everyone within the city limits.

But I ended up liking him despite my best efforts. Grudgingly at first, of course, but then with a sort of mad envy. I didn't just like Syrus; I wanted to become Syrus. I'd sought magic and power to protect myself, but Syrus showed me that magic and power can be handled like a toy, a way to wring more pleasure from the world.

Gods, I was an idiot. I try to smile like Syrus, that smug half grin that makes you wonder if he's actually listening or just watching the door for someone more interesting to show up. The men both launch into their groggy hunting stories, interrupting one another to make the wolves more massive and themselves more heroic.

So my illusions worked. Even if the rest of the hunting party are as tight-lipped as priests, these two will spread tales of the horrors of the Daggers all over the finer establishments of Silver City. But there's no trace of magic around them, so I have yet to find the Towers's operative.

Which leaves Kira. She's here hunting the fox who stole the moon, apparently. She doesn't feel like magic, and she doesn't move like a mercenary. So why in the nine hells would she be here with the Towers?

I suppose that's what I need to find out. I pull in a deep breath, shift slightly to make sure the tent in my pants has subsided, and then push back from the table.

"Excuse me just a moment, gentlemen," I say, with Syrus's opaque smile.

And then I walk to the bar to fetch the second bottle of wine and two new glasses before heading to the staircase.

CHAPTER 9
REZNYK
SOMETHING YOU WANT TO KNOW

The third floor is clearly where they keep the cheaper rooms. The second floor had a plush, crimson carpet and rooms spaced so far apart the hallway felt like it belonged to a castle. But the third floor's landing has a beaten-down carpet that probably started life as a deep forest green but is now a sort of seasick lime. The doors here are much closer together, and the roof slopes down on either side, giving the third floor a pinched feeling.

The sense of magic is thicker up here too. Whatever magic the Towers brought with them, and whoever's controlling it, it's here. I might have just walked into a trap. Magic prickles beneath my skin as I step gently onto the sickly green carpet. There's a strange, rhythmic creaking sound in the hallway, like a rusty hinge banging open and shut, open and shut.

Oh. Right. My cheeks burn as I recognize the sound of bedsprings getting a thorough workout. I ease down the hallway on my tiptoes, holding my breath. The metallic creaking is coming from the first door on the right. And so is the warm rush of magic. I hesitate for a moment, long enough to hear the gasps and muffled slapping sounds accompanying the protests of the bedsprings. Whoever came here from the Towers, it's not Fyrris. It's probably not an Exemplar at all; they're sworn to celibacy, and this would be a very public place to break that vow.

I'm oddly disappointed. I'm not even worth sending an Exemplar? And I'm such an easy target that whoever is hunting me can spend the afternoon fucking instead?

I shake my head. This is all good news, really. With any luck, I'll get all my questions answered tonight and slip out before the Towers know I'm here. I pass the door, letting magic tremble across my skin.

The fourth door on the left is open a crack. I pause, my heart pacing inside the cage of my ribs, magic simmering under my skin, and my cock taking quite an interest in the muffled sounds that are still floating through the hallway. My fingers tighten around the neck of the wine bottle; I force them to relax. And then I push the door open.

My mind goes blank.

The woman, Kira, is sitting on a bed pushed against the window. It's the only thing in this little room, just one massive bed under one massive window.

And she's not wearing pants. My mind trips over itself as I try, and fail, to stare at something other than the vast expanse of bare skin and tight curves curled under her body.

"Oh," she says. "I wasn't sure you'd come."

She blinks at me. In the gray light falling through the window, her eyes are the bright blue of the ocean lined with a delicate shadow of kohl that I swear she wasn't wearing when I met her downstairs. Her lips look darker too. Shinier.

"Of course," I stammer.

Hells below. She got dressed up for me. And she took off her pants.

All the blood in my body is abandoning my brain in favor of my cock, and if I don't move soon, things are going to get awkward. I smile at Kira, step into her room, and pull the door closed behind me. Then I look around desperately for somewhere to sit that isn't the bed.

"How did you escape those mighty hunters?" Kira purrs.

She shifts on the bed, patting the wrinkled duvet next to her. And I realize she's not completely without pants; she's just wearing a pair of loose shorts, like something an off-duty Guard might toss on. They make her look even less like Lenore, who would choose an excruciating death over wearing something like that.

"Well, it wasn't easy," I reply, finally abandoning my quest to find somewhere to sit other than a bed in a tiny room that clearly only contains a bed. "I had to fake my own death."

I sink down on the edge of the bed. Kira pulls the wineglasses from my hands. She sets them on the windowsill, then takes the wine bottle.

"I'm surprised that worked," she says, raising an eyebrow at me. "They didn't just continue talking at your corpse?"

"I had to do it twice," I reply.

Kira grins at me in a way that makes me glad these pants aren't any tighter. She lifts the bottle, fills both glasses, and then offers one to me.

"So, here's an idea," she says. "Have you ever played Questions?"

"I'm familiar with the concept," I reply, as I take the glass from her outstretched arm. "Answer the question honestly or take a drink?"

"Oh, you have been a teenager, then?" she replies, with another wicked, wicked grin.

"Is that a question?" I reply. "Should I take a drink?"

Kira takes a sip of wine. It leaves her lips glistening, and for the first time in a very long time I want to know how a woman tastes. How all of her tastes.

"Gentlemen first," Kira says, tipping her glass to me.

"Did you invite a gentleman?" I reply. "Should I move over to make room for him?"

She giggles. It's a delightful sound, like bubbles rising in a glass of frost wine.

"Just go," she says. "Ask away. I'm sure there's something you want to know about me."

I smile at her. There are so many things I want to know. Why is she working with the Towers? What do they want? Why didn't they send an Exemplar to collect me? And what would it take to finally be free of the godsdamned Towers of Silver City?

And none of those are even close to acceptable questions for a woman I'm trying to seduce. So I take a sip of wine, stalling for time, and then ask the least imaginative question possible.

"Are you married?"

Kira lifts an eyebrow at me. "Is it a problem if I am?"

"Don't answer a question with a question," I say. "That's cheating."

She grins. "No, I'm not married. Are you?"

I contemplate taking a sip of wine instead of answering and letting her wonder, but I shake my head. "I'm not. Are you betrothed?"

She giggles again, a sound that makes me feel like I've just taken a shot of whiskey.

"I am completely, and in every way, romantically unattached," she answers. "Does that answer your question?"

I meet her eyes and then, slowly, take a sip of wine. She stares at me before collapsing into another round of giggling.

"Okay," she says, waving her hand at the space between us. "Your turn."

I glance through the rain-streaked window, where the light is slowly fading from the gray sky. "Have you ever been in love?" I ask.

She frowns, and I realize too late that it's a terrible question. I should be keeping things light and flirty, damn it, so that she'll drop her guard, not trying to probe her life history.

"No," Kira says, in a soft voice. She's staring at the wineglass cupped in her hand as though the murky crimson pooled inside holds some sort of answer. "I mean, I've had plenty of lovers, but I never felt like one was any more special than another. It would be nice, I think. Falling in love."

I laugh before I can stop myself. It's a cruel sneer, a sound like the edge of a blade, and I regret it as soon as it's out. Kira stares at me; I fumble to recover.

"It's not nice at all," I mutter.

"Oh? You've been in love?"

"Once," I reply. A shiver runs down the back of my neck,

and I twist my head, trying to shake the memories before they can swarm up and choke me. "Anyway. You've had plenty of lovers?"

Kira smiles again. Some of the chill creeping up my arms dissipates.

"Plenty," she replies. "You too, I assume?"

"Is that your question?" I ask.

"Don't answer a question with a question," she chides, her eyes dancing in the dim gray light. "That's cheating."

I grin at her. "One," I reply.

"Oh, bullshit!" she snaps as she slams her wineglass down on the windowsill.

"Is that your question?"

"There's no way," she says, shaking her head. "You can't look like that, act like that, and only have had one lover. You're such a liar."

"I had no idea romantically unattached women in hunting lodges were so easy to offend," I reply.

Kira looks like she's trying not to smile as she refills her wineglass, then moves over and tops off mine. Her loose shirt falls open even further when she bends forward, which might be intentional. Either way, I lean forward to meet her. And to cover the bulge in my pants. Kira sips from her wineglass and crosses her arms over her chest.

"Let me guess," she says. "This one partner you've had. She's the one you loved?"

I force myself to smile, although my chest feels like a sliver of ice just lodged in there. And then I take a slow, deliberate sip of wine. Kira huffs, then tosses her hands in the air.

"Liar," she mutters.

"Taking a drink isn't lying," I retort. "It's literally how

the game works. Remember? Answer the question, or drink."

Kira looks like she's contemplating slapping me. A sense of panic flutters inside my chest; this whole situation is getting away from me. I want to seduce her, damn it, not piss her off.

"But, as you seem to find that offensive," I say as gently as I can manage, "we could make this more interesting?"

Kira cocks an eyebrow at me. It's an expression that shouldn't be so damned suggestive. "Fine," she says. "I'll bite. What's your idea?"

I set my glass down on the windowsill. "No more wine," I say. "Answer a question. Or kiss me."

My heart freezes. I meant it to sound playful and suggestive, but there's a moment of raw panic as Kira weighs my offer. Magic hisses under my skin. I pull it back. Finally, Kira's lips curve into a smile.

"You want to kiss me?" she asks.

I lean forward, resting my hands on the mattress. Her eyes widen. I hesitate just long enough to let her pull away. She doesn't. I shift forward and press my mouth to hers.

It's just for a heartbeat, just long enough to brush my lips against the soft warmth of hers. Then I pull back, my eyes watching hers, my entire body tight and hard with anticipation.

Gods, the pull of it. I haven't done this dance in ages. I used to be good at this, damned good, giving and taking pleasure as easily as drinking and laughing. But that was years ago. Before Lenore. Before the amulet.

Now, I feel too hot and too cold at the same time. This tiny room is pulsing around the corners, my cock is so stiff it aches, and I realize too late I should have avoided that second bottle of wine.

This all used to be part of it, toying with my own body along with everyone else's, walking the knife's edge of my limits. But now I feel like the knots I tried to tie have just fallen apart in my hands, and when I meet Kira's pale blue eyes, I'm not sure who's doing the seducing anymore.

And then she rocks forward and presses her lips to mine.

CHAPTER 10

KIRA

THAT'S CHEATING

He's a liar, sure, but he's a gorgeous liar, and this has been a very long and painful trip. Spending multiple nights on the ground listening to wolves debating whether they want to kill you before they eat you is not exactly a vacation.

And it's not like things were easy before this trip either. Gods above, I was so happy when the Towers came for me. I could have kissed their feet, those two white-clad Exemplars who told me I came from magical lineage and it was just a matter of time before my hereditary potential revealed itself.

That was three years ago. Since then, I've done nothing but sneak around in the darkness and learn to fight, badly. There has to be something about my family in the Archives, but after all my nights paging through nearly illegible sheets of parchment by candlelight I'm no closer to discovering who they were than I was when I was scrubbing outhouses in the orphanage. And no closer to discovering that magical potential I'm supposed to have. Sometimes, when I cross the main courtyard in the Towers, I feel like

I'm walking around with an axe over my head, just waiting for it to fall.

So, yeah. If there's a chance to have some fun with this guy, I'll take it. His claim that he's only had one lover is idiotic, but do I care? No.

Well, not that much, at least.

I lean forward as he pulls back and push our mouths together once more. He freezes, then opens for me, his lips parting, his tongue sliding over mine. He tastes like wine, good wine, and gods, he knows how to move his tongue. I slide toward him on the bed, then run my hand up his arm.

He groans into my mouth when I sink my hand into his hair, and there goes any last remnants of restraint I might have had. He meets my kiss, our lips pressing and searching, his hand tracing a path up the bare skin of my arm. The space between my legs is already slick and aching.

I break away, panting. His dark eyes gleam in the misty half-light filtering through the window. I know what he's going to say, and I wish I didn't. That stupid line about only having one past lover is a setup, I'd bet my life on it. He's about to ask if I'd like to be number two. Gods, I hate that I'm about to fall for something so damn stupid.

"It's my turn," he says.

His voice is deeper and thicker, almost a growl. For a moment, I'm so focused on the hungry gleam in his eyes that I can't remember what in the nine hells he's talking about.

Oh. Right. Questions. I try to breathe, then nod.

"Of course," I say. "Go ahead."

He gives me that strange half smile, the one that feels almost predatory. I brace myself for the stupid line I know is coming. Would I like to be number two?

Fuck, that's stupid. And fuck yes.

"Where are you from?" he asks.

I blink. That's so far from what I expected to hear that, for a moment, I'm not sure how to respond.

"Wouldn't you like to know?" I stammer.

He leans in. I expect another bruising kiss, the kind I feel in every part of my body, but instead his lips close on my neck. I shiver as my skin pulls taut. His tongue flicks across my neck, and his breath whispers past my ear.

"Answering a question with a question," he purrs. "I've been informed that's cheating."

I shift on the bed, trying to relieve the throbbing pressure between my legs without pulling away from his lips.

"S-Silver City," I hiss as my pulse thunders in my skull.

His teeth close around my earlobe. Holy hells, I haven't felt this wound up in ages. I'm about to explode; there is no way a man with only one previous lover would be so good with his mouth. I close my eyes, swallow, and try not to lose it as his tongue flicks against my skin.

"You?" I ask, in a strangled sort of voice. "Where are you from?"

His hand traces a path down my arm and dances across the bare skin of my thigh, teasingly close to the aching heat in my core.

"Blackwater," he whispers, his breath hot against my neck, his fingers slowly edging up the inside of my thigh.

The sound that comes out of my mouth is more of a whimper than an actual word. I take a breath and try again.

"I— I've never heard of Blackwater," I say, trying to pretend we're still having a conversation and his fingers aren't dancing along the hem of my shorts while his lips trace a path down my neck.

"Of course you haven't," he replies, with a growl that echoes between my legs. "You're from Silver City. As far as you're concerned, the world ends at the far bank of the Ever-Reaching River."

I groan in response and then, to keep from grabbing his hand myself and pressing it against the pulsing, aching heat between my legs, I sink my fingers into his hair and drag him down with me, until I'm flat on my back on the mattress, my nipples hard as stones against my shirt, his lips and tongue driving into me.

He breaks our kiss, and I stare up at him, the contours of his mouth outlined by what little light remains in the storm-darkened night sky. His hair falls over his shoulders, and his eyes gleam in the darkness. Some part of me remembers wolves—

And then his hand is back on my thigh, sliding up the inside of my shorts, and I can't stop the whimpering moan that slips from my lips. His finger parts the wet folds, sliding inside of me, hesitating just before the bright shining ember of pleasure at the crest of my sex.

"Why are you here, Kira from Silver City?" he rasps. "What are you hunting?"

He touches it, and pleasure burns through me, bright and hot as flame licking dried kindling. I cry out; his hand pulls back, leaving me panting.

"Gods," I stammer. "Just take off your damn pants and fuck me!"

He grins at me in what's left of the light. His finger slides back, tracing a path up and down the slick folds of my sex, lingering just before the hot bud at the top.

"Are you going to answer the question?" he asks.

Damn him. He knows exactly what he's doing, but why does he care? He's taking the whole Questions thing way too far. I gasp, a short, sharp inhale, as I try to think of something witty. His finger drifts across the top of my sex, sending another tremor of pleasure through my entire body.

"Oh, fuck," I moan. "That's not fair."

He makes a satisfied purring sound. "You want me to stop?" he says, brushing that finger across the spot that makes my body pull tighter than a bowstring.

"No!" I gasp. "Gods, no!"

"Then answer the question."

I pant, trembling, entirely pinned by this man's long, talented fingers.

Well, fuck it. It's not like he'll believe a word I have to say.

"We're hunting a man," I say, in a voice that sounds like I've run all the way here from Silver City.

"Oh, interesting," he replies.

His finger settles on the top of my sex. Pleasure sears through me like lightning ripping the summer sky apart. He bends over me, his hard chest dragging across my breasts.

"What will you do when you find him?" he whispers.

I cry out as his teeth close around my neck, pain mingling with intense pleasure, and my gods, I'm close. I'm going to explode like a firecracker. My hips rock against his hand, driving into him. The length of his cock presses against my thigh through his pants, and his breath comes hot and fast against my neck.

His hand stops. He pulls away, panting. I make a sound like I've just been ripped from something beautiful.

"Well?" he asks, letting his beautiful fingers slip down the wet, aching split of my sex. "Are you going to kill this man?"

It takes me a moment to even remember how to form words. "He— He stole something," I stammer. "We're getting it back."

"Ah," he replies.

He leans into me again, but this time I'm ready for him. His fingers dance over my clit, pleasure burns through me, but I bring my hand to his waist and shove it down the front of his pants.

He gasps when my fingers brush the head of his cock, and his fingers freeze between my legs. I rub my thumb across the tip of his cock; he shivers. When I draw my fingers down the length of his hot shaft, he makes a moaning sound that feels like it was torn from the very bottom of his soul.

His cock pulses in my hand, and his body curls over mine. His head presses into my shoulder. He gasps like he's forgotten how to speak. When I close my fingers around his shaft, his entire body tightens.

"I have questions too," I whisper into his neck.

He groans. Gods, he's close; I had no idea. I turn toward him, kissing his neck, tasting sweat and lingering rainwater as his pulse beats against my lips. I run my hand up and down his shaft until his hips rise and fall against mine, and his gasping moans thread together, becoming desperate, incoherent panting.

"Where the fuck is Blackwater?" I say, as I nip the edge of his earlobe.

I almost stop touching him, but gods, I'm a liar. I don't give a fuck where Blackwater is. I just want to make this gorgeous man come undone before me.

"It— It—" he pants.

I press my lips into his neck, biting and licking as I thrust against his hips with my fist, fucking him hard with my hand, until his entire body moves with mine and he's gasping against my neck, completely under my thrall, all his questions forgotten.

"Ah, fuck!" he cries. "Fuck!"

His breath hitches, his cock thickens, and I pull back to watch his face as he falls apart in my hand.

His body rolls like a wave, he makes a stuttering sound that's almost speech, and heat spills across my fingers as his cock pulses again and again against my palm. When it finally stops, his head sinks to my shoulder. He trembles against me, panting like he just fought something, and my hand is covered with the heat of his seed.

Well, damn. There goes the evening. I pull my hand out of his pants and wipe it on the sheets.

I'm sure he'll kiss me on the forehead and leave, just like every other man I've ever tumbled with. Once the cock is satisfied, the night is over. I want to smack myself for getting carried away. Instead, I scoot out from under him and prop myself up on my elbow as he gasps like he's drowning beside me.

"Sorry about your pants," I say.

It's almost too dark in the room now for me to see his expression. He sighs, and the mattress shifts as he moves.

"They're not even my pants," he replies.

Gods help me, I laugh. It's not fair that he's gorgeous and funny. At least he's a godsdamned liar to balance it out, because there's no way in the nine hells a man with so little experience would be that good with his hands.

"Here," he says. "I'll show you where Blackwater is."

Great. A geography lesson. I try to swallow the simmering coals of my arousal as the mattress shifts once again.

And then he's next to me. His finger traces a path along my collarbone, sending shivers across my skin and another deep, aching throb through my sex.

"Let's say this is Cassonia," he murmurs.

I hum in agreement. I don't want to admit that I probably couldn't find Cassonia on a map, and honestly, I couldn't care less where Blackwater is. But I'm not going to say anything that might stop those lips from touching my skin.

His hand slides under my shirt, tugging the fabric up as his long fingers trace a path between my breasts. His hand shifts, and his fingers run across the hard nub of my nipple.

"Then these," he whispers against my neck, "must be the Iron Mountains."

This time, my murmur of agreement sounds more like a moan. He makes a soft noise in the back of his throat, like a swallowed laugh, and then he pulls my shirt up to my neck and drops his mouth to kiss the tight bud of my nipple.

"Oh, gods," I moan as I grab the blanket in my fists and hold on.

His tongue flicks across my nipple, dancing and teasing. When he pulls back, the loose fabric of his shirt drags across my bare stomach. It's too dark to see his expression, but his voice sounds like he's smiling.

"So this," he says, "must be the Ever-Reaching River."

His shirt covers my stomach as he bends between my breasts, kissing a path down my chest. My hips twist against the mattress, meeting the hard wall of his chest. His breath is hot on my skin; I'm panting and aching when he runs his hands down my waist.

"And here's the great Silver City," he says, running a finger across my navel.

"Oh?" I gasp. Gods, I want to beg, but I think that's just going to make it worse.

"Mmmm," he purrs against my skin.

His lips trace a path down the curve of my trembling stomach.

"This is Deep's Crossing," he says, after kissing my skin.

He moves to the side, dragging his lips across the crest of my hip.

"The Port of Good Fortune," he whispers.

I'm burning. I'm dying. I know exactly what those fingers can do, and if he doesn't touch me soon, I'm going to go up in flames.

"Blackwater," he whispers, sending sparks across the inside of my thigh and a burst of heat between my legs, "is a little south of the Port. And a little east."

He kisses a path across one of my thighs as his hand drags up the inside of the other. I feel the bite of his teeth hidden behind those velvet lips, and I'd be crying for more if I could even remember how to form words.

Then his fingers slide inside me. My hips buck against the bed as I make the kind of noise that would make a stone god blush.

"There we are," he says, from the darkness. "Blackwater."

His mouth joins his hand, teeth and tongue against the nub at the head of my sex while his fingers thrust deep inside of me, and I surrender to my fate. My hips beat against his mouth, driving into his tongue, and he meets me stroke for stroke.

There's nothing calm or gentle about the way he devours me. No, we're beyond the teasing now, beyond the playing. This is hard and harsh and fast, pleasure burning through my body like waves in a storm, drowning me, destroying me. I wrap my legs around his shoulders and hang on as he drives me toward that cliff, that sweet oblivion. And when I start to crest, he goes even harder, until I swear I see feast day fireworks streaking across the ceiling of this dark little room.

I fall back against the mattress, gasping for air as my soul leaves my body and hovers against the ceiling for a few heartbeats. He kisses the inside of my thigh, then lies down next to me.

"Holy hells," I pant, when I finally remember how to use my lips to form words.

He makes that sound again, the soft, half-swallowed laugh.

"Does that answer your question?" he says.

I don't even remember the question, but I make a little purring sound of agreement anyway. After what he just did with his mouth and fingers, I'd agree to damn near anything. His arm settles across my stomach and his body curls against mine. It feels good, the warmth of his skin on mine.

"Damn," I whisper into the darkness. "It's nice to be number two."

"Hmmm?"

"You know, since you've only had one lover before," I say, running my fingers along his arm.

I'm teasing him and I know it, but come on. It's such a stupid lie.

"Oh," he replies, in the voice that sounds like he's smiling. "Well, that depends on how you define lover."

"Right," I snort. "Gods, you didn't tell me you're a magistrate."

He laughs, sharp and loud. I get the feeling the laugh startled him.

"Magistrate?" he says. "Why in the hells would you think that?"

"What, you're telling me you're not?" I reply, with a grin. "After using technical legal definitions of sex and lovers as pillow talk?"

He laughs again. This time it sounds more relaxed.

"I assure you, I'm not a magistrate."

"That sounds exactly like something a magistrate would say," I mumble as I close my eyes and roll over.

"Hmmm," he replies. "And how would you know what a magistrate sounds like in bed?"

"Shut up," I reply.

His soft laugh brushes the back of my neck, and I sigh. As his arm settles around my waist, I let myself fall into sleep thinking about how damned good it feels to share a bed with someone.

CHAPTER 11

KIRA

HEADING OUT

Something very close to me is moving. I freeze, holding my breath and opening my eyes as sleep evaporates. I'm facing the window. I see the ragged edges of moonlit clouds scuttling across the ebony sky.

The mattress shifts under me, jostling my memories. Right. The man who came in from the storm, Reznyk. The one who claimed he's only had one lover, depending, of course, on how you define lover.

I roll my eyes as his feet tap the floor. He's moving quietly. I make my breathing steady, in and out, so he'll think I'm asleep. There's a scrape against the floor; he's probably pulling his boots out from under the bed. Then the rustle of cloth as he stands up. My muscles pull tight.

Is he going to rob me? I'm not the most likely mark in this hunting lodge, but then again, he is inside my room. I listen to his boots tap across the floor and wait for the rustle of him going through my bag. I tucked a dagger under the mattress, of course, but it's going to be tricky reaching it. And, if I'm being honest, I'm not very good with weapons. In my three years of training, I've mostly tried not to stand out. So, if this man tries to rob me, my best bet is to scream.

I might prefer to die of embarrassment.

There's a creak, and a thin rectangle of light falls across the dark window pane. I see the watery reflection of Reznyk's shirt, then the blur of his face as he looks back over his shoulder.

And then the door closes, leaving me alone in the darkness.

I exhale slowly. He didn't try to rob me. What a gentleman.

As I drift back into the world of sleep, it occurs to me that I have very low standards when it comes to sexual partners.

∾

THREE SHARP KNOCKS against the door wake me yet again. I force my eyes open, meeting the sun's weak light filtering through thick gray clouds.

"Morning, sweetheart," Zayne's voice says from the other side of my door. "You both awake in there?"

I growl something at the closed door.

"Lovely," Zayne replies. "Throw a blanket over whatever you don't want me to see because I'm coming in."

The door rattles, then opens. I sit up in bed. My head immediately reminds me that I had the better part of two bottles of wine last night. I wince, then run my fingers through my hair. Zayne pulls the door shut behind him. I don't even have it in me to ask how in the nine hells he has a copy of my room key. This bastard probably stole a master key as soon as we checked in.

"Ah," Zayne says. He looks disturbingly chipper for how

early it must be. "Mister tall, dark, and handsome left last night, I take it?"

"No, I shoved him under the bed," I growl.

Zayne grins at me. "I love it when they leave afterward," he says. "Nothing worse than those awkward early morning conversations. There's just no good way to ask someone what their name is after you've fucked them, you know?"

"Are you here for a reason?" I ask. "Or is this your twisted idea of fun?"

"We're heading out," he says.

"What?" I glance at the window again. It looks like the sun hasn't even come up yet. "Now?"

Zayne nods. "Yes. Now. Best we leave before the hunting party wakes up and starts to count their shills."

I rub my fingers against my throbbing temples. "Really?"

"Hey, we won those rounds fair and square," Zayne replies, holding his hands up in front of his chest. "We just don't want things to get awkward."

"Right," I reply. I'd roll my eyes, but that would probably just make my headache worse. "What about the tracker?"

As far as I know, the tracker the Towers hired for us is still missing. Zayne just grins at me.

"What about him?" he replies. "I got more information out of five minutes of cards with those idiots than we did in five days of his tracking. But if you want to wait for him..."

Zayne waves his hand in the air and lets his voice trail off.

"Fine," I say. "I'm getting up."

"Excellent," Zayne says, leaning a little closer. "After all the fireworks last night, I think Tholious is in a bit of a rush to leave."

"Fireworks?"

"Tholious and Matius had a falling out," Zayne says, with a perfectly innocent smile. "Matius stormed out of the lodge. I think he spent the night in the stables."

"Really?" I reply, fascinated despite myself. "Over what?"

Zayne shrugs. "Something about whether or not Tholious is going to value their relationship and how they could start over somewhere new. I didn't ask about the details, sweetheart. But both of them look like death warmed over this morning."

Zayne winks, then eases out of my room and pulls the door closed behind him. I groan. Training with the Towers's Guards for the past few years taught me that most of them are absolutely incurable gossips. And what's worse, it made me realize I'm an incurable gossip too. So I drag myself out of bed and pack up my few things, lured by the promise of a bit of drama.

But neither Matius nor Tholious says a damn thing as we set off up a dirt smear that's hardly even a suggestion of a road. The wind is cold, the sky looks like it's holding back tears, and the mud sticks to my boots like manacles around my ankles. Matius and Tholious look like they're trying to outdo each other by setting the hardest pace. Eventually, they pull ahead as Barrance and Girwin fall back, leaving me panting up the mountain with only Zayne for company.

"This pace is fucking ridiculous," I pant when we stop to drink from the creek that's frothing at its banks. "Just how much money did you steal from those people?"

"I didn't steal a single shill," Zayne replies, wiping his sleeve across his mouth. "I did, however, win quite a bit."

"So that's why we're running into the mountains," I reply.

"No," Zayne replies. "We're running into the mountains because the lover boys are having a spat, and they're subjecting the rest of us to the misery of their relationship."

I smile, despite the fact that every part of my body hurts.

"Hey, at least you got laid last night," Zayne says. "He was a pretty fine specimen too. Did you find out what he was doing at the Golden Peaks?"

That's the kind of thing Zayne would have discovered immediately. I feel like an idiot as his name surfaces in my mind yet again. Why is the name Reznyk so familiar? For some reason, it makes me think of the Towers, although I can't place anyone there with that name.

"No," I reply. "He said he's from a place called Blackwater."

My cheeks burn as I remember his lips tracing a path down the map of my body. Zayne laughs.

"Yeah," he sneers. "Of course he is."

"What? That's not a real place?"

Zayne shakes his head, then starts back up the road that's more of a muddy streambed. Wind shakes the trees above us, sending pebbles of cold water down on my back.

"Blackwater was a real place," Zayne says. "It was south of the Port of Good Fortune, a real bastard's den. The whole place burned to the ground about twenty years ago. Now it's a bit of a legend."

"Oh." I frown, trying to think of a place that would be considered more of a bastard's den than the Port.

"We see it all the time," Zayne continues. "Little shits who want to join the Guild come in claiming they're from

Blackwater. It's what idiots say when they're looking to impress someone."

"Great," I mutter.

And just like that, I feel even worse about my life decisions.

CHAPTER 12

REZNYK
SILVER BLOOD

"Shit," I mutter to the wind.

I lower the spyglass and rub my hand across my face. I'm sitting with my back to the wind, hidden by the trees, watching the meadow where I attacked the hunting party with my illusions.

A few raindrops filter through the pine needles to fall against the back of my neck. The clouds have been writhing all day, and the air is heavy with another incoming storm. If the party tracking me had any sense at all, they'd start setting up camp in the meadow now, before the rain really sets in.

I raise my spyglass once more, trace the ragged edge of the forest, and find the shivering figures standing in the meadow. There are five men dressed in dark traveling clothes, two of whom appear to be having an intense difference of opinions.

And there's Kira.

Her cheeks are bright red. Her long hair is pulled back into a loose braid. She looks cold, exhausted, and somehow even more attractive than she did last night. Part of me wants to run down there with my teakettle and a dry blanket. I sigh, then lower the glass once again.

She is hunting me.

I knew it when I first saw her, this woman who looks so much like Lenore in the middle of the Dagger Mountains with men who must have been hired by the Towers. Hells, she told me herself last night.

Gods, I'm an idiot.

My plan to scare the Towers away from the Daggers failed. Clearly, the men in the meadow below weren't afraid of the hunters' stories about magical wolves who disappear when you shoot them.

Great. I glance toward the dark peaks looming above me. If I'm fast, I could slip over the ridge tonight and vanish in the forest on the far side of my valley. Another scattering of raindrops beats against my face and the low rumble of thunder drifts on the wind. If I'm fast, and possibly suicidal, I could attempt to cross the pass. In the dark. During a storm.

But they would keep hunting me. Kira told me they're after something stolen. That's not exactly an accurate description of the amulet, but what else could they mean? I stare at the spyglass in my hands, then back at the clouds hanging heavily above the meadow. If I cross the pass, they might follow me. They might discover the wolves, and what lives with the wolves.

I shiver under my cloak. Strange, feeling like I have something to protect. I could kill them, of course, but—

The taste of wine on her lips. The gasp she made when I leaned forward and ran my fingers up the inside of her thigh.

Thunder rumbles again, closer this time. I lift the glass and run it across the meadow, stopping at Kira. She's talking with the man next to her, who's tall and far too handsome. She leans toward him. Something inside my chest twists painfully. Magic trembles under my skin. I set the spyglass down, cup my hands together, and push magic through the wind and rain. It solidifies against my palms, becoming something cold and smooth and sharp.

I stare at the blade of magical fury I created. We were all good at something, the four Elites of the Towers. Aveus created illusions, Syrus could heal, Pytr controlled flame.

And I killed. I made weapons that sliced the air, weapons that shattered the straw-stuffed targets in the courtyard. I made weapons that would melt inside their victim's body, clogging their blood vessels.

My vision blurs. The weapon vanishes, nothing more than rain and mist. But when I look down at my hands, I can still see it, coated in blood that will never wash away. Silver blood.

"Godsdamn it," I snap.

I push myself to my feet as a rain-soaked gust of wind slaps me in the face. I can't run. I can't kill them.

There's no Exemplar in their little party, which means no one in that meadow knows what the amulet looks like. They won't know what it actually is, or what it was meant to do.

Hope flickers inside my chest, a tiny whisper of a spark in the gathering storm. If I can convince them I don't have it, that I'm not a threat to the Towers, will that be enough? Will they leave the Daggers?

I shake my head. It seems like a fool's hope, that I could reason with anyone sent by the Towers. It's far more likely this whole thing will end in blood. And I don't want to see Kira again—

No, that's not true. Of course I want to see her again,

preferably naked in an enormous bed with another bottle or two of wine to split. But I want to be the stranger in the lodge who rescued her from those mighty hunters when I see her again.

I don't want to see her as what I truly am. The Godkiller.

Magic hisses under my skin. I close my eyes and try not to think about Kira sitting on her bed in those tiny little shorts, her lips dark and her eyes hastily lined with kohl. As if she needed to make herself look any better.

I open my eyes and stare at the meadow. The sun has already dipped below the lip of the mountains; shadows fill the hollow below like wine fills a cup. It was only a dream, the night I shared with her. I'm never going to have a chance to play that role again.

I mutter curses under my breath as I run my gaze over the meadow, wondering where they're going to set up camp. There are no good options, really, but they'd have to be idiots to set up near the river. It's already swollen with rain, and I'd bet all my shills it's going to spill its banks tonight.

But they're not by the river. They're not by the far edge of the forest either, and they're no longer standing in a shivering huddle and arguing.

Something that's almost fear traces a path up the back of my neck as I bring the spyglass up. There, on the edge of the meadow, I catch a fluttering glimpse of the last of the men vanishing into the woods below me.

They're climbing. In the dark and the rain.

Toward me.

CHAPTER 13

KIRA

THIS IS A TRAP

I squeeze my jaw shut to stop my teeth from chattering. I can't quite make out what Tholious and Matius are saying as they argue in low, sharp tones a few steps ahead of us, but I get the gist of it. Matius, like the rest of us, thinks we should stop in this field. Because it's freezing, it's getting dark, it's starting to rain again, and none of us feel particularly like dying tonight.

Aside from Tholious, that is. The darling of the Towers seems to think we should all throw ourselves against the mountains until we break our necks. Another gust of wind blasts down the cruel peaks looming above us. I lean over to Zayne.

"Can't you overrule him?" I whisper.

Zayne shakes his head. "I'm the leader of the Guild's representatives," he replies. "But the Guild is employed by the Towers, and technically, Tholious speaks for the Towers."

"That's bullshit," I grumble. "Can't we at least take a vote?"

The wind howls, tugging my cloak away from my body

and sending me a burst of the argument between Tholious and Matius.

"—just because you think suicide is easier than leaving the Towers to be with me—" Matius growls, waving his arm at the mountain like he's trying to prove his point using the ominous scenery.

Tholious's reply is drowned out by a wet slap of rain from the heavy clouds. Great. I pull my cloak tighter and try not to think about how nice it probably is at the Golden Peaks right now.

"You just want to watch them fight," I grumble to Zayne.

Zanye crosses his arms over his chest, then grins in the gathering darkness. "I've got a bet going with Girwin. Fifty shills say they break up permanently before this trip is over."

"That's disgusting!" I say, smacking him on the arm.

"Tell that to my bank account," he replies.

Matius stomps past me, his hood pulled low over his face and every line of his body tight with rage. Tholious turns toward the rest of us and clears his throat. His cheeks are flush, his pale hair is flat against his head, and rain streaks down his cheeks like tears. I can't help but think of what I just overheard about suicide.

"We push on," Tholious declares.

"Fucking bullshit," Matius mutters under his breath.

"This is my expedition," Tholious replies.

Tholious is looking at all of us, but I think he's only really seeing Matius. For a heartbeat the air between them is thick, like it's about to ignite, and then Matius turns away and the moment dies. Tholious picks his bag up and turns toward the mountains. There are two paths out of this valley, the hunters said. They explored the easier route and didn't find any direwolves or magical, murderous fugitives. That leaves the steeper, narrower path for us, the one that leads to the base of Desolation Peak.

Great. I sigh as I step into line behind Tholious.

"See," Zayne whispers as Tholious vanishes into the darkness beneath the pines. "This is why I never mix business and pleasure."

I growl at him, then turn my attention to not dying. But, as I drag my exhausted feet up the mud-choked path, I have to admit the man has a point. The rain picks up as the light fades from the sky, and soon we're climbing in the dark, using rain-slick tree trunks to pull ourselves up a slope that's all tangled roots and boulders that hit right in the shins. Behind me, Matius is uttering a string of curses whose sheer vulgar creativity would be impressive under any other circumstance, and I'm playing a fun little game with myself called *Is this the most miserable thing I've ever done?*

Yes, I determine after yet another boulder bites me in the kneecap. I'd rather clean the orphanage latrines every single day for the rest of my life than be here right now. The Daggers, I decide, are as close to the nine hells as I've ever come.

"Sweet screaming gods," Zayne pants from in front of me. "Finally."

I look away from my feet for the first time in hours. We've reached the top of a small ridge. The sharp edges of Desolation Peak glint in patchy moonlight that filters through the clouds. From this angle, Desolation Peak is the first in a string of mountains leading off into indecipherable darkness.

"You're fucking kidding me," Matius announces.

I turn away from the mountain and see a tower.

My breath catches in the back of my throat just as a distant flash of lightning paints the underside of the storm clouds piled over the valley behind us. The tower clings to the far edge of the ridge like it's holding on for dear life.

And, at the base of the dark stone monolith, there's the warm orange glow of a fire.

Someone is waiting for us.

Another shiver forces its way through my body. Suddenly, standing on the edge of a mountain in the rain doesn't seem so bad. Because we came here to hunt the man who killed an old god, and that ugly stone fortress perched beneath the mountains looks exactly like the kind of place he would be hiding.

Or, not hiding. Waiting, like a spider waits in the middle of its web.

Tholious clears his throat, but whatever he might have said is lost in another blast of wind and rain that hits my face like needles of ice.

"Great," Zayne mutters. "So much for stealth. That fucker clearly knows we're coming."

I turn from the tower to the dark forest below me. Somewhere down there is the Golden Peaks Hunting Lodge, with the warm bed where I spent part of last night curled in the arms of a gorgeous man who was so polite he didn't even rob me on his way out.

And what are the chances that I could find that place again on my own? Without slipping in the mud and breaking my neck or getting hopelessly lost in these damn mountains? With a sigh, I bring my gaze back to the ground and concentrate on following Tholious as he plods slowly toward the bright orange glow at the base of the tower.

As we follow the narrow lip of the ridge, the fire tucked inside the bottom of the tower casts its warm glow over rain-lashed trees and slick stones. Our slow progress gradually reveals an arched opening at the base of the structure that seems completely unguarded. Like there's just a roaring fire inside a cozy, welcoming shelter in the middle of the uninhabited Dagger Mountains for absolutely no reason.

"Okay," I whisper. "This is a trap, right?"

"Of course it's a trap," Matius hisses from behind me.

"And we're walking right into it," Zayne replies.

Tholious stops, perhaps sensing some of the fear that's radiating off of my body, and the mercenaries gather behind him. I place myself between Zayne and the nearest boulder, just in case I can hide from the Godkiller who robbed the Towers.

"Hello?" Tholious calls.

Zayne makes a soft choking noise, like he's trying not to laugh, and I have to agree with him. Hello? That's a bold opening move, Tholious.

A figure appears in the doorway. I freeze; the night suddenly feels much colder. With the fire behind him, I can't make out the man's features, but he looks massive.

"Hello," the figure replies.

Shit. Something about that voice—

"Master Reznyk Thorne," Tholious replies.

Oh shit, shit, shit. I make a strangled gasping sound, then slam my mouth closed.

That's why the name Reznyk was familiar. Reznyk Thorne was one of the four Elites. I never knew which one of the four stole the amulet, and I never had a damn thing to do with the Elites before they vanished from the Towers, so his name didn't exactly sink in.

Still, how could I have missed this?

"We come from the Towers of Silver City," Tholious

continues, in a voice that's far more confident than our situation actually warrants. He's standing on the Godkiller's doorstep, covered in mud and flanked by four exhausted, drenched mercenaries. Plus me. He should probably start apologizing, or maybe begging for his life.

Tholious falls silent. Another bolt of lightning dances across the sky, throwing the world into sudden silver light.

And it's unmistakable. The man standing in the archway of the evil-looking ruined tower in the middle of the Dagger Mountains is the same man I invited up to my room last night. Zayne whistles, soft and low under his breath.

"Holy hells," Zayne whispers. "You fucked the Godkiller."

"Shut up," I hiss.

"You're lucky he didn't kill you," Zayne continues.

"Stop," I growl as thunder rumbles across the mountains.

"At least now we know what he was doing in the lodge last night," Zayne says, under his breath. "Did he want you to whisper sensitive information about the Towers as foreplay?"

My cheeks burn; thank the gods it's too dark for him to see. I drive my elbow into Zayne's ribs. The bastard doesn't even flinch.

"We've come to request an audience," Tholious announces, oblivious to the way I'm trying to murder Zayne with my elbow.

"Really?" Reznyk replies. "In this weather?"

Tholious falls silent. Reznyk leans against the side of the arched entryway into the tower. Firelight plays across the curve of his full lips as he crosses his arms over his chest and raises an eyebrow. He looks perfectly satisfied, like he'll wait all night while Tholious stammers in the rain.

"Perhaps we could discuss this in the morning," Zayne calls.

"Excellent idea," Reznyk purrs.

He doesn't move. The warm glow of the fire licks his features and plays across the folds of his cloak and the long, dark hair curling around his shoulders. He looks dry, warm, and somehow even more murderously sexy than he did last night. Thunder rumbles in the distance, echoing off the peaks surrounding the tower. I shiver beneath layers of wet cloth. Zayne whispers something that sounds like *fuck*. Finally, Tholious speaks.

"May we seek shelter here?" Tholious asks.

His voice is softer, like he's lost some of the cocky bravado he first had when he announced us. Reznyk shrugs, as if it's all the same to him whether we stay in the rain or come by the fire he clearly lit to lure us in.

"For tonight only," Reznyk says. "And do not climb the stairs. I doubt you'd like what you'd find," he finishes, with a wicked grin.

With that, he retreats behind the curved entrance. There's the sound of a door slamming shut, and then we all stare at each other as rain howls around the tower.

"Fuck it," Zayne mutters. "Let's go in."

Zayne pushes past me, and the other mercenaries follow. Matius gives Tholious so much space it would be funny under any other circumstance.

And we all walk directly into the trap.

CHAPTER 14

REZNYK

YOU HAVE SOMETHING WE WANT

As I expected, I didn't get much sleep.

After climbing down the broken wall from the second story of the keep and crossing the grass to my cabin, I pulled the shades so the group from the Towers wouldn't see firelight coming from the cabin's windows, even though I didn't honestly expect anyone from that group to investigate my tiny wood cabin. They have every reason to believe I live in the keep, after all. Isn't that drafty old ruin exactly where a Godkiller would live? Besides, I told them not to climb the stairs.

I laugh, although it sounds cold and hollow on my lips. But it's the truth; they won't like what they'll find if they poke around. That ruined keep is filled with broken furniture and cold stone. Even if they manage to break the lock on the highest floor, they'll only find a room filled with mirrors, and I'm not sure the blond who called me Master Thorne has enough magical training to recognize my wards, even if he finds them.

Honestly, it's a little insulting. They didn't even send an Exemplar to come collect me. I think I recognize that blond from the Towers, although we were discouraged from socializing with the Entrants and Novices, especially after Syrus seduced one of them. Still, there's something about his bland good looks that seems familiar, and the buzz of magic centered on him.

And Kira looked like she was considering bolting off the cliff.

Great. Nice to have that effect on women.

I sigh, force myself up from the table, and peek through my curtains. The eastern horizon holds a blush of pink beneath a racing scrum of clouds. It's going to be another unsettled day, and the mountainside will still be slick with mud. It will not be a good day for traveling.

Which shouldn't bother me. These people need to leave the Dagger Mountains. Now. So what if they break their necks on the way? The important thing is that they scurry out of here before they can get close to the wolf pack, or close to what the wolf pack is hiding.

I pull my cloak from the wall, shake it gently, and tug it over my shoulders. Then I ease the door open, slip outside of my cabin, and walk around the back of the keep. Wind tugs at my cloak, heavy with the promise of yet more rain. I spare a glance at my garden, which looks utterly defeated in the predawn light, before climbing the collapsed wall into the second floor of the keep.

I wait until I smell woodsmoke curling through the long chimney that connects all four floors of the tower. I walk down the stairs slowly, catching scraps of conversation as they float up with the smoke and the scent of frying bacon, trying to pretend I'm not just listening for her voice.

The door into the first floor, the one I slammed shut last night, is no longer closed. It's open a crack, just enough to let me know someone's been through.

It's a message. My hand hesitates over the doorknob as I stare at the bright slit of firelight falling across the cold stone stairs. This opened door says *we're not afraid of you* as clearly as if they'd scrawled the words across the walls with paint.

I wonder who did it and how far they went. The man who said they've come to request an audience is the most likely suspect, but somehow my shills are on the other man, the one who suggested they come inside. The one Kira leaned over to talk to in the meadow.

Something unpleasant twists inside my chest. I try to swallow it.

Or maybe it was her. A vision of Kira pushing open that door and tiptoeing up the stairs catches in the back of my throat, cutting off my breath. Maybe she came looking for me last night.

I shift quietly on the stairs, trying to swallow that thought too. Even if Kira did come looking for me, it was probably with a blade in her hand.

And somehow, that's still a very sexy mental picture.

Godsdamn it. I push the door open with a slam that sounds like an explosion and then walk through. Everyone stops to stare at me. It's almost funny, the way they freeze with their mugs or forks in midair, the way even the fire seems to die down when I enter a room.

Yes, almost funny. Isn't this what I always wanted? This kind of power, this type of control? I wanted to be so strong no one would dare to attack me, didn't I?

Well, here I am. I force myself to smile at the five men and one woman cowering before me. They look terrified.

I feel like shit.

"Good morning," I declare.

I don't mean it to sound threatening, but somehow it

still does. Kira looks at the floor, then steps back, like she's thinking about slinking through the arched opening and vanishing into the woods.

That does it. They have to get out of here, all of them. I don't belong with people anymore. I clear my throat; the man in the back with the copper hair flinches.

"You requested an audience?" I say to the blond who buzzes with magic.

It feels like a silver chain, the haze of magical energy that surrounds him. No one in the Towers has magic in their body, of course. That privilege is reserved for elves and dragons. Humans rely on magic that's been pulled from other sources and trapped inside metal.

All humans except me. Oh no, the magic I stole is trapped inside my body. I'm a living myth. Or a nightmare.

I push that thought away as I stare at the man before me. He's no Exemplar. Still, he must be an accomplished student of the Towers to be trusted with one of their silver chains. I watch his neck bob as he swallows, and then he nods.

"Yes," he says. "Please."

"With me," I reply, gesturing to the open door.

Before I turn, my eye catches on Kira. Her cheeks are flushed, like she's been running, and her fiery hair is pulled back into a loose bun. I nod at her before I can stop myself. She gives me the tiniest flicker of a smile.

Perhaps not everyone in this room is afraid of me. Something inside my chest leaps. I turn around before my expression can give anything away. With the man from the Towers trailing me, I climb the stairs to the room on the third floor, which I prepared earlier this morning.

It's the most intact room in the keep, save the one I've locked and filled with my wards. The bottom floor was clearly for carriages and livestock, the second floor for storage, and this room must have been where people actually lived.

I've cleared away and burned most of the rotten furniture and mouse-filled mattresses, but I spared a rather grand desk and a single chair. It's all elven, functional and pretentious at the same time, perfect for making an impression.

We come through the staircase and find the third floor exactly as I left it. One massive elven chair sits alone in the center of the room, with the desk pushed up against the far wall. I stroll across the dusty floor and settle in the chair, channeling Syrus's casual arrogance with every muscle. And then I try not to smile as the blond fuck from the Towers looks around the spartan room for another place to sit. And finds nothing.

Finally, he gives up and turns to me. He looks like he's trying to be serious, maybe even threatening, but there's a strange shadow in his eyes and a tic in the muscles of his jaw. He wasn't in the common room of the hunting lodge during the storm, I'm sure of it, and I suppose I can see why. He'd make a bad card player.

Does that mean he was upstairs, giving the mattress that workout? And if so, who was up there with him?

"So," I finally say, once the silence between us has grown past awkward and into almost painful territory. "What is it you wanted to discuss?"

The man glances at his feet, then stiffens his spine. There's something almost apologetic in his expression. It's a strange way to begin negotiations.

"Master Thorne," he begins.

I bristle but try not to show it. Master Thorne is what Fyrris called me when he wanted to humiliate me.

"I've come to propose a trade," he says.

I raise an eyebrow.

"I believe you know what the Towers want," he continues.

I say nothing. A gust of wind blasts the keep, sending puffs of dust scuttering across the floor. The man glances at his hands, as if he's got his whole speech printed on the inside of his palm, and then back up at me.

"You have something that belongs to the Towers," he says. "An amulet. We believe you used it to kill the last old god on this continent."

"I killed the last old god with an ebony crossbow and a silver bolt," I reply. "Just like the Towers trained me to do."

The man flinches, like he's been slapped, but then recovers. "And the amulet?" he asks. "It trapped the magic, right?"

"No," I reply. "I left the amulet behind."

For the first time, the man looks defiant. He pulls himself up straighter. "Sir, I can feel the magic in this room," he says.

"Oh, you can?"

I grin, then raise my hand before my chest. I tug on the magic simmering beneath my skin.

A flame bursts into life between the cage of my fingers. I open my hand and let it float across the space between us, dancing and hissing like a fallen star. The man recoils like it might bite. I let it explode. Sparks rain down across the stone floor. The air smells vaguely like burned metal.

"Tell me," I say. "Do you see an amulet? Or one of your Towers's little silver chains?" I wave a hand at the walls. "What about pipes? Do I have those damned pipes that carry magical energy to the Exemplars? Do you think I'm hiding arcanite behind these walls?"

The man shakes his head. Then he sighs, runs his fingers through his hair, and meets my eyes.

"We're prepared to make a deal," he says.

"I don't have the godsdamned amulet," I lie for the second time.

"We'll give you the woman," he says.

My mouth falls open. Wind howls across the broken stone of the old keep like a beast in pain. The blond man glances down at the floor, then at me. He doesn't look proud of what he's just said. Somehow, that makes it even worse.

"You fucking monster," I spit.

He says nothing. A gust of rain spatters through an open hole in the wall that might once have held a glass windowpane.

This explains everything. Why Kira looks so much like Lenore. Why the Towers dragged her out here in the company of a man who's authoritative enough to speak for the Exemplars but not dangerous enough to be an actual threat.

Fyrris is behind this, I'm sure of it. The absolute bastard.

But Kira didn't tell me she was here to be offered up in some backroom bargain like a side of meat. No, she said she was here to hunt a man who'd stolen something.

Oh, gods above. I feel sick as I ask my next question.

"Does she know?"

Finally, the man has the decency to look ashamed. "I haven't told her yet," he admits. "I haven't told any of them."

I lose all interest in pretending to be Syrus and pull myself upright in the chair. Rage burns through my body; magic pulses in time with my heartbeat. I could incinerate this man right here, turn him into nothing but a smear of ash against the far wall.

But I was once a part of the Towers too. I know how they work.

I drop my head into my hands. This room is so silent that I hear a distant burst of laughter from the first floor as it echoes up the very long chimney. I shake my head, then stare at the messenger before me.

"You," I begin, "are an absolute waste of blood and bone for agreeing to do this."

He doesn't bother to argue.

"Why her?" I ask. "Did she do something wrong? Is she being punished?"

The man squirms. "No. Not that I'm aware of. Fyrris said you—you'd like her."

And there it is. Fyrris really did just find someone who looks like Lenore, yank her out of her life, and shove her into the Towers, just in case he ever needed to bribe me.

I drop my head into my hands once again and wait for the rage seething inside my chest to subside enough for me to speak. When I look up, the man is staring at me like he's expecting to get punched.

"Who do they have of yours?" I ask.

He blinks. "Excuse me?"

"Please," I snap, waving my hand in the air between us. "The Towers trained me too, you know. I'm sure you didn't volunteer for this little errand. What are they holding over your head?"

The man's back stiffens. He crosses his arms over his chest. He's not going to tell me. Fine, I can work with that.

"I want out," he blurts.

My eyebrow lifts as I stare at him. He looks angry,

defiant almost, but there's a pink tinge creeping up his cheeks.

"I...have someone," he continues, in a softer voice. "I want to make a life with him. Outside of the Towers."

"Shit," I spit.

Him? It's the redhead, isn't it? He wasn't in the common room either. Now the squealing mattress makes sense.

"Fyrris told you he'd let you go?" I ask. "Just like that?"

The man's face grows redder. A crease appears on his forehead.

"He did, didn't he? And you believed him," I finish.

"It's a simple trade," the man growls. "Give the Towers the amulet you stole, and you get the woman."

"And you get your freedom," I reply, not bothering to hide the sarcasm dripping from my voice.

"You have to be lonely," the man says.

"You have to be desperate," I snap.

We glare at each other across the room. For a heartbeat, it's like looking in a mirror. All the ambition that must have brought this man to the Towers, that blind desire for power and control. And how quickly that desire turned into desperation to escape.

"No," I finally say. "Even if I had the amulet, which I do not, I wouldn't trade a human life for it. You can tell Fyrris to go fuck himself."

An expression flashes across the man's face, there and then gone, like the night landscape illuminated by a flash of lightning. And in that flash, he's a broken man, staring at the ruins of the dreams he built that allowed him to survive the life he's been forced to live.

Once again, it's like looking in a godsdamn mirror.

He turns away. His boots echo on the floor, their heavy smash bouncing back to me, amplified by the empty room.

"Wait," I say.

The man freezes at the top of the stairs. He doesn't turn around.

"You don't have to go back to the Towers," I say. "You can stay here. Let the others carry your robes back to Silver City. They can say you found nothing and died in the attempt."

The man turns around slowly. When he meets my eyes, it's with the saddest smile I've ever seen.

"See," he says. "I knew you were lonely."

With that, the hollow thud of his bootsteps fills the room as he descends the staircase, walking toward the light and laughter of the group that brought him here.

CHAPTER 15
KIRA
WE NEED YOU

Tholious looks like the negotiations with the Godkiller did not go well.

He's scowling when he comes back down the stairs, and he pulls Zayne outside without a word for the rest of us. Matius ignores him, like he's been doing ever since we dragged ourselves inside this stone tower last night, and I wonder if the icy distance between the two of them bothers Zayne and Girwin as much as it's bothering me.

Not that I care about Tholious's love life, particularly. It's just awkward to feel like I've wandered into the middle of someone else's relationship problems, and the only escape is pouring rain and possibly wolves.

"We're leaving," Tholious announces.

I look up to see him standing in the arched entryway with his arms crossed over his chest. Zayne slouches next to him with a pout. I frown. I don't think I've ever seen Zayne slouch before.

"Why?" Barrance asks. "We ain't got the amulet, right?"

97

Tholious looks up at the ceiling, then turns back to Barrance.

"He said he doesn't have it," Tholious replies, in a voice that's a bit too loud.

Ah. He's not talking to Barrance. He said that for the benefit of the Godkiller, who's probably listening in on our conversations. The thought makes me feel uncomfortable, like my skin is too hot even as I shiver in the cold wind blowing through the doorway.

Gods, I hardly slept. I spent most of the night staring at the door Reznyk closed when he left, torn between hoping the Godkiller wouldn't come through looking for me and hoping that he would.

Shit. I'm an idiot, and I'm lucky the Godkiller didn't murder me in the hunting lodge. The gods know he had ample opportunity.

"So that's it?" Barrance says, coming to his feet. "We're just gonna leave? Go back to the Towers empty-handed? How are they gonna like that?"

Tholious rolls his eyes, then points at the ceiling.

"What the hells is that supposed to mean?" Barrance replies. He steps forward with a scowl. "I don't know how they do things in the Towers, but in the Guild, we don't leave the job half done."

"Barrance," Zayne growls. "Stand down."

The two men lock eyes. For a moment, the air inside the old tower feels thick and heavy, ready to explode. Then Barrance turns away, spits on the ground, and kicks his backpack.

"Anybody else have a problem with the plan?" Zayne asks.

His smile is tight, and his eyes are hard. By the time it occurs to me to ask what the plan is, we're walking down the ridge in a thick, gray drizzle as the old tower vanishes in the fog behind us.

"This is probably far enough," Tholious suddenly announces, with a glance over his shoulder, as if he's expecting Reznyk to suddenly waltz out of the freezing mist.

Zayne makes a sound in the back of his throat that could be taken for agreement. Tholious drops his pack to the ground. We've stopped in a little hollow just below the lip of the ridge. The Godkiller's tower is out of sight, and the forest drops away beneath us, one long, steep, and muddy pitch to the meadow where everyone but Tholious wanted to spend last night.

"Kira," Tholious says.

I turn toward him. Tholious looks like something hurts, and for a moment I wonder if Reznyk did something to him this morning. Did he get some sort of magical injury? Is he about to explode and take us all out? Gods, from the look on his face, that's a real possibility.

"Yeah?" I ask, wondering if I should take a step back.

"The Towers need you," Tholious begins, in a halting voice that makes me think this conversation is about as much fun as the fight he's having with Matius. "We all need you, I mean. For this."

He falls silent. Rain drips off the pine boughs all around us, and somewhere a bird calls out, the same rapidly falling four notes, over and over.

"Okay," I say, when the silence starts to feel awkward.

Tholious sighs, then looks down the mountainside and toward the meadow. The clouds are beginning to lift, although tatters of mist still hang heavy over the forest. Maybe he's estimating how far we are from the hunting lodge. Or maybe he's just trying to avoid making eye contact. When he finally turns back to me, there's a hard edge in his expression that I'm not sure I've seen before.

"Reznyk does have the amulet," Tholious whispers.

"'Course he does," Barrance grumbles.

Tholious ignores him.

"That whole place feels like magic," Tholious continues. "Especially Reznyk. I think he's wearing the thing, but if not, he's at least got it somewhere close by."

Zayne snorts. "If only someone had seen him naked," he mutters under his breath.

I scowl at Zayne like I'm trying to set him on fire with my mind. Tholious makes an awkward cough. Hells. At least Zayne didn't tell Tholious that the Godkiller was in the hunting lodge with us. With me. Naked.

Still, Tholious's words burn. The whole place feels like magic? Really? Shouldn't I have noticed magic buzzing around the old tower last night? Or what about the night before, when I had as much of my body as possible pressed against the man who stole the amulet?

Although I could swear to the fact that Reznyk was not wearing an amulet that night. Not that I'm about to bring that up just now.

"Kira, that's why we need you," Tholious says.

I glance up and blink. How much of this conversation did I just miss?

"He's lonely," Tholious continues, "and he's got the amulet. One person might succeed where a group did not."

That bird calls again, four sharp notes like glass falling against stone.

"Excuse me?" I finally say.

Tholious makes a face like he's about to be sick. "We need—" he begins. "I mean, I need, uh. You need to hurt yourself."

Barrance grins. Matius looks horrified.

"What?" I say.

Tholious's neck bobs, like he's swallowing poison. "You need a reason to go back there," he says, "and to stay there. Maybe a twisted ankle?"

"That's fucking absurd," Matius snaps, glaring at Tholious. "How is this easier than the two of us leaving now for Cairncliff—"

"I'll do it," Zayne says.

His face is a closed door. Something deep inside of my chest curls in fear. I've laughed with Zayne quite a bit since we left Silver City. I've gotten to know him, and some part of me has come dangerously close to considering him a friend.

I almost forgot who he actually is. A hired mercenary from the Guild. The leader of a group of hired mercenaries.

"What?" I say again, only this time it's less of a question and more of a wheeze.

"You fuck him," Barrance replies. He makes a disgusting hand gesture, just in case I wasn't sure what those words meant. "Then you take the amulet back."

"One of us will be waiting for you in the hunting lodge," Tholious says. His face has gone so pale I think he might pass out. "I'm sure you'll be able to sense the amulet. That much magic can't be hidden for long. Once you find it, come down the mountain."

My mouth falls open, but the scream building inside my lungs doesn't come out. Instead, I stare at the five men around me and suddenly wish I was the one who had some sort of magical injury that was about to explode. It'd be worth it just to take them all out.

Instead, I try to smile, to be the polite and invisible Kira from the Towers, but my mouth refuses to cooperate. What I'm actually thinking bursts out instead.

"You're sending me up there," I snap, "just because I have tits?"

Barrance shrugs and nods.

"You have Towers training," Tholious replies. "You can find the amulet and bring it back."

"You have more training than me!" I say. "Why don't you go up there and fuck him instead?"

"He already knows who I am," Tholious replies. "He doesn't know who you are."

I take a breath. I need to tell Tholious everything; that I've never had any magical training in the Towers. I've never sensed so much as a spark of magic, ever, in my entire life.

And that the Godkiller does, in fact, know who I am. He knows quite a bit about me that these five men will never know.

A hand closes around my arm. I jump. The words die in my throat as I meet Zayne's eyes. He's frowning, but his grip on my arm is gentle.

"Kira," Zayne says under his breath. "Let's go."

There's something behind those words, something more he's trying to tell me. I shake free of his arm, then glare at Tholious.

"Fuck you," I snap at him.

Tholious recoils, but it's not enough. It's not nearly enough. I try to think of the worst insults I've ever heard, something that will haunt this son of a bitch to his very grave.

"You—" I begin. My vision blurs, and my voice cracks. "You're a bad person!"

Gods, that was pathetic. I turn away and wipe my

sleeve across my face so Tholious won't see my tears. Then I grab my pack and stomp off, toward the ridge, my breath catching in the back of my throat and my body trembling.

What in the hells am I going to do? Find my way down the mountain alone? Return to the Towers empty-handed, with no magical potential, no amulet, and Tholious there to say I didn't do my part? Hells, after years of sneaking around at night, digging for the truth, and acting invisible, the last thing I need is a reputation as a troublemaker.

Fuck. Fuck them all, every single son of a bitch who dragged me from the Towers when I was so close to finding what I needed.

And fuck me too for not recognizing the name Reznyk. For not finding it even mildly suspicious that a gorgeous man traveling alone in the middle of a storm would be so interested in my life story.

"This is far enough," Zayne says from behind me.

I collapse on a rock, my chest heaving and my eyes burning. Zayne sits down next to me. For a moment we're both silent as patches of sunlight race across the valley that's spread out before us.

"Look, sweetheart," Zayne finally says. "I'm going to hurt you. But before I do that, I want to give you an idea."

I sniff, then wipe my eyes. Zayne brings a hand to the back of his neck as he turns toward me. The clouds lift, and in a sudden burst of light I see the stubble on his cheeks and the fine lines tracing paths out from his eyes like rivers cutting through the forest.

He doesn't look like he wants to be here. And that's not much consolation, but I suppose I'll take it.

"Don't come back to Silver City," Zayne says.

I blink. "What?"

Zayne shrugs, then glances out across the jagged peaks that rise to scrape the clouds behind him.

"This guy," Zayne continues. "Reznyk. We already know he likes you well enough. Ask him to take you somewhere else, to help you get set up. You play your cards right, and I bet he will."

"What?" I say again. "Why?"

Everything I know is in Silver City. Before Fyrris chose me for this godsdamned expedition, I'd never even left the city.

"Because I wouldn't even want Barrance to go join the Towers," Zayne says. He's smiling, like always, but his eyes are hard.

I open my mouth. Nothing comes out. My shoulders curl forward as a gust of wind blasts down the mountain, carrying one final smattering of rain.

"The Towers took one of ours," Zayne continues, in a low voice. "Years ago. His name was Aveus. They turned him into one of the Elites."

He says Elites like some people say shit. I stare at him. I know the name Aveus, vaguely at least. He was another one of the boys in black who we were all supposed to ignore. And now there are no Elites, and we're supposed to pretend there never were.

"What happened to him?" I whisper, as though the Towers could hear me asking forbidden questions all the way up here.

"Gone to chase the moon, I suppose," Zayne replies, with a shrug. "We didn't exactly keep in touch."

Zayne stretches, then shifts on the rocks until he's sitting directly below me. He bends forward to pick up the heavy boot holding my left foot.

"It was a power move," Zayne says. "The Towers

wanted to show the Guild who was really in charge, so they took the boss's favorite. And it worked." He rolls my boot back and forth in his hands, like he's warming up to give me a massage. "The Towers are shit, sweetheart. Don't go back there."

"But you still work for them?"

"I work for anyone who's got the shills," Zayne replies, with a grin. "But you aren't getting paid, now, are you?"

I frown. Of course I'm not getting paid. No one gets paid; serving in the Towers is honor enough. Isn't it?

"Look at me," Zayne says.

I meet his eyes. In this light, they're a strange, murky green, like water at the bottom of an abandoned well.

"Scream," Zayne says.

He twists my foot. Something pops. A bolt of pain howls up my leg. My vision goes white, then red.

I scream.

CHAPTER 16
REZNYK
I'M NOT A HEALER

They've been gone for maybe two hours when I hear the scream.

I drop the bucket full of weeds I've pulled from the wet garden and narrow my eyes at the horizon, as if I could see them. Stupid of me; they're long gone. Still, my heart races as I bend down for the bucket, then dump the weeds over the fence for the rabbits. It's hard to tell with a scream, of course, but that sounded like a woman.

No, not a woman. That sounded like Kira. And what are the chances some scream-worthy accident would befall Kira so close to my keep?

Why, they're probably the same as the chances that a woman who bears such a striking resemblance to Lady Lenore Castinac would wander the Dagger Mountains with a man from the Towers and four hired mercenaries.

I sigh as I stretch my back, then rub the sore spot that always flares up after bending over in the garden all morning. The mist is burning off, although the wind still carries an occasional fistful of rain. Still, it looks like it's going to be a beautiful afternoon.

I walk to the front of the keep and stare down the ridge. Judging from the scream, they're in the forest just below the lip. Or at least that's where they've set their trap.

They must think I'm an idiot. I turned down their barbaric offer to trade a human being like a bundle of turnips in the marketplace, so now they're using Kira as bait.

My chest aches. I press my knuckles into my skin as I frown at the horizon. I've seen a lot of bastards do a lot of shitty things. Still, this bothers me. The casual cruelty of the whole thing. The way Kira smiled at me in the hunting lodge when she told me she was hunting the fox who stole the moon.

She thinks she's part of it, whatever she was told their little group is doing. I remember the way Tholious frowned when he said he hadn't told her yet, and magic flickers across my skin, hungry to be turned into a weapon. Gods, this is why I live alone.

I'm walking before I even realize I've made a decision. The wind tugs my hair back from my face and flutters the edge of my cloak. This isn't the first trap I've walked into, and the way things are going, it won't be the last either.

I'm halfway down the ridge when I see them climbing toward me. I stop, cross my arms over my chest, and wait as the wind toys with the edge of my cloak. It's the man who was standing with Kira in the meadow, the handsome one who was playing cards with the hunters.

Kira has her arm around his shoulders, which makes something inside of me pinch. Magic hisses along my skin as I imagine how easily I could form a blade and slice that man's head clean off.

But their embrace doesn't look especially passionate. Kira is scowling and limping; the man helps her struggle over the rocks. I don't see anyone else on the ridge, which means they've either gone ahead or they're very good at hiding.

It's a strange trap. I stand and wait for the pair to make their way to me. The man grins as they approach; Kira looks down at her feet, her cheeks as dark as sunset and her hair pulled back in a tight bun. In the shifting light, it's less like Lenore's dull amber and more like molten fire.

"Well, good morning again," the man declares.

I don't respond. He doesn't seem to care.

"Kira had a bit of an accident," he says.

Kira sits down heavily on a rock. She's panting. Magic prickles beneath my skin, like it always does when I'm close to a creature in pain.

"That's convenient," I finally say.

"Not for me," Kira snaps.

Our eyes meet, and the mountain air sizzles. I look away quickly, before those angry blue eyes can do any more damage to my insides.

"She twisted her ankle," the man continues, stating the perfectly obvious. "She can't make it down the mountain."

I say nothing. The wind gusts between us, flinging scraps of clouds across the sky. I'm beginning to feel the outline of this particular trap, and I don't care for it.

"So," the man says, "can we stay with you for a few days?"

"We?" I reply. That was unexpected.

The man gives me a perfectly charming smile. It's the kind of smile that makes me think he has a dagger in his palm and he's about to use it.

"Or she could stay here," the man continues, waving his hand at the windswept boulder-covered ridgeline. "Until the wolves find her, at least."

"Zayne," Kira says. There's a note of panic in her voice that lodges in my chest like a sliver of ice.

"I don't relish the thought of a member of Silver City's Mercenary Guild poking around my home," I say.

"Just Kira, then," Zayne replies. "I'm sure you'll take good care of her."

There's a twist to his lips that makes me think he knows exactly what happened in the hunting lodge. But Tholious didn't seem to know, which means both Kira and this man must have reasons for keeping their mouths shut.

I bring my fingers to the bridge of my nose and close my eyes. I have to admit, it's a rather brilliant trap. I told Tholious I don't want the woman, but what choice do I have now? Zayne is right; she can't make it down the mountain on one leg. And what kind of monster would I be to refuse to take her in?

So I'm supposed to bring her to the keep. And then she'll tear the place apart looking for the amulet, which she'll take back to Silver City as soon as she can.

And then Fyrris and his bastard Exemplars will realize the amulet doesn't have the magic it's supposed to hold. Which means Fyrris will keep searching for another source, another old god to slaughter.

"Shit," I hiss under my breath.

I glance at Kira, trying not to stare too obviously. She's gasping for breath. Sweat has pressed loose strands of hair against her forehead. She looks miserable, exhausted, and mad as all nine hells.

Gods, she's beautiful. It's partially her resemblance to Lenore, but there's more to it than red-gold hair and full lips. Lenore was beautiful like a flower grown inside a hothouse, something delicate and refined. Kira is beautiful like a mountain, something that will be even more breath-taking after a few storms.

Part of me stirs a little lower, and I tear my eyes away from Kira. Maybe she's here to destroy the home I've made. Maybe she's here to stab me while I sleep. Or—

My gaze drifts over her again, pulled like a moth toward a lantern. She's scowling at the man next to her like she wants to drive a rock through his skull.

Maybe she's just here. Maybe the Towers have someone of hers, and maybe she's got about as much choice in this as I do.

Less, actually. Because I could turn around and leave the two of them to figure out this problem alone while I drink the rest of the wine I stole, my cabin door locked and the shades pulled. And I wouldn't put it past a member of the Mercenary Guild to actually leave Kira out here, on the rocks, by herself.

"Fine," I say.

I meet the man's gaze. He's not smiling anymore.

"Get the fuck out of here," I snap.

The man gives me a little bow, then turns on his heels. I sigh as I watch him trace a path through the boulders. When he disappears, I settle down on a rock near Kira. She's avoiding my gaze so thoroughly it's impressive.

Fine. I need to convince her that I'm not a threat to the Towers, and she needs to believe I don't have the amulet that's wrapped in cloth and hidden beneath the floorboards under my bed.

I just don't know where to begin.

"Hey," Kira says.

Her voice is soft and quiet, almost embarrassed. I look up, and she looks away.

"I, uh, appreciate you not mentioning what happened in the hunting lodge to Tholious," she says.

I clear my throat. "Me too," I say. "I mean, I appreciate you not mentioning it."

She smiles. It's like the sun breaking through the clouds.

"Thanks," she replies. "And, you know, thanks for not killing me, too."

Her smile fades. The world feels colder without it.

"Of course," I reply. "It's very rude to kill someone on the first night. I'd wait until the second or third night, at least."

Our eyes meet, and something flashes between us, an echo of the spark that turned into a fire in the hunting lodge. I clench my jaw against the sudden rush of heat in my core.

"Shit," she says. "I'm sorry. I didn't mean that the way it sounded."

She exhales slowly. Her jaw is clenched, and she's holding her body in a strange, stiff way that looks exhausting. I glance over my shoulder, trying to estimate how long it would take her to reach my keep without help.

Quite a while, I would guess.

"May I see your ankle?" I ask.

"What?" Kira says, with a tight smile. "Aren't you going to buy me a drink first?"

"Only if we play Questions afterward," I reply.

Her cheeks darken, and for a moment she's very interested in the rock beside her. Then she shifts and lifts her left leg.

"Go ahead," she says, with a wince.

I catch her boot with both hands. Magic pricks at my skin, making my palms feel hot. I run my fingers carefully along the worn leather at her ankle. Her breath catches, but she doesn't make a sound.

"What happened?" I ask as I start to undo the laces.

Kira growls something that sounds like *fucker*. I decide to let the matter rest.

"May I look?" I ask, once the laces are undone and magic is screaming beneath my skin like a pot at full boil.

"Don't tell me you're a healer," Kira replies through her clenched teeth.

"I am not," I say, meeting her gaze. "And I'm not a magistrate either."

Her lip curls in the slightest suggestion of a smile. It doesn't do much to make her look less terrified.

"But I might be able to help," I finish.

A gust of wind ruffles Kira's cloak. She turns toward me, and there's just enough of a glimmer of fear in her eyes to give me an idea about what really happened to her ankle.

I look down at her open boot and the wool-wrapped ankle inside. It's already swelling and it feels hot, but I don't see any blood or obvious broken bones. Still, it looks like it hurts. A lot.

It's too bad the men who came with her are hiding. Because right now, I'd like to kill them all.

"I won't do anything you don't want me to do," I say. "Ever."

She looks away, and her shoulders tremble. The wind carries my words to be locked away inside the mountains. Magic sparks and dances over my fingers.

"I have some skills," I begin, haltingly. "I was never a healer, but I— I can probably make things a little better."

I fall silent. My heart beats against the inside of my chest. She knows about the amulet, so she must know what

I've done. The price I paid for the magic trapped inside my body.

Kira blinks, then wipes her eyes with her sleeve. "Fine," she says. "Go ahead. It's not like you can make things much worse."

I try to give her a reassuring smile as I lift her ankle with both hands. She's wrong, of course.

If there's one certainty in life, it's that things can always get worse.

CHAPTER 17

KIRA
DESOLATION PEAK

My whole leg throbs, and my teeth are clenched so tightly my jaw aches. Lifting my ankle sends a wave of pain through my body that makes the bacon I had for breakfast flip over in my gut.

"Okay?" he asks, with a frown.

"Sure," I reply.

He nods. "I have to take your boot off," he says. "That might be uncomfortable."

"I bet," I growl.

Godsdamn it, I've had enough with strange men holding my feet. Reznyk is gentler than Zayne, but still, I'm an idiot for letting any of this happen. This is the man who killed the last old god, for fuck's sake.

Fear curls inside my gut as Reznyk peels back the top of my boot and Zayne's words come back in a whisper that rattles around inside my skull. *You're lucky he didn't kill you.* The Godkiller frowns at my sock like he's trying to read something in there, and part of me screams to just tell him to forget it, that there's nothing he can do here to help me.

But maybe he can. I think of the amulet again, that

stolen artifact the Towers are so desperate to recover. If the Towers weren't enough to awaken whatever magical potential I've been hiding all these years, then maybe his amulet is what I need. Maybe I can march back to the Towers with the amulet and some new abilities of my own.

And maybe that will be enough to convince the Exemplars to finally tell me the godsdamned truth about my family.

"Okay," Reznyk says. "Here goes."

He tugs on the heel of my boot. For the second time this morning, I scream as a bright bolt of agony sears through my body. Tears sting my eyes, my vision blurs, and I try to swallow the sob that's battering the inside of my throat.

"Gods, I'm sorry," Reznyk mutters.

My ankle feels hot, like he's wrapped it in steamed blankets. Panting, I rub at my eyes. Reznyk stares at my foot with the sort of concentration I associate with tightrope walkers at Crown Day festivals. Both his hands press against my ankle, and I feel—

I take a breath. The pain recedes slowly, like water trickling down a drain. I blink as the sun breaks through the clouds, flooding the world with light.

"W-What did you do?" I whisper.

He looks up at me. Light plays across his dark hair and full lips. His eyes aren't black, like I thought in the hunting lodge. No, they're a deep, rich brown, like a garden just before it's planted. And then his forehead contracts as he looks away.

"I'm sorry," he says. "I was never very good at healing."

"You are a healer," I gasp.

"No." He shakes his head. "Syrus was the healer. I just —" He shrugs. "I do what I can. But it's not much."

I stare at my wool-wrapped ankle cradled in his hands, waiting for it to start throbbing again.

"Syrus Maganti?" I ask as my mind catches up to his words.

It's a name everyone in Silver City would recognize. The sixth son of the Maganti family, Syrus was the most infamous of the four Elites of the Towers that we're supposed to pretend never existed.

Reznyk gives a distracted nod, then shifts my ankle to one hand and points with the other.

"I named that mountain after him," he says, pointing to a row of jagged peaks stretching behind the stone keep. "See the smaller mountain next to it? That's Veloria. They're inseparable as always."

He's smiling in a way that makes me think whatever he just did to my ankle took more out of him than he wants to admit. I decide not to tell him that Syrus vanished from the Towers a year ago and Veloria remained behind as a Disciple, colder and quieter than ever.

"So what mountain is Aveus?" I ask, using the name Zayne told me, wanting to change the subject.

"Off by himself," Reznyk replies, pointing to the last peak in the row.

"And which one is you?" I ask.

Reznyk grins at me. "Right behind you."

I turn to glance over my shoulder, as if I expect the massive peak I've been staring at all morning to have moved while Reznyk was doing whatever it was he just did to my body.

"That's Desolation Peak," I say.

Reznyk's smile evaporates. The air feels colder without it.

"Well, that's fitting," he says, turning away from the

mountain and back to me. "How's your ankle? Did I make any difference?"

I wiggle my toes as gently as possible, then twist my foot in his hands. It hurts, but the pain is softer than before.

"Better," I say, although my breath catches in my throat as I speak.

He looks disappointed. I suddenly realize what's just happened.

"Oh my gods," I mumble. "You just used magic."

Numbly, I tug my foot out of his hands. Reznyk lets it go. He looks more tired than he did this morning, when he was waiting for Zayne and me to hobble up the ridge with his arms crossed over his chest. I realize I'm staring at the dark fabric of his shirt, looking for a bulge that might be the amulet he stole from the Towers.

"That's what I do," Reznyk says. His voice is colder, just like the wind.

I bend my leg, pull my foot into my lap, and run my fingers across my ankle. Reznyk healed me. He used magic to repair what Zayne just did to my ankle.

And I didn't feel anything.

CHAPTER 18

REZNYK

I CUT MY HEART OUT

Magic prickles my skin as I pull the door shut behind me, cross the room, and kneel on the floor. Despite the closed door and the pulled curtains, I hesitate as I stare at the loose board under my bed, the only one that's not nailed down.

I left Kira in the bottom of the keep, next to the remains of the fire. But I can't leave her there forever. Hells, every room in that decaying tower is miserable. I would know; I spent almost a month living there while I repaired this cabin. I wouldn't wish that cold, drafty ruin on my worst enemy. And Kira—

I sigh. Kira is, technically, my enemy. She told me she's hunting a man who stole something, and she's going to get it back. Hells, she twisted her own ankle to be here. She is a trap in every possible way. I need to find out what she wants and then get rid of her as quickly as possible.

But she's alone. And she's injured.

I bite my lip, glance back over my shoulder, and then reach forward. Magic skitters over my fingers as I push through the wards I've placed around this floorboard. Kira might not find it, of course. But I'm not that much of an idiot. I pry the floorboard up, then lean back on my knees.

The amulet is here, nestled in cloth resting on the black earth. My teeth sink into my lower lip as my heart thuds against my chest. The key to hiding something is to put it somewhere idiotic, right? Put it somewhere ridiculous, somewhere no one would ever think to look. And a loose floorboard under the bed has got to be the first place someone would look.

I reach for the ball of fabric. At some point I realize I'm humming that stupid tavern song under my breath, the one about cutting my heart out so you can't hurt me anymore. I don't stop. I feel like I'm whistling past a graveyard.

The slick, dark metal of the amulet winks up at me as I lift it from the bundle of fabric. There's not much magic in the damn thing, I made sure of that, but still, I don't like it. The Towers made this thing to trap magical energy, and the metal feels hungry in a way that's deeply disconcerting. I don't even like looking at it, much less touching it. But I can't leave it here, just like I can't leave Kira in the keep.

"I cut my heart out," I whisper under my breath, the tavern song coming out in rusty, uneven tones. "Sunk it to the bottom of the sea."

Magic skitters up my arm as my fingers close around the amulet. The metal is cool and smooth and much heavier than it looks. My arm burns as I lift it.

"I cut my heart out," I whisper as I come to my feet. "Now there's nothing left inside."

I peek through the window before I leave. There's no sign of Kira. The way she was moving, I doubt she's left the keep. Still, I tuck the amulet beneath my cloak when I leave the cabin, and I walk quickly to the garden.

Somewhere no one would think to look. I stop at the far

end of the garden, by the scraggly carrots and the pile of old wooden planks I pulled from the keep. Someday I'll turn this scrap wood into a shed to store buckets and rakes and other garden stuff I've cobbled together, but for now, it's just another heap of crap.

"I cut my heart out," I whisper.

I get down on my knees, push the rake aside, and move a broken bucket. Then I shove the amulet between two splintering planks of wood and pull the bucket over the gap.

"So you can't break it anymore," I say, finishing that stupid song in a hurried whisper.

I stand up and wipe my hands on my pants. I should have left the damn thing behind, I tell myself for the thousandth time. I should have thrown it into the Ever-Reaching River, or tossed it off the top of a mountain.

But things like that have a way of coming back, don't they?

A shiver climbs the back of my neck, and I turn toward the crumbling keep. Where I can't leave Kira.

CHAPTER 19
REZNYK
NOT GOOD AT COMPLIMENTS

I spend the rest of the day cleaning the cabin and fixing dinner. Somewhere between going back to the keep and finding Kira asleep on the ground next to her pack, nailing down the loose floorboard so it looks like every other floorboard in the cabin, and making the most elaborate dinner I've made in months, I come up with a plan. It's not a good plan, exactly, but it worked once already, right?

Yes. Questions. We'll play Questions again, Kira and I.

The sun is sinking toward the valley as I walk back to the old keep. The wind has died, and birds call to each other from the forest just below the ridge. It's been a singularly beautiful day. I hesitate before the arched entryway, wishing I could hold on to this moment before I plunge ahead with my stupid plan to get rid of this woman as quickly as possible.

Gods, if only I could pretend we were back in the hunting lodge and nothing had changed. Or, hells, maybe I could pretend I've lived a different sort of life, become a different sort of man. Maybe then Kira and I could be something other than enemies.

"Hey," Kira calls from the shadows inside the keep.

I step in and find she's sitting against the far wall with her leg propped on a piece of wood.

"Good afternoon," I say, and then I immediately feel like an idiot.

She smiles. Something inside my chest clenches like a fist. Gods above, I wish she didn't have such a lovely smile.

"Thank you," Kira says. "Whatever magic thing you did this morning, it— It helped."

"It didn't help much," I say, glancing at her ankle on the piece of wood.

Kira grins. "You're not very good at taking compliments, are you?"

I blink. She waves her hand in the air.

"It's fine," she says. "You're here to do what? Send me on my way?"

"Not at all," I reply as I cross the room. "I'm here to invite you to dinner."

I hold my arm out to her and try to ignore the rush of heat when she wraps her hand around my bicep.

"You're going to feed me?" she says. There's a twist in her voice that sounds like she's teasing me, but I don't know her well enough to be sure.

"What kind of monster do you think I am?" I ask.

Kira doesn't answer that particular question. She's hardly limping as I lead her around the crumbling far side of the keep and into the shadows that pool beneath the mountains I've named for the other Elites, the men I once called my brothers.

"Oh!" Kira cries. "That's where you live!"

In the gathering evening shadows, the twin windows of

my little cabin glow with the light of the fire. I pulled back the curtains and left the door propped open, and the spiced aroma of the stew I made for dinner hangs in the air.

I have to admit, it does look pretty cozy. I smile at her.

"What, you didn't think I lived in the old tower?" I ask. "Not even the owls want to live in that thing. It's cold as the hells."

I let go of her arm, then step into the tiny cabin and sweep my hand past the entrance, like I'm beckoning her into a grand ballroom. She grins as she steps over the threshold.

"You have a cat," she exclaims, with a level of glee that's almost certainly not warranted.

"I don't have Xavier," I reply as Kira heads toward the bed and the scruffy tomcat curled at the edge. "He just tolerates my presence."

Kira smiles at me, then sinks down next to Xavier and his death claws.

"Careful," I say. "He can be a little touchy."

But he's already rubbing his head against Kira's hand and making me look like a liar. I shake my head at the furry little asshole as I fill two bowls from the stewpot and set them on the table. I only have one chair, so Kira will have to make do sitting on the edge of the bed.

"Dinner is served," I announce as I pour wine into two wooden mugs.

"Damn," Kira says as she scoots across the edge of the bed to my table. Like everything else in the cabin, the table was made with only one person in mind; two bowls and two mugs only barely fit on it.

I sit down and try not to notice the way Kira looks at the stew, biscuits, and wine. I wasn't trying to impress her, exactly, but this is the most elaborate meal I've cooked in

123

months. Sometimes I can't even be bothered to boil potatoes, and I just eat them raw and disgusting.

Tonight, though? I took my time. I used some of the dwindling spice supply I bought in Cairncliff and the last of my flour. I cooked beans from the garden with new potatoes and the few tomatoes that survived the last frost. I only realize how nervous I am when Kira tries the stew, looks at me, and smiles.

"It's delicious," she declares.

I shrug, like it's nothing. Like I didn't have to teach myself how to cook by failing and burning things over and over. Kira looks down at the meal, then back up at me.

"You don't eat meat, do you?" she asks.

I nod. Something inside of my throat pulls tight.

"You didn't eat anything at the lodge," she continues. "I wondered why."

"I don't," I answer. "Eat meat, that is."

My heart thuds dully, and my mouth feels dry. It's such a stupid, simple thing for her to notice. With all the birds and fish and deer in these woods, I should eat meat. I should have an entire cellar full of salted deer haunches and smoked trout.

I just can't bring myself to kill anything. I haven't been able to spill blood since the old god died in my arms.

Kira makes a little humming noise, then continues to eat her stew. Next to her, Xavier comes to his feet with a great show of effort, stretches, and then flops down again.

She didn't ask why. She doesn't even seem to think it's odd, my preference for vegetables. I swallow hard, then shove a spoonful of stew into my mouth. My cheeks feel hot. I'm starting to regret the slug of wine I had before I walked over to the keep.

Fuck, I need to focus. I need to remember who I used to

be, back when seducing someone for money or information was one of the easiest things I did with my hands. I need to know exactly what Kira wants and how I can make her leave, and I know the easiest way to do just that.

Kira's spoon scrapes the bottom of her bowl. I push mine to the side, my appetite evaporated, and then reach toward the sideboard and the second of the four bottles of wine I stole from the Golden Peaks Hunting Lodge.

"Here's an idea," I say as I dig the cork out with my knife. "What about a second round of Questions?"

CHAPTER 20
KIRA
STRAIGHT FOR THE JUGULAR

Y ou've got to be kidding me.

I freeze with the last bite of biscuit in my mouth. Yeah, I wasn't sure how Reznyk was going to handle the awkwardness of having slept together two nights ago, but I wasn't expecting this. I didn't think he'd just go for it.

The cork comes out of the bottle with a pop. Reznyk frowns.

"Is that a no?" he asks.

I swallow hard and try not to stare at the way his fingers hold the knife. It doesn't help that I remember every single thing those fingers can do, and gods help me, some part of me is about to tell him to skip the teasing and just take off his damned pants.

"No," I say. "I mean, that's not a no."

I shake my head. Gorgeous men, damn it. They turn me into a babbling mess every time. I grab my mug and finish the wine inside.

"Yes," I say. "Questions. Great idea. You start."

He fills my mug, then his. The scent of red wine swirls through the little cabin that's so freaking adorable it makes

126

me want to laugh. I'm sure Tholious and the rest of them pictured the legendary Godkiller living in the old keep, maybe hanging upside down like a bat at night. He doesn't seem nearly so intimidating now that I know he lives in a damn cottage. With a cat.

"Okay," Reznyk replies.

He lifts his wooden mug, swirls it, and takes a sip. He's looking at me in a way that makes heat purr between my legs, and suddenly I find it in my heart to be grateful to Tholious for stranding me up here.

"Are you here to steal the amulet for the Towers?" Reznyk asks.

I laugh. It's like an explosion bursting through my lips. I'm lucky I already swallowed my wine or I'd be spraying it across the room. But Reznyk isn't laughing. He's not even smiling.

He's serious.

"Shit," I say. "You go straight for the jugular, don't you?"

"You're answering a question with a question," he replies. "I've been told that's against the rules."

I snort. "Fine. Yes. Tholious sent me here to find the amulet."

"That's your plan?" he asks, with a raised eyebrow.

"That's not my plan," I snap. "Nobody asked me about my plans."

"What are your plans?" he replies, as the ghost of a smile curls his lips.

"Nope," I say. "It's my turn to ask a question."

I take another sip of wine, and he does the same. It's good stuff, this red wine. Honestly, it's far better than it should be, given we're in a literal shack in the middle of nowhere.

"So," I say, putting my mug down. "Why did you steal the amulet from the Towers in the first place?"

He blinks. I lean back on the bed, waiting. If he's going straight for the jugular, so will I.

"I didn't steal it," he replies.

I make a skeptical sound in the back of my throat. Reznyk shakes his head. He takes another sip of wine, then turns to me.

"The Towers gave me the amulet," he says, in a lower voice. "They trained me how to use it. I just didn't give it back."

"So you're, what, borrowing it?" I ask. "For an extended period of time?"

He laughs under his breath. It's a nice sound, a warm sound.

"You could say that," he says.

His eyes meet mine. I'm already warm from the wine, but his dark gaze sends a tremor of heat straight to my core.

"Why did you join the Towers?" he asks.

I laugh. It's not warm, like his. No, this is almost a bark, resigned and bitter.

"Shit," I say.

I glance around the inside of his little cabin. The sky outside the windows is ridiculously gorgeous; streamers of clouds painted scarlet and gold against an indigo sky. The mountains march to the sea behind the ruins of the keep, and I could almost believe we're the only two humans in the entire world up here. I hated them yesterday, but now, I have to admit the Daggers have their moments.

My fingers tap against my mug as Reznyk's question hangs in the air between us. I could drink, sure. I could throw back the wine and ask him a question, or even tell him to fuck off. But then he'd think I have something to hide, wouldn't he? And I've spent the past three years trying to convince the world that I have nothing to hide.

"I grew up in Silver City's orphanage," I begin. My voice is rough, like it's catching on the edge of something. "You probably know it from the Towers. Just across from the courtyard with the chickens?"

He nods. I take a very long drink of wine, suddenly deeply grateful for alcohol and its many gifts.

"Yeah," I say. "So, obviously, no one adopted me. I just, you know, hung around. At some point I went from living there to working there. And then," I continue, neatly glossing over several humiliating conversations with Dame Serena about my options in the world of work, which mostly boiled down to maid or whore, "three years ago, some Exemplars came to the orphanage. They pulled me into the drawing room." My voice pinches, then dies, and my eyes sting. I blink, then throw back the rest of my wine.

"Anyway," I say. "They told me I wasn't just a nobody orphan. Apparently, my parents were Exemplars, and I had all this magical potential." I can't help the bitter twist to those words. Maybe he won't notice.

"So that's how I came to the Towers," I finish, conveniently leaving out the last three years where I've failed to live up to that magical potential in any way, no matter how small or simple, and I've filled my time covertly searching every corner of the Towers for some record of my vanished parents.

I set down my empty wooden mug. Reznyk looks like I've just slapped him across the face. I ignore him, grab a fresh bottle, dig out the cork with my own knife, and fill both of our mugs. My body buzzes softly with the hum of wine. I'm about to compose a song of thanks to Esyn, goddess of love and drunkards. I usually avoid her blessings, because I can't afford to get drunk, slip up, and let someone at the Towers know what I actually think, but I would not have wanted to tell Reznyk that whole stupid story without her help.

"My turn," I announce as I set the bottle down.

"Okay," Reznyk replies.

I lean forward, resting my elbows on the table. Fuck the amulet. There's something else about him I'm dying to know.

"Why only one?" I ask.

He blinks. It's rather adorable, the look of confusion that flickers across his very kissable face.

"What?" he replies.

"Don't answer a question with a question," I say, with a grin. "Why've you only had one lover? I mean, depending on your definition of a lover, of course."

I thought that might make him smile. Instead, the little furrow in his forehead gets even deeper.

"You're, um, not bad-looking," I stammer. "I'm sure you've had plenty of opportunities. Why limit yourself?"

He reaches for his drink. My heart sinks.

"Don't tell me it was The One," I snap. "What? The woman you loved broke you? Ruined you forever?"

Finally, his lips curve into a wicked grin. "It wasn't because of her," he says.

"Thank the gods," I grumble.

"You know, you look a bit like her," he says.

I glare at what has to be a lie. He brings his mug to his lips. I try to stifle a momentary flare of jealousy for that mug.

"Not going to answer?" I say, not bothering to hide my disappointment. I laid my entire stupid history out on the table, and then he dodged my question. What did I expect?

Reznyk sets his mug down, then turns to look at the glorious sunset that's flooding the sky and spilling in through the open front door.

"I was raised in a brothel," he says quietly.

"No shit?" I reply.

He turns to me with a smile, but there's a strange shadow over his features.

"You know, I don't think I've ever said those words out loud," he continues. "But, yes. No shit. I was raised in a brothel in Blackwater. *The* brothel in Blackwater, in fact."

I whistle, long and low. He grins at his mug of wine.

"I learned about sex," he says. "As you can imagine. I learned quite a bit, listening to the ladies share their tips and tricks over breakfast every morning."

"I noticed," I mutter.

He meets my eyes. The air between us grows thick and hot. Then he turns away and runs his hand across the back of his neck.

"But I saw the dark sides too," he says. "Men spending everything they had for one more night with a woman. Sobbing, screaming at the doors. I saw a woman waiting for her husband outside the gates with an axe in her hands." He speaks slowly, as if he has to pull the words back through all the years that have built up between then and now.

"I— I think I was afraid," he continues, looking at me in a way that's almost apologetic. "Sex can make you crazy, right? It can make you blind. So I told myself I'd wait. That when I had the kind of sex that could make a child, it would be special. It would mean something."

He shrugs, like that's something to be ashamed of.

"Gods," I sigh. "What did she say to that? The One, I mean. That's a lot of pressure on a girl, I'd imagine."

131

He shakes his head. "She didn't know."

I almost spit out the last of my wine.

"You're kidding!" I cry. "You spent your whole life waiting to have perfect sex, and when you finally had it, you didn't even tell her what it meant to you? What in the hells?"

"I didn't——" he begins. His cheeks look darker. "I mean, we didn't have that kind of relationship."

"You were fucking but not talking?" I snort. "What kind of relationship is that?"

"It's my turn to ask a question," he says. "What's your plan to steal this amulet that I clearly told Tholious I don't have? Where are you going once you have it?"

"No," I reply, waving my hand in the air as if I'm brushing away his stupid-ass question. "Seriously. How could she be The One if you couldn't even talk to her about your feelings? How is that even love?"

Reznyk brings his mug to his lips, then frowns at it.

"We need more wine for this," he announces.

He puts his mug down, reaches for the sideboard, fumbles, and then grabs the last bottle. He digs at the cork with his knife. It comes free with a loud pop.

"Oh!" I cry. "Is that frost wine?"

Reznyk frowns at the label. "Shit," he says. "Frost wine. Guess the hunting lodge'll be sending someone up here next."

"You took this from the hunting lodge?" I ask as he pours a stream of sparkling frost wine into my mug.

"Absolutely," he replies, with an adorable drunk smile. "I stole it."

I take a long sip of frost wine, letting it dance across my tongue. I haven't had frost wine in years, and I've never been able to afford a whole bottle. My gods, I was wrong about the Daggers. I want to live here now.

"All right," I say, bracing myself on the table as the room swims gently around me. "Tell me about The One."

Reznyk swirls the frost wine in his mug. There's a dreamy, distant look on his face that makes me feel like I'm about to be sick. Whoever this woman is, I hope she knows what she threw away.

"She's—everything." He hesitates. Takes a breath, then takes a sip of frost wine. "Everything I'm not, I mean. I was nobody. Am nobody. And she— She has everything. Like a queen. The Lady Lenore Castinac."

"Great," I mutter.

"Everything I did, I did to gain her approval," he says. A frown creases his forehead, and my stupid, drunk heart aches. "I thought that was the life I wanted. Trying to win her over. To make her happy."

"I don't think that's love," I say.

Reznyk takes another sip of wine, then shrugs. "Maybe. Maybe not. All I knew was that I would do anything, steal anything, build anything, burn anything, just so I could lay it all at her feet."

Something cold creeps across the back of my neck. I put my mug down as my gut twists and the amazing stew I had for dinner presses against the back of my throat.

"Is that why you killed the old god?" I whisper. "Did you do that for her?"

Reznyk freezes. The color drains from his face.

"No," he whispers. "No, that was—"

He lurches backward, knocking his chair over. Then he sways forward, pressing both hands against the table.

"I—I'm sorry," he says. "I had too much wine, and I— I can't talk about this."

He turns, then stumbles through the open door. The cat on the foot of the bed raises its head to watch him go.

"Shit," I mutter to the cat.

I pick up my mug and finish my frost wine. Then, just because no one can stop me, I pick up Reznyk's mug and finish his frost wine too. And then I push myself off the bed and stumble after him.

The night air is cool against my cheeks. The first of the stars dance in their velvet sky. Reznyk is sitting on the ground outside his cabin, staring down at the forest below us. I sit down next to him, reach for his arm, think better of it, and drop my hand back to my side.

"I stole a necklace once," I say.

My voice is rough, and I remember what Reznyk just said. I've never said these words out loud either.

"Well, I didn't exactly steal it," I continue. "It was during a Crown Day festival. You know?"

He makes a sad sort of noise in the back of his throat that probably means he remembers Crown Day in Silver City. I push on.

"It was the first time I snuck out of the orphanage," I say. "I had a borrowed dress and a couple glasses of wine, and gods, I felt like the queen of the world." I smile at the stupid memory. "Anyway. You know how they rope off the area by the fountains? How it's for the golden ticket holders?"

He nods. I look down at my hands as my cheeks burn with wine and memories.

"When it's late enough, they don't really care anymore," I say. "I waited till the guard turned around, and then I slipped under the rope and grabbed a glass of wine and just acted like I owned the place."

Reznyk makes a sound that's almost a laugh.

"I looked down when I stepped on something that went crunch," I continue. "And it was a necklace. No, not just a necklace. It was—"

My voice fades. How can I describe it? Sure, gold and diamonds and something that looked like a butterfly.

But it was also something incredible. I'd never seen something that beautiful before, never held anything like that in my hands. When I picked it up and wiped the mud off the butterfly's cracked golden wing, I actually thought I might cry.

"I took it," I said. "And a moment later, I see this woman put her hands to her neck. She says something real loud. Everyone around her freezes." I take a breath, remembering how my entire body went cold.

"That was my chance, right?" I say. "I should have gone up to her, said I found what she lost. But then I looked down at myself, and I saw an orphan in a borrowed dress who snuck under the ropes to be there. And—"

My voice fails again. The memory lives in my mind, one of those bright, shining moments when every other breath of my life pivoted on a single decision. I could have done the right thing. Nine hells, maybe she would have rewarded me.

But I'm nobody. I shouldn't have been there in the first place. I looked down at the wine splashed across the front of the dress that the gods only knew how many women had worn before me, and I realized that moment could swing in another direction.

I could be called a thief. That night could end with me in prison.

And there was something else too, something darker and crueler than fear of being called a thief. My fingers wrapped around that shining gold necklace, and some part of me claimed it. It was my pretty thing now, my beautiful gift. I didn't want to give it up.

"So, I spent the night in the outhouse," I say. "All damn night. Until all the stalls closed and the guards gave up and went home, and then I buried the stupid necklace in the orphanage gardens."

Reznyk makes a sound like he's trying to laugh. "Are you comparing finding a necklace in the dirt to murdering an old god?" he asks.

His voice is rough, like it's had to travel a very long way to reach me. I put my hand on his arm.

"No," I reply. "I'm just saying I know what it's like to have something in your past that you don't want to talk about."

He inhales. It's a sound that's caught halfway between a word and a cry. He leans forward. His shoulders tremble.

"It— It had silver blood," he whispers. He turns to stare at his open palms, his long fingers spread across his folded legs. "So much blood. I— I can still see it on my hands."

He makes that sound again, the choked sort of cry. His head drops. I scoot closer to him, until my thigh presses against his leg, and then I cover his hands with my own.

"Reznyk," I whisper. "They just look like hands to me."

He inhales. The night air presses down all around us, and the first of the starlight plays off his eyes and his lips as he turns toward me and begins to lean closer.

Godsdamn it, it is not fair for him to be this gorgeous. I so badly want to fuck this man senseless, but he's drunk, he's just poured his heart out, and he's clearly still in love with The One. I'd have to be a real asshole to take advantage of him in that many different ways.

I close my eyes, then softly touch my forehead to his.

When he sighs, I swear I can taste the frost wine on his breath.

"It's okay," I whisper. "It's okay, Reznyk."

And then, because my self-restraint has its limits, I push myself away from him, come to my feet, and drag myself back into the cabin. My last thought before passing out on the bed next to the cat is, hey, my ankle doesn't hurt at all anymore.

CHAPTER 21

REZNYK

I wake up feeling like my brain is trying to break through the back of my skull and make a run for it. Sunlight pounds its blinding hammer on my temples specifically, and my mouth feels like it's been packed full of sand. I groan, roll away from the brutal onslaught of light, and press my nose into a scruffy patch of grass.

Great. I blink at the dirt as memories of last night come together like the broken pieces of a shattered vase. Opening that bottle of frost wine. Deciding sleeping outside was a fantastic idea. Babbling to Kira about silver blood on my hands.

"Shit," I mutter.

If she only knew how much blood these hands have spilled.

I flop over again, then tip my head so I'm staring at my cabin. The door I vaguely remember stumbling through last night is still open, which means Kira is long gone. She probably trashed the place on her way out, searching for that damned amulet. I lift my hands and press my palms to my eyes.

What in the nine hells was I thinking? Alcohol is an acquired tolerance, for fuck's sake. I can't go from not drinking anything in months to sharing that many bottles and still expect to function like my old self.

Gods, my old self would be kicking me in the ribs right now. I'm an idiot. I'm lucky she didn't slit my throat on her way out. I wouldn't be especially surprised if the Towers had asked her to do that too.

Damn it all, maybe I am lonely. If that's part of my punishment, then hells, I certainly deserve it. I lower my hands. The birds are too damn loud this morning, and they're everywhere, screaming their heads off, and someone singing—

I blink, even though it makes me wince. Singing? Really? Am I hallucinating on top of being hungover?

Magic buzzes under my skin as I shift to my side, then pull myself up to sitting. Xavier's scruffy head appears in the open door. He regards me with his usual expression of disdain.

And then, yes, singing. It sounds like that damn tavern song about cutting your heart out, sung in a distracted sort of half-hum. My gut lurches as I come to my feet. I spit, then again, waiting to see if I'm about to lose it.

No. I'll hold on to whatever it is I have. I take a deep breath, then walk back to my cabin.

It's blessedly dark inside, and it smells like stew and strong tea. I hesitate on the doorstep, staring at the only other human who's been inside this place since I rebuilt it. She's standing by the hearth, her thick, fiery hair pulled back into a messy bun and her rather tight pants giving me a lovely view of one of the finer backsides I've ever seen.

"Oh," she says, turning around. "Good morning, sunshine."

Kira doesn't look especially well this morning either, which is at least some consolation.

"You too," I reply. My voice sounds like I've just gargled broken glass.

"Have a seat," she continues, waving at my chair. "I'll bring you something."

"If it's wine," I growl, "I don't want it."

"If you have any more wine, I wasn't able to find it," she replies.

I sink into the chair. She crosses the small distance between us.

"You're still limping," I say.

"It's better than it was," she says as she sets a mug down in front of me.

She turns back toward the fire. Guilt twists inside my chest. Syrus could have healed that ankle perfectly.

"There's plenty of stew left from last night," Kira announces. "Honestly, I think it's even better this morning."

Her words fade as I stare down at the table. The sweet, thick aroma of strong black tea rises from my mug like an angel coming to lift away my hangover.

She made me tea. I turn from the mug, one of a half dozen I've carved on endless rainy days, and watch as Kira fusses with the big copper pot I salvaged from the keep. She's still favoring her ankle, but other than that, she looks perfectly at home.

Kira turns around. I try to act like I wasn't staring at her.

"Everything okay?" she asks as she limps back to me, then slides a bowl of stew across the table. "I hope you don't mind that I made tea," she continues. "You don't have much, at least not that I could find. But after last night I thought we could both use some."

I shake my head, which does nothing to settle the throbbing in my skull. "It's fine," I say.

And then, because I'm not sure how to tell her that I can't remember the last time anyone made anything for me without expecting shills in return, I pick up the mug and bring it to my lips. The tea is strong and hot. I drink it slowly, letting it wage its silent war against the throbbing in my skull. Xavier wanders back inside as morning sun stretches itself across the floorboards, and Kira bends down to scratch him behind the ears. He rewards her with a deep, gravelly rumble of a purr, something it took me months to hear. Little bastard.

I realize I'm smiling as I watch her, this woman who looks almost like she belongs here. She laughs more than Lenore. She smiles more too, and she shows the bright edge of her temper far more easily. Lenore was always calm and composed, still waters revealing very little of the depths below. And Lenore would never spend the night in a place like this, I realize as the warmth of the mug I'm holding sinks into my hands. She would never make tea. Not for me, at least.

Three years ago, was it? Kira said that's when she was approached by the Exemplars of the Towers. I finish my tea as my smile evaporates. Three years ago I was falling in love with Lady Lenore Castinac in Silver City, and I thought no one knew.

The back of my throat suddenly tastes bitter. I take a tentative spoonful of last night's stew to cover it. Kira's resemblance could be the result of a direct family connection. Lenore's red-haired, blue-eyed father, Lord Rameur Castinac, is hardly a paragon of fidelity. It makes sense that his illegitimate daughter would end up in Silver City's orphanage.

But I haven't sensed any magical potential in Kira, and I certainly didn't sense any in Lenore or in her rather terrifying father. Maybe there's something I'm missing. I'm hardly an Exemplar of the Towers, after all.

"So," I say, pushing my now-empty bowl away. "There's still a question you haven't answered."

"This again?" Kira replies. At her feet, Xavier shakes his head like he's disappointed. "Look, I don't know about you, but I'm in no shape for another round of Questions."

"Just one then."

Kira sighs dramatically, and I have to fight to keep my eyes off the swell of her chest.

"Fine," she says. "If I don't want to answer, I'll just drink the last of the tea before you."

"Fair enough," I reply. "What are your plans?"

Kira stares at me. Outside the open door, the throaty scream of a thrush echoes off the rocks and bounces around inside my skull. This godsdamned hangover is putting up a good fight. Later today, I'll limp over the ridge and come back with willow bark to chew. That will beat it into submission.

"What do you mean?" Kira finally asks.

"Last night, you said no one asked you for your plans," I reply. "You were generous enough to tell me the Towers's plan for you, but I still don't know what you have in mind for yourself."

She frowns at me in a way that makes me think she's waiting for the punchline.

"You can't stay here," I continue, even though the words make something inside my chest twist. "So, where do you want to go? It doesn't get any simpler than that, right?"

Her gaze drops to her hands. Guilt pulses once more inside my chest. I try to strangle it. She can't stay here, damn it. She's beautiful, she made me tea, and she needs to get the hells away from here before she realizes what kind of monster I really am.

"I— I don't know how to answer that," Kira says. Her voice is so soft it's almost a whisper. "No one's ever asked me that before."

Of course not, I realize, like an idiot. The Towers don't ever ask. They just pound you into the shape they want and then send you toward their target. If you shatter on the way, hells, they've got a quiver full of replacements.

"Give it time," I say, running my fingers up the back of my neck. "It wasn't an easy question for me to answer either."

She blinks a few times, then runs her hand across her eyes. I'm expecting her to push the issue, to ask me how I made my decision or what it was that I wanted or even where that damned amulet is, but she doesn't reply. I push back from the table, then come to my feet.

"I'm going over the ridge," I announce. "Don't follow me."

Her eyes widen, and her neck pulses as she swallows.

"Shit," I mutter as my head throbs. "That's not a threat. Just, rest your ankle, okay?"

"Sure," she replies, with a frown. "What's over the ridge?"

"Nothing."

Her frown deepens. I sigh, then rub my fingers against the blinding ache in my temples. I'm not very good at this anymore. I've been alone too long.

"There's a meadow," I finally say. "With willow bushes. I need to do something about this godsdamned hangover. Chewing willow bark will help."

And there's a pack of direwolves, I don't dare to say, that is descending the side of the mountain this morning.

With an old god watching them that nobody, not even the Towers, knows about.

CHAPTER 22

KIRA

IT HAS TO BE HERE

"Okay," I mutter under my breath. "Amulet."

I glance suspiciously at the cat curled on the end of the bed. Sure, he looks like a normal, ragged tomcat, but maybe he's not. Maybe he's something magical. With a sigh, I lean over and give him a scratch behind one of his battered ears. Magical or not, it looks like he's led a rough life.

"Tell me the truth, Xavier," I ask him. "Are you magical?"

The tip of his gray tail twitches in an annoyed way. I can't tell if that's an answer to my question or not. I glance at the windows, as if Reznyk might be peeking in, just waiting to catch me in the act of interrogating his cat. There's nothing out there but a beautiful morning.

"Gods, this is stupid," I mutter under my breath.

I stand up, wipe my hands on my pants, and close my eyes. Tholious said that much magic would be impossible to hide. He said I'd be able to sense the amulet. I take a deep breath, inhaling lingering smoke from the fire mixed with tea and the aroma of vegetable stew that really was better this morning.

Nothing here feels special. I open my eyes and stare at the cabin, realizing too late that I have no idea what the amulet looks like. Maybe I should have asked Tholious to sketch it for me.

Frowning, I turn toward the door. I searched the cabin as soon as I woke up, turning over every mug, pressing on each floorboard, and running my fingers along each dusty rafter. I didn't find anything, aside from a few spiderwebs in the rafters. My eyes rest on the crumbling stone tower where I spent the night with Tholious and the mercenaries.

It has to be there. And I have to find it before Reznyk comes back.

But now the morning is fading into gloriously sunny midday, and I've found absolutely nothing.

I mean, sure, there's a bunch of crap in here. The second floor has a collapsed wall with a trail of rubble that ends in the grass beside Reznyk's garden, and so much junk it would take me a lifetime to sort through it. The third floor only had a beaten-down desk and one lonely-looking chair in the middle of the room.

And the fourth floor has a door. I stop in front of the rough wooden door, hold my breath, and close my eyes. The air is cold in the keep. It smells like dust and things that have been forgotten. Wind sings across the stone as I reach for the door.

Something sharp jumps into my skin when I touch the knob. I pull back, shaking my fingers. It's not uncommon, of course, that bite of lightning that sometimes jumps out of metal. But was that normal? Or was it magic?

And, damn it, shouldn't I be able to tell the difference? Both of my parents were Exemplars, after all. If the amulet is behind that door, I should know.

I huff, sink to my knees, and stare at the lock. It looks simple, like the original locks on the orphanage pantry. Hells, I could probably pick this in my sleep. Unless it's a trap, and some kind of magic that I can't sense is going to kill me if I try.

"Fuck," I mutter under my breath.

I am here to find the amulet, damn it. Find it, bring it back to Silver City, and learn the truth about who my parents were and what happened to them.

I reach for the pocket I sewed into the lining of my vest, pull out my lockpick set, and select what I'm going to need. I clench my jaw when I bring the pick and tumbler to the lock, but there are no further sparks, no bursts of deadly magic. Just the soft click of the lock yielding to the right kind of pressure. And then the door swings open. I pack my kit, hold my breath, and cross the threshold.

Nothing happens.

This room is the weirdest of all. My gasp echoes off the stone walls. My own reflection stares back at me from every surface.

Mirrors. Reznyk hung mirrors on each of the four stone walls, massive ones and tiny ones, high against the ceiling and resting on the floor. I count seven of them, with two polished pot lids propped against the south wall.

It's like he's created a room solely to admire his own reflection, although the angles are all wrong. Each mirror gives a shattered, distorted glimpse of my body; my boots in the potlids, the top of my head from the mirror against the rafters. None of them are hung in a way that would help Reznyk decide if his cloak matches his pants.

Gods, it's creepy. Still, I suppress my shiver and search every mirror, running my hands along the sides and peering at the stone behind it. Nothing.

Finally, I tiptoe backward out of the room, watching the mirrors like I'm a child afraid of my own reflection. I pull the door closed behind me. The lock settles into place with a click. For a heartbeat, I fool myself into thinking the Godkiller will never know I was here.

Right. I haven't been caught snooping around the Towers, but I'm a Guard. Guards go everywhere. Here, I'm an unwanted guest who was supposed to stay put. As I walk down the stairs, the children's story about the pirate's wife unfurls behind me. Open any door you want, the pirate told her. Just don't go to the top of the tower.

"Shit," I hiss.

By the time I emerge in the open room where I first spent the night, my heart is hammering a marching tune and my ankle throbs.

I went to the top of the tower. I broke into the only locked door in the place. I didn't find the bones of all Reznyk's previous wives, not like the pirate's wife in the story, but I sure as the nine hells went somewhere I wasn't supposed to go.

My gaze settles on something by the open door. It's my pack, still hunched against the wall where I dumped it yesterday. I press my hand against my chest as my mind sorts through my options.

Reznyk doesn't want me here. He said as much this morning when he told me I can't stay. I haven't found the amulet, but I did find a creepy room filled with mirrors.

That doesn't mean anything to me, but it might mean something to the Towers.

I bite my lip, then glance back over my shoulder like I'm expecting Reznyk to come running down the mountain behind me. The thought makes me shiver, and not entirely with fear.

Which is another reason to leave. I know who he is and what he did, but I still can't make myself hate Reznyk. Not after last night. Not even if he did kill the last old god in the world. And I'm here to rob him, damn it.

But I don't have to rob him. I could go back to the Towers without the amulet. I'll tell the Exemplars everything I found. Hells, I'll tell them he doesn't have the amulet. Maybe then they'll leave him alone, and they'll let me go back to my life in the Guard and my nocturnal snooping around the Archives.

I cross the room, pick up my pack, and swing it over my shoulders. My ankle pulses in protest, but I clench my jaw and ignore it. This dull ache is a lot better than the screaming pain of yesterday. Besides, it's only a day's walk to the hunting lodge.

If I'm fast, I'll make it by tonight.

CHAPTER 23

REZNYK

RESCUING YOU

I flinch. The willow branch in my hand snaps in two as magic sears my skin.

One of my wards just snapped. I blink at the broken branch. Magic churns under my skin. That was close. Close enough to hurt. Panic pulses through my skull. Magic reaches across the meadow and down the ridge, feeling for anything out of place. If someone came for Kira—

No. If another human came into this valley, I'd know. No one could make it this close without warning.

Which leaves only the obvious option. I shade my eyes and stare down the ridge to the ruined keep. From here, a shoulder of rock hides my garden and the cabin. All I can see is the very top of the tower. The locked room where I keep my wards. Including the tiny ward that protects the lock on the door.

That must be where Kira is. When I woke up this morning, I thought she'd be long gone. But I'm an idiot. Why would she leave in the night? Why not wait for me to give her the perfect opportunity to search the place and then run?

I remember the mug of tea she handed me, and how strange it felt to have someone do something for me with no expectation of return. Except she did expect something in return, didn't she?

My hands clench into fists, mangling what's left of the willow branch. What did I expect? She told me exactly why she was here. I'm the fool who let myself get distracted by a mug of tea and a shapely backside.

I shove the willow branch into my pocket and begin my descent down the mountain. I move slowly, letting my rage subside as clouds chase themselves across the sky and the wind picks up, carrying a hint of rain. Kira's not going to find anything in the tower. I might as well let her exhaust herself looking.

By the time I reach the cabin, it's clear she's gone. Xavier prowls restlessly by the door, then sprints outside as soon as I open it, as if he too can't wait to leave.

I know what I'm going to find, but I search the tower anyway. Her pack is gone. Aside from that, she didn't touch much. The chair on the third floor is still in the center of the room, and the crates are still piled haphazardly around the second. She even closed the door to the top room and locked it behind her. I open it, then walk through the room, feeling my wards.

Nothing. She could have broken them all, left a room filled with shards of glass and shattered wards. She could have torn the cabin apart, thrown bedding into the fire, ripped up the floor boards. Instead, she moved like a ghost, almost as if she were trying to deliberately obscure her presence.

Finally, I check the garden. I feel the amulet's dull,

hungry pulse without even moving the broken bucket covering its hiding place. I stare at the pile of scrap wood with my arms crossed over my chest for a long time, trying to think of a better hiding place. Wishing I could burn the thing, or drown it, or finally be free of it.

A tremble flows across my magic, a sudden spike of interest from the wolves. The pack has moved down the valley, following the elk as they seek fresher pastures. As the sun sinks toward the jagged western horizon, the wind carries a howl past the keep.

And I think of Kira, alone in the woods, with an injured ankle.

Good. As long as she's away from here. The wolves are following elk into the other drainage. If she's heading to the Golden Peaks Hunting Lodge, she has nothing to worry about. And where else would she go?

I walk to my cabin, pull open the door, and stand on the threshold. The stewpot has been washed and hung on the wall, next to the two mugs from this morning. She shoveled the ashes out of the hearth. Nine hells, she even made the bed.

I close my eyes and breathe as my magic chases the wolves. They're excited about something, but from here, I can't tell what. Something small, and trembling, and afraid.

I pull the door closed and lope down the ridge. Kira's tracks are easy to spot once I drop below the boulder field. She's following the road to the meadow, of course, just like I thought. She'll be in the hunting lodge before nightfall—

The trail washed out halfway down the mountainside.

I freeze, staring at the ground before me. Water broke across the trail to the lodge, carrying sand and stone into the other drainage. On the far side of the break there are a few large, smudged boot-prints pointed toward the Golden

Peaks Hunting Lodge. The men who came with Kira. The bastards who wanted to trade her.

But on the fan of scattered sand and mud left by the stream, there's another print. It's smaller, fresher, and pointing directly away from the Golden Peaks. Away from any roads, in fact, and into the drainage where the elk have gone and the wolves have followed.

My magic trembles with the low, distant hum of another human in pain. I glance at the sky. The sun is close to the western horizon. There's not much daylight left.

A long, slow howl rises from the forest around me. The excitement of the hunt pulses through my magic, tugging me forward. The washed-out drainage below me is steep; I find two places where the tracks reveal that Kira slipped, and my gut clenches with a mixture of rage and guilt. Gods above, how could she have been so stupid?

How could I have let her go?

Howls and yips surround me. I still can't see the wolf-pack, so for a moment it feels like the forest itself has started to cry. There's a distant, heavy crash, the sound of breaking branches, and panic floods my magic. Grief and rage, terror and thrill. The hunger of the wolves. The fear of their prey.

And then, suddenly, I see Kira. She's standing on a rise in the forest, her back to a tree and a little silver blade trembling in her fist. Her wide eyes flash in the fading light. Her blade points directly at my chest. I raise my hands in the air.

"The wolves won't hurt you," I say.

Already, I feel the wolves withdrawing as their prey crashes further down the drainage, running blindly into the pack's ambush at the mouth of the valley.

"What about you?" Kira growls.

I blink. She's leaning heavily against the tree. Pain comes off her in waves, radiating from her ankle like heat from a fire. Godsdamn my lack of healing abilities.

"Kira," I say, in the same sort of voice I used with Xavier when I tried to get him to eat after fishing him out of the river. "I'm not going to hurt you either."

The blade trembles. "I broke into your weird mirror room," she says, almost like she's daring me to challenge her.

"I know."

Her shoulders drop. "Then why are you here?" she asks.

It's a good question. I'm not sure how to respond.

"Why are you here?" I reply, answering a question with a question.

Kira pulls her hair back from her face in a way that manages to look indignant, despite the circumstances.

"I'm leaving," she says. "You said I couldn't stay. So, I'm going back."

"Back to where?"

She scowls at me. "The hunting lodge."

"You're going the wrong way."

Her mouth opens, then closes. She shakes her head. "Fuck," she finally mutters. "I knew it."

"And you're hurt," I say, as gently as I can manage.

She shakes her head, like she's trying to dismiss the way she's resting all of her weight on just one leg.

"I'm fine," she says. She pulls in a deep breath, then tucks the little blade back into a sheath on her belt. "If you could just point me in the right direction—"

"Really?" I say. "You're going to keep going? At night? With the wolves?"

A howl that almost sounds like a human scream rises from the woods behind her. Kira flinches.

"Shit," she hisses. "Why do you have to live in such a terrible place?"

"Because I'm a terrible person," I answer.

"That's not funny," Kira growls.

"It's not meant to be," I say.

"You're not terrible," she snaps.

"You don't know anything about me."

"I know you take in strange women who show up uninvited on your doorstep," she says, with a strange expression on her face. "And you even use your magic to heal them."

I swallow. My throat suddenly feels tight. Kira glances at her empty hands, then up at me.

"And— here you are," she continues, in a small voice. "Even though you know I'm supposed to rob you. You could have let me die out here. You'd have one less thing to worry about if I got eaten by wolves."

"I'm not going to let you die," I say. It comes out as a growl.

"I know," Kira replies. The ghost of a smile dances across her face. "Because you're not a terrible person."

My face feels hot. I turn away. She's wrong, but I can't find the words to prove it. Kira makes a strangled coughing sound.

"So," she says. "Did you happen to bring any of that willow bark?"

She's watching me with an apologetic smile, like she's asking for something she doesn't expect to get. Or perhaps she's trying to make a joke. I sigh.

"No," I admit. The willow branches are still on the table in my cabin, where I threw them before sprinting down the mountain like a maniac.

Her smile fades. The pain radiating from her body makes the magic in my body churn. There's a crash from

155

the forest, and then a scream. Kira flinches. A moment later, the wolves begin their victory howl. I close my eyes. Joy and grief flicker through the connection between my magic and the creatures of these mountains. The elk's death is life for the wolves, and my gods, there is so much pain in this world and so little I can do—

Wait. My eyes snap open. That's not entirely true, is it? There is something I can do to alleviate some small measure of the pain swirling through the Daggers tonight.

"You know I'm not very good at healing with magic," I begin. "But, if you'd like, I could try to help—"

"Gods, yes, please!"

I realize I'm smiling as I kneel in the pine duff in front of her.

"Sit down," I say. "I'll do what I can."

She does. I remove her boot carefully, then cradle her ankle. The pain isn't as sharp as it was yesterday. Still, the dull throb of it sinks into my fingers. And, horrifyingly, some lower parts of me take a sudden interest in what my hands are doing.

Stop it, I tell my godsdamned cock as I let magic flow through my hands and into Kira's body. She makes a sound that does nothing to dissuade my cock. I grit my teeth and do what I can.

When I'm finished, I set her foot down on the ground. Her eyes blink open, and she smiles at me in a slow, tired way that makes me wonder what she would look like first thing in the morning, with the sun filtering through the windows to dance across her hair.

Fuck. I'm sitting far too close to this woman, but standing up is going to reveal my pointed interest. I try to find something to stare at that's not the curve of her lips or the way her chest presses against her shirt.

"Thank you," Kira says. Her voice is thick, and gods, she looks exhausted. "Now, how do I get to the lodge?"

"You're not going anywhere tonight," I reply.

She glances over her shoulder, toward the fading sounds of the wolves' victory party.

"The wolves won't hurt you," I say. "The pack caught the elk they were chasing. They'll spend the next few days eating."

Kira doesn't look like she's found much comfort in my words.

"I'll stay with you tonight," I say, like the idiot I am. "I'll keep watch."

Kira nods slowly. "I'll leave first thing in the morning," she says. "I'm sure I can make it to the lodge now."

I glance at the sky as it gently fades to indigo. Two stars dance there already. No, make that three.

"We're closer to the keep," I say.

Kira frowns. "You said I couldn't stay there."

"You can't," I reply. "Not forever, I mean. But I did tell your mercenary friend that you could stay until your ankle healed."

"My ankle is fine," she growls.

Gods, I'm smiling again. When did that happen?

"It's going to be rather inconvenient if I have to keep rescuing you," I say.

Kira gives me a look that could freeze water in the bottom of a well.

"Besides," I add, "I can think of a few things we can do together while you're there."

CHAPTER 24

KIRA

IF I WAS TRYING TO KILL YOU

Gardening.

He meant gardening.

I've been here for almost a week, working with Reznyk in his garden while we joke and tease and talk about Silver City. There's no reason for me to pretend to be something I'm not around him, no need to bite my tongue or avoid attention.

It's a strange feeling, not having anything to hide.

The days have been beautiful, filled with sun and enough wind off the mountains to keep the temperature comfortable, but the nights are cold. This morning, when we sat on the ground outside the cabin sharing the last of the tea he stole from the hunting lodge, there was more gold than green in the trees rippling below us. The scraggly potatoes and spinach growing in his garden don't have much time left.

Reznyk has been horribly, torturously polite ever since Zayne dropped me on his doorstep like a demented gift basket. He's friendly. He's funny. He's got a sly sense of humor that winks like a blade in his palm, and I don't think

I'll ever get tired of the way he laughs when he's not expecting to or the expression on his face when I actually surprise him.

I like him, damn it. I like him quite a bit. If we were together in the Towers, I'd be coming up with any possible excuse to get him alone and flirt like mad.

And he never touches me. He pulls away if I bump into him in the garden; he shrinks against the wall in the cabin when I walk past. Every night ends with me in his bed and him on the floor, in my bedroll.

Last night, after he blew out the candle and darkness settled its warm haunches around the corners of the cabin, I told him there was plenty of room in the bed. He laughed. I told him we should at least trade off nights in the bed, and he said it was better for my ankle. I told him my ankle was perfectly fine. He rolled over and pretended he couldn't hear me.

Whatever happened between us in the Golden Peaks Hunting Lodge, it's not going to happen again. Reznyk couldn't make that any clearer if he climbed one of the mountains and screamed it from the summit.

I huff at the washbasin in front of me like it's getting on my nerves. Reznyk wants me gone, and my ankle feels fine. It's time to finally answer his last question: What do you want?

I wipe my wet hands on my shirt, then drag the sudsy basin away from my clothes before tipping it over and watching the soapy water disappear into the grass. When I turn back to the cabin, it looks like I've tried to decorate the place with my wet clothes dancing in the sun. Almost like I'm marking my territory, warning any other woman that I've claimed this little cabin and the man inside.

I sink my teeth into my lip and try to throttle that

stupid thought. It's been disturbingly insistent, the part of my mind that keeps telling me this cabin in the Daggers feels like the home I used to dream about. That I could make this work, staying here in the mountains, just me, the man who killed the last old god in the world, his cat, and his cherished memories of the only woman he'll ever love.

Yeah. That would be great.

"Is that a rug?"

His voice makes me jump. I turn and see Reznyk grinning as he walks across the grass. Behind him, my shirts and pants and embarrassingly ragged underwear hang next to the little wool rug I was going to put in the cabin.

"Oh," I say. "Yeah. I found it in the keep. I thought it would look good in the cabin, once I got it washed."

"Was it on the second floor?"

I nod. "The washbasin too. I probably don't want to ask where you've been doing your laundry, do I? Do you do something magical with it? Some sort of dark, forbidden, dirt-removing sorcery?"

"There's a pool in the meadow," Reznyk replies with a grin as he waves his hand in the direction of Desolation Peak. "That's where I wash everything. No magic involved."

"Ah," I stammer, trying not to imagine Reznyk washing himself in a mountain stream. "The forbidden meadow."

"It's not forbidden," he says, as he walks up to me.

"Right. Then what was that ominous 'don't follow me' about on the first morning?"

"First, I was hungover," he replies. "And second, you were limping. But if you want to go to the meadow, sure. I'll take you there tomorrow."

I'm suddenly very aware of how close Reznyk is to me. His lips curve into a smile, and the late afternoon light falling through the windows makes his dark eyes dance. I shift awkwardly, unsure how to start the conversation about my plan. It seemed so much easier in my mind. And away from the effects of Reznyk's damn smile.

"How is your ankle?" he asks, completely oblivious to the effect he has on me.

"Still just fine," I say.

"Good," he says.

I swear, I can feel the rumble of that voice in my bones. I take a step back before I melt.

"And, uh, I've been thinking about your question," I say. My voice trembles, and I turn away before my cheeks catch fire. "About my plan."

"Do you have an answer for me?" He raises an eyebrow, and his lips curve into that damn half smile. I can't tell if he's trying to flirt with me or trying to kill me with raw sexuality.

"Maybe," I admit.

Gods, he is close to me. I can smell him, that thick, rich scent that has me remembering the hunting lodge in all sorts of embarrassing ways. My teeth tug on my lower lip as I curse myself for being such a damn coward.

He might be waiting for me to make the first move, right?

"I have something for you," Reznyk says, reaching for a pocket.

He pulls out a piece of linen, then unwraps it, revealing a dozen tiny crimson berries. He smiles at me again. My cheeks burn.

"Try one," he says.

"Are they poisonous?"

He laughs, soft and low in the back of his throat. "Kira, if I was trying to kill you, I'd do something much more effective than poison."

"Is that supposed to make me feel better?" I reply. Gods, I can't stop smiling at him.

"Absolutely," he says. "Poison can be very painful. And it's not always effective."

"This is a lovely topic of conversation," I mutter.

"Look, I'll eat one too," he says, popping a berry into his mouth. Then he picks up a second berry and holds it out to me in his long, delicate fingers.

"Trust me," he says.

I open my lips and take what he's offering. He smiles at me as I crush the tiny crimson orb between my teeth. Juice floods my mouth, tart with a hint of summer sweetness. Reznyk's smile widens. Red berry juice spreads across his lips. It makes him look wild and possibly dangerous.

"There aren't many left this time of year," he says.

I take another berry, then hold it out for him.

"Please," I say. "They're delicious, and I'll feel bad if I eat them all."

For just a heartbeat, he hesitates. Then his lips close around my fingers. Heat pools in my core as our eyes meet. The air between us is suddenly thick and heavy, and the sun is far too hot. Then he pulls away and grins at me with red-tinged lips.

"So," he says, holding out the last berry for me. "What's your plan? What is it you want?"

I take the berry and shrug as sweetness spreads across my tongue. The first answer in my mind, the stupid, impossible answer, is that I want to stay here, sitting in the autumn sunshine and feeding berries to this man until all the worlds end.

I sigh. "I've thought about this a lot," I begin as I stare at a group of clouds chasing themselves across the sky. "And don't laugh, okay?"

"I promise," he replies, in that deep voice I feel between my legs.

My fingers twist together over my stomach. "It's going to sound stupid," I say. "But what I really want is to learn about my parents."

Reznyk says nothing.

"They were Exemplars," I continue. "I've tried to find out more about them, but—" I hesitate. I'm not quite ready to admit to all my nocturnal snooping inside the Towers. "I don't think the other Exemplars want to tell me the truth. Not until I show some flicker of magical potential, at least."

I blink at the clouds as my vision blurs.

"That's not stupid," Reznyk says.

"So, that's my answer," I finish, with a shrug, like this means nothing to me. "What I really want is to go back to the Towers with some sort of, I don't know, magical energy. Magical potential. Something to prove I'm ready to learn the truth about my family."

Reznyk frowns.

"I'm sorry," I say. "It sounds idiotic when I say it out loud."

"No, it doesn't," he replies, in a soft voice.

Something chirps in the forest below us. It's followed by another, softer cry from farther away. I exhale slowly, wishing I could melt into the mountain and stay here forever.

"Maybe the Towers wanted you for some other reason," Reznyk says, in that strange, soft voice. "And they didn't tell you."

I laugh. It sounds like something breaking.

"Yeah," I snort. "Maybe they were really hard up for an orphan who can't sense magic."

"Here," Reznyk says. "Sit down and give me your hand."

He settles into the grass beside me, holding his palm out. I sit down next to him, wipe my eyes, and press my palm against his. He smiles as his long fingers close over the back of my hand, and I feel warmer. Some of the hopeless desperation I've carried with me all over the Daggers dissolves into the grass.

"Do you feel that?" he asks.

I shiver. I'm so close I feel the heat of his breath on my lips. I feel a lot of things, honestly; an ache between my legs, heat in my cheeks, a tight knot in my chest. Is that what magic feels like?

"I— I don't know," I reply, in a low whisper. "I would know, right? If I felt it?"

Reznyk frowns, then lifts my hand like he's holding it out to the sun. He stares at our interlocked fingers like he's trying to read something written in another language.

"Now?" he asks, in a low whisper.

He's so close to me. He's staring at our intertwined fingers, and I'm staring at him, at those thick lashes, the curve of his jaw, the hint of tart red juice on his full lips.

Is this what it feels like to have the potential to shape magic? Is magic the reason why I ache when I'm around him, why I can't stop thinking about pressing my lips to his or tangling my fingers in his dark hair?

Or maybe he's been waiting for me after all. Maybe all I need to do is give this a little push.

I lean forward and press my lips to his.

He freezes, then pulls away with a gasp that leaves me feeling cold.

"That's what I feel," I whisper as his dark eyes meet mine.

"I— feel that too," he replies, his voice thick and rough, like rope.

He turns away. His hand drops mine, and the moment shatters like glass.

My chest feels hollow. Godsdamn it, I know better. I turn toward the dark, cold mountains and blink until my vision clears. Why do I keep torturing myself by reaching for something I can't have, something he doesn't want to share?

Reznyk told me how he feels on my first night here. He's in love with Lady Lenore Castinac back in Silver City, the woman he had perfect sex with, that queen who has everything.

And I'm not her.

CHAPTER 25
REZNYK
THERE'S SOMETHING ELSE

T close my eyes.

What in the nine hells am I doing? I should be avoiding Kira, not holding her hand and pressing magic into her palm. She was sent by the thrice-damned Towers to find the amulet. All I need to do is convince her I don't have the damn thing so she'll go back to the Towers and tell them there's no reason for anyone to come back here ever again.

Kissing her is absolutely not a part of that plan.

Besides, some dark whisper of intuition suggests, Kira's flirty innocence and her sad story would make one hell of a cover. I don't think it's likely Kira's been faking it this whole time, of course; she'd have to be damn good, better than any spy or assassin I've ever met, to go this long without slipping up once.

Still. If that's a cover story, it's brilliant. And if it's not, it's just so damned cruel.

I should tell Kira that the Towers lied about her magical potential. I just ran enough magic through her hand to make my skin burn, and she didn't so much as flinch. I don't think she felt any of it. Although what she did feel—

I shift on the grass, then press my knuckles into my chest as if that's going to loosen the knot under my ribs. Gods, this pull between us is making everything worse. What kind of idiot was I to take her up on her offer in the hunting lodge?

Fuck. The same kind of idiot I am now.

I know why the Towers came for Kira three years ago. That would have been when I started to pursue Lenore in earnest, when she stopped being just another pretty face in a crowd of silk dresses and started to be something more. A vision of a possible future, one where I didn't have to be alone.

My failed attempt at romance is the reason Kira gave her life away to the Towers. I'm behind the lie of her magical ability. Fyrris might have whispered the words into her ear, but he did it because of me and Leanore Castinac and my godsdamned idiotic heart. Because I thought I'd get away with it, that I could fall in love like a normal person.

That's a joke. My entire life is just a trail of ash and bones. I shake my head, then drag my hand through my hair. This would all be so much easier if we hadn't slept together. If I hadn't gone to the damned hunting lodge. If I hadn't murdered the old god without using the amulet and then run screaming from the consequences.

Damn it. I turn back to Kira. Suddenly, I feel very old. But was there ever a time when I felt young?

"Kira," I say. My voice sounds strange, like it's coming from somewhere very far away. "I should tell you."

Her shoulders rise and fall. It looks like she's bracing herself. Of course. She has to know what's coming.

"About your, uh, magical potential," I begin. "I'm so sorry. But I don't feel it."

She makes a sound that's almost like a laugh, until I catch the expression on her face. She presses her palms against her eyes, then shakes her head.

"Of course you don't," she mutters. "No one does."

She drops her hands, then tilts her head toward the sky. Tears glint in the corners of her eyes. Afternoon sunlight plays off the strands of hair that have escaped from her braid, and I stare at the lips that just touched mine with a sort of hunger I'm not sure I've ever felt before. She makes that sound again, a whimper she's trying to disguise as a laugh.

"Whoever my parents are," she says, under her breath, "they're probably disappointed with me."

I turn to stare at my own hands, like the coward I am.

"There's something else," I continue.

Kira inhales softly as the world holds still around us. Wind ruffles the gold and emerald leaves of the forest beneath us. For a moment, I wonder if I actually have the courage to do this.

"The man from the Towers," I say. "The one you came with, the blond."

"Tholious," Kira says. The tone of her voice suggests there's not much love lost between the two of them, thank the gods.

"He offered me a trade for the amulet," I say. "He didn't look happy about it."

She turns toward me, and I have to look away.

"What was it?" she asks.

"They offered me you," I confess, even though something hot and sharp twists in my gut when I say the words. "And, maybe that's why the Towers—"

Kira laughs. It's hard and bright, like the edge of a blade. And then she buries her face in her hands and laughs again, although this time it's more like a sob.

"Fuck," she cries. "Why am I even surprised?"

She barks another laugh, then wipes her eyes and stares at the clouds shape-shifting their way across the sky.

"Of course," she mutters, as if she's talking to the air. "There's nothing special about me. There never was."

"That's not funny," I snap.

"It's not meant to be," Kira replies.

"I've known a lot of people with magical potential," I say. "The world would be better off without most of them."

Kira laughs again, softer this time. My chest aches as I open my mouth, searching desperately for the words to express all the myriad ways Kira is incredibly, heartbreakingly special.

"I wanted a rug," I blurt.

Kira blinks at me. Tears shimmer in her eyes.

"I rebuilt the cabin months ago," I continue. "It's better than the keep, but it's still too damn cold in the morning. I kept telling myself I'd get a rug out of the keep, but— You're the one who actually did it."

I snap my mouth closed before I can say anything even more idiotic. A tear slides down Kira's cheek as she shakes her head.

"Thanks," she whispers.

Her lips curve into something that might, one day, blossom into a smile, and my gods, I have never wanted to kiss anyone like I want to kiss her right now. The wind pushes a strand of hair across her lips. I could reach out and tuck it behind her ear, then lean closer—

I clench my jaw, then turn away. She can't stay here, damn it, and kissing her would only make it harder to send her away. I stare at the distant peak of the mountain I named after Aveus, master of illusions, and try to tell myself the sting in my eyes is due to the wind. Behind me, Kira clears her throat.

"So," she says, speaking slowly. "I have another plan. A backup plan."

"Oh?"

I glance at her, but she's not looking at me. She's frowning at the mountain I've named after myself. Something cold whispers across the back of my neck.

"I, uh. I don't think I want to go back to Silver City," she says, in a voice that's hardly more than a whisper. "Not now. Not after—that."

"Oh?" I say again.

My stupid heart leaps at this, almost like it's been waiting all week for those exact words, and suddenly I'm picturing things I didn't even know I wanted. Kira in the cabin, holding a mug and watching snow fall through the window. Taking her hand and pointing out the direwolves, showing her the yearling pups as autumn leaves blanket the forest floor.

"I just— I don't know where else to go," Kira continues. "Maybe the Port of Good Fortune? I don't know."

Right. Of course. I try to drown those dreams of Kira curled up on the bed in the cabin, watching snow fill the valley below us like tea in a mug.

She doesn't want that. No one would want that.

"I know someone in the Port," I say, thinking of Dreures. He's an asshole and a professional criminal, but he still owes me a favor. That should be enough to render him trustworthy. I hope.

Kira makes a humming sound. She looks at me, then away, and then back at me. She's smiling, but there's something hesitant about it, like it's been pulled too tight over something else.

"You could come with me," she says.

A hint of what I feel about that idea must flicker across my face, because her eyes drop.

"Not like that, I mean," she continues, speaking fast, like she's trying to bury what she just said in a flood of words. "Not like, you know, a partner, or whatever. Not even for long. Just, maybe you could help me get set up? I mean, hells, I don't even know how to get to the Port of Good Fortune. I've never even been outside Silver City, at least not until I came here."

I feel cold. The damned amulet glints in my memory, shoved under a broken bucket in the garden, of all the stupid places to hide it. I think of the direwolves crossing the ridge in the sunlight.

And I think of the old god who travels with them, the last creature of pure magic left in this world. If the Towers come hunting for the amulet, bringing ravens and Exemplars and all the things that are sensitive to the delicate pull of magic, they'll find the wolves.

They'll find the old god.

And then some other idiot will be handed an ebony crossbow and a silver bolt, and the entire world will be lessened.

"No," I say. "No. I can't leave."

"Reznyk, you don't have enough food!" Kira blurts. "Trust me, I ran the orphanage larder for years. You've got two, maybe three months of food stored in your root cellar. It's not enough for the winter!"

"I know," I growl through clenched teeth.

Kira blinks. She looks like someone just smacked her.

"So, what in the nine hells are you thinking?" she snaps. "You're just going to sit up here and starve?"

I turn away from Kira and stare down at the valley below us. Spots of green wink from the sea of gold. There are more golden leaves today than there were yesterday. Soon, there will be so many leaves falling in that valley that I won't be able to ignore what they mean anymore.

"I'll go to Cairncliff for supplies," I say.

I don't mention the fact that I've already spent most of my shills in the Golden Peak Hunting Lodge.

Kira laughs. "Really? That's, what, a five-day trip? Do you have any idea how much food you're going to need when the snow really piles up?"

Not really, no. But I don't want to sound like an idiot, so instead of answering her question, I stumble to my feet and turn away.

"I can't leave," I snarl.

Which is, I have to admit, a very shitty excuse.

CHAPTER 26
REZNYK
THE FORBIDDEN MEADOW

"Morning, sunshine," Kira says, with a shy little smile that twists like a knife inside my chest.

I try my best to smile back. She lit the fire and hung the teapot over the flames, and now the scent of the flowers she's been using as a tea replacement swirls through the air in the cabin, a soft counterpoint to the rising woodsmoke. Xavier lifts his head from the foot of the bed and stares at me with his wide, green eyes. A wave of annoyance radiates from his person.

I know. Spending the night in the old keep was a bad choice. I woke up shivering so violently it hurt. But somehow, freezing my ass off in the keep felt safer than trying to sleep in the same room as Kira after that kiss.

Kira hands me a steaming mug. The shadows under her eyes suggest she didn't have the most restful night either, but she doesn't say anything.

Good. Probably best for both of us if we ignore yesterday's hand-holding and everything that came after. Now I know Kira wants to go to the Port, and she knows I'm not going with her. Later today, we can start to make plans for her trip.

But first, I have a promise to fulfill. I take a slow sip of what Kira's handed me, which tastes like wet grass, if I'm being honest, as I lean against the doorframe and watch her rotate the last of yesterday's turnip in a pan.

"It's not much of a breakfast," she says, when she turns back to me. "But you're fresh out of bacon and eggs."

"Damn, I knew there was something I forgot to pick up at the market this morning," I reply, as she hands me a bowl with a warmed-up lump of boiled turnip in it.

Our eyes meet. She smiles in a way that gives me a sliver of hope. Perhaps we can go back to the way things were, that tenuous balance of teasing and flirtation that seemed so close to friendship.

At least until she leaves forever.

I swallow the last mushy lump of turnip, then shake my head, as if I could knock that thought away.

"So," I begin as I slide my bowl back to its place on the sideboard, "are you ready to see the meadow?"

The direwolves feel close, but still on the far side of the peak, I think. And the weather is clear. It's going to be a beautiful day to climb the ridge.

"Oh!" she replies. "The forbidden meadow?"

"The very same," I answer.

"I don't know," she says, with a grin. "Isn't that where you keep all your secrets?"

"Only the darkest," I reply.

"Great!" she cries, but then her smile fades and she looks at me like she's about to tell me something I might not want to hear. "You don't need to do this, you know," she says.

My throat pulls tight. I blink, then look away. Past the

fire she lit, the tea she brewed, the breakfast she prepared out of the dinner she cooked last night. It's already hard to imagine how this place will feel without her.

"I know," I say, clearing my throat. "But it's going to be a beautiful day, and there's not much to do around here."

That's a blatant lie. There are at least a hundred things I should be doing around here, but I'd much rather show Kira the late summer wildflowers blooming in the meadow than worry about the damned garden or split even more firewood.

"Well, if you'd like," Kira says, with a shy sort of smile.

"Please," I say, after giving her a little bow. "Allow me."

I hold my arm out for her like I'm Syrus Maganti about to escort her to a dance in the private section of the Crown Day festivities, and together, we leave the cabin.

The wind picks up as we climb the ridge, tugging Kira's hair back from her neck. Magic buzzes and flickers in the air, making it hard for me to determine where exactly the direwolves are roaming. Clouds scurry across the face of the sky, leaving dappled shadows over the forest below us. I watch sunlight wash across the stony faces of the mountains I've named after the other Elites, the only friends I've ever had, and once again it occurs to me that Tholious might have had a point, damn him.

I have been lonely. Nine hells, I'm befriending the mountains.

"Shit," I mutter under my breath.

"What's that?" Kira calls down from above me.

She's pulled herself up the steepest part of the ridge, just below the lip of the meadow. The wind has done a commendable job of ruining her tight braid, and now loose strands of amber hair flutter around her cheeks. Her skin is slightly darker now, after a week of working in the garden with me, and her full lips part as she catches her breath. The sound of the stream clattering down the stones beside us fills the air, interrupted by the occasional shriek from the fat little rodents who've claimed this part of the ridge for their kingdom.

She looks happy up here, on the far edge of the world. And now I'll never be able to look at this part of the ridge without remembering the way she's smiling at me right now.

"Nothing," I call up to her. "Almost there, that's all."

I lean back and watch as she pulls herself up the final pitch, sunlight glinting off her hair and the wind ruffling the back of her shirt. When she reaches the edge of the meadow, she makes a soft little cry, a sound that's partly surprise and partly a whispered, reverent prayer.

I join her. Together, we stare at the tiny, perfect world cupped between the mountain I named for myself and the other three peaks I named for my fellow Elites. Below us, the stream cuts a winding curlicue through emerald grass. Willow bushes hug the edges, thick and whispering in the breeze. Seed heads rock and bob, dotted here and there with late summer blossoms of crimson and gold.

"Hells, Reznyk," Kira says, turning back to me. "It's beautiful up here!"

There's a wild sort of joy in her expression. For a heartbeat, she looks so perfectly at home here that I can almost believe she's a part of this place, that I stumbled on Kira just like I stumbled on the ruins of the keep and the wolves.

The wolves. Their presence tugs on my magic again, and I turn to stare at the far rock field, the low saddle between Syrus's peak and Aveus's peak. Kira walks into the meadow with her arms spread, like she's ready to embrace the whole place.

"Is this where you found those berries?" Kira calls.

She crouches in the grass, halfway to the stream, beaming like she's just found a pile of gold in the leaves. I turn away from the mountains and join her.

"Nicely done," I say, when I see the little red sphere between her fingers. "I thought I found them all."

"Here, you should have it," she says, holding her hand out to me.

Our eyes meet; heat floods my body even as the presence of the wolves flutters and dances across my magic. My breath catches in the back of my throat.

"You go ahead," I reply. "Here. Let me show you the place with the best view."

Kira is silent as we walk along the meadow's ragged edge, the place where the rock field quietly abandons itself to the vanguard of the grass. The thrum of the wolves' awareness grows stronger. By the time we reach the flat-topped boulder overlooking the meadow, I can't ignore it any longer.

The wolves are coming over the ridge.

"Kira," I say in a low voice.

She turns to me. I press my finger to my lips, then point to the low saddle between the two peaks. She follows my gaze. Sun dances off the rocks, and the wind rustles the leaves on the willow bushes. Somewhere in the distance, a hawk calls for his mate.

And then the first of the direwolves climbs into view.

It's the old male, the leader. He stops at the edge of the ridge and sniffs the air. Kira gasps, then slams her hand over her mouth. The male stares down into the meadow, his gaze traveling over the two of us as if we are of no more significance than the boulder we're sitting on. Kira's breath catches; her arm presses into my side.

"It's okay," I whisper. "They're not interested in us."

The old male lowers his shaggy head, then picks his way slowly down the rock field. One of the rodents screams a warning as the wolf's mate crests the ridge. The birds fall silent.

Another female crosses, and then the four pups gallop over the ridge, all long legs and dangling tongues. They jump on each other and wrestle, the opposite of their leader's stately descent.

"Those are the cubs," I whisper to Kira. "Born this spring. They were tiny."

I hold my hands up, trying to estimate the length of the direwolf pups when I first saw them, but Kira's eyes don't leave the far ridge as the rest of the direwolf pack pours over the pass and drops below the meadow. I count them, as always, my chest tight as a fist until I see the entire pack is safe.

The old wolf stops at the far edge of the meadow, looks at us once more, and then leads the parade of his pack into the forests below. I exhale slowly, thanking all the gods who are listening that those damned hunters are gone.

"Reznyk." Kira's voice trembles, making my name a sort of panicked whisper. "What's that?"

I know what they are before I turn back to the ridge. I can feel them, like eyes on the back of my neck or a pocket of cold water welling up from the bottom of the ocean. Something ancient, something impossible. Something magical.

Slowly, the old god crests the top of the pass. They look almost like a direwolf this morning, although smaller, and the longer I look at them, the more fluid their body becomes. Now a wolf, now more of a deer, and now a pool of inky smoke pouring down the side of the ridge.

I turn to Kira. She's crying. Tears trace glistening tracks down her cheeks, even as she smiles. Her mouth opens with a sort of wonder that doesn't belong in this mundane world of turnips and washing basins.

I reach for her hand. Our cold fingers intertwine as we watch the last old god in the world. They rest at the fringe of the meadow, long enough to stretch and shake, their body like feathers, like silk, and then like fur. They sniff the ground, a sort of snorting huff that echoes off the stones, and then they turn and follow the wolves.

Even after they vanish over the ridge and the birds resume their songs, Kira and I watch the spot where they disappeared.

"Was— Was that?" Kira whispers.

My gut twists, and my chest feels tight. I nod.

"But, I thought," she stammers. "I thought the last one was—"

Her voice cuts off, mercifully. I swallow, trying to drown the bitterness rising in the back of my throat. It's bad enough knowing I murdered an old god in the abstract. But after seeing one?

Now she knows exactly what a monster I am.

"I thought they were all gone," Kira finally whispers.

"That's what everyone thinks," I say. My voice sounds like stones grinding together. "No one knows there's an old god still living in the Daggers. As long as I'm here, no one ever will."

She makes a sound in the back of her throat, something sharp and sudden. I turn to see what's happened. She's staring at me through a haze of tears.

"You're protecting them," she whispers.

Her voice twists inside me like a knife. Suddenly, it's too

much. Seeing the old god, knowing that Kira understands what I've done.

I drop off the boulder and onto the grass. Kira's voice follows me, calling my name. I turn around. Kira is right behind me, reaching for me. The look on her face hits me like a punch to my gut.

"Stop it!" I scream.

Kira blinks. "Stop what?"

"Stop looking at me like I'm some kind of hero!"

"Hero?" she says, in a voice that's almost as loud as mine. "Reznyk, you're going to starve up here so you can protect the last old god. You're an idiot!"

I exhale. The sun winks on the tears in Kira's eyes, and her shoulders sink as she sighs.

"You're idiotically heroic," she says.

CHAPTER 27
REZNYK
BLACKWATER

I sink to the grass and bury my head in my hands. My mind howls.

Hero? Never.

Screaming, blood, and flames. That's what I am. That's all I'll ever be.

Cloth rustles as Kira sits down beside me. She doesn't say anything, and for a long time, I sit with my knees pulled up to my chest, cradling my head as the sun warms my shoulders and the birds and insects of the high mountains sing all around us. Finally, I raise my head and stare at the patch of bare stone the old god just crossed.

"I didn't come to the Towers like you," I begin. My voice is rough, like the rasp of a file against wood. "I wasn't invited. I— I sought them out."

I fall silent. That's not the start of the story. But it's not a story I've ever had reason to tell, is it? I clear my throat as a dragonfly's glossy wings catch the light by the stream.

"You know where I'm from," I say.

I can't quite bring myself to meet her gaze, but I watch out of the corner of my eye as she nods.

"It was a small, nasty place, Blackwater. Smugglers and crime lords, mostly. Hells, as a kid, I thought it was normal for ships to come into the harbor at night with no lights." I chuckle at the memory. "The brothel was the biggest business in town."

I close my eyes, searching for a way to describe it, but the words don't come. Looking back, I can recognize what kind of place the Siren's Song was. But to me, at that time, it was full of magic and wonder and women who played games with me or told me stories or snuck me treats from the larder. I was a child, and the Siren's Song was my home.

I sigh, then pick a blade of grass and twirl it between my fingers.

"Madame Drenaris ran the brothel," I say, choosing my words carefully. "She was also my mother. But she didn't run the town. Lord Murus did."

I drop the blade of grass at my feet. A sudden breeze ruffles the seed heads in the meadow and makes the willow leaves wink silver and green.

"Like the Maganti family and Silver City?" Kira asks.

"No," I say. "Not at all."

A shiver crawls up the back of my neck. The Magantis, Syrus's family, run Silver City like a business. Sure, every deal they cut has something in it for them, but ultimately, they do well when the entire city does well.

Lord Murus ran Blackwater like he was holding it against a wall with a blade to its throat. He was going to take all he could and kick the corpse into the harbor.

"Murus wanted the brothel," I say. "But it was more than that. He wanted my mother too."

"As a wife?" Kira asks. "Or a, uh, concubine?"

"I'm not sure," I answer. "I didn't understand it as a

child. I still don't quite understand it now. She used to say men like him only want something beautiful so they can put it in a cage."

Kira laughs low in her throat, and I wonder if most women have experienced men like that. It's not a happy thought.

"They went back and forth for years," I continue. "Screaming messengers. Threats. Stones thrown through windows."

"Gods," Kira whispers. "That must have been terrifying."

I shrug. I should have been afraid. But my mother never showed fear. She told me I was safe, and so I was. Madame Drenaris was the heart of the Siren's Song, and the heart of my childhood. I never doubted her.

"It came to a head when I was about ten years old," I say. "My mother sent me to the Port of Good Fortune with a few of the younger girls. She said it was so we could see the feast day celebration."

My voice fails. I close my eyes. Wind dances across my face and tugs at my hair. Even now, after so many years, the pain is still sharp.

"When we returned," I begin, my voice soft and slow, "it was gone. The entire place. Burned to the ground."

I shake my head, trying to dispel the scent of ash and cinders that lingers in my memory.

"I tried to confront him, Lord Murus. I ran all the way to his estate, screaming and raising my fists. But Scarlet caught me. She was one of the girls who'd taken me to the Port. She bought me taffy." I pause, sorting through the jumble of memories I usually keep locked in the dark. "She caught me in the middle of the road outside his estate, and she said, 'Not now, Reznyk. He'll only kill you too.' She probably could have gotten something from Lord Murus, if she'd turned me in. But she took me with her instead."

I pause, then stretch my legs.

"We went back to the Port. There was nowhere else to go, really. Scarlet found a place, another brothel. I stayed on for a while, running errands. But the owner didn't really want me there, so I found...other work."

I fall silent, remembering.

"I learned how to fight," I finally confess. "I learned how to hurt people. How to steal. I learned what it means to have the kind of power that makes people afraid of you, and I— I wanted it."

I suck in a breath. I'm afraid to look at Kira, to see myself reflected in her eyes, so I turn toward the valley instead, where the shadows of clouds dance across the green and gold leaves far below.

"And then," I continue, "one day, two men in long white robes came to the Port. I don't know who they were or what they were doing, but they pulled me like a flame calls to a moth. I followed them for days, until I finally got close enough to steal the thing that had been screaming out to me." I take a breath, then continue. "It was a silver chain."

"You robbed an Exemplar from the Towers?" Kira asks.

I close my eyes so I don't have to look at her, and nod.

"I didn't know they were from the Towers. I had no idea what the chain actually was," I continue. "But some part of me knew what it could do. So I wrapped it in a handkerchief and talked my way onto a sloop headed for Blackwater."

I pull my legs up to my chest and drop my head to my knees. Memories swirl and dance like flames. I've never told anyone what happened in Blackwater that day, and the words are slow in coming. I remember the smell of the muddy harbor at low tide, the wind pushing in from the ocean as the sun set over the swamps. A thousand tiny, hidden creatures sang in chorus as I walked up the hill to the estate of Lord Murus, the stolen silver chain wrapped around my fist, strange magic crackling across my skin.

I don't remember all of it. My memories are full of holes, like silk spread over a fire. I'm not sure how I got into the estate, for one, or how I ended up in the drawing room with Lord Murus on his knees before me.

But I do remember what he said to me.

"Murus," I begin. "When I found him, he—he said he'd take me in. Said he'd raise me. As his son."

I open my eyes and stare out across the valley, where the leaves hold more gold and crimson today than they did yesterday. I remember the way Murus's hands trembled when he told me he'd be my father, that he would teach me everything he knew. That I would rule Blackwater when he was gone.

Next to me, Kira mumbles something under her breath. It sounds like a curse. She understands. More than anyone else, I would guess. A woman raised in Silver City's orphanage would know exactly what it means when someone offers you a family. I clear my throat.

"Like I said," I continue, "I didn't know what the silver chain would do. When I let the magic go, I— I didn't think it would explode."

Here my memories go black again. I remember jets of flame shooting from the chain on my fist, waves of super-heated air, the scent of ash, and a strange, horrible gasping sound, like the earth herself had just taken a breath.

And the next thing I remember is staggering to my feet as Blackwater burned below me.

"I only wanted to stop Murus," I say. My voice is thin,

like it's been pulled tight over something sharp. "To make him pay for what he did. I didn't want to destroy his estate. I didn't realize the wind would carry the flames—"

My voice cuts off, like I'm being choked. I wipe my hand across my eyes. Maybe it was the wind that carried the flames. Maybe it was the force of my hatred and rage combined with the magic I'd stolen, magic I had no idea how to control.

Whatever the cause, Blackwater burned to the ground that night. By morning, there was nothing left of the town Murus promised me but cinders and ash.

"I spent a long time in the swamps, after that," I whisper. "Years later, when I finally made it back to the Port, I felt that pull again. There was another Exemplar on the docks, with another silver chain. This time, I didn't steal it. I followed him to Silver City. To the Towers."

I open my mouth, but slowly realize there's nothing left to say. I could apologize, but what difference would that make? I heard the screams of the people who died in the flames. I still hear them. No apology could ever right the wrongs I've done.

I turn away from Kira, unable to force myself to meet her gaze. She'll be horrified, of course. Anyone would be horrified by what I've done, what I am.

And I didn't stop with Blackwater, did I? No, I ran straight to the Towers. I learned how to control the magic in those silver chains, how to kill and destroy with elegance and precision. I became a monster, or perhaps I was already a monster. Hells, I even betrayed the Towers. They sent me to murder an old god and trap their power in the amulet.

But I didn't use the amulet. I took the magic of the old god for myself, so that not even the Exemplars of the Towers could make me bow.

So here I am, the monster of the Daggers. Master of my own destiny. Powerful beyond my wildest dreams. Feared by all, even those who once claimed to love me.

And completely alone.

CHAPTER 28
KIRA
WHY YOU'RE HERE

"Gods," I whisper under my breath.

Reznyk acts like he can't hear me. He's turned away, so all I can see is the slight tremble in his shoulders, the way he's holding his knees to his chest like he's trying to keep himself from falling apart.

"How old were you?" I ask. "When you stole the chain from the Exemplars?"

He ignores me. I reach for him, let my fingers brush his shoulder.

"Reznyk?"

He shivers, then pulls away.

"I don't know," he mutters, answering me without turning around. "Thirteen, maybe? What does it matter?"

The wind catches in his long black hair, pulling it toward me. I swallow hard as Zayne's words float back to me. He sees it all the time, Zayne said, little shits claiming they're from Blackwater in order to impress someone.

But what Reznyk just told me is horrifying, not impressive. Some distant part of my brain whispers that perhaps I should be afraid of the man who stole a silver chain from an Exemplar and used it to destroy an entire town.

But all I can see is a terrified kid who lost his mother and his home. Shit, Silver City orphanage is full of scared, angry kids. They'll throw a punch at a grown man just because they don't want to be the first to flinch.

I held those kids as they cried themselves to sleep. I rubbed their backs and made them tea and tried to convince them there was more to life than fear and incandescent rage.

Sometimes it worked. Barcus became a blacksmith, using his fists to create instead of destroy. Maryam started to smile after a year in the orphanage, then to laugh, and then she was married with a sweet little baby of her own, and she would come by with a plate of cookies and gossip about the other women in the marketplace where she worked.

And sometimes they snuck through the windows at night, those wild, broken children, off to rob the Maganti estate or to join the Mercenary Guild or to wash up weeks later on the banks of the Ever-Reaching River with knife wounds in their gut.

Suddenly, I remember the way Reznyk's eyes danced in the light as he stared at me. Something cracks open inside my chest, and gods above, is this what magic feels like? Like something just broke open inside of you?

Or is this what it feels like to fall in love?

"Shit," I announce.

I push myself to my feet and rub my hands along my arms. Reznyk continues to stare across the valley like he's convinced he can make me vanish if he ignores me long enough.

"So that's why you're here?" I ask.

Wind tugs at his shirt and ruffles his hair. Reznyk sits there like a boulder.

"You're going to die up here, starve to death, as what, some sort of penance?" I push. "Because you feel bad about what happened when you were a child? You think that's going to make anything better?"

He ignores me.

"You think dying here is better than going to the Port of Good Fortune with me?" I cry.

The wind carries my words, making them sound shrill and brittle. My face feels hot. Gods help me, I'm about two heartbeats away from completely losing it.

"Damn it!" I snap.

I spin away, gulping air as I stare at the sheer stone faces of the mountains Reznyk named after his friends, and then I stumble down the slope and into the meadow. Flowers bob in the sun. Tiny insects hum and buzz, all going about their business as if winter wasn't hunched on the far horizon with its teeth bared.

I stop at the edge of the stream, just before a low tangle of willow bushes. Little golden birds flit and dart through the leaves. I press my palms over my eyes and try to slow the frantic beating of my heart. So what if Reznyk doesn't want to come with me? So what if he wants to stay in the Daggers through the winter with enough food for a month or so? Why do I care so godsdamn much about him?

"Kira?"

His voice sends a tremble through my body. I lower my hands slowly, then turn to find Reznyk standing behind me with a strange expression on his face. He looks almost lost, like he's not sure where he's standing or how he got here.

"It's not like that," he says, softly.

I laugh. It's a terrible reaction, possibly the worst thing I can do, but I can't stop myself. He's just so full of shit. For all his dramatic posturing in the keep, his slamming doors and making ominous pronouncements about not following him, some part of him is still just a scared little kid with stolen magic who doesn't know what in the nine hells he's doing.

I cross my arms over my chest and raise an eyebrow.

"Not like what?" I finally ask.

He winces. "It's not personal," he says. "It's not about you. It's about them."

He looks down the slope of the ridge where the old god vanished with the wolves into the dusky pine forest, and that thing inside my chest cracks open once again. It's like a wound, like he's injured me in some secret, invisible way.

"Shit," I mutter, eloquent as ever. "Look, Reznyk, how old do you think the old god is?"

He blinks like he's never considered this.

"Old, right?" I continue. "Older than the wolves."

"Maybe even older than the mountains," Reznyk says.

"And they've survived," I say. "All that time. Without a protector."

Reznyk turns away. He looks like something hurts.

"The Towers—" he says. It's almost a whisper, like he's afraid of being overheard.

"The Towers have no reason to come up here," I say. "Hells, they only sent us up here because of you. You could be drawing the Towers closer to the god just by being here."

He shudders, then spins away. I raise my hand and let it fall.

"Don't stay here," I finally say. "You don't have to come with me, but please. You deserve better than this."

Reznyk growls, something low and violent that echoes

across the meadow. When he spins to face me, his eyes are wide and wild. His lips pull back in a snarl.

"No, I don't!" he screams. His shoulders tremble as the wind pulls his cloak and hair back. "You don't understand!"

He looks down at his hands, his open palms, his fingers curled like talons. They're trembling. The air around them is hazy, almost like mist rising from a river, and some dim, distant part of me wonders if that's magic, if I'm finally coming into my birthright.

But a much, much larger part of me recognizes those hands for what they are, magical shimmer or not. The gods only know what Reznyk is seeing. But whatever it is, it's not the truth.

"Reznyk," I say. "They're just hands."

He makes a choking sound. When he looks up at me, his dark eyes shine in the light.

"You know what I am," he says, in a voice as rough as the mountains. "You know what I did. You should know—" His voice chokes off. His hands curl into fists as he shakes his head, his black hair falling over his face like a veil. "There's no place for me," he whispers. "Not anymore. Not now."

"Oh, fuck that!" I snap.

His head snaps up, shock rippling across his features.

And I kiss him.

It's awkward and clumsy, my lips hitting his so hard I feel the bite of his teeth through his skin. Blood blossoms on my tongue. He pulls away. I reach for him.

"You don't have to earn your place in the world," I say. "You're just here, same as the wolves and the flowers. And—"

My throat pulls tight, suddenly horrified by the words bubbling up inside of me. What difference is it going to make how I feel? I'm not The One, and I damn well know it. But I think of that scared little kid, the one who lost everything and couldn't see a way out, and I have to try.

"I don't want you to die," I say.

I drop my hand. Reznyk catches it as it falls. He meets my gaze, that strange, inscrutable look in his dark eyes, and the whole world stops, frozen in this brilliant autumn afternoon, this golden alpine meadow suspended in amber.

And then he pulls me into his arms, and the world bursts back into life. The soft rasp of his shirt presses against my cheek. I'm surrounded by his scent, rich and thick and magical. His chest rises and falls. Below the threads of birdsong, and the soft hiss and rustle of the wind, I hear the low, throbbing beat of his heart. Or perhaps it's my heart echoing against his chest.

"Thank you," he whispers into my hair.

His lips brush my forehead, and another laugh bubbles up from somewhere deep inside of me. I shake my head against his chest.

"Hells, Reznyk," I say, turning up to meet his gaze. "That's not much, saying I don't want you to die. That's not even—"

His lips catch mine, stopping me before I can tell him how ridiculous he's being, and my words evaporate. Because Reznyk is kissing me again, finally, and I'm falling apart in his arms.

It's not soft or gentle, the kiss he's offering. It's not a tender, hesitant first kiss or a gentle thank you. No, this is hungry. This is the kind of kiss he gave me after two bottles of wine and a full game of Questions. It's a kiss of hunger and hard edges, a kiss with ragged desperation in its hidden teeth.

And my gods, I open for it like a flower. His arms tighten

around my waist as I reach up, my fingers twisting in his black hair, my tongue dancing with his, sliding and embracing, falling away only to come back together, harder and deeper. I kiss him with every spark of sexual frustration that's been churning inside me ever since lightning arched through the night sky above the Daggers and showed me the man who made me scream the night before, standing in the shelter of a ruined tower with his arms crossed over his chest.

And he gives it right back, his lips and tongue pressing into mine so hard it's almost a struggle, almost a test of strength. There's no more room for the part of me that whispers he doesn't love me and that the ache in my chest is going to hurt so much worse if I don't stop—

Hells, it's too late. I plunge into our kiss, desperate for more of him as my body goes up in flames, kissing him like I've never kissed anyone before as his hand slips under my shirt and goes up my back, scattering sparks across my bare skin. I press into him, shifting my hips until the hot ache between my legs meets the iron between his, panting as our bodies ripple together, and no one should be able to make me feel so damn good without even taking off my clothes.

He moans, a sound so deep and low I swear I can hear it in my very core. A moment later he breaks our kiss, then traces my jaw with his lips. I twist against him, the place between my legs hot and wet and aching, and my gods, how can he do this to me with just a kiss?

His mouth drops to my neck. I tilt my head back; clouds tumble over themselves as my gaze rakes the sky. Reznyk's arm closes around my rib cage as his teeth trace a path down my neck.

I break our kiss just long enough to drop my hand from his hair, trail it down the wall of his chest, and slide my fingers into the waistband of his pants. His entire body pulses when my fingers meet the soft head of his cock; he makes a sound that might be the most erotic thing I've ever heard in my life. I bring my lips to his neck, kissing and biting, following the trail of sweat as my hand wraps around the steel of his cock.

"You might need another pair of pants," I whisper.

He trembles, his entire body pulling tight. "Fuck," he groans.

I tilt my hips, grinding the ache between my legs against his thigh as I run my hand up and down his cock. Gods above, it's not fair! I want this man inside me more than I've wanted anyone in the past.

If I ever meet this woman he loves, I promise myself as he gasps in my arms, I'm going to punch her in the fucking face.

"Fuck," Reznyk rasps again.

He trembles again, then pulls back, out of my reach. His mouth is on mine before I can protest, driving hard, one hand tight around my waist while the other rips at the waistband of my pants. He tugs them down so violently I hear something rip, and then his hand presses between my legs and all thought vanishes.

He doesn't break our kiss. No, if anything, he drives into me harder as his hand parts my thighs, fucking me with his tongue and his fingers, ripping me apart while I'm still standing. His thumb drives into my clit as my thighs rock against his, and his gorgeous fingers slide into me, curling, pressing against that spot from the inside as I cling to the back of his shirt, my body cresting, cresting—

I explode like a feast day firework, breaking our kiss to scream his name, something that I've never done before. But his thumb doesn't stop, he drives into me even as pleasure breaks inside my body, and the world dissolves around us as I shatter longer and harder than I ever thought possible.

The world comes back to me slowly, floating in bits and pieces. Clouds drifting across their cerulean sea. Birdsong, the chatter of flowing water. Reznyk's arm draped around my waist, his cloak spread out on the grass below me. Somehow, we're on the ground, my pants shoved down to my knees, my lips sore and swollen and hungry for more.

"Oh my gods," I mumble as Reznyk pants beside me. "I might never walk again."

He laughs softly. I turn to see him staring at me, the sun filtered through his dark hair, that same strange expression in his eyes. He's looking at me like I'm a message written in a language he's never learned to read, and my chest aches in all the secret, cracked places that split open around him.

It's terrible, I realize as he stares at me. It's every bit as horrible as all the tavern songs say, falling in love.

And it's not nearly enough.

I roll over on my side and slide my fingers under the hem of his shirt.

CHAPTER 29
REZNYK
DANGEROUS WORK

This woman is going to kill me.

I've tried so hard, damn it. I sleep on the floor; I never touch her. I've been so very good at keeping my hands to myself and my eyes off Kira's ass. And her chest. And her lips.

Partly because of some whisper of intuition that says getting physical again wouldn't be a great idea, but mostly because I have no idea how to proceed. I've had friends and a lover, but never in the same package. Kira started as a lover. She's gotten dangerously close to being a friend.

No. If I'm being honest, Kira is a friend. Hells, she's more than a friend. I've had friends before; Syrus, Aveus, and Pytr, the three other Elites in the Towers. I never told them what brought me to Silver City.

I've never told anyone about Blackwater.

It should have sent her screaming. Instead, she acts like it doesn't even matter, the smoldering trail of destruction that seems to follow me no matter where I go. I should find it infuriating, the way she dismissed what I just told her.

But it's hard for me to feel anything over the constant

throbbing of my desperate cock. Gods, I can't drain that bastard enough. Just listening to Kira catch her breath next to me is enough to keep me hard.

Kira's fingers slip under my shirt and trace a path up my chest. My brain shuts down, all of my best intentions vanishing like mist before the rising sun. A moment later her lips meet my neck. My eyes snap open, catching wisps of clouds as they tangle together in the sky. I try to say something but it comes out as a strangled groan.

"Mmmm," Kira purrs against my ear as her fingers dance across my chest. "Tell me something, Reznyk?"

"Anything," I manage to say.

"I think I forgot where the Port of Good Fortune is," she says.

Something flashes in her eyes, and the explanation I was about to offer dies on my lips as the memory of that little room in the hunting lodge comes rushing back. Kira's naked body on the bed, my tongue tracing an imaginary map through the mountains of her breasts and the valley between her legs.

"Oh?" I stammer. "You need me to show you where that is again?"

"I might be able to find it," she replies. "If you take off your shirt."

I obey, because I'm an idiot and because it has been a very long time since a woman told me to take my shirt off. When I lie back down on the grass, the sun filters through Kira's fiery hair as she grins at me.

"Right," she says, tracing a finger over my collarbone. "This is Cairncliff, then."

"Cassonia," I reply.

Her smile widens, and then she bends down to run that wicked tongue over my skin.

"Like I said," she replies. "Cassonia."

I groan as her lips trace a path down my chest. One of her hands toys with my nipple, and I grit my teeth against the sudden impulse to roll her over onto the ground and drive my tongue into her sweet mouth.

"The Iron Mountains," Kira says, before she closes her mouth over my other nipple.

I try to say yes, but it comes out as another moan. Kira grins at me like a hunter standing over her fallen prey as her hair fans out across my chest, silk over my skin. Then she looks down at my chest and frowns.

"Damn," she says. "You have a lot of scars."

"It's dangerous work, being a magistrate," I say.

"You're not a magistrate," she replies.

"No," I say. "I'm not."

Our eyes meet. The air between us burns. Her fingers drop below my chest, tracing a path through the tangled curls toward my abdomen.

"Right," she says. "So here's Silver City."

She kisses my navel, then lower, and lower. I close my eyes as my entire body throbs with her touch. Gods, maybe this is a mistake, but I wouldn't stop her for all the shills in Silver City.

She stops at the waistline of my pants, then rubs her hand along my cock as she argues with the lacing.

"If Deep's Crossing is here," she says, tugging my pants down to kiss the top of my left hip. "Then that must mean—"

She pulls my pants down to my knees, then lets her lips trace a line across my trembling skin, from my hips to the base of my shaft.

"Oh, here we are," Kira says. "The Port."

And she takes me in her mouth.

I make a sound that's not even remotely close to human speech. Kira's fingers wrap around my shaft as her tongue flicks over the soft head, and then she's swallowing me, sucking me off like she never wants to do anything else in this world.

My gods, she's good. I try to hold still, but my hips rise to meet her, my body responding no matter what my mind says. I have a moment to think about how long it's been since anyone has done this to me, and then my thoughts are buried by waves of pleasure. I feel my climax building, hot and fast at the base of my cock, and hells, she's so good. This is so good—

And suddenly it's not enough. My eyes snap open. I want more in a way I haven't felt in years.

"Kira," I gasp.

I twist my hips on the grass, pulling away from her sweet, soft lips. She looks up at me, mouth glistening, eyes wide.

She's so beautiful it hurts.

Longing throbs inside me, a deep, pulsing ache. No, this isn't enough. We're not playing Questions above the hunting lodge anymore. She can't stay here, and I can't leave with her, but whatever this is between us, it's more than just another tumble in the sheets.

I want it to be more.

I lean forward and run my fingers along her cheek. "Kira," I whisper. "You're—"

But my voice fails me. I don't have a word for someone who makes me laugh, who works by my side, and who is so godsdamned sexy she makes me ache. She's more than a friend, more than a lover, much more than a night in a hunting lodge.

So I kiss her instead. She's shy at first, her lips slow to open, as if she's afraid she's done something wrong. I lean back, pulling her into the grass with me, kissing her softly, slowly. Kissing her like we have nothing else in this life to do, as if the entire world will wait in sunlight and birdsong while I kiss the woman who has become more than my lover.

I roll over her, pressing her shoulders to the grass as I tug off my pants. Slowly, I run my hand down her body, pull her pants off, and spread her thighs. Her eyes fly open, as blue as the sky above the Daggers.

"Reznyk—" she gasps, as if she knows what I'm thinking.

I nod, then come onto my knees. Her legs spread out before me; my gods, men have killed and died for less than this. My breath catches in the back of my throat. My cock strains forward, like it's trying to find the heat of her body with or without me. Kira frowns. The air between us trembles.

"Are— Are you sure?" Kira says.

I lean forward, my hands sinking into the grass above her shoulders, covering her body with mine. The heat of her rises to meet me; my cock brushes the curls between her legs, and I can't stop the moan that rips out of my throat. My arms tremble with the effort of holding myself back. Somehow, I find my voice.

"I'm sure," I whisper, in a voice as ragged as the edges of the mountains that surround us. "If there's a child, I— I'll—"

My throat closes around the sheer impossibility of the thoughts rising inside me. It doesn't matter what I say. If there's a child, I'll find a way to care for it. I'll make a way with fists and blood, if I need to.

Kira's head shakes against the grass, her hair tangling with the flowers. "The Towers," she says. "I drink the tea."

Of course. The nasty contraceptive tea everyone inside the Towers is forced to drink once a month, preventing any unnecessary complications despite the Towers's loosely enforced policy of celibacy.

"Still," I start, but my voice catches on something in the back of my throat.

Because, in that trembling heartbeat of a moment, I almost want to plant a seed that will grow. To have the promise of a future.

I shake my head, then begin to tip my hips forward. She's hot, wet, and sweet, and she makes a noise as I begin to enter her, a sort of gasp. She watches me as I move inside her, as slowly as I can, letting her surround me.

Gods, she feels good. My muscles tighten with the effort of holding back, entering her slowly. I gasp for breath as my shoulders roll, every part of me burning, drowning. Something shimmers in the edge of my vision. I break Kira's gaze, turn away for a heartbeat.

Magic dances in the air all around us. It's rising from me like steam off a river, slipping free as my focus shifts to the dance between us. It looks like sparks, or stars, golden fragments of pure magic swirling around us. I close my eyes, ignoring the subtle pull of magic as I sink into Kira's body.

Then I'm inside of her, fully inside. She makes another sound, a cry that's almost my name. Magic races across my skin; for the first time since the old god died in my arms, I don't try to hold it back.

I move my hips slowly, pulling out and returning in long, slow waves. When I open my eyes, sparks of magic wink and dance in Kira's hair. Her mouth is open; sweat beads on her neck and chest. She reaches up and sinks her fingers into my hair.

"Fuck," she growls. "Fuck, don't stop!"

Her hips rise to meet me. Magic flares and sparks down my arms. Pleasure burns at the base of my spine; my control is thin as the edge of a knife, sharp and cold. I bring one hand to the place where our bodies join and sink my fingers into the curls of Kira's sex until I touch the hard, hot nub of her clit and she screams.

I move faster, panting as sweat stings my eyes. Kira gasps and trembles beneath me, her legs wrapped around my waist, my name coming out in broken gasps, and my gods, she feels good. I want more, more of her, more of this, all of this, forever—

Kira screams again as she comes undone beneath me. Her sex pulls tight, closing as I slam into her hips, plunging deeper and deeper, ecstasy flooding my body, exploding from deep inside of me, seed pulsing through my cock in waves, filling her, a cry ripping through my throat that I couldn't swallow if I tried.

My body curls forward. I collapse with my head against her shoulder, my breath ragged and uneven, the world spinning on without me as the last of my seed spills between Kira's sweet legs. Kira gasps. Her arms tighten around my back.

"Are— Are you doing that?" she whispers.

I turn away from the safe haven of her neck. Magic spins around us like a field of golden stars.

"Shit," I groan. "Sorry."

"No," she whispers. "It's beautiful."

I kiss the soft skin of her neck, then roll onto the grass and drape my arm across her stomach. The magic is dissipating; already the golden sparks look more like mist and less like stars.

"Does that happen every time?" Kira asks.

I laugh, but it comes out sad and low. "No," I say. "I didn't have magic until I killed the old god. This is their magic, trapped inside my body."

Once again, this is the kind of statement that should horrify any rational person. Kira should react to this with shock, or possibly rage. Instead, she folds her arm over mine and watches me with those perfect blue eyes like she couldn't care less who or what I've murdered.

Hells, this woman is insane. Suddenly, I want to do this all over again. Kissing. Pulling off her clothes. Sinking into her, losing myself so fully that the magic trapped inside my body escapes to dance against the clouds.

I sigh. "I tried to stop it," I admit. "At first. When the old god was dying, I felt the magic leaving their body. I thought that's what I wanted, for their magic to come to me. But, when it happened, all I wanted was to stop it. To keep them alive."

I turn away. That's yet another thing I've never told anyone, how my courage failed at the moment of my victory. How desperately I tried to undo the very thing I'd trained for years to do.

"Hells," Kira whispers.

I blink at the sky. The magic is all but invisible now, just a slight suggestion of golden mist rising above us.

"I tried to set it free," I whisper. "For months afterward, I tried to let it go. I ruined the Towers's plan and ran from them, moving at night, hiding in the forest during the day and trying to get rid of it. I pushed magic into the world for hours, illusions and flames and spears, until I passed out. But every time I woke up, it was still here."

I touch my fist to my chest and try to laugh. It comes out as more of a whimper.

"Maybe the magic didn't want to leave," Kira says.

I turn to frown at her.

"Oh, you haven't considered that, have you?" she asks, with a wicked grin. "You didn't think to ask the magic what it wanted?"

"Magic doesn't want things—" I begin, but then stop.

Kira wouldn't know. She's never felt the pull of magic trapped inside silver chains or pipes. The Towers never trained her how to manipulate it.

But, some strange part of my mind whispers, that doesn't mean she's wrong. The magic inside of me doesn't feel at all like the magic I used in the Towers, or the magic I freed from the silver chain to destroy the city of Blackwater. I'd assumed, when I stopped to think about it at all, that the difference was because this magic came from an old god while the magic inside the Towers came from other places I'd rather not think about.

But maybe it's more than that. This magic is living, not trapped and static. It hums and purrs inside of me, instead of hissing like an angry caged animal.

I smile at the woman who's surpassed every single one of my expectations. More than a lover, more than a friend. Whatever that is.

"Kira," I say. "You're brilliant."

And then I stop her objections with a kiss.

CHAPTER 30

KIRA

IS THIS MAGIC?

After all that, I told Reznyk last night after we stumbled down from the meadow in the glorious haze of a singularly fantastic sunset, you'd better spend the night in the bed with me.

And he did. We fell asleep tangled in each other's arms, woke in the night for slow, dreamlike sex, and then collapsed once more, the sheets a hopeless tangle around our feet, the gray cat giving us a dirty look from the hearth.

I sigh as early morning light falls through the window to paint the stones of the hearth. I feel strange, light and fluttery, like something with wings is trapped inside my chest and it might just burst into song. Beside me, Reznyk's dark hair spills over the pillows. His shoulders rise and fall with his breath. I smile as I remember Zayne saying he loves it when they leave in the middle of the night.

Not me. I love it when they stay. What's better than waking up to find you aren't alone in the dark?

I pull my arm out of the covers, reach for Reznyk, and then hesitate. The gods only know where he slept after I invited him to travel to the Port of Good Fortune with me, a suggestion that was apparently so offensive that he had to stomp off and curl up in some dark corner for the night.

Some of the fluttery feeling in my chest dissipates. I kick my feet out of the blankets as gently as possible, then step out of bed. There's a chill in the air this morning, although the sky is clear and the sun will soon chase it away. Still, winter is creeping toward the mountains. What was it the Exemplar said before we left? We have two months until snow closes travel in the Daggers?

And Reznyk probably has no idea what winters are like up here. Hells, the man probably never saw snow until he joined the Towers in Silver City.

I shake my head. I should be basking in the glow of a half-dozen orgasms this morning, damn it. Not lost in a tangle of worries about the future that's loping toward us like a direwolf with its teeth bared.

I stop at the door and glance back at Reznyk. The sun filters around his shoulders, almost making him glow, and suddenly I remember the golden lights dancing around us in the meadow when we made love, like a private world of stars.

I push the door open, step into the light, and let it close softly behind me. I can't stop what's coming any more than I could stop the sun rising this morning. I'm going to the Port. Reznyk is staying here. But he gave me something incredible last night. Whatever happens next, I'll have that to hold onto.

Still, my throat feels tight and the shimmering flutter in my chest has vanished as I walk across grass thick with dew toward Reznyk's garden. I decided sometime in the night that I'm not going to leave this cabin until I sit him down and tell him exactly what he's going to need to make it through the winter. How much butter, salt, and flour. How many bags of beans and potatoes. I stocked the orphanage larder for years; I plan on giving him a very thorough list and then making him swear on whatever it is he cares about that he'll do whatever it takes to get that shit up here.

I don't think it's a conversation he'll enjoy. And if I'm going to greet him with that, the least I can do is make breakfast first.

The fence around Reznyk's garden is more of a suggestion than an actual barrier. Still, I walk to the gate instead of stepping over the fence. The rising sun hits the garden first, making last night's dew sparkle. I watch my breath as it rises like smoke before me. It won't be long until that dew is frost, and then snow.

I run my hands up and down my arms as I walk through the scraggly rows of vegetables, looking for something that could conceivably serve as breakfast. Maybe I can convince Reznyk to get some chickens, although then he'd have to build a coop and then worry about filling their beaks all winter.

The carrot patch has a few ragged survivors from whatever rodent ate the rest from the ground up. I pull those, then yank a fat beet from the soil and try to stop thinking about all the things that would actually taste good for breakfast. Like bacon.

Frowning, I search for something to carry the vegetables so I can wash them off in the stream. There's a stack of old wooden planks nearby, with a rake and a bucket.

Perfect. I bend down and grab the bucket.

The handle comes off in my hand.

"Shit," I mutter, reaching for the rest of it.

I tug the bucket away from the pile of wood and realize there's a jagged crack down the side. If I put any weight in this thing, even carrots, it might snap in two. With a sigh, I lean down to tuck the bucket back into its final resting place.

Something glints in the sunlight under the old planks.

A shiver crawls up the back of my neck like a cloud passing before the sun. It can't be anything important, that flash of metal under the old wooden planks. Maybe it's a trowel, or part of a hinge that rusted and fell apart.

Still, I set the bucket down and crouch by the stack of wood. My breath catches in the back of my throat as the sun shines off the hidden piece of metal. When I reach for it, prickles dance along the back of my arm.

My throat feels like a vise, twisting until it's closed. The birds singing from their hidden perches in the bushes suddenly feel like they're far away, part of another world. Even the warmth of the sun on my skin feels distant.

Is this magic? After all this time, am I finally touching my potential?

My fingers brush something cool and smooth, then close around it. I pull back, gasping like I've been shocked. Something inside my chest writhes like a snake. My fingers slowly unfold, revealing a metal disc.

I know what it is. Even before I run my fingers around its smooth edges and pull it into the sun, before I see the strange patterns carved into the dark metal, some part of me recognizes what this is. What it has to be.

It could be a leftover artifact from the ruined keep, some sort of decoration or seal. Maybe it was part of a door that long ago rotted into the earth.

But it's not.

It's the amulet.

This is what the Towers gave Reznyk before they sent him to kill the old god. It's what Tholious was supposed to bring back from the Daggers. Hells, it's what I'm supposed to bring back. I rock back on my heels, set the metal disc in the dirt, and rub the fingers that touched it.

I felt something when I reached for it, didn't I? Something cold, like walking down a dark alley and hearing footsteps behind me.

For the Towers to want this amulet, for Reznyk to hide it from them, it's got to be powerful. More powerful than anything I've ever seen or touched. Tholious said I'd be able to feel it. And I did. Didn't I?

I swallow hard. If anything is going to awaken my magical potential, it's this.

My jaw clenches as I reach for the amulet. My fingers brush its polished surface. I feel— something? Maybe? A whisper of fear, like a dark cloud on the horizon. Is that what magic feels like?

I pull my hand back. Reznyk did something when I finally admitted what I really want, the bone-deep ache of my missing magical potential and the knowledge that would come with it. Who my parents were. Who I really am. He replied by taking my hand in his, then holding our hands out to the sun.

Is that what I'm missing? The sun? I glance down at the amulet, hidden in the shadows of my body, and then at the brilliant morning sun behind me.

Maybe magic responds to sunlight, just like the rest of us. That amulet's been hidden in the shadows for the gods only know how long. Maybe it's lost something, down there in the dirt. Maybe it needs light to spark magic. Hells, why not?

I grab the amulet with both hands, then come to my feet. Its smooth metal is cool and strangely heavy against my palms. I spin toward the sun, like I'm carrying the world's weirdest divining rod. My gut pulls tight as fear again skitters over my skin, chased by restless excitement.

Is that magic? Please, gods, let that be magic. Let this be the key to unlocking the secrets the Towers are hiding about my family.

Sunlight spills over my hands and warms my fingers, but the metal of the amulet remains stubbornly cool and inert. I take a few steps through the garden, closer to the sun. Stop. Hold my breath.

Nothing. I walk to the gate, then through it, until I'm on the grass before the cabin, my arms outstretched, the amulet winking in the light of the rising sun. Blood throbs through my hands; my arms ache with the effort of holding it. My throat feels tight, like there's a rope wrapped around my neck. There's a soft, creaking sound from behind me, something that rises over the usual morning chatter of birds. A whisper of wind dances over the back of my neck.

Is that magic? Is any of this, anywhere, magical?

"You found what you were looking for."

I jump. The voice is so deep that I almost don't recognize it. I spin, my arms trembling, the amulet clutched against my chest.

Reznyk stands in the doorway, rage heavy on his brow. And it is Reznyk, even though it takes my mind a moment to decide. It's his face, his clothes, his tall, lean body.

But I've never seen him with that expression on his face. Everything about him is suddenly hard, from his obsidian eyes to the way his lips pull back over his teeth.

"Reznyk," I gasp. My heart tries to leap out of my chest as he stalks toward me. "I was—"

"You were good," he purrs, his voice soft and low and more threatening than a rumble of thunder. "Better than I imagined anyone from the Towers could be."

"What?"

My brain feels like it's stumbling, trying to keep up. No one in the Towers has ever called me good. At anything.

"And you got what you wanted," Reznyk continues as he paces closer to me. Gods above, his eyes are so cold. "I hope you're proud."

"Reznyk, I—"

His hand flashes in the space between us, closing over my wrist. His fingers clutch the amulet in my hands. A pulse of heat flashes across my skin. I stare at him. His lips pull back in a snarl.

And then the air is forced from my lungs, and the world vanishes.

CHAPTER 31
REZNYK
YOU HAVE WHAT YOU WANT

The ground slams into my feet. My vision flashes white, then crimson. Magic screams all around me, howling like it's in pain, a grisly echo to the agony inside my chest.

I cut my heart out, the old song goes. Gods, if only that were possible.

There's a crack, then a boom, like a roll of thunder. My legs tremble. The ground sways beneath me. Exhaustion hits me like a punch to the gut, and I stagger backward.

Dragging Kira with me. She gasps once, then again, and finally I manage to force my hands to let go of her wrists. My vision swims as I fill my burning lungs.

Trees. I'm staring up at a dance of interlaced branches, soft pine needles filtering the rising sun. Magic shrieks under my skin, hissing and spitting like it's been injured. I stare at the trees, then drop my gaze.

I can't look at her. Instead, my eyes fall to the metal amulet in her hands. It hums with magic it's just pulled from my body, an obvious trap waiting for someone foolish enough to fall in.

Just like Kira.

My eyes sting. I clench my teeth and force my hands into fists. Where the fuck are we? What in the nine hells just happened? I step back, then back again. Water chatters in the background, a river going about its daily business as if nothing in the world has changed. Pine trees whisper overhead. Birds sing.

Did she trap me? Drag me somewhere horrible? Am I just now waking up?

I risk a glance at the woman who just ruined me. She's gasping for breath, her eyes wide, the amulet clutched to her chest. Exactly like she looked this morning, when I opened the door of my home and realized who she really was.

No. Kira didn't do this.

I look down at my own hands, at my skin hissing and burning with magic.

Travel magic? That's a myth, a story to tell children. I've watched the old god for months, and I've never seen them use anything like travel magic. Hells, the Towers stalked my victim for years. If travel magic existed, wouldn't the old god I slayed have used it to escape the silver crossbow bolt I fired into their heart?

My hands tremble, then blur. Silver blood pours down my fingers, pooling around my wrists, dripping to the pine needles below my feet.

Shit. I'm falling apart. And the woman who ruined me is right here for it.

I force myself to step back, gasping as the forest spins around me. There's a sort of path behind me, leading through an opening in the trees. I stagger toward it, see what's below us.

And suddenly I know exactly where we are.

Oh, gods. I'm going to be sick. I force it down, then turn back to Kira with a snarl I couldn't stop even if I wanted to.

"Go!" I scream, stabbing my hand toward the opening in the trees as silver blood drips from each of my fingers.

"W-What?" she stammers.

"Go!" I snarl, as my voice cracks. "You have what you wanted! Leave this place and never come back!"

She turns toward the opening in the trees, toward the path that will take her down the slope and into the Golden Peaks Hunting Lodge that's sitting like a jewel in a ring in the valley just below us.

Somehow, the magic inside my body combined with the amulet and made something entirely new; travel magic that brought Kira exactly where she wanted to go. Perhaps the amulet wants to go home, some distant part of my mind whispers.

I turn on my heels and force my body to run.

Branches whip my face. Behind me, Kira screams my name, over and over, until it has no more meaning than the whisper of the wind or the shriek of the birds.

I run until I collapse, vomiting on my hands and knees, and then I push myself up and stagger forward until I collapse again, gagging on my empty stomach, every part of my body singing with pain.

Time folds in on itself. I curl into a ball, dragging my cloak around the tattered remnants of my body as memories beat against the inside of my skull. A river of silver blood flows over the grass. Sparks, carried by the wind, rain down on the roofs of Blackwater. The murky water of the bay reflects the pyre, until the entire world is burning.

And through the flames, I see Lenore's face when she met me at her window.

I moved slowly through Silver City, careful to avoid any

places that might recognize me. Still, I couldn't betray my vanity entirely. I stole enough shills to visit one of the tailors Syrus always talked about, using the old god's trapped magic to cast an illusion over my face.

So I looked good when I climbed the steep road to Fyher's Landing and stole into the Castinac estate. When I used my new magic to lift myself to her window, the same window I'd climbed into a dozen times as one of the Elites.

But that was when I wore black. Before I had the magic of an old god and a new suit in scarlet and gold.

Now, I looked like the type of man who would be allowed to approach a daughter of the Castinac family, like someone with the money and power and sheer arrogance to claim Lady Lenore for himself.

I'd crushed the boy I once was into the dust, burned him in the ashes. Now nothing could stop me.

But Lenore didn't smile when she opened her window and found me waiting for her. She didn't kiss me, as she once had, or unbutton her gown or lead me to her bed. Instead, she stared at me with her hand over her mouth until my dreams began to leak out of my chest, dripping to the cobblestones like silver blood.

"Reznyk," she finally said, in a hushed whisper. "What are you doing here?"

"I came for you," I answered.

She stepped back, away from me. Her eyes widened with something that I could not bring myself to admit was fear.

"They're looking for you," she whispered, as if I didn't know. "The Towers. They said you stole something, and— and killed something."

"I did," I said. "Lenore, I'm powerful now. More powerful than I was. More powerful than the Towers."

She stepped back again, until there was an empty room between our two bodies.

"Come with me," I said.

I wanted to sound powerful, confident. But I did not.

Lenore shook her head. "No," she whispered, her eyes darting to the thick burgundy carpet and then back to me. "Reznyk, you know I'm betrothed."

"But," I stammered. "I love you."

I'd never told her before. Hells, I'd never said those words to anyone before.

She shook her head, then tucked her hair back behind her ear.

"I know," she whispered. "But I won't leave Silver City. This is my home."

I opened my mouth, but she spoke before I could embarrass myself any further.

"I don't love you," Lady Lenore Castinac said. "I'm sorry."

Her eyes met mine. I took a step forward, reaching for her, my queen of light and beauty, the woman I dreamt of in the forest as I struggled to control the magic inside my body, to escape the men sent to kill me. Lenore was the reason I dared sneak back into Silver City, even with all of the Towers on my tail.

"Stop," she said. "I will scream, Reznyk. The guards are just outside my door."

Our eyes met again, but this time, there was nothing soft in her expression. She had become a stranger, beautiful and untouchable. I could spend what was left of my life throwing myself at her feet, like the ocean against the rocky shore.

It would break me. And she would remain unchanged.

Even now, years later and with an entire mountain

range between us, that memory tears something out of my throat. It's a harsh, barking sob, and I cover my head with my hands to hide it.

CHAPTER 32
KIRA
CRAWLING BACK

I scream for Reznyk until my throat gives out.

After that, I'm on my knees in the middle of the wilderness making strange choking sounds that aren't even remotely human. I collapse onto my hands, dig my fingers into the pine needles, and gasp for breath as my mind continues to scream every curse I can imagine after Reznyk's horrible, beautiful ass.

And then I just cry.

It's a stupid reaction, this flood of tears. Because none of this is a surprise, is it? Reznyk told me he loves another woman, and I knew it, even as I teased him and flirted with him and rode him so hard I almost blacked out.

We fucked like gods. But that doesn't change the fact that his heart belongs to someone else.

And I told him what I wanted. My magical potential, my link to the family I never knew. A chance to go back to the Towers with my head held high and claim the position my parents left me.

I rock back on my heels and drag my hands across my face, wiping tears, snot, and sweat on my sleeve. Reznyk saw me with the damned amulet. He must have thought I was going to steal it. Hells, he probably thinks that was my intention all along.

But I also touched whatever magic lies in the damned thing. Because here I am, on a hillside overlooking the Golden Peaks Hunting Lodge.

Reznyk brought me here. He's furious. I get it. I'd be furious too, if I was in his place. But I told him I wanted to go back to the Towers once I found my magical potential, and here I am. The first step in a very long journey back to the Towers.

The amulet must have worked, then. Why would Reznyk have brought me here if I didn't have any magical potential? He knows I won't return to the Towers without it. Hells, without magical potential, the Towers would probably get Tholious to trade me off to some other loner who has something they want. But now I have what they want.

Hells, now I am what they want.

I turn to stare at the hunk of metal glistening in the pine needles next to me. It looks almost oily, like it's shining with something I can see but can't touch.

"I did it," I whisper.

My voice sounds like it's been dragged through the dirt for days. I clear my throat, gag, and try again.

"I have magic," I announce.

The wilderness does not respond. From somewhere behind me, an insect lets out a long, shrill scream. I stare at the amulet in the dirt like I'm expecting it to do something. My gaze climbs away from the tug of the metal circle and drowns in the trees where Reznyk vanished. He ran like I was going to chase him, like maybe I had a crossbow and a bucket of arrows and I was going to shoot him in the back if he lingered.

My eyes burn. I sniff, then wipe at them with the back of my hand. I could follow him, chase him into the woods.

But Reznyk clearly doesn't want to see me again.

Pain rolls through the great, throbbing emptiness in my chest. Even if I could find him, somehow, in this maze of trees, what could I possibly say that would convince him I wasn't trying to steal this damn thing? Or that I don't want to go back to the Towers?

I blink. That's not true. I have magic, now. Of course I want to go back to the Towers. That's my plan.

And he wants to be alone with his wolves and the last old god in the world. That's his plan. I'll bring the amulet back to the Towers and no one will ever have any reason to bother him again.

Look at that. We're both getting what we want, aren't we? I drag a ragged breath over my lips. I feel absolutely nothing. Shouldn't success feel a bit more, well, victorious?

It takes me a long time to come to my feet, and even longer to turn my shoulders away from the darkness beneath the trees and toward the path leading down the hill. Tholious said someone would be waiting for me in the Golden Peaks Hunting Lodge. I try to imagine who it's going to be as I drag myself down the mountain.

It turns into a stupidly beautiful day. The sky is brilliant, filled with thin wisps of clouds spinning overhead like they're writing a message in some language I can't understand. Birds cry and respond all around me, flecks of gold dance in the thick bands of sunlight slanting through the trees, and my shattered heart knocks on inside of my chest.

"This is what I want," I whisper to the forest that looks

like it came straight out of the pages of a children's story book. "I have magic."

The forest ignores me.

"Kira?"

I jump, startled by the sound of my own name. The Golden Peaks Hunting Lodge comes into bleary focus. I've been staring at my own feet for so long I didn't even realize how close I was to the lodge's front door.

A man who was sitting by the fence comes to his feet and tucks something into his belt. It takes me a moment to drag his name from my memories.

"Matius," I say.

My voice sounds exactly like I've spent most of this past morning screaming obscenities into the woods. Tholious's one-time lover doesn't seem to mind. He meets my gaze. There's something shadowed and broken in his eyes that echoes the hollow ache inside my chest. He walks over to me, and together we stare at the amulet cradled in my hands.

Maybe this is what magic feels like. Crushing emptiness and regret.

"You don't have to tell me anything," Matius says.

I look up at him, but he turns away. There are shadows under his eyes, and a tight, almost angry set to his jaw. At the beginning of this idiotic journey, he and Tholious couldn't stand to be separated. Hells, they'd make up all sorts of flimsy excuses to bed down together somewhere out of sight from the rest of us and make muffled moaning sounds for hours.

But Tholious left Matius at the hunting lodge with that haunted look in his eyes. It doesn't take a tactical genius to figure out what must have happened between them after all their fighting.

Great. Two walking romantic disasters, side by side.

"You don't have to tell me anything either," I reply.

He nods. The corner of his lip twitches in what might be a half-hearted attempt at a smile.

"You want to leave now?" he asks. "Or wait until——"

"Now," I say.

He nods again. The look on his face makes me think he understands everything I haven't said. I tuck the amulet into my pocket, then follow Matius into the hunting lodge. He brings me a glass of wine, which I down in a few massive gulps despite the fact that it's the middle of the day, then vanishes into some back room. I stare through the windows and try not to think until Matius reappears and announces that our horses are ready.

I've never liked horses. We couldn't even afford to look at horses in the orphanage, so I never got the hang of standing or walking around those massive, deadly beasts, let alone riding one. But Matius stares at me like riding a horse is the very least one could ask out of another human being, and between the bone-deep ache in my chest and the glass of wine I just chugged, I can't even summon my usual horror of all things equine.

I manage to clamber onto the horse, which shifts and snorts like it can tell I'm a bad person, and then I cling to it for dear life as Matius leads me down the road. We ride in silence as the world goes on around us, following a river that threads its way out of the Daggers.

At some point, Matius stops his horse, and we share a lunch of bread and cheese that tastes like sawdust on my tongue. When the light begins to leak from the sky, Matius leads his horse away from the road and into a little patch of beaten-down grass.

"You want a fire?" he asks.

It's the first thing he's said since we left the hunting lodge. I shake my head. He unties something from the back of my horse's saddle that turns out to be a bedroll, then hands me another bit of bread, some hard cheese, and half of a peppered salami. It all tastes like ash. Finally, he pulls a flask from his hip pocket, takes a deep swig, and passes it to me without a word.

I drink something that burns going down and makes my sore legs go numb. Matius takes another pull, then stares at the stars as they dance above us, cold and silent.

"I didn't even like him at first," Matius says, in a voice that's so quiet I'm not entirely certain he's talking to me. "Tholious, I mean. I thought he was a prick. Stuck up. Stubborn. Far too devoted to his precious damned Towers."

He laughs. It's a rusty, sad sound, like the hinge in an abandoned building creaking open in the wind.

"Turns out, I was right," Matius finishes. "Tholious is a prick. And nothing will ever drag him away from the Towers."

He drops his head to his knees and makes a sort of snort that he probably wants me to think is a laugh and not a cry. My gut twists around the few bites of bread I was able to stomach. I think of Reznyk in his tower, waiting for us to climb his mountain and steal his amulet. Welcoming me even though he knew who I was and where I came from. Healing my ankle, sharing his frost wine. Telling me his secrets.

And now, he must feel just like Matius.

Because here I am, crawling back to the Towers.

CHAPTER 33
REZNYK
THE PERFECT TRAP

I climb the mountain like someone's chasing me. By the time I reach the ridge, my muscles are screaming, blood pulses as it oozes slowly out of scrapes on my knees, courtesy of a large boulder I didn't notice until it was too late, and magic hisses and spits under my skin like it's trying to scold me. The sun sinks into the west, filling the sky with its fire. The crimson glow of the dying sun makes the stones of the keep look like they're streaked with blood. I ignore it all. None of it matters.

Was it all calculated? Her casual flirtation, her wit as sharp as a dagger, that irresistible combination of ferocity and vulnerability, the way she could go from looking like she wanted to punch something to looking like she was about to cry on the turn of a coin. Was it all an act?

Godsdamn it. I grind my teeth until my jaw aches. A friend and a lover. Someone who made me laugh. Someone who made me feel safe enough to talk about things I've never talked about before, to share secrets better left buried.

That woman was the perfect trap.

225

I kick open the door of my cabin. It swings inward, creaking slightly. Xavier lifts his head from his place on the hearth.

I gasp like I've been punched in the gut.

Her memory is everywhere.

There's the plate Kira used last night. Her bedroll pushed against the far wall. The jumble of blankets on the bed where we made slow, sweet love not even a day ago. There is a word for it, some horrible part of my mind whispers. A word for a friend who's also a lover, for a person who shares your bed, your dishes, your home. Someone who knows the very worst about you but doesn't run away.

Wife.

My mouth tastes like blood. I gag, then spit through the open door. It wasn't just that she seduced me. Hells, I've seduced plenty of women in my time, and a few men too. I've stolen shills and information, and once even a set of vault keys. That's all part of the game; my body is another tool at my disposal.

But Kira didn't just seduce me. She won me over, godsdamn it. She made me fall in love. And then she robbed me.

I rock back on my heels and blink as my vision swims. Why, damn it? She could have stolen the amulet her first night here, or the first time I left her alone and climbed to the meadow. Why wait until after we—

I spin around, barely making it through the door before retching again. There's nothing in my stomach, so what comes out is a thin stream of bitter emerald acid. I stare at it for a long time as a glorious sunset throws itself against the indifferent mountains. My mind slowly stumbles over what I'm going to do next.

Yes. Good idea.

I reenter my cabin like a rampaging army. I grab the

plate Kira used last night, the bundle of flowers drying above the hearth that she'd been substituting for tea. I rip the blankets from the bed, all of them, and kick her bedroll through the door. I take everything she held, everything that smells like her, and throw it into a heap on the grass.

And then I send fire magic into it.

The fire is slow to start, the magic strangely unresponsive. I'm trembling by the time flames finally start to lick their way up the mountain of bedding and clothes and plates and cooking pots. I sink to the ground before the pyre, pull my legs into my chest, and stare at the flames as they consume everything Kira touched.

Another whisper of magic tugs at my consciousness, the lupine pull of the wolves. I turn toward the mountain I named for myself and see the old male wolf in the distance, watching me with eyes that gleam in the last of the light. I nod at him; he ignores me, as usual. His pack follows, walking slowly, nervous around the scent of smoke, close enough that I can see the shimmer of their eyes in the fading light.

When the wolves vanish over the ridge, I let my head drop onto my knees. The fire crackles and hisses. Wind rustles the pines below the ridge and sings over the broken stone of the ancient keep. My knee aches where it met the granite of the mountain. Magic settles over my skin like a heavy cloak.

Something prickles the back of my neck. It's cold, like a snowflake melting on my skin. I lift my head slowly.

The old god sits on the grass between me and the keep.

Their body is small tonight, with delicate paws and a large tail, like a fox. They're so dark they look like a hole punched straight through the face of reality. Their silver eyes stare at me, moonlight reflecting from the bottom of a well.

My heart catches before staggering on. They've never come this close before. I open my mouth, but words don't form.

I think of all the things I want to tell them, all the apologies I should make. The horrors I've seen, the blood I've spilled, the crushing weight of those memories.

The black hole in my chest where my heart should be.

My eyes sting. The old god's body swims through a haze of tears, small and still and perfect, sitting on the grass and watching me with wide silver eyes. I swallow, part my lips, but my throat closes tight around whatever words I might say. I have nothing to offer this ancient creature of pure magic. Nothing but my broken self and the stolen magic trapped inside that I can't shed.

"I'm sorry," I manage to whisper.

The old god tilts their head to the side and blinks, blackness swallowing silver, silver emerging again.

"Don't you want to kill me?" I ask, as my tears make the world swim and the magic trapped inside my chest hums, low and soft, like a mother rocking her child. "I deserve it."

The old god twists their head to stare at the mountains. Something that looks like steam rises from the shifting corners of their body. This close, I hear their breath, a slow, even rasp, like wind through leaves.

"You should hate me," I say. "For—for everything I've done."

I stare at my hands in my lap, expecting to see rivers of silver blood. But they're empty, holding nothing but the night air. Kira's words come back to me as a whisper. *They just look like hands to me.*

I turn back to the old god. Their body ripples in the moonlight.

"I hate myself," I admit, although my voice breaks when I speak. "I should die for what I did."

An owl cries from the forest below. His haunting call hangs in the air between us. The old god's head shifts, then tilts upward. Their body lengthens and grows as it rocks back on its haunches, and now it looks more like a bear, sniffing the night air.

Slowly, they drop forward, falling onto silent paws that are now almost as large as my chest. Their great silver eyes blink once more, slowly. Magic flows from their body like water down a mountainside, making the flames of the fire flicker and dance. They turn and trot toward the ridge of naked stone, first on four legs, then on six, and then their body blends with the shadows on the mountainside and they are gone.

I stare at the spot where the old god stood for a long time as the fire crackles before me and the light of the rising moon bleeds across the sky. My body aches, my heart howls, but slowly, strangely, an odd sort of peace laps at the edges of my consciousness.

I've lost everything. Again.

But there's a certain liberation in knowing you've lost, that it's not worth fighting anymore. I drop my head to my knees and let out a long, slow exhale. Xavier makes a chirping sound from the door of the cabin, as if he's asking me why in the nine hells I've just burned all the blankets I have.

"It's complicated," I mutter into the darkness.

A flicker of annoyance drifts across my magic, radiating from Xavier, the resident king of annoyance. I lift my head to stare at the flames.

"It'll be fine," I say, talking to the cat and not to myself. "I'll just go into the keep, find something else we can use—"

But my voice fades, because now I'm picturing the keep. Not the second floor, that great jumble of junk that's probably hiding at least a few more moldy old blankets, but the root cellar. Something in the fire hisses, then releases a great stream of sparks. I think of the potatoes down there, the handful or two of carrots, the stack of turnips and beets.

Kira was right. It's not enough food. My breath catches like there's something lodged in the back of my throat. It was never enough, and I knew it.

Because that was my plan, even if I didn't admit it to myself. I wanted to die here, quietly, in the snow, releasing the magic caged inside my body. And releasing my spirit to follow the wolves forever.

Something shoves my arm. I turn to see Xavier aggressively rubbing his head against my elbow. There's a strange rattling coming from the ragged old tomcat, and it takes me a moment to recognize it as his ugly rumbling purr. I cup his chin, then run my fingers down the soft velvet of his back. If my spirit chases the wolves, who will light the fire for this ragged old bastard?

"Xavier," I whisper into the gathering night. "I've got to get more supplies."

CHAPTER 34
KIRA
CONGRATULATIONS

"You may enter," Fyrris declares from the other side of the room.

I shiver as my heart flails around inside my chest. I glance to the side, as if I'm looking for Matius, but he's not there. He left hours ago, at the gates of the Towers before the last bell chimed, and I can't blame him. I know why he wouldn't want to enter this place.

It just happened so quickly. We spent seven days together, dragging ourselves out of the Daggers, across the Sea of Grass, and onto the barge at Deep's Crossing that carried us back to Silver City. We rarely spoke, but the silence that grew between us felt almost comfortable. It's like we'd both been wounded in the same battle, and we were limping home together with injuries no one else would be able to understand. When I first saw the brilliant white Towers of Silver City rising above the Ever-Reaching River, I turned to Matius.

But the words didn't come. And I spent the rest of that day, as the barge beat on against the current and the

Towers grew larger, trying to think of how to tell him how grateful I was for his quiet companionship and how sorry I was for what happened between him and Tholious.

Even as we walked together through the streets of Silver City just hours ago, my fingers clenched around the damned amulet hidden in my pocket as I turned the words over in my head and then silently dismissed them all. None of them fit.

And then we were at the gates of the Towers, and Benja took my arm and told someone to notify Fyrris, and Matius frowned like that invisible wound we shared was suddenly much harder to bear, and all I could think to say was a whispered thanks before the gate shut between us and Benja pulled me into a small room and fired round after round of questions at me, until the answers all blurred together. The only one that seemed to matter was the first.

"Do you have it?"

I nodded, then pulled the amulet from my pocket. It gleamed in the light like it was covered in oil. I stared at it as Benja asked me question after question, waiting to feel something.

Nothing. There's nothing at all inside of me.

Finally, another Guard came to the door and whispered something to Benja. I was handed the amulet, then led through the main courtyard and into the very same room where I'd been told to prepare for a journey to the Daggers with Tholious. Only there's no Tholious here tonight. Now the room holds only Fyrris and another Exemplar, a woman wearing white robes and a scowl.

Fyrris frowns at me like he's disappointed already. "Enter," he says again. "And be seated."

I stumble into the room and sink into a chair.

"Where's Tholious?" I ask. My voice sounds like a rasp dragged over splintered wood.

Fyrris makes a face that suggests I've just said something off-color. Some insane part of me wants to apologize.

"Tholious is indisposed," the woman replies.

She gives me a smile that makes me think she personally stabbed Tholious in the back. I shiver. My fingers tighten around the slick sides of the amulet cupped in my palm. Matius is going to be upset about this. Despite everything, I don't think he would want Tholious dead. But since when do we get what we want?

"Show us," Fyrris says, with an impatient gesture toward the table.

Right. He might have been more delicate with Tholious, or more polite with Zayne and the other mercenaries. But I'm no mercenary and no star pupil. I reach forward with the amulet. My fingers feel stiff; it takes more effort than it should to pry them away from the smooth metal.

The amulet falls to the table with a solid thump, a sound far louder than its size would suggest. My mouth feels dry. Slowly, I pull my hands away from the amulet of the Godkiller.

Fyrris and the woman both stare at the damn thing like I'm not even here. Minutes slide by silently, dragging cold fingers across my skin. I wonder where Matius is right now, and how he'll react when he hears about Tholious. I wonder if the sun is shining in the Daggers, if it's streaming through the window of the cabin—

Fyrris makes a snorting sound. His hands hover over the amulet like a man trying to warm himself over the ashes of last night's fire.

"Not much in here," he mutters.

"I felt it," I announce.

Fyrris and the woman ignore me. She runs her fingers over the thing, and her expression tightens.

"Maybe we have to dig deeper," Fyrris says.

"Or maybe I'm correct, and there's a synergistic effect between the device and the wielder," the woman says.

Fyrris scowls like that's the stupidest idea he's ever heard.

"That's not how we designed the arcanite containment system," he growls. "The nightmare steel alone should contain the entire force of the creature."

The woman leans back in her chair and crosses her arms over her chest. There's a look on her face that suggests this is not their first argument.

"We'll do what we can," Fyrris declares. "Hopefully the next one won't have the same complications."

"Syrus is more docile," the woman replies. "We've got that going for us, at least."

I can't stop the little gasp that slips from my lips. I thought Syrus was dead. I thought all the other Elites were dead.

Both Exemplars turn to stare at me. The woman looks like she's surprised I'm still here, and I realize making any sort of noise was a mistake. I should have slipped out of the door like a ghost.

"Did you see him use this?" Fyrris asks, waving his hand over the amulet.

I shake my head.

"Was he wearing it?" the woman asks.

I shake my head again. Now both of them look disappointed. Their white robes gleam in the low golden glow of the lanterns on the walls.

"Very well," Fyrris says. "You're dismissed."

I come to my feet, then hesitate before the door. My heart flutters in the back of my throat. I feel like I'm standing tiptoe on the point of a blade. I turn back to Fyrris.

"Sir?" I ask.

"Is there a problem?" Fyrris replies.

My pulse hammers inside my skull. My gut shifts like it's looking for a way out. Still, I have to ask. I felt the magic. I came back to the Towers.

I'm ready.

"Shall I join the Entrants?" I say. "I'm ready for my magical training."

The air in the room turns to ice. For what feels like a very long time, nobody says anything.

And then Fyrris laughs. It's cold and brittle, the sound of something breaking. The woman next to him starts to laugh too, until the stone walls ring with the sound. My eyes sting. Something bitter and sharp climbs the back of my throat.

"Kira." Fyrris grins at me like the rattlesnake who sang to the mice. "You'll join the Guards."

I try to breathe, but my throat is too tight. The room spins. My heartbeat pulses crimson behind my eyelids. My hands curl into fists. I've tried so hard to be silent here, to blend in and follow the rules. But I can't just let this go.

"I felt the magic," I say again. "In that, that damn thing. I felt it!"

"Do not push the limits of my gratitude," Fyrris snaps, in a voice as low and cold as the snow. "I was not making a request. You will serve the Towers as a member of the Guards, or you will not serve the Towers at all."

I feel like I've been punched in the gut. "But my—my parents—" I stammer.

Fyrris said they were Exemplars. Gods know I've

memorized every story I've ever heard about Exemplars, and I've paged through those dusty records until my eyes watered.

Perhaps they died in the explosion that ruined the Broken Tower. Perhaps they traveled to the far continent in search of more magic. But someone here has to know who they are, what in the nine hells happened to them, and why they didn't want their own daughter.

The woman laughs again. It's a sound that brings back every nasty memory I have of parties and festivals, of the highborn lords and ladies on the other side of the crimson ribbon or the crystal panes of glass.

"Your parents?" the woman says. "You're one of Lord Castinac's many bastards, girl. Your mother was a whore who died on the birthing bed."

Fyrris scowls at her. I gulp for air in a room with walls that are closing in all around me.

"Then—why?" I manage to whisper.

It doesn't make any sense. Why pull me from the orphanage? Why tell me to develop my magical potential?

"So that you could serve as a Guard," Fyrris says, folding his hands neatly on the table in front of him. "Or you will leave the Towers in a coffin. Do I make myself clear, Miss Kira Silver?"

Like Tholious, my mind howls. The woman said he was indisposed, which I assume is her polite Towers way of saying he's been murdered and sunk to the bottom of the Ever-Reaching River. Maybe it even happened in this same room. I try not to look down. If there's blood on this floor, I don't want to see it.

I manage a nod. My hands are shaking so badly it takes me several tries before I can get the doorknob to turn. Benja stands in the hallway just outside the door, his arms crossed over his chest, waiting.

"I hear you're officially joining the Guards," Benja says. "Congratulations!"

I press my hands to my eyes and try to breathe. Benja takes my elbow, then gently leads me to the Guards' quarters.

CHAPTER 35

REZNYK

VISITORS

"I'm not having this argument with you again," I tell the cat.

Xavier narrows his eyes at me. He looks like he's willing to fight me to the death if I try to move so much as a single hair on his person. I sigh, then lean back on the bed.

"Pillows are for humans," I declare. Again.

Xavier settles his head on the only pillow we have left, and then he begins to purr. Aggressively.

"Fine!" I snap, throwing my hands up. "You're right, I shouldn't have burned all the bedding."

I stand up, groaning as my body creaks in protest. Thin morning light leaks in through the window. Somehow, it only makes the room feel colder.

"You know, you could at least act happy to see me," I tell Xavier.

Xavier closes his eyes, his victory assured. The tip of his tail curls around his body and flicks like a metronome. I sink down in the chair, then toss a fresh log onto the low embers of the fire. My feet throb, and my back aches in at least a dozen new and interesting places. .

This entire month has been a slog through the nine hells.

I went to Cairncliff. I didn't have many shills, but that's never been a problem for me, especially not in a quaint little tourist town like Cairncliff where rich visitors practically beg to have their purses lifted. I was sorely tempted to drown myself in ale in one of Cairncliff's many dockside pubs, but in the end, I was too afraid to let down my guard.

So I slept in the Spirit Wood and picked pockets until I had enough shills to buy what seemed like a truly absurd amount of food. Then I had to wait for a spot on one of the few carriages that cross the mountains and bribe the driver to drop me as close to the Daggers as I could get. The old man driving the carriage laughed as he took my shills.

"Let me tell you, son," he said. "She ain't worth it."

"Excuse me?" I asked.

"You think you're the first?" He shook his head. "Hells, I see it all the time. Some lady broke your heart, so you're off to live in the wild. That's about the measure of it, ain't it?"

I gave him a polite smile that could mean whatever he wanted it to mean. He laughed again.

"You're a damn fool," he said. "But then again, I figure I was too at your age."

I dragged the first of my four crates out of his carriage and kept on smiling.

"Listen, kid," he said, lowering his voice. "I do this route once every two weeks till the snow flies. You get tired of eating squirrels and talking to frogs, you just wait for me here. I'll be by."

Something pinched in my chest, the nerve that twists whenever I'm offered something I clearly do not deserve. A cloud of insects bloomed around my face as I dragged the crates off the road. It took me almost three days to climb down from the mountains and reach this road; it would take me twice as long, I guessed, to walk back with however many supplies I could carry.

My heart sank as I contemplated my shitty decisions. The man clucked behind me, and the carriage creaked and groaned as the horses began to pull in their traces. The four remaining people in the carriage, two gruff older men and a young couple, all stared at me like I'd stripped naked on the side of the road and started dancing.

"Don't worry," the man driving the carriage said as he started to pull away. "Even broken hearts heal, kid."

"I very much doubt that," I muttered under my breath.

That was the last time I talked to another human.

It took me three trips to carry all the food back to the keep. By the time I hauled the last bags of flour, hard cheese, and dried beans over the ridge yesterday afternoon, I was seriously doubting whether keeping myself alive over the winter was a noble enough task to warrant this much effort.

And then my wards shattered.

I dropped the pack filled with dried beans and stared at the sky. It happened fast, one quick bolt of rage and panic cracking the wards, leaving me breathless. At first, I thought something inside my body had snapped in half. But I was still standing; my blood was still mostly on the inside.

"Fuck," I huffed.

I yanked the pack back onto my bruised shoulders, limped into the cabin, and collapsed into bed, leaving Xavier very annoyed by my insolence.

I was too exhausted to do anything but let the broken wards wait until morning. And now, instead of spending all day in bed with my head on the one musty pillow I have yet to burn, I have to see what fresh horror is coming for me.

With a groan, I shove myself out of the chair and limp to the door. Frost sparkles from the grass, and my breath hovers before me like mist rising from the swamps. The forest below is mottled with gold around the skeletal black fingers of naked trees. It would almost be beautiful, if I wasn't so worried about what it means. What do I know of winter, really?

I try to shake that thought out of my head as I drag myself up the stairs of the old keep. My footsteps echo off the cold stone. The key catches in the lock on the top floor; I have to rattle it before it gives way. Magic flickers over my skin as I cross the threshold and greet the empty eyes of the mirrors holding my wards.

Shattered glass spills across the floor at the base of the southern wall.

Of course. I close my eyes, then bring my hand to pinch the bridge of my nose. Sure, it could be nothing. These traps go off for anything magical, save the old god. Maybe some elves passed through. Hells, maybe some dragons came to Cairncliff on vacation.

But it's not nothing, is it?

I feel it in the way the shards of glass shiver as I sweep them up. Whatever set this off, it was subtle. An Exemplar, or one of the Towers's silver chains, that would have blown the glass all the way across the room.

No, this was softer. It was closer. And something about it feels damned familiar, like seeing a face across a crowded market that I should be able to recognize. I twist magic in my palms as I leave the keep and walk beneath skies rapidly filling with low, heavy rain clouds. Blades, arrows, bolts; I can make them all. And they might as well be flowers for all the good they've done me over the past two years.

Not that it matters. Whatever is coming will be here soon enough.

Xavier lifts his head off the pillow as I slam the door behind me. His tail flicks with annoyance as I throw more wood on the fire, then stretch my cold fingers toward the hungry flames.

"Well," I tell Xavier. "Looks like we're going to have visitors."

THE KNOCK COMES JUST after dusk.

It's been raining for hours, so it's hard to tell when the light first started fading from the churning, gray skies. Magic has been skipping and flickering under my skin all day. It's a strange, hesitant sort of pull, nothing at all like the confidence of the wolves or the annoyance of a cat penned inside all day by lousy weather.

There's something almost familiar about this subtle dance of magic, although I can't figure out why. It feels like a half-remembered dream. Still, even with the steady tug of magic that's been dancing across my remade wards all day, I didn't expect anyone to climb up the ridge in the rain. Or to knock politely.

I set down my mug of tea, push back from the chair, and pull my magic tight around my fists. If it's an assassin, I'll shove enough sleep magic into them to knock them out for a week. It's not likely that an assassin from the Towers would be foolish enough to knock, but hells, if I could predict what the Towers were going to do, I'd never have fallen into Kira's beautiful trap.

"Hello?" a voice calls, muffled by the rain.

It's a man's voice. He sounds hesitant, like he's not sure what he expects to find behind this door. I guess that makes two of us. I clench my jaw, draw my cloak around my shoulders, and rattle the doorknob. There's a sort of stomping sound on the other side, like whoever is there just took a step back. Good.

I pull the door open, then lean against the doorframe and narrow my eyes at the two men standing just outside my cabin. They're soaking wet, and they look exhausted. The tall blond stares at me like he's waiting for me to draw a weapon.

Oh. Oh, shit.

I can't begin to understand what he's doing here, but the man from the Towers who told me he would give me Kira in exchange for the amulet is here, on my doorstep, looking like he's just been kicked in the ribs and he's about to beg for more.

"Tholius?" I say.

He nods but doesn't turn away, like he's still preparing for a fight. But I don't see any weapons, and there's no magic thickening the air between us. There's very little magic coming off of him at all; if he's carrying one of the Towers's silver chains, he's already used it. And the distant echo of magic that would hold would be just enough to snap my ward.

The man behind Tholious clears his throat. I realize I recognize this one too. He was one of the mercenaries who came up here with Kira. Matius, maybe? Anger rises hot and thick inside my chest at the thought of Kira, although I'm not sure if I'm mad at the men who brought her to my doorstep or mad at myself for being such a dipshit and falling for her.

"What," I finally manage to stammer, "the fuck?"

CHAPTER 36

KIRA

WE NEED TO KNOW EVERYTHING

There was frost on the cobblestones in the main courtyard this morning.

It's gone now, washed away by the constant gray rain beating at the whitewashed walls of the Towers, but it crunched under my boots this morning. I glance out of the window and through the veil of rain to the Barrier Mountains. The peak of Victory Mountain glistens with snow. Soon, all the foothills will wear that white shawl.

The Daggers are smaller than the Barriers, and further south. Still, it won't be long until they get their first snowfall. A shiver runs up my arms as I picture snow drifting around the windows of the little cabin, Xavier the cat curled in the window and watching it fall.

At least they're safe, Reznyk and Xavier. At least the Towers will leave them alone now that they have the amulet. At least I gave him that.

"Kira?" a voice calls at the door. "Are you there?"

Because no one is here to see it, I roll my eyes as dramatically as I want. Gods above, I could lock myself in the outhouse and Benja would still find me.

"I'm here," I say.

I pick up the sharpening stone from the bench beside me and make a half-hearted attempt to run it along the dull edge of the dagger on my lap. Not that I think Benja will make a fuss about the fact that I clearly shut myself in the armory closet in an attempt to find some privacy.

The door creaks open. The torch on the wall flickers with the push of wind from the courtyard. Benja gives me his usual hesitant smile. Benja's a decent guy, friendly and approachable without pushing too hard, and he's fairly easy on the eyes. He's probably interested in me, and I should probably be interested in him too. But his dark hair reminds me of someone else, and that hesitant smile only makes me think of another smile that was like the edge of a blade winking in the darkness.

Godsdamn it, what is wrong with me? I shake my head, put the sharpening stone back down, and try to look normal. Benja doesn't push or ask what's going on, which is very decent of him. I should find it attractive, just like I used to. Before something broke inside of me, and now I can't seem to get the pieces of my old life to fit back the same way.

"It's always the same message, isn't it?" Benja says.

"What?" I reply.

I've spent the past month feeling like I'm ten heartbeats late to every conversation around me. Still, that was especially confusing.

"I mean, the message I have for you," Benja continues. "It's always the same."

"What message?" I ask.

Benja winces slightly. "Fyrris wants to see you."

"What?" I say again, as a chill twists inside my chest. "Why?"

"You really think he'd tell me?" Benja asks.

I shut my mouth. No, of course Benja wouldn't know. We're only Guards, after all. I put the dull dagger back on its rack and set the sharpening stone in its cradle as my heart knocks around inside my chest.

"Same place?" I ask Benja.

He nods. "You want me to walk you there?"

I shake my head. I'm a Guard; I don't need an escort. I try to turn away before I meet Benja's eyes, but I don't quite make it. He gives me a look like he's not quite sure who I am anymore, or like the person who came back wearing Kira's body is a total stranger.

Hells, I can't blame him. I feel like that too.

The main courtyard is empty, filled only with rain and shadows. The sound of murmured conversation flows out of the open doors to the dining hall, making me realize how late it must be. I wasted the entire afternoon in that armory closet, staring through the window and wondering if leaving the Towers in a coffin would really be worse than living here right now.

I hunch my shoulders against the rain and walk past the sad little door to the Archives without giving it a second glance. I haven't been back there since that woman in the white robe told me the truth about my worthless lineage. Why would I? My parents weren't Exemplars. There won't be any records about me in those dusty rooms.

I'm nobody. Nothing.

I shiver as I enter the same cold hallway Benja brought me to before I left Silver City with Tholious and the mercenaries. No one has lit the torches in here yet. The hall is filled with the early gloom of the rain. It gives the place a strangely solemn air. I walk quietly, as if I'm trying not to disturb the peace. Ahead of me, an open door spills its

247

golden light across the polished stone floor. Something flutters inside my chest. It takes me a minute to recognize the feeling.

It's fear. I'm afraid.

Great. The first thing I've felt in days, maybe weeks, and it's fear. I feel like smacking myself across the face, but that would be awfully loud.

"—all these weeks. I cannot believe it's useless without him," a voice rumbles from inside the room. "After everything we put into crafting the nightmare steel. It should have absorbed all the old god's magic."

I freeze. Fear tugs at the skin on the back of my neck.

"Well, we don't have much choice," a woman replies.

My heart stops. That voice belongs to the woman who was in the room with Fyrris when I arrived. The one who shattered my entire world with one sentence. *You're one of Lord Castinac's many bastards.*

"If it won't work without him," the woman's voice continues, "then we need to capture him. Just like I've been saying. He can make it work again, I'm sure. With enough persuasion."

They're talking about Reznyk. They have to be. I force myself to breathe as my pulse hammers at my temples. The man makes a murmur of assent.

"Of course," he says. "And we know what he wants."

Feast day fireworks explode inside my skull. Capture him? Gods, no.

Reznyk is safe in the Daggers. I took the only thing he had, and I brought it here. There's nothing the Towers would want from him anymore.

But I think of Reznyk holding my broken ankle in his hands and making the pain vanish. I remember golden sparks swirling around us when we made love, like the stars themselves fell from the sky to dance for us.

The magic the Towers want was never in the amulet. Godsdamn it, the magic is in him.

Somehow, I manage to put one foot in front of the other until I'm standing in the pool of light spilling through the open door. And I clear my throat. Loudly.

"Kira," Fyrris announces, from the other end of the long, polished table in the middle of the room. "Enter."

There's a scattering of parchment spread across the table. It appears to be building plans and layouts. I try not to stare too hard at any one thing as I make my way to the same chair I sat down in twice before.

"Where are the rest of them?" the woman asks.

I blink as my mind stumbles over possible answers to that strange question.

"Coming from further away, of course," Fyrris replies. There's a cold edge to his voice. Once again, I decide the two of them don't get along.

Fyrris slides a piece of parchment across the table toward me. The parchment has been divided into four equal partitions with ebony ink and notes scratched along the edge.

"Do you know what this is?" Fyrris asks.

I frown as I weigh my various options. I manage not to say *a piece of parchment*, *a rectangle*, or *fuck you, you're a godsdamned monster*. The woman makes a little snorting sound.

"Tholious told us about the fortress where you found the Godkiller," Fyrris continues, ignoring the woman. "We need you to confirm a few details."

"Of course," I whisper.

"And you said you found the amulet in a garden?" Fyrris says.

Panic flares inside my mind like lightning flashing across a thundercloud. I look down at my hands as my cheeks burn. The woman makes another snorting sound.

"Kira Silver," Fyrris says, in a voice that's probably supposed to be reassuring. "It's very important you tell us exactly what happened."

"There's more to it than the amulet," the woman adds. "That man, Reznyk, he did more than kill an old god. Somehow, he took the amulet, our amulet, and he ruined it. It no longer works the way it's supposed to."

I glance up. They're both staring at me in a way that makes me want to shrink into the chair.

"We need to know everything," Fyrris says.

My breath catches. Everything? Reznyk's smile dances through my mind, the way the wind lifts his hair, the way his dark eyes dance in the sun. The feel of his lips. The sound of his laughter. The scars across his chest.

And the answer comes to me.

I blink, then wipe my sleeve across my face like I'm embarrassed. And I am, but not for the reasons they'll assume.

They want a story about the amulet? One that makes Reznyk a villain and the Towers the heroes? One that will scare them away from his lonely little cabin in the Daggers?

Well, of course they do. And if I do that, if I tell them what they want to hear, they'll forget about me. I've only ever been a means to an end for them. I keep my mouth shut, do my job, and I'm invisible.

And if I'm invisible, perhaps I can just walk through those open gates. I lean forward and take a deep breath.

I'm going to tell them everything they want to hear.

CHAPTER 37

REZNYK

WHAT DO YOU WANT FROM ME?

Tholious and Matius stare at me in the reflected glow of my fire. Rain runs in rivers off of their cloaks and pools at their feet. Behind me, a flicker of interest runs through the bond I have with Xavier. The cat doesn't want to admit it, but he's curious about the two men standing on my doorstep in the storm.

So am I. I raise an eyebrow and wait until the silence between us grows heavy and awkward, filled with rain and unspoken questions. The blond man, Tholious, clears his throat. I feel like he's about to speak, but instead he turns to the man behind him and nods his head.

"Just to be clear," the mercenary says, "we don't approve of what you did to Kira."

I blink. A gust of wind brings a thin veil of mist through the door, prickling my skin.

"Excuse me?" I ask.

"Matius," Tholious hisses under his breath.

The mercenary shrugs. "Someone had to say it," he replies.

"What I did to Kira?" I stammer as my mind lurches toward some possible response.

Kira came here to steal from me. She played her role so well she could have convinced the gods themselves, and then she took what she was after and left.

Well, sort of, my mind whispers. I used travel magic to shove her down the mountain. But that was after she'd stolen the amulet. Wasn't it?

I shake my head like I'm trying to knock those thoughts loose.

"Did you come all the way up here to tell me that?" I ask.

"Forgive my partner," Tholious says. "It's been a very long trip. May we come in?"

I stare at them for what feels like a long time. They're both carrying packs but no visible weapons. They're wearing simple traveling clothes, brown and mud-splattered green, not the black I associate with the Mercenary Guild of Silver City. They're effectively unarmed. They're asking for hospitality. And yes, they do look like it's been a long trip.

I might have fallen a long way from my upbringing in the legendary Blackwater brothel, but hells, not even I can turn away weary travelers seeking hospitality in the middle of a storm. I step back, then wave my hand at the hearth.

"Come in," I say.

I put on another pot of tea as Tholious and Matius shed their wet cloaks and stack their packs beside the door. There's only one chair, and I try to act like I'm not watching as they both look at the chair, then at each other, and then settle on the floor.

I take the chair. This is my house, damn it. We sit and stare at each other as the fire hisses and spits. I'm tempted to keep my tea to myself, but when the kettle sings, I pull it from its hook above the fire and pour tea into three carved wooden mugs. Tholious takes both cups, hands one to Matius, and then clears his throat again.

"The last time we spoke," Tholious begins, "you made me an offer."

I stare at him. He holds my gaze, although his hand trembles, sending little ripples across the surface of his tea.

"I don't remember making you an offer," I say.

His face is so pale I wonder if he's about to pass out. Still, he doesn't turn away. I wonder if he was brave before he went to the Towers, or if he had to grow brave to survive whatever they did to him there.

"You told me I could stay here," Tholious says. His voice is clear, but the echo of it trembles.

"Oh," I reply. "Right. That."

I take a sip of tea as that conversation comes pouring back to me. He offered me Kira in exchange for the amulet. I told him to go fuck himself. He said it was a good trade. I asked him what the Towers used to coerce him into making that offer.

And he said he wanted out.

"Let me guess," I say. "Fyrris didn't release you from the Towers."

Tholious finally looks away. A hint of pink creeps across his cheeks.

"I can't serve the Towers anymore," Tholious says, in a voice that's almost a whisper. "It's not worth losing him."

His gaze settles on Matius. Their eyes meet, and something flickers in the space between them that's so small and beautiful it makes me want to drive my fist through the wall. I grit my teeth against the dull, scraping ache in my chest.

"Great," I mutter.

"We can pay," Matius adds. "We've got shills."

"Oh, lovely," I snap. "I'll just walk around the corner to the nearest bank, shall I? Shills are so useful up here."

Matius narrows his eyes. For just a heartbeat, I have the distinct impression that he's considering punching me. Magic simmers under my skin. I almost hope he tries.

"I lied to the Towers," Tholious says. "I made it sound like you had a godsdamned fortress up here just so they'd leave you alone."

I turn back to him. The bravery and defiance that met me on the doorstep is gone. He puts his mug on the floor and shakes his head.

"I've got family down the river in Deep's Crossing," Tholious says, "but that's the first place the Towers will look. The Mercenary Guild said they'll cover our tracks, but they can't take the risk of hiding us. We had to go somewhere off the map, somewhere no one would ever think to look, at least for a few months. Until the Towers give up."

He turns toward the soaking packs dripping water onto my floor, then back to me.

"We brought all the money we have," he says. "We're not asking for charity."

I frown at the packs, then at Tholious, and finally at my rapidly cooling cup of tea. My mind keeps circling back to what Matius said. *We don't approve of what you did to Kira.* What in the gods' many names do they think I did to her?

"What exactly do you want from me?" I finally say.

"A place to stay," Tholious says.

"A place to hide," Matius adds. "In a month, the Mercenary Guild will hold my funeral. Two months after that, they'll report back to the Towers that they found a body in the river they think is Tholious."

"Three months?" I ask. "Do you know how much snow there'll be up here in three months?"

For the first time since I opened the door and met his gaze, Matius looks uncomfortable.

"It doesn't have to be with you," Matius says. "You know these mountains. Is there another place? A cave, maybe?"

"Oh, for fuck's sake," I mutter.

I drag my hand through my hair, then stare at the men sitting on my floor, a mercenary from the Silver City Mercenary Guild and a Disciple of the Towers who just showed up on my doorstep like children lost in the woods.

It's another trap. It has to be, but—

"Why me?" I ask. "Out of all the places for you to go, why here?"

Tholious blinks. "Because you offered," he says.

I laugh. I can't help myself; it's just such a stupid answer.

Only much later, after I've set Tholious and Matius up in the third floor of the keep with a stack of firewood big enough to turn the place into a sauna, the rain has faded, and stars shine through in patches torn from the shifting gray clouds, do I realize that was the first time I've laughed since Kira left me.

CHAPTER 38

KIRA

WE HAVE THE BAIT

"He did wear the amulet," I begin.

Fyrris and the woman both lean in closer, their eyes wide and gleaming, like wolves watching a wounded deer. I shift on the chair, the live coal of shame burning in my gut. Good. That will make this little fable all the richer.

"I didn't notice at first," I continue, spinning the lie like I spun so many nighttime stories for the children in the orphanage. "Because he wore it under his clothes. Next to his skin."

The sound of footsteps echoes through the room, drifting in through the open door behind me. Guards, probably, making their evening rounds.

"I'm not a thief," I say, although the memory of the golden necklace I pulled from the mud of a Crown Day festival burns in my mind, just one more lie added to my tale. "I couldn't sneak into his quarters to take it from him while he slept. I mean, not with all the magic and traps he has."

Fyrris and the woman both nod.

256

"So," I continue, letting my voice drop as I turn to stare at my fingers tangled in my lap. "I seduced him."

The woman makes a little grunt, like that's exactly what she expected.

"That's how I found the amulet," I continue. "And, once he fell asleep, I was able to take the amulet from around his neck."

My vision prickles with the hot burn of tears. This must be exactly what Reznyk thinks happened.

"What else did you notice?" Fyrris says.

I glance up, fear and disgust waging a little war in my stomach. If Fyrris is about to ask what positions we used, I swear to the gods—

Someone clears their throat behind me. I jump in my chair. Fyrris glances up, then makes an impatient hand-waving motion.

"Yes, come in," he snaps.

The sound of footsteps fills the room. I turn and see Zayne enter, followed by Barrance and Girwin. Zayne gives me a polite little nod. My fingers fold into fists as I remember my promise that I'd punch that bastard the next time I saw him, even as my mind screams about what a terrible idea that would be. Barrance gives me a lascivious grin that destroys any hope I might have had that the mercenaries hadn't overheard my whole seduction story. Girwin says nothing. Of course.

Matius isn't with them. I stare at the empty hallway behind Girwin for another heartbeat, waiting to see the man I'd come to think of as my friend melt out of the shadows. But there's nothing.

My heart sinks as I turn back to Fyrris. I can't blame Matius. Of course he doesn't want to set foot in the Towers. Still, I'm surprised at the dull ache in my chest I feel in his absence. It's a strange reminder that some small part of my heart might still be alive.

"Tell us more about the Godkiller's tower," Fyrris says, once Zayne and his mercenaries are settled around the table.

I take a deep breath, then tell Fyrris exactly what he wants to hear. I lie beautifully, extravagantly, describing exactly the kind of place a Godkiller would have for his lair. Magic. Traps. Wolves.

Fyrris and the woman eat it up. Zayne brings his hand up to cover his mouth. Finally, I run out of things to say and shut my mouth.

"Exactly what we expected," the woman says to Fyrris.

Fyrris nods. "An attack would be...difficult. We'll send a messenger first. Make an offer." He turns back to me. "Kira, tell me. Did the Godkiller talk about anyone else? Anyone who was special to him?"

My gut clenches like a fist. *We know what he wants*, they said as I lurked in the shadows outside the door. Was I really foolish enough to think they were talking about me?

"Did he mention, perhaps, a woman?" Fyrris continues.

"He did," I admit. My voice trembles, and the back of my throat tastes bitter.

"What about her?" the woman asks. Her eyes gleam like she's about to pounce. I don't think I've ever seen her look so interested in what someone has to say.

"He said there was—someone," I begin, forcing the words out. "In Silver City. He wanted to, uh, bring her up there. To his tower," I add, trying to build the story they want to hear.

"Who is she?" Fyrris asks.

"I don't know," I say, as my mind screams her name. *Lady Lenore Castinac.* I feel like the walls of the room are closing in all around me. "He just said she— She looks like me."

I let my head drop and blink as my vision swims. The woman hits the top of the table with her open palm.

"There," she declares, like she and Fyrris have just resolved a long-standing argument. "We have the bait. We set the trap. We'll bring the Godkiller back and make him fix the damn thing."

A chill dances up my neck. They really are going after Reznyk, then. It's not enough that they have the amulet I stole.

My mind conjures up another picture of the cabin in the snow, only this time the windows are broken, the door is kicked in, and Xavier hides shivering under the bed.

"But how are we going to acquire her?" Fyrris asks. "You can't just grab a Castinac off the streets."

A Castinac. The woman's words come back like a scream in the night. *You're one of Lord Castinac's many bastards.*

"That must be where we come in," Zayne says, in a voice like a low rumble of thunder in the distance.

I stare at Zayne for a moment, wondering what in the nine hells he could do to help me now, before I realize he isn't talking to me.

But by then it's too late. Because even as Zayne and the mercenaries start haggling about levels of criminality and reimbursement plus expenses, my mind has already settled on a very specific way Zayne could help me.

I stare at my own hands until Fyrris finally notices I'm still here and barks that I'm dismissed. No one even looks at me as I slide my chair back and walk out of the room, closing the door behind me. Gods help me, I'm invisible again.

Which is why no one cares that I stand in the entrance to the dark hallway, rocking slowly on the balls of my feet, as Silver City's bells toll and another Guard walks by, nodding his head without bothering to ask what I'm doing.

I wait in perfect, uninterrupted silence for the mercenaries. Because I have another job for them.

After all, I did steal the amulet. No matter what I intended when I picked the damn thing up, I left the Daggers with Reznyk's magical amulet in my hands. I thought I gave him what he wanted, that we'd both be safe once the Towers had the amulet.

I was wrong.

And now I need to warn him about what's coming.

CHAPTER 39
KIRA
THE TRUTH

B y the time Zayne and the mercenaries leave the room at the end of the hall, wind has joined its old friend rain, and together they're throwing fistfuls of water through the open door. Thunder rumbles in the distance, like the growl of some hungry beast. It's almost enough to mask the sounds of heavy boots in the hallway behind me.

I step away from the wall and fall into place beside Zayne. He nods, the briefest possible acknowledgement of my continued existence, and then pulls his hood up and over his face before stepping outside. I follow him. A gust of wind tosses rain into my face.

"Kira," Zayne whispers, his voice hardly audible over the constant drum of rain against the cobblestones. "You want something?"

Panic pulls my throat tight. I swallow hard. It's one thing to turn words over inside the quiet comfort of your own mind, and quite another to say them out loud.

"Yes," I whisper. "I need to go back. To the Daggers. I can pay."

Zayne doesn't respond. We turn toward the main gate. Wind rips at my clothes. Rain streaks down my face as disappointment pools inside my chest. Why did I think Zayne, of all people, would help me? Gods, this idea was doomed from the start.

Zayne stops. The Guards inside the entrance house stare through the window at us. Behind me, Barrance grumbles a few choice expletives.

"Good to see you again, sweetheart," Zayne announces. "Glad the ankle's recovered."

I'm about to tell him to go fuck himself when Zayne leans forward and tugs me into a hug. My back stiffens.

"Tomorrow night," he whispers. "At the Next Best Gander. Give the Towers a good cover story, okay?"

Before I can reply, he pulls back and slaps me on the shoulder hard enough to knock a spray of water out of my shirt. And then he's off, melting into the shadows on the other side of the gate with Barrance and Girwin at his heels. The Guards inside the entrance house watch him go.

The Next Best Gander? That dockside tavern has long held the reputation for being the filthiest and most dangerous pub on the waterside; I've never been inside it. The shiver that steals across my skin isn't entirely due to the rainwater trickling down my spine.

But, hells, it's not like I'm doing anything with my life here in the Towers. And, after so many years of pretending to be a ghost, it's not like anyone around here is going to miss me. Or even notice that I'm gone.

With a sigh, I shove my hands in my pockets and splash across the courtyard toward the Guards' dormitory.

~

"So, uh, I know it's a lot to ask," I say, staring at my hands as my cheeks burn. "But, I— I mean, if it's not too much trouble. I just need to get away."

I dare a quick glance at Benja. He's still watching me with a mixture of shock and deep, deep concern, like I've just told him I'll walk off a broken leg or not to worry about that arrow through my shoulder.

Shit. Maybe someone here will miss me after all. The thought should make me feel better, but it doesn't.

"Oh," Benja finally says.

The lump in his throat bobs as he swallows. The air in this tiny room is stale and musty; it feels like we're standing inside an abandoned boot. Benja gives me a smile that's probably supposed to be comforting but instead looks a little like he's desperate to find the nearest outhouse.

"Yeah, that's fine," Benja says.

My mouth falls open. It's that easy? I begged and stammered about how desperately I need a few weeks off to go reconnect with the damned orphanage, and it's that easy?

Benja rubs the back of his neck, then winces. "Look, usually when someone comes back from an expedition, they get a leave of absence," he says. "I mean, you can guess why, right?"

I blink. I'm not at all sure what he's talking about. He gives me another pained smile.

"I know it's hard," he says. "The things we do here. The things we see—"

He shakes his head. When he turns back to me, it's with a different expression on his face.

"You have to remember," he says. "They're not like us, Kira. The Exemplars, the Disciples, the Elites. Especially the Elites. They look like us, sure. But they're not like us."

Benja meets my gaze. Despite the stuffy heat of the

room, I feel like I've just fallen into something very cold and very dark.

That's how he can do it. Whatever Fyrris asks him to do, whatever makes people scream in the middle of the night, I'm now certain Benja is part of it. And he can walk away in the morning with his heart a clean slate. Because they aren't people. Not to him.

"I know you came here hoping to be one of 'em," Benja continues, shaking his head. "A lot of us did. But, I mean, thank the gods you're not, right?"

I force myself to breathe, in and out, just like a normal human being, but my mind howls inside my skull, and all I can see is Reznyk, hunched over in the meadow, staring at hands that once spilled the blood of an old god. Certainty closes around my heart like a fist.

I can't be a Guard for this place anymore.

The Towers are full of monsters.

"So, um, it's okay then?" I ask. "To take some time off?"

"Yeah," Benja says, "it's fine. We'll cover for you. Like I said, we all know what it's like."

I know, my mind screams. That makes it even worse.

I walk out of the tiny front office with its smell of mildew and damp clothes, across the courtyard, and through the main gates. My throat pulls tight as I step beneath the shadow of the gate, but no one stops me. The Guards inside the entrance house nod at me, certain that I have some reason for leaving, or just certain they don't give a shit. I'm another invisible Guard, after all. They'd be more interested in me if I were a rat scurrying across the cobblestones.

The warm glow of a late autumn afternoon fills the streets of Silver City, turning the air to melted gold. All around me, the city hums with life. A donkey pulls a cart filled with hay. Children who probably came from the orphanage shriek as they race down the street. Far above us, the gleaming white Towers thrust into the brilliant azure sky. I'm at the steps of the orphanage in just a few minutes, and sitting in Dame Serena's tiny study a few minutes after that. Some part of me wonders that the geography of my entire life can be circumvented so quickly.

"So," Dame Serena begins, after we've exchanged pleasantries and she's caught me up on all the gossip, "what brings you here, Kira, my dear one?"

She calls every single child here *dear one*. Still, hearing it makes my chest ache and my eyes sting. I might as well be five years old again, reading a string of letters and looking up to see one of her rare smiles.

I threw this all away. Dame Serena, and the children who listened to my stories every night, and the pantry I learned how to manage after years of picking every lock and stealing every sweet. I left the orphanage the same day Fyrris arrived with his beautiful lies about my parents and my potential, convinced I was moving on to something better. I didn't want to come back here unless I was wearing the white robes of an Exemplar, ready to share the secrets of my illustrious parentage with all the people I left behind. But something better never arrived, did it?

I try to swallow the lump in my throat. "I— I left quickly," I stammer.

"Yes, you did," she replies, with a nod. "They gave you a good offer."

It's not a question. Her mouth pulls tight in a way that makes me think she has her own opinions about the Towers, but she's polite enough not to offer them.

"I never got to ask about my—"

My voice cuts off. We don't talk about where the children in the orphanage come from. Dame Serena tells them they are each a blessing, that they were delivered by birds or fish or foxes, and she is so fortunate to have them now. It's only when someone leaves the orphanage that she unlocks the box on her desk, pulls out her massive ledger, and reveals what little she knows of their history.

I glance at her desk pushed against the wall, and the locked box in the center. In all my years in the orphanage, that's the only lock I never picked. I wanted to believe it didn't matter, that I didn't care where I came from.

And maybe I believed that lie. At least until the first time Fyrris opened his mouth.

"Your history?" Dame Serena asks, finishing my sentence.

I nod. My throat feels tight, and my hands are trembling. Dame Serena pulls herself up in her chair and clears her throat.

"I knew your mother," she says.

I blink. For all the time I've spent imagining my mother as an Exemplar, I never pictured her as an actual person, a human with friends and family, someone who might have known the same people I know.

"We grew up together," Dame Serena continues. "Here, of course."

My breath catches. My mother was an orphan?

"She wanted to keep you," Dame Serena says. "Difficult, in her line of work, but not impossible. She came to me for advice." She shakes her head. "If she had survived, Margot would have made a wonderful mother."

I open my mouth, but nothing comes out.

My mother wasn't an Exemplar, and I was no long-lost princess of the Towers like the bedtime stories I made up for the children. She lived here, in these halls. I spent my childhood in her home, and I never knew.

"As for your sire," Dame Serena continues, with a tight twist of her lips that reminds me of the expression she made when she mentioned the offer the Towers gave me, "I'm fairly certain I know him as well."

"Lord Castinac?" I ask.

Dame Serena looks almost surprised.

"Yes," she replies. "Yes, I believe so. He would deny it, of course, if you were thinking of approaching him, and you know there's no way to prove it. But he did make a rather sizable donation to the orphanage after your mother's death."

I blink, then turn toward the room's one small window set high in the stone wall. I can see the gleaming edge of a white tower standing like a bulwark against the wild blue sky.

The Towers really did lie to me. I have no magical lineage. I don't belong there, or anywhere else. Being the bastard daughter of a nobleman means exactly nothing in this town; I can think of at least a half dozen other children in the orphanage right now who could claim something similar.

I truly am nothing special.

The gods only know what the Towers wanted with me when they pulled me from the orphanage with a story so blatantly false I should have seen through it years ago. But I fell for it, and Dame Serena didn't stop them. Maybe she didn't want to interfere unless I asked. Maybe she's afraid of the Towers.

No, there's only one person who ever told me the truth. I remember the way the wind tugged at Reznyk's hair as he held my hand in the sunlight. He looked almost apologetic when he said I don't have any magical potential, as if it was his fault that I'd swallowed that stupid lie years ago.

And then I betrayed him.

My eyes sting. I press my palms to my face to cover the flood of tears before it can spill down my cheeks. Dame Serena makes a clucking sound. Her chair groans as she comes to her feet.

"I'll give you a minute," she says.

The door creaks as she closes it behind her. And then I'm alone, in the only home I ever had, the place I left without a second thought, surrounded by a lifetime's worth of mistakes.

CHAPTER 40

KIRA

THE NEXT BEST GANDER

The necklace is exactly where I buried it.

The delicate golden butterfly winks at me in the dim glow of the streetlamp on the far side of the garden walls. I run my dirt-streaked fingers over its delicate wings.

I should feel something, shouldn't I? But my chest is as empty as the night sky. It's just cold metal, this necklace, no different from the garden spade I used to unearth it. I pile dirt back in the hole, toss a handful of straw over it, then come to my feet and cross my arms over my chest.

It's cold already. My breath forms a cloud in the soft glow of the streetlamps. On the far side of the garden wall, hooves rattle and a cart creaks as someone makes their way home for the night.

Dame Serena told me I'm welcome to stay, just like that. Not for the night or until I felt better. I'm welcome to stay, period, for as long as I want. I could spend the evening, or spend the rest of my life here, working in the garden, managing the pantry, wiping noses and telling stories about orphan children who discover their parents were magical.

It wouldn't be a bad life, staying here in the orphanage. It would certainly be better than sneaking through the Towers in the dark, searching for records of parents who don't exist.

But Fyrris would find me. A dog barks in the distance; I shiver. Benja told me to take as much time as I need. Still, that doesn't mean forever. Fyrris might not miss me for a few weeks, possibly even a handful of months. But if I tried to stay here for years? I swallow hard as I tuck the golden necklace into my vest, close to my heart. There's more to it than being afraid of Fyrris, with his stupid lies and threats.

Reznyk was kind to me. He told me the truth, even though he knew exactly who I am, where I came from, and what I was doing.

And I thought he was safe. I thought the Towers were done with him.

I creep through the darkened garden on my toes, just like I did when I snuck out to go to the Crown Day festivities. The old apple tree still spreads its limbs against the far garden wall, although by now almost all of its leaves have fallen and the few apples that remain look almost as wrinkled as Dame Serena. Still, the branches feel solid enough to hold my weight.

I climb the old tree to the top of the wall, then drop into the alley below. The sound of my boots against the stone echoes like a firework. I freeze, my breath catching, but the only reply is the scurry of some small creature startled from its hiding place at the far end of the alley. I pull my hood up over my head and leave Silver City's orphanage for the second time in my life.

The city is quiet by the time I make it to the docks. My

heart pounds in the back of my throat, but the fear I'm expecting has yet to show up. I should be afraid, of course. This area isn't known for being welcoming after dark, and I very much doubt Zayne is completely trustworthy.

I swallow hard as I stare at the round sign featuring an angry goose's open beak, complete with tiny, serrated teeth. The Next Best Gander, the sign reads in sharp, dark letters. The image isn't exactly welcoming.

But it's too late to turn back.

I push the door open. It swings inward with a sigh, revealing a dimly lit room filled with rough-hewn tables and chairs. There's a bar on the far side, and a hearth with a low, flickering fire. At first, I think the room might be empty. Then I see an older woman at the bar watching me closely, two men hunched over tankards by the fire, and a figure in black sitting in the back corner.

Zayne, of course. I take a deep breath and walk toward him. His eyes follow me closely, but he doesn't move. I stop in front of the table and stare at him. There's a candle between us. Its weak light sends strange shadows dancing across his pale face. He looks tired, and somehow even more dangerous than he did when he was sitting next to Fyrris, making plans to abduct a noblewoman.

"Well," I announce. "I'm here."

Zayne raises an eyebrow. I feel like a complete idiot.

"Have a seat," Zayne says, gesturing toward the chair in front of me like he's offering me something.

I collapse into it. Zayne taps his finger on the table and stares at me like he's expecting something. Payment, probably. I tuck my fingers into my vest and feel the hard edge of the butterfly's golden wing.

"I've got a question for you," he says.

I pull the necklace from my vest and slide it across the

table. It's not as beautiful as it once was, not in this low light. Gods above, please let it be enough.

"Payment," I whisper.

The corner of Zayne's mouth curls up. He covers the necklace with his hand, and then it's gone, just like a magician's trick.

"Appreciated," he says. "But that's not my question."

"So?" I say.

My heart is beating like a bird trapped in a cage. Zayne crosses his arms over the table and leans forward, his strange, green eyes on mine.

"Why?" Zayne says.

I blink. He grins at me in a way that makes me feel like he's indulging me. Suddenly, I'm remembering that I did promise myself I'd punch this bastard the next time I saw him.

"Why what?" I snap.

He leans back in his chair. "Why go back to the Daggers? You forgot something up there, sweetheart?"

"Fuck you," I reply.

He grins at me. "That's not usually how someone asks for my help, you know."

"You broke my ankle," I say.

"And you came back to the Towers."

I huff, then stare at the rough wooden table and the empty place where the golden butterfly necklace just vanished.

"I made a mistake," I admit.

Zayne makes a purring noise in the back of his throat. "Nothing wrong with that," he says. "Although most people can't bring themselves to admit it. You going to fix it?"

I nod. My eyes sting, but my gods, I am not going to cry

here. I've cried enough. Now it's time to do something about the mess I made.

"I'm going to try," I whisper.

"Good enough," Zayne says.

His hand floats over the table again. When he pulls it back, there's a smooth wooden disc in the place where I put the golden necklace.

"Some of my clients are bringing a shipment to Cairn-cliff," he says, in a low voice. "They're looking to avoid undue attention, so they're traveling to Deep's Crossing, then taking the road past the Daggers."

I keep my damn mouth shut, although I wonder what he means by *my clients*. Is he talking about the Mercenary Guild, or does Zayne have some side business that's even worse than murdering people for money?

"They can get you as far as the road to the Golden Peaks," he says, glancing up to meet my gaze. "Can you make it from there?"

I sink my teeth into my lower lip. That road was pretty straightforward, right? I'd remember if there were any major turns, wouldn't I?

"Sure," I say.

"One more thing," Zayne adds. "If you see any friends there, tell them I say hello."

"What the—"

"Great," Zayne continues, cutting me off with a wide smile that does nothing to help my confidence. "You'll need this."

He pulls something out from under the seat at his side and hands it to me. It's a dark pack, like the one I carried on our first expedition into the Daggers. I take it, and I have just enough sense not to paw through it while sitting in the middle of the Next Best Gander.

"And this," Zayne continues, picking up the wooden disc and pressing it into my palm. "Find the *Maiden's Revenge*. She's small, dark, and low to the water. She's leaving at first light. Give this to the captain. He'll take care of the rest."

The wooden disc feels strangely cold against my skin. I stare at Zayne as my body cycles through every single emotion I've ever experienced in a mad hurricane of panic and second thoughts. The fire of terror, the brittle frost of fear, and finally the hollow, empty feeling that's lived inside my chest ever since I stumbled into the Golden Peaks Hunting Lodge with that damned amulet in my hands.

In the end, I just feel tired. I shake Zayne's hand, walk to the docks, and let strange hands tug me onto a low barge that stinks of fish and unwashed bodies.

CHAPTER 41

REZNYK

TRUST

There's another dead animal strung up on the grass.

Something hot and sour rises in the back of my throat. I turn away from the naked red flesh, the soft fur splayed out next to the corpse, but not before my mind spits out the word rabbit.

Gods, what in the nine hells is wrong with me? I've killed animals before, damn it. I've killed more than animals. Why do I feel like I'm going to be sick looking at a dead rabbit?

"Fuck," I mutter under my breath before dragging my eyes up to the place where Matius sits in the first light of the rising sun, fiddling with the ancient bow.

My food stores were the first thing I showed Tholious and Matius. Tholious crossed his arms and stood in the doorway of the half-collapsed cellar. Matius walked the length of the room, running his fingers along bags of beans and potatoes, wax-encrusted wheels of hard cheese, metal canisters of flour and tea, all the things I bought in Cairn-cliff and carried back here, step after painful step.

"Well?" I finally asked, tired of watching him pace the room like judge, jury, and executioner.

"It's not enough for three," Matius declared.

Of course it's not. I tried not to let it show, but I felt like sinking into the stone floor.

"But it could be," Matius continued. "If we do some hunting."

I kept my mouth shut. That's a normal thing to do, hunting for food. It's what I should have been doing all along. So I ignored the twinge in my stupid, weak heart as Matius set traps for rabbits and refurbished elven bows that were probably ancient when my grandparents were born. He told me he wants to take down a deer before the snow flies.

It's what the Towers trained me to do, killing large animals. But I didn't offer to help him, and he didn't ask.

Matius shades his eyes as I approach and stand beside him. He doesn't smile, exactly. Tholious has been almost embarrassingly polite around me for the five days they've been here, but Matius still treats me with cool disdain, as though we're on two different sides of some old family feud. I'm not sure which one of them irritates me more.

As I watch, Matius loops a string over both ends of the bow. That string is probably rabbit gut, I realize as my stomach lurches over the raw potato I had for breakfast. Matius tugs gently on the new string.

"That looks solid," I offer.

He snorts. "It looks like it's going to explode in my face."

"Are you always this argumentative?" I snap. "Or is this something you reserve for people who are trying to help you?"

Matius grins as he tips the bow in his hand. "You know what the worst part of being in the Mercenary Guild was?"

"The murders?"

"Not even close," he replies. "The worst part was not being able to tell an asshole to go fuck himself."

"Lovely," I mutter.

He's such a charming individual, Matius. I'm so glad I decided to open what passes for my home to this gentleman.

"If someone had the shills, we'd do whatever they said without a word of complaint," Matius continues. "Even if they were ten pounds of shit in a five-pound bag. We smiled, and we got the job done."

"You're not doing a job for me," I reply.

"I know," Matius says.

There's something predatory about the smile he gives me. It makes me wonder just how far behind he left Silver City's Mercenary Guild.

"Who are you doing a job for?" I ask, not expecting an answer.

Matius stretches, then unhooks the string and coils it around his fingers.

"No one," he says. "I'm a free agent now. And that's why I can tell you to go fuck yourself."

"Right," I reply.

Like hells he's a free agent. The Towers sent them here for something, although I haven't been able to make out what it is yet.

"Are you always this suspicious?" Matius asks as he tucks the string into a pocket in his vest.

"Of men from the Towers who just happen to show up on my doorstep?" I say. "Actually, I think I'm not suspicious enough."

Our eyes meet. There's something hard in his expression that I don't understand. Matius has plenty of reasons to hate me, naturally. I murdered an old god; everyone in the world has a reason to hate me. But the simmering anger in his eyes feels more personal. Or maybe he's just a bastard.

"You've got problems with trust," Matius says. He comes to his feet beside me.

"Trust?" I snap. "You broke a woman's ankle, then sent her to fuck me for—"

I see the flash of his palm, but he's far too fast for me to avoid it. Matius's hand hits my cheek. My head rocks back. White spots explode across my vision as blood coats my tongue. Magic surges forward in response, hissing and spitting across my skin. For just a moment, it forms spikes across my knuckles. And then the moment fades. Pain sings through my body. I spit blood at Matius's feet.

"What in the hells was that?" I snap.

"Don't talk about Kira like that," Matius says, in a low voice.

"The fuck do you care?" I growl.

Rage throbs behind my temples. My ears ring. I frown at the man standing in front of me like I'm trying to read something written on a wall that's on the other side of Silver City.

For all I can tell, Matius really is in love with Tholious. The way they watch each other when they think I'm not looking would give it away even if I hadn't heard the noises they make at night that are horribly amplified by the empty stone walls of the keep.

But maybe I missed something. Maybe he's in love with Kira instead?

I run my hand across my mouth and stare at the streak of blood left behind. My lip stings where Matius's hand split it open. I bet the Mercenary Guild taught him that, how to slap someone with a flat palm for maximum damage. That bastard probably knows thousands of ways to hurt someone. Like breaking an ankle.

I scowl at him as magic ripples under my skin. Matius, for what might be the first time in his life, looks mildly ashamed.

"What you did to her was wrong," Matius says, in a much quieter voice. "And I'm not afraid to say it."

"What I did to her?" My voice is rising. "What, take her in? Heal the ankle you bastards broke? Give her—"

I snap my mouth closed before I can say more. What I did to Kira is none of this man's business.

"I brought her back to Silver City," Matius growls. "You think I didn't notice? You fucked her up."

My mouth falls open and stays that way. A hawk cries in the background, his shrill warning call, just in case any other hawks out there were thinking about moving into his territory.

I fucked her up? Nine hells, she's the one who took the amulet. I'm the one who burned all my godsdamned pillows. I snap my mouth closed and cross my arms over my chest.

"You're here for the same reason," I finally manage to spit through my swollen lip. "But whatever the Towers sent you up here to steal, whatever they think I still have, you're not getting it."

For a heartbeat, we're both perfectly still. The wind whispers around us, cool against the fire of the cheek this bastard just smacked for no reason. Matius frowns at me.

And then he laughs. I rock backward, not sure if he's about to take another swing at me.

"Shit, you do have trust issues," Matius finally says, wiping his eyes.

"Don't fucking touch me again," I growl. "Or I'll—"

"What's so funny out here?" Tholious calls from the yawning opening at the top of the pile of rubble.

I shake my head, whatever idle threat I would have made dying on my lips. I'm not going to hurt either of them, and Matius knows it. The Towers know it too. Why else would they send these two?

I turn away as Tholious steps through the hole in the wall, two steaming mugs in his hands.

And then my wards explode.

CHAPTER 42

KIRA

HOW HARD COULD IT BE?

T his was a terrible idea.

Even with Zayne's pack, which holds a change of scruffy clothes, hard biscuits, a bedroll, and several daggers, I'm completely unprepared, totally alone, and possibly lost.

It was better with the smugglers of the *Maiden's Revenge*. They treated me with a cool sort of professionalism, and the captain even pressed a few shills into my hands a week later, when their caravan stopped in the night on the road to Cairncliff.

"For helping us load the carts in Deep's Crossing," he said, with a little nod.

I was absolutely certain my help wasn't worth that much coin, but I took it anyway. The mountains looming up on either side of the road seemed larger and steeper than before, and the wind blowing off them was so cold it cut through my cloak like a knife.

"Golden Peaks Lodge is that way," the captain said, nodding at a smaller track branching off from the road we'd been following. "I'd travel at night, if I were you," he continued, staring at the road in a way that made me think he was seeing something more than packed dirt and bedraggled grass. "Someone's been through here. Earlier today, I'd guess. You'll want to keep out of sight."

"Thanks," I said.

He nodded again. For a moment, I thought he was going to say something more, like trying to talk me out of doing something that was so clearly idiotic. But one of the horses stamped the ground behind him, another man said something low and thick that I couldn't quite make out, and he turned away. I stepped into the shadow of the trees as their carts passed, nearly silent in the thin moonlight.

Then I took a deep breath and turned toward the road to the Golden Peaks Lodge. It took us two days to reach this road from the lodge, I think, when I was traveling with Matius. But that was on horseback. And I hadn't exactly been paying attention.

Still, I reasoned, how hard could it be? It's just walking, after all. I could walk through the nine hells if I had to.

And I've been cursing myself ever since. At least with the smugglers, I could pretend I wasn't making a horrible decision. I could let myself slip into the fantasy that I'd decided to run away from the Towers, from my entire life in Silver City, and load mysterious crates from a barge into nondescript carts to travel dangerous mountain roads at night.

But now? Now I'm stumbling through the woods, at night, alone, with nothing but my bad choices to keep me company. Zayne's heavy pack cuts into my shoulders, my feet squawk with protest after every step, and I'm only vaguely certain I'm still on the right road. I'm following some sort of cart tracks, at least. Every now and then I stumble across another pile of fresh horse manure, so I'm close to them, whoever they are. And they must be going somewhere. Hopefully to the Golden Peaks Lodge.

"Kira," I huff to myself, "you're an idiot."

I stop and glare at the sky, as if it's to blame for my stupid decisions. The stars are vanishing one by one. The sky is the faded gray of clothes that have been washed until they're threadbare. The jagged black peaks of the Daggers look sharper in this light, but no closer. There's no sign of the Golden Peaks Lodge, and no sign of the carriage I'm following.

I'm low on food, I have at least another night of walking ahead of me, if I'm not lost already, and my damn feet throb so badly I feel it in every other part of my body.

"Shit," I say.

Things were bad in the Towers. So I went and made them all much, much worse.

Why? Because I fell for someone who told me at the start he was in love with another woman. And now, apparently, I'm going to wander around the Daggers until I either find him and apologize for being such an idiot or just keel over and die.

Reznyk was right about falling in love, damn it. There's nothing at all that's nice about this ache in my chest, nothing warm and syrupy like those stupid tavern songs.

I should have listened to him, I tell myself as I shove aside a thicket of scrubby bushes and collapse on the ground. I should have punched Zayne in the nose instead of letting him break my ankle. Hells, I should have broken Tholious's ankle and left him to seduce Reznyk.

My eyes close. I'm still rattling through my regrets when sleep drags me to another world.

CHAPTER 43
REZNYK
WHAT DID YOU DO?

My wards don't just go off. They shatter.

It hits me like a punch to the gut. I sink to my knees, air rushing out of my lungs. Even as I reel from the punch of magical energy, I can't help but notice how very cold the ground is this morning through the thin layer of frost the sun has yet to burn away.

"What happened?" Matius snaps.

He's at Tholious's side in an instant, one arm around his lover's shoulders. Tholious meets my gaze, his eyes wide and his face suddenly pale. One of the mugs rolls slowly across the stones, leaving a steaming trail of tea.

"Something's coming," Tholious whispers.

"Magic?" Matius asks.

Tholious nods. Matius's lips pull back in a snarl.

"It's them, isn't it?" Matius growls.

"Shit," I pant, as I struggle back to my feet.

I knew it was coming, and still, I'm surprised. Just like with Kira. Damn it, you'd think I would know better by now. I turn to the two men who must have led the Towers here to betray me and try to summon the rage I should feel.

But rage doesn't come. It's like trying to throw one of the weapons I used to make out of magic into the heart of a living creature. I hesitate, grasping for the way I know I should feel.

It's so cold in the shadow of the keep this morning. In the pale morning light, Matius and Tholious look less like assassins from the Towers and more like two boys who lost their way in the forest and turned into strange, wild men.

"What did you do?" I finally say. I mean it to sound like a threat, but it comes out as a sigh.

And then Matius pulls out a knife.

It winks in the sun, bright steel shattering the thin light around it. I take a step back without thinking. I didn't even notice he was carrying a knife; yet another reminder of how far I've let my guard down around these two.

"Did you do this?" Matius snaps.

He takes a step toward me, raising the knife. Magic simmers across my skin.

"Did you sell us out, you pathetic son of a bitch?" Matius screams.

The edge of the blade trembles as it moves closer to all sorts of places I'd rather not have a blade. Before my brain can sort through the jumble of questions pulsing inside my skull and pick one to force through my mouth, Tholious steps forward and puts his hand on Matius's shoulder. Tholious makes a soft sound, like a purr, then leans forward to whisper in Matius's ear.

"It's not him," Tholious murmurs.

The knife doesn't move. Matius's eyes flash at me like lightning arcing across the underside of a thunder cloud. I open my mouth, but I still can't get anything to come out.

This is the bastard who set me up, right? Tholious and Matius have to be the reason something with enough magic to shatter all my wards just crossed into this part of the Daggers. So why the fuck is he pointing a blade toward my throat?

"Maybe he made a deal," Matius growls, but there's a tremble in his voice that echoes the subtle shake of his blade.

"Hells," I snap. "And you said I have trust issues."

Tholious makes that sound again, the little purring noise. "No," Tholious whispers. "He hates the Towers as much as we do."

Tholious turns to me. His eyes shine like chunks of ice. He's staring at me like he's asking a question, but that would be absurd. All of this is absurd.

"Of course I hate the Towers," I spit, answering his unspoken question.

I'm about to continue, to point out the fact that they must have set me up and not the other way around, but Matius makes a sound like he's been punched in the chest. A moment later, the mercenary sinks to his knees. His knife falls, stabbing the cold ground. When he looks up at Tholious, it's with a strange, pleading expression I wouldn't have believed his face was capable of making.

"It really is them, isn't it?" Matius whispers. "It's the Towers."

Tholious flicks his head to the side, the barest suggestion of a nod, and then he sinks to the ground beside his lover and wraps his arms around his shoulders.

"I'm sorry," Matius whispers in a voice I'm suddenly certain I'm not supposed to overhear. "I promised we'd outrun them."

"Don't take this on yourself," Tholious replies as he sinks his head onto Matius's shoulder.

Well, this is awkward.

I take one step back, then another, until I'm well out of earshot for their strange, whispered, huddling conversation. Hells, they're really committing to this act. They're almost as good as Kira.

My chest aches. Pain comes in waves, like an echo of shattering magical wards. I remember the look on her face that morning. She was standing right here, the amulet in both her hands, almost like she was offering it to the sun. Or gloating about her discovery.

Or bringing it to me, some traitorous part of my mind whispers. But why would she do that? To shove it under my nose and ask why I'd been lying?

I can't stop the flood of images that tumble through my head. Kira with her hair pulled back, grinning at me as the light of my fire caressed her cheeks. Kira spinning in the meadow, her arms flung wide, as wild and free as any of the creatures of the Daggers. It's only too easy to imagine Kira flinging open the door of the cabin, slapping the amulet down on my table, and saying something sarcastic and teasing and perfect about forbidden amulets and secret hiding places.

My eyes burn. I force them closed and turn to the wind, focusing on the sting of cold air against my skin. That never happened. The Kira I knew, or thought I knew, was a fiction invented by the Towers. She was a tool, a weapon pointed directly at my weakest parts.

And she broke me. All she had to do was make me forget who I am, and what I am. She opened the door to another world; I'm the fool who thought I could walk through it. After everything I've done, I still thought someone could love me.

Gods, I should know better by now.

Someone coughs. I blink open my eyes, then run the

287

back of my hand across my face. Hopefully they'll think it's just the wind that's made my eyes water.

"We need to go," Tholious says, soft and low, like I'm an animal he's afraid of spooking.

When I turn, a shadow flickers across the man's face, there and then gone. It's less than a heartbeat, that little ripple of hesitation, but it makes me pause.

He doesn't completely trust me. Despite his reassurances to Matius, some part of Tholious thinks I might have actually called the Towers down on my own head just to be rid of the two of them.

Because I'm a monster. And that's what monsters do.

I sigh. Then, because it has to be said, I say it.

"They aren't here for you," I declare.

Tholious stares at me. His eyes are wide. For a moment, he looks almost startled.

"They want the Godkiller," I say. "Not you."

Tholious frowns. Wind ruffles the edges of my cape. A hawk screams as it circles over the forest of shifting scarlet and gold.

Magic trembles across my broken wards, moving fast and straight at me. It's not Fyrris, at least, who broke the wards. I don't think it's a human. But one of the Towers's ravens would be just as dangerous to Tholious and Matius. I narrow my eyes at the rising sun.

"Get inside the cabin," I say. "Lock the door. Pull the shades. They're coming."

CHAPTER 44
REZNYK
WE'LL LET HER LIVE

Two ravens fly over the ridge, moving low to the ground as the light of the rising sun glints off their sharp beaks and dark, beady eyes. I don't have time to run to the top of the keep, to pretend I live anywhere other than the cabin where I've just shoved the two men who are either my only friends or my dangerous enemies.

Instead, I walk toward the ravens as they approach. The wind rips my cloak back and cuts through my clothes. One of the ravens carries something in its black claws that flashes in the light like a small piece of metal. It doesn't feel magical. Still, there's something ominous about that little wink of light clutched in the bird's talons.

I stop once I pass the keep, cross my arms over my chest, and await my fate. The ravens climb high, circling the area first. Clever. I'm not certain if this is the same pair I tried to bribe months ago, but I feel like it is. There's something familiar in the way their tentative magical awareness brushes against mine.

"What are you looking for?" I call up to them. "My army?"

Annoyance flickers across the bond between us. It's strangely satisfying to know I'm getting under their avian skin. Finally, one of them descends. It's the one with the piece of metal in its claws. As it approaches, I see the metal is gold, in an oval shape, and it's connected to a thin chain.

There's something familiar about that shape. Something that feels very, very wrong.

The first raven settles on a rock that's not quite within reach while the second stays above us, flying in low, slow circles. Keeping watch. The golden oval gleams in the sunlight, tugging at my memory. I recognize it, I'm sure of it. But from where?

In one smooth motion, the raven bends down, grabs the piece of gold in its ebony beak, and then tosses it to me. Its thin chain streams behind it like the streak that follows a meteor. I grab it out of the air. The metal is cool against my palm; the chain bleeds through my fingers.

The raven watches me with dark, impassive eyes, saying nothing. My throat feels tight. My heart beats in the back of my skull. I imagine turning around, stalking toward the keep, ignoring the ravens. Or tossing whatever this is over the edge of the ridge, losing it in the autumn forest below.

But in the end, I have to know.

I unfurl my fingers slowly, one at a time, revealing the pendant like a woman taking off her clothes in front of her lover for the first time.

And then I stare, numb, at the golden locket in my palm. There's a delicate floral filigree around the edges and an ornate C in the middle. It could be a forgery. If the Towers were motivated enough, they could find a goldsmith to create this.

But the clasp looks real enough. And, when I press my fingernail against the seam, the locket opens without a sound. Inside are two tiny oil paintings, one of a man with cheeks as red as his hair, the other a stern-looking woman with black hair long and loose over her shoulders.

My pulse hammers inside my skull. Something bitter climbs up the back of my throat, and I realize the locket is trembling.

I've never seen this locket open, but I know those pictures. They hang above the entryway to the Castinac's manor, which was as far as I was ever allowed to enter. The nights I climbed the arbor to Lenore's bedroom to see this locket against the bare skin between her breasts were strictly unsanctified.

I close the locket, then force myself to lower my hand before the tremble gives me away. The raven meets my gaze.

"How dare you," I say. It comes out thin, like a whisper.

The raven ruffles his feathers.

"We have your mate," he says.

Panic closes its cold fist around my chest. But, no. He's not talking about Kira. Kira is back at the Towers, where she belongs. No, this is Lenore's pendant, the third daughter of the Castinac family. They think she's my mate.

Which means those crazy sons of bitches actually attacked the Castinac family.

"Taking her was a mistake," I say, in that same thin voice.

"Maybe," the raven replies, with another ruffle of his feathers. "Maybe not. You meet us in the meadow before the sun sets, and we'll let her live."

"And if I don't?"

The raven shakes his head, then spreads his wings. With a little hop, he's in the air, banking fast as his wings beat against the sky. His partner makes a low, gurgling croak. For a moment, I'm surprised to hear such a normal raven sound coming from one of the Towers's birds. Then they both drop below the ridge, leaving me alone with the dull throb of my heart and the cold golden locket that belongs to the woman I once loved.

I turn toward the western horizon, then toward the forest, as the cold of the locket sinks into my body. I don't have long until sunset. I can't see the meadow from here, but I'm sure Fyrris is there, waiting for me. Maybe with Lenore, or maybe that was just an empty threat.

It didn't feel empty.

Slowly, with legs that feel like they've turned to stone, I face my little cabin.

Were Matius and Tholious part of this? If so, it's not in a way I can understand. The Towers knew where to find me without those two, and Fyrris must have known about my relationship with Lenore for years. Maybe they didn't come here to betray me after all. Maybe their story is true. And Kira—

I freeze as the thought hits me in the gut.

Kira took the amulet. But the Towers are here, asking for me. Threatening to hurt someone they think I love to get me. And they didn't bring Kira. No, Fyrris still thinks I'll come running to save Lenore.

Maybe Kira wasn't a trap. Maybe all she ever was to the Towers was a trade, something for Tholious to offer in payment. Because she looks a bit like Lenore, and Fyrris thought that would be enough for me.

Maybe I was wrong. About everything.

Suddenly, I'm remembering that morning in the garden. Kira holding the amulet out to the sunshine, her brow furrowed in concentration as the metal gleamed in the light. She didn't look like she had anything to hide. She never looked like she had anything to hide.

I thought she was a master, the greatest deceptionist I've ever met. But, as the wind swirls around me and Lenore's golden locket digs into my palm, another far simpler explanation finally surfaces.

Maybe Kira was telling the truth.

All of it, from the start. She told me in the hunting lodge that she'd come to track a man who stole something. She was chasing the lie the Towers fed her years ago, that she had magical potential. I told her the truth when I said I didn't feel her potential, but why would she trust me after years of listening to the Towers's lies?

The look on her face flashes through my memory once again.

Kira wasn't trying to hide the amulet that morning. Gods help me, maybe she was trying to use it. Maybe she was looking for the magic the Towers promised her years ago.

I stumble, then sink to my knees. My heart feels like a hole punched through my chest; my throat is so tight it's hard to breathe. I sink my fists into the thin grass. There's another truth now, something as bright and hard as the golden locket in my hand.

The Towers are here. In my mountains. If they come up the ridge, it's not just the old god I'm hiding. They'll find Tholious and Matius. I don't quite consider the two men who crashed on my doorstep friends, but still, wouldn't the Towers assume they mean something to me? Just like they think Lenore means something to me?

My gods, the Towers attacked the Castinacs. They must be desperate to cross the invisible line that protects the rich and powerful families of Silver City. What would keep them from torturing Tholious and Matius to make me dance?

Or Kira? If they ever found out how I feel about her—

Slowly, I push myself back to my feet. Magic bristles around me, hot and sharp. I've been running for years, ever since the old god died in my arms. But I can't run now. I have too much to protect.

The Towers trained me to be a killer.

It's time for me to live up to my potential.

CHAPTER 45
REZNYK
AN OFFER

I wait until the ravens are swallowed by the gold and scarlet forest below before I push the door of my cabin open. Tholious and Matius are sitting on my bed, leaning against each other. Matius stares at the floor while Tholious absently runs his fingers down Xavier's spine. The old cat's rough purr fills the cabin. Little bastard. It was months before he let me pet him like that.

Both men turn to stare at me as the door swings open. Tholious clears his throat.

"We'll go over the mountains," he tells me. "Once the sun sets. The Towers's ravens won't fly in the dark."

I don't have it in me to point out all the reasons why that's a horrible plan. Instead, I uncurl my fingers and toss the little locket with its portraits of the Lord and Lady Castinac onto the table.

"Like I said," I announce, "they're not here for you."

Both men stare at the table. Tholious's hand freezes just above Xavier's ruff.

"What—" Tholious begins.

"They have a Castinac," I say. "In the meadow above the hunting lodge."

Matius snorts. Tholious turns to me with wide eyes.

"They want to make a deal," I continue.

Bitterness twists around my words. I can't help but remember the first deal Tholious offered me, Kira in exchange for the amulet. What if I'd taken it? Would it have made any difference?

"It's Lenore, isn't it?" Matius asks.

I frown. There's no way he should know about my relationship with Lenore, but hells, he is from the Mercenary Guild. Secrets are as important to their trade as blood.

"Who?" Tholious asks.

"Lady Lenore Castinac," Matius says, meeting my eyes. "A noblewoman with a taste for dangerous men. Looks a bit like Kira." Matius shakes his head, then rubs his hand across the back of his neck. "I should have figured that out weeks ago."

"The Towers just made enemies of the Castinac family," I say.

"If the Castinacs know the Towers took Lenore," Matius says.

"They'll know," I say. "Because I'm taking Lenore back."

Tholious raises his eyebrow in a way that makes me think he's about to disagree.

"The Towers are desperate," I explain. "And that makes them weak. I'll bring Lenore back, she'll explain to her family what happened. The Towers have plenty of enemies."

I take a deep breath as the idea forms in my mind. I spent so long running from the Towers; it's almost liberating to imagine fighting back.

"I'll find them," I say. "Together, we'll bring the fight to the Towers."

Tholious exhales in a whoosh. Matius comes to his feet.

"What can we do?" Matius asks.

I cross my arms over my chest and run my eyes around the cabin. It's small, this place. It was small when it was just me. With two people, and with snow piled all around, it might feel tiny.

But that's all right. They have the keep, and the mountains. And they're in love. Hells, for all I know it'll feel like a honeymoon.

"You're not coming," I say.

Matius scowls like he's about to argue. I ignore him.

"Stay here," I continue. "The Towers don't know you're here. There's food, there's firewood. And—"

My throat closes around the words I'm about to say. I glance down at the bed I once shared with a woman who felt like a friend, and then at the ragged gray tomcat. It's small, but they'll manage. The three of them.

"Watch over Xavier," I say. It comes out as a whisper, more of a plea than a demand.

Tholious comes to his feet, making Xavier twitch his tail in annoyance. He looks like he's about to say something, but instead, he pulls me into his arms. My back stiffens as he gives me an awkward hug. When he releases me, Matius takes my hand.

"I might have gotten some things wrong about you," Matius says, with a strange smile. "I apologize for that."

I don't understand, but I nod anyway. It's unsettling, having Matius look at me without that angry glint in his eyes.

"If we survive this," Matius says, tilting his head toward the door, "Drake's Rest. At the Port of Good Fortune."

"Excuse me?"

Matius's grin widens. "It's my favorite pub. Right on the water. You can't miss it. We'll meet you there, once the snow melts."

My breath catches. I hadn't thought past getting down the mountain. Matius is already planning a reunion.

"We'll give you back your damn cat," Matius says.

I open my mouth, but the words don't come. Matius drops my hand. I turn toward the door. The light of the rising sun spills across the threshold.

"What are you going to do?" Tholious asks, in a low voice.

I stare at the jagged face of the mountain I named after myself as magic pulls tight around my body.

"What they trained me to do," I reply. "I'm going to destroy them."

THE SUN SETS FAST this time of year, making the meadow a full day away.

I sprint down the mountainside, my sides heaving and my lungs burning, racing that great fire in the sky as she plunges toward her dark rest. Leaves flutter down all around me; the shadows hold a chill they probably won't shake for the next six months. It's almost too easy to imagine the entire world is dying.

At least the direwolves are far away, with the dim pulse of their magic suggesting they're beyond the mountains. At least Kira is safe, for now.

At least this is going to mean something.

I stop, panting and restless, when I see the meadow spreading before me through a break in the trees. I know what trick I'm going to pull. It worked with the hunters, after all. I close my eyes, tug on the magic, and make a long, low howl rise from the forest. And then another, closer to the meadow.

They're illusions, but hells, not even an Exemplar will know for sure. Anyone from the Towers will sense magic, but they won't know exactly what I'm doing with it. Not unless they try to wrap their arms around one of my illusion wolves, and I'll just have to hope whoever they sent isn't that stupid. I make a few illusion wolves pace through the trees behind me, straighten my cloak, and walk toward the meadow as the sun sinks behind me in all her fiery splendor.

I want to look like I belong here, like I'm a part of the Daggers. I want to look like everything I do is intentional.

A raven sounds a sharp cry of alarm. As I emerge from the trees, the shadows on the far edge of the forest slowly draw together into recognizable shapes. There's a carriage, large and black, and four horses with their heads down in the thick meadow grass. A raven ruffles its feathers on the top of the carriage; the second one must be above, making slow circles in the dusk. A man sits on the box seat, the reins in his hands, his eyes fixed on the ground for plausible deniability. Fear trembles through the air, rising from the nervous horses chained to the Towers's carriage.

When I'm close enough to the carriage to make out the gleam of the raven's eyes, the door opens.

There's a swirl of white fabric from the shadowed interior of the carriage, and the low, boiling hiss of magic. It feels like that carriage holds at least three of the magic-imbued silver chains, possibly four. Has the trapped magic in those silver prisons always felt that angry, I wonder, and I never noticed?

And then Fyrris, Exemplar of the Towers, steps out of the carriage and into the meadow below my mountains.

Fuck me. Fyrris actually left his precious Towers. I suppose I should feel flattered.

We stare at each other as dusk gathers her shadows below the trees. Some hidden creature of the woods calls softly for its mate. One of the horses snorts and stomps, fearful of the illusion wolves.

"Master Reznyk Thorne," Fyrris finally says. "You're late."

I don't bother glancing at the sky. I know the sun has already set.

"I didn't want to come," I reply.

Fyrris sneers like he's disappointed with me. It's such a familiar expression that it would be almost funny, under different circumstances. Kill an old god, steal their power, evade the Towers for years, and I'm still a disappointment. Fyrris clears his throat.

"Come out," he says, almost under his breath.

My chest closes like a fist around my heart. There's another rustle of fabric inside the carriage, and then a woman steps down from the door. She moves slowly, with grace and poise, as if she's used to having an audience.

Screaming gods above. She's wearing a fine burgundy dress that's streaked with dirt and ripped at the hem, as if she was kidnapped in the middle of an elegant party. Her hands are bound together with coarse rope, and there's a gag of scarlet cloth across her mouth. She looks like she's been crying, Lady Lenore of the Castinac family.

Our eyes meet. A shiver flashes through the magic pooled around my body. Lenore's eyes widen in recognition, then drop to the grass. She knows who I am, and it gives her no comfort.

"You fools," I growl.

I step forward before I even realize what I'm doing.

"That's far enough," Fyrris says.

I stop. Magic trembles across my skin; my heartbeat feels very loud inside my skull. Behind me, illusion wolves pace restlessly beneath the shadows. Lenore glances at me again, raising her head just enough for me to notice a fading bruise below her right eye. It's an old bruise. Either the Towers had her for longer than it took to reach the Daggers, or the bruise didn't come from Fyrris.

Fear, rage, and an angry, hopeless sort of desperation wrestle for control of my mind and body. The magic under my skin howls for release. Did I really once believe I could grow so powerful that nothing could hurt me again? Was I ever such a fool?

I draw back, clench my hands into fists at my sides, and try to regain some of my dignity. Fyrris knows how to twist the knife. But I can't let him win. Not this time. There's too much at stake.

"I assume you're here to make me an offer?" I say, my voice as cold as the wind that blows off the mountains.

"Very astute," Fyrris purrs. "We're here to make a trade, as I'm sure my associates told you."

He nods gently toward the raven on top of the carriage, who is watching this with black, impassive eyes. I say nothing.

"We have the amulet," Fyrris continues.

"Good for you," I reply.

Fyrris ignores me. His white robe ruffles in a gust of wind that shakes fistfuls of leaves from the trees behind him.

"You've done something to it," Fyrris says. "Something you need to undo."

I cross my arms over my chest and stare at him. I did nothing to that thrice-cursed amulet. It was created to trap the power of the old god and bring that magic back to the Towers, to help the Exemplars spread their torture and manipulation across the ocean. I couldn't let that happen.

All I did with the amulet was leave it behind. The magic of the old god entered me instead. I thought it would kill me. I almost hoped it would.

Fyrris sighs, like this entire conversation is a waste of his precious time. "You come with us," Fyrris says, "and the woman lives."

He nods to Lenore. She makes a choked sort of cry, muffled by her gag. Her eyes widen.

"A life for a life," Fyrris announces, with a smile that makes me feel sick. "Romantic, is it not? After all, how many lovers get to make such a sacrifice?"

My jaw clenches as rage hammers my temples. Magic bristles under my skin. I pull it tight in my palm, feeling the hard edge of a weapon beginning to take shape.

"Untie her," I growl.

Fyrris makes a tsk-tsk sound with his tongue, then shakes his head.

"It's such a simple offer," he says, in that same disappointed tone. "Even you should be able to understand that."

One of the illusion wolves behind me growls with my frustration. The closest horse makes a skittish whinny. The man holding the reins barks something in response, and a whip flashes through the gloom. The horse's fear spreads through my magic like blood in the back of my mouth.

"Untie her," I say again.

Fyrris rolls his eyes. Magic trembles across my skin. The blade I created is sharp and cold against my palm. How many times did I do exactly this in the Towers's training yards? How many targets did I destroy?

Fyrris turns slowly, keeping his eyes on me for as long as possible. My illusion wolves step out from the shadows to flank me, their eyes bright as daggers in the fading light. Lenore shakes her head. Her eyes are wide, like she's trying to tell me something. Fyrris grabs the rope holding Lenore's hands together.

His eyes leave mine. I raise my hand. The world is suddenly very clear, a perfect moment frozen in time. The white folds of Fyrris's robe beneath his dark hair. The pale line of his exposed neck. Red skin, like the inside of the rabbit, dead and spread across the grass outside my cabin.

Rabbits in the grass, nibbling on clover. There were seven babies this spring, black and gray, tumbling over each other in the sun—

I clench my jaw against the memories. The magical blade flies from my fingers. Too slow, too damn slow—

A sharp crack shatters the calm. My magic burns. Fyrris grins at me from inside his protective shield, a silver chain flashing from between his fingers. Lenore staggers away from him, then rips the gag from her mouth.

"It's a trap!" she screams.

I turn toward Lenore, dimly aware of the carriage driver behind her coming to his feet. I pull magic into my palm, feel the cold weight of another blade.

There's a crossbow between the driver's legs, one he's raising toward me. The sick pulse of nightmare steel rises in the air. Even from here, I feel the hunger in that metal. Magic sinks to my core, as if it's trying to shy away from the emptiness of nightmare steel. The blade in my palm shivers like a living thing.

I meet Lenore's eyes.

"Run," I tell her.

I spin, then throw the blade I made. It shatters against Fyrris's shield even as a new blade forms in my hand, cold magic against my skin. I raise my hand, open my mouth to scream at the man who made me into this—

My words die with the twang of a crossbow's string. Magic solidifies around me, forming a shield even as memories surge forward.

I fired the crossbow. I sent the silver bolt into the heart of the old god, even as they stared at me with eyes so dark they looked like all the stars had fallen from the night sky, even as their body began to burn. Before I pulled the bolt from their side and tried to stop the flood of silver blood, before I cried and begged and screamed as their magic sank into me, I fired the crossbow.

I killed the god.

Nightmare steel punches through my magic. Pain screams through my body. I sink to my knees, staring at the sliver of metal jutting out of my shoulder. It's not even that big, the nightmare steel arrow that just hit me. Is that all it takes, some part of me wonders, to stop the Godkiller?

The carriage driver drops the crossbow and sprints forward, moving much faster than any carriage driver should be able to run. He's carrying something dark in his hands, something that makes my skin crawl. Fear and rage flow from the horses; the great black carriage begins to strain against the brake. Fyrris screams. There's another flicker of trapped magic from his silver chains. One of the horses rears. The carriage totters on its great black wheels.

In the corner of my vision, Lenore sprints into the woods. She's not afraid of the wolves, some numb part of me realizes. Or she's more afraid of Fyrris than whatever horrors await in the Daggers.

The carriage driver reaches me, and I see what he's holding. Chains. Nightmare steel manacles close over my wrists. The magic trapped inside my body screams. With the last shard of my strength, I make my illusion wolves howl as they vanish beneath the trees.

Then his fist meets my temple, and the world goes dark.

CHAPTER 46
KIRA
DON'T COME ANY CLOSER

Something's wrong.

My breath catches and my heart races inside its cage. Gods, what in the nine hells is coming for me now? I turn off the road and crash into the woods, wincing as branches snap beneath my boots.

It was bad enough when I passed the Golden Peaks Hunting Lodge this afternoon, just as the sun dipped below the horizon and the wind howled down from the peaks.

Some part of me knew what to expect. Everyone at the lodge called us late-season guests, after all, and winter is stalking these mountains like a wolf stalks a deer. Still, the sight of the Golden Peaks standing silent and empty, with their windows covered by heavy shutters and a massive chain through the handles of the front door, made something inside of me snap.

I already knew I was alone up here. The Daggers are uninhabited, and the only other human here is someone who already told me, in no uncertain terms, to leave and never come back. But perhaps I'd been clinging to some stupid fantasy after all, like that the Golden Peaks would open their doors to me or I'd see Reznyk sitting in the common room in his black cloak and we could start over again from the beginning.

But the lodge has closed for the winter. And I'm alone.

And then wolves started howling.

I pushed up the road anyway, despite the sound of wolves in the distance, as the moon rose above Desolation Peak and cast her white glow over the forest, making it look like I'd fallen into some other world, like the Lands Below, where legends claim an elven kingdom was trapped for five hundred years. Eventually, the wolves stopped howling. I tried to tell myself that was a good thing.

But now? I'm hunched in the shadows below a bunch of ragged pines, panting as my heart hammers against the inside of my chest. Something is wrong, but what?

The forest is strangely silent in the chill night air. There's an occasional rustle in the leaves as some small, hidden creature searches for its dinner, followed by the distant call of an owl who must be keeping watch over the road. Slowly, another sound drifts through the still air in the valley. A low rumbling interspersed with clicks.

It's such a familiar sound it takes me a moment to realize how strange it is to hear it here, in the Daggers. I've heard that click and rumble almost every day of my life, after all. There are always carriages clopping up and down the streets of Silver City.

I hold my breath as the hoofbeats grow louder. The carriage creaks and the horses' harnesses rattle as the wheels rumble over the road. They're moving fast, much faster than I would want to drive a carriage through the woods in the dark.

A moment later, it explodes from the shadows and flies past the trees where I'm hiding, a blur of black wood and frothing horses. I'm dimly aware of the gleam of polished metal, the clatter of hooves against stone, and the labored breathing of terrified animals.

Then it's gone. The creaks and clattering fade, swallowed by silence. My heartbeat drums against the inside of my skull. The owl cries again, further away this time. Slowly, the little forest creatures resume their nocturnal scurrying. I step out of the trees and stare down the road, my mind as numb as my body.

Panic batters my thoughts like a moth throwing itself at a lantern. My teeth sink into my lower lip. I force myself to turn away from the road that just swallowed the carriage and keep walking.

There are no towns in the Daggers. No farms, no villages. This time of year, there's not even a hunting lodge. There is no reason for a carriage to be on this road. Hells, there's no reason for anyone to be on this road. Isn't that why Reznyk lived here?

Lives. He lives here.

My eyes sting. In my mind, I see his cabin, the windows broken and the door smashed in. Blood on the front steps. Xavier huddled under the bed, terrified and hissing. Or sprawled across the cold grass, his spine snapped—

And now I'm running. Tears leak from my eyes. My breath tears at the inside of my throat even as my mind howls it can't be true, Reznyk is safe inside his cabin.

But why would there be a carriage?

I burst into the meadow where Tholious first told us we were going up the mountain, at night, in a rainstorm. The moonlight makes it look like this meadow is already filled with snow. All but the carriage tracks that cut deep into the grass.

And the woman.

My breath catches. I freeze. I'm trembling all over, and my heart feels like it's about to explode.

The woman is making her way through the meadow very carefully, favoring her right leg, with her long, elegant skirts bunched in one fist. A tangle of loose hair falls down her back. Something comes out of my lips, but it's not even close to human speech.

The woman stops. Her eyes meet mine. Her back stiffens. She drops her skirts and clasps her hands in front of her, a scowl on her face, something shiny held in her fist.

Oh. Oh, gods, she's holding the smallest little knife I've ever seen.

After everything I've been through, from the Towers to the Next Best Gander to the smuggler's boat to the gods-damned carriage that just tore past me, a woman in an elegant gown pointing a butter knife at my chest is just funny. I can't stop the laugh that presses against the inside of my mouth, but I do try to turn it into a cough.

"Don't come any closer," the woman growls.

She holds the knife out like it's a holy symbol and she's facing a demon. I walk into the light, holding my empty hands out toward her. Gods, my feet hurt.

The woman steps back. The tiny knife trembles in her fist. Dirt streaks her elegant dress, and there's something on the right side of her face that might be blood.

She's a long way from home, Lady Lenore Castinac.

And she doesn't look that much like me after all.

CHAPTER 47

REZNYK

NIGHTMARE STEEL

"What about the woman?" a voice growls from the darkness.

I open my eyes. Pale moonlight shifts through slats of wood. The world is shaking all around me, creaking and pitching to the thunder of hooves. My wrists burn under nightmare steel manacles, and my shoulder throbs around the nightmare steel arrow embedded in my flesh.

The carriage. I tug at the manacles, sending a bolt of pain through my shoulder that's so sharp it makes me gasp. The dull panic of the horses flows through my magic. They're obeying the commands of the carriage driver, but only barely. It wouldn't take much to get them to panic completely.

I reach for my magic and find only a dim flicker. In nightmare steel, I can't even conjure a simple illusion. Not even one wolf.

"Should I go back to finish her?"

I freeze. That's the man who shot me, the carriage driver with a crossbow between his legs that was loaded with a nightmare steel arrow. The trap Lenore warned me about. The one I walked straight into.

And he's talking about Lenore. I feel cold.

"No," Fyrris replies. "It's not worth the risk. These damn horses could turn us over. Let the wolves finish her."

His voice is strangely muted. It takes me a moment to realize he's leaning through the window in the front of the carriage, speaking to the driver. And I'm crumpled on the floor, my head hitting the underside of the seat every time the carriage jostles.

I try to speak, but my voice comes out a garbled moan. I close my eyes, gathering my strength. My shoulder feels hot and wet; not a good sign. If I could just pull the arrow out.

I lift my hands slowly. The nightmare steel manacles are heavy, and moving them makes me feel like I'm going to be sick. Waves of pain wash over me as my shoulder screams.

When my hand closes around the nightmare steel arrow in my shoulder, I gag. Bile rises in the back of my throat, hot and bitter. Nightmare steel burns my palms. Magic screams inside of me, pulling back, trying to drag me away.

I force my fingers to close around the steel shaft. I feel like I'm on fire, everything screaming, everything burning. When I yank on the arrow, the pain is so intense that my vision flashes white, then crimson. The taste of blood fills my mouth.

I pull harder. Barbs on the arrow drag through my flesh, searing skin and magic. A sound comes out of my mouth, but it's nothing human, nothing I've ever heard before. There's a low, wet pop, a sound like mud or shit, and the arrow is free. It clatters to the carriage floor, leaving me shivering.

"What in the hells are you doing?" Fyrris mutters above me.

My eyes flutter open. The world swims around me, pale moonlight and the luminous glow of bright white Exemplar robes. Like the Towers, white against the night sky.

There was a time when I thought that meant something. The Towers were a beacon, a place where I could become a different person.

But they just made me more of a monster.

Fyrris frowns at me as his hand dips into his white robes. There's something odd about that expression on his face, something I haven't seen on Fyrris before. Plenty of other people, of course. Lots of people were afraid of me. But Fyrris—

Fyrris pulls a silver chain out of his robe. The surge of trapped magic batters the air, its angry churn hissing against my skin. I try to pull away as he drags the chain toward me, its trapped magic howling for release.

The chain hits my arm. It's hot, then cold, as the imprisoned magic inside bleeds into my body only to beat helplessly against the nightmare steel. Fyrris's lips twist into a scowl. He's pushing magic through the chain, but whatever is inside of me is pushing back.

"Damnit," Fyrris growls.

The chain drops to the floor of the carriage, emptied of magic. The air smells burnt. My gut heaves as I gag on something that tastes like blood. I'm shaking now, trembling so violently my head hits the underside of the seat and I can't stop myself.

Fyrris pulls another silver chain from his robes. Magic arcs through the air between us, briefly illuminating the dim interior of the carriage.

"You bastard," I growl as Fyrris leans over me. "You stinking son of a—"

Fyrris presses the silver chain against my cheek. Magic screams through my skin, burning as it escapes the chain. Sleep magic, some dim, distant part of me realizes.

And then the world goes dark.

CHAPTER 48
KIRA
KIDNAPPED

"Who in the hells are you?" the woman demands.

She probably means to sound tough, like she's the kind of woman who knows how to use that tiny knife she's holding. But she just sounds like what she is, a terrified noblewoman running from wolves in the middle of nowhere.

"I'm here for Reznyk," I say.

She lowers her knife and frowns at me. "Why?"

I open my mouth. Close it. Open it again.

That's a very good question, and I have no idea where to begin answering it.

"I— I owe him," I stammer. "I came here to warn him—"

"About the Towers?" she asks.

I blink. I know what she's going to say. There's no other reason why a carriage would be tearing through the Daggers in the middle of the night like all the nine hells were chasing them.

"I'm too late," I whisper.

The woman slips her butter knife back into some secret fold in what was once probably a very expensive dress.

"The Towers took him," she says.

Her voice trembles as she speaks. That little tremble cuts through my clothes like the north wind off the mountains.

She loves him too. She must. I feel so empty that the realization just bangs and bangs around inside of me. Reznyk must be The One for her too. She was the bait, just like Fyrris said in the Towers.

And that means Reznyk sacrificed himself to save her.

"Shit," I say. It comes out as a whimper.

I close my eyes as a wave of exhaustion washes through me. I've been running since I told Benja I needed to visit the orphanage, and for what? Did I really think I could beat the Towers?

"He's still alive," the woman says. "They chained him, but they didn't kill him."

She pushes her hair back from her face and stares at me like she's trying to evaluate what level of hell she's going to have to wade through next. She looks tired, this woman Reznyk loves. Tired, cold, and very far from home.

"I have a plan," she says, like she's measuring her words with a silver spoon, "although I may need some help."

Damn it. I so dearly wanted to hate Lady Lenore Castinac. I wave my hand in the air, telling her to go on. She smiles for the first time.

"All I need," she says, smoothing down the front of her ruined evening gown, "is to get to a town."

The expression on my face must reflect some of what I'm feeling, because she frowns.

"I am a daughter of Lord Castinac," she declares. There's an edge to her voice that implies I should be

MEREDITH HART

impressed by this. "Anyone living along the Ever-Reaching River will recognize that name."

"Right," I mutter. "No offense, but you don't exactly look like a lady at the moment."

She huffs, then tosses her head back. There's a twig tangled in her long hair.

"I'll tell them what happened," she says, as though that's obvious. "Anyone from any respectable family will leap at the chance to help the Castinacs."

"What happened?" I say, although I'm certain I already know.

The Towers said they had the bait. Clearly, the trap worked.

"I was kidnapped," Lenore says, with that same little tremble in her voice.

Her eyes grow wide. For just a moment, I can see exactly how she would look on the marble floor of some noble-man's house. A beautiful woman in a ruined gown, holding back tears as she explains how desperately her very rich family must want her back.

"Great," I reply. "And why the fuck do you need me, then? Am I your kidnapper?"

"You're my handmaiden," she replies.

I laugh. Lenore pouts, like she can't understand what fault I could possibly find in her brilliant plan.

"You're kidding, right?" I say. "You got kidnapped with your maid? Who in the nine hells is going to believe that?"

Lady Lenore clears her throat, then crosses her hands demurely in front of her waist.

"I would love to hear your plan," she replies.

I sigh, then sink my teeth into my lower lip. Moonlight shines off the granite face of Desolation Peak. Somewhere

316

up there is Reznyk's cabin, maybe with the door bashed in and the windows shattered.

And Reznyk is in a carriage racing toward Silver City. And the woman he loves is here, asking me to help her get back home.

"Great," I mutter again.

Some numb, distant part of my mind lurches toward the inevitable. Climbing to Reznyk's cabin won't help him now. But maybe, if I can make it back to Silver City, back to the Towers, I can do something. And hells, if Lenore's plan doesn't work out, I still have a dagger and a pile of shills.

I'll think of something.

CHAPTER 49
REZNYK
MORE BLOOD ON MY HANDS

Magic drags me through a sea of darkness studded with brief, occasional flashes of consciousness. I wake in the bottom of the carriage, my head thudding against the wall, a boot resting on the small of my back. Someone is humming a song, low and off-key, and by the time I recognize the tune as that old tavern song about cutting your heart out, sleep claims me again.

I wake at night, the darkness so thick I almost panic, imagining they've draped a hood over my head. But there's no warmth around my face, no brush of fabric on my skin. Just the bite of frost in the still, silent air. I manage to lift my head, only to smack into the wooden planks just above me.

I'm still in the carriage, then. Slow waves of exhaustion radiate off the horses and tug at the edges of my bound magic. They must have stopped to rest. The sad wail of an owl floats through the air, followed by a low, muffled snort from outside the carriage, possibly a horse, possibly the man who shot me.

This is my chance to escape.

I try to turn, to move, and a brilliant bolt of pain sings out from my shoulder. I wince and try to grit my teeth around the moan rising in the back of my throat. Magic simmers like a nest of hornets inside my body. Fyrris's sleep magic can't escape the nightmare steel either; we're uneasy rivals trapped in the same prison, wild beasts locked together in a cage, circling each other warily.

The taste of nightmare steel coats my mouth and tongue, a thick, acrid sting. I close my eyes against the darkness, and I see Lenore running toward the woods. Please, gods, my mind whimpers. Let her run toward the mountain. Let her climb the trail and find Tholious and Matius. Together, they could travel to Silver City—

But my mind replies with images of Lenore's dress tangled in thorns above a pile of bones picked clean by ravens and vultures. Cold sinks into my body. Lenore never left Silver City. Why would she climb the mountain? How would she even find the trail? Even Kira got lost in these mountains, and Kira is smarter and tougher than Lenore.

Truth cuts through me like a blade. There's no way Lady Lenore Castinac could survive the Daggers. That's another death on my conscience, more blood on my hands. Gods, is there anyone in my life I haven't failed?

When sleep magic surges forward and drags me down, it's almost a relief.

I wake again to angry voices, the thick odor of unwashed bodies, the constant jostle of the carriage. Pain throbs through my arm, pulsing like a second heart. I try to move, then clamp down on the groan slipping through my lips. A man grunts above me.

"I'm saying," the man mutters, "he's waking up."

The carriage squeaks and rocks. Exhaustion washes over me; the poor horses are ready to drop.

"Dose that fucker again," the man says.

"Do not presume to tell me how to do my job."

Fear settles in my gut, low and heavy, like a stone. That's Fyrris speaking.

"That much magic should have killed him," Fyrris continues.

"That right?" the man answers.

There's a heavy shifting sound above me, and a burst of pain explodes in my lower back. I grunt as my vision flashes red. Magic burns under my skin.

"Like I said," a man growls. "He's waking up."

"Not for long," Fyrris replies.

Captured magic hisses in the air, the angry churn of one of the Towers's silver chains. Someone yanks back my hair. I make a sound as Fyrris presses another chain to my skin, something low and animal. Magic burns into my body and drags my screaming consciousness down with it.

Somewhere, a river chatters in the distance, rising and falling, hissing and muttering. I listen to the river as bird-song twists with the music of the water, hoofbeats, and the creak and groan of motion. Moving. In motion. Being moved.

I let the river carry me, magic swirling in my wake.

CHAPTER 50
KIRA
PLACES NOT EVEN A KING CAN GO

T he worst part of Lady Lenore's stupid plan is that
it worked.

We reached the main road just as the sun was
setting on our second day of traveling. The first two
carriages we saw didn't meet whatever invisible criteria
Lenore used to judge such things, so we hid in the bushes,
holding our breath as the horses snorted past.

The third carriage was the charm. It was black, with gilt
trim all around and massive, scarlet wheels. Two riders on
black horses escorted the thing, one in front and one
behind, and the man on the box seat wore a ridiculous hat
that probably meant something important to other people
with absurd wealth.

Lenore grabbed my hand and yanked me onto the road.
The guard in front of the carriage pulled up short, his horse
snorting and pawing the ground, one hand on the hilt of his
sword.

Lenore burst into tears. And the rest of the plan fell into
place, just like magic.

She'd been kidnapped by bandits, Lenore said. She

managed to run from the men who'd abducted her, but now she had no way to get back to her family in Silver City.

It was an absurd story. How would a woman in a full evening gown manage to outrun a bunch of bandits in the woods? And why in the names of the many gods would the bandits also abduct me? Are noble captives worth even more ransom money if they happen to have their own handmaiden?

Not one of the men voiced an exception. Instead, the carriage door opened, and an older couple with rosy cheeks practically ran to embrace her. Lenore was hustled into the plush crimson interior of the coach; the guard riding in the rear even brought out a bottle of wine to help soothe her nerves. I got shoved on the box seat, next to the man in the stupid hat, who spent the entire drive sniffing loudly every time he looked at me.

And now here we are, sitting in the largest estate in Deep's Crossing, watching the rising sun stream through crystal windows in a room that's about a million times nicer than the room in the hunting lodge where Reznyk showed me how to find Blackwater.

I shove the last slice of buttered bread into my mouth and try to find it in my heart to be annoyed with Lenore and her plan. But all I can manage is grudging respect. An expensive dress, a lovely smile, and a sad story will, apparently, take you pretty damn far in this world.

An older woman opens the door, gives Lenore a small bow, and brings in a steaming washbasin. She places it on the table beside the mirror and the velvet dress someone brought in with breakfast, then glances at the rumpled pile of blankets on the floor where I slept and frowns. Maybe handmaidens are supposed to fold their own blankets?

The woman clears her throat. "When you're ready, the

Lord and Lady are expecting you, my dear," she says, with another nod to Lenore. "On your own time, of course. You've been through quite the ordeal."

She gives Lenore a sympathetic smile, yet another little head bob, and then backs out of the door. I grit my teeth.

"What about me?" I mutter under my breath as soon as the door closes.

"Excuse me?" Lenore says.

"You've been through quite the ordeal," I say, mimicking the older woman's voice. "What about me? Haven't we both just escaped from kidnappers?"

Lenore stares at me like I'm an idiot. I stare right back.

She's taller than me, Lady Castinac, and thinner. Her skin is creamy where mine is spotted with freckles, and her features are sharper, like she's carved out of something harder. Still, the resemblance is impossible to ignore. We have the same curve to our lips, the same arch to our eyebrows, and the same fiery gleam in our hair. It's on the tip of my tongue, the truth of how we're related. But Lenore speaks first.

"Servants are powerful," she says, in a voice so low it's almost a whisper. "That's your strength. There are places not even an elven king can go. But maids? They go everywhere."

I snort, then cross my arms over my chest.

"Thanks," I reply, barely suppressing the desire to roll my eyes. "That's so inspiring. Is that what you tell your own maid?"

Lenore sits down at the table, then turns her back toward me.

"No," she says. "I tell my own maid to fix my hair."

I stare at the mess of tangled red curls cascading down

her back. There's a stick caught in that chaos. No, make that two sticks.

I bite back my sigh, cross the room, and pick up the wooden brush on the table. I have a lifetime's experience pulling sticks and leaves out of children's hair to make them presentable for dinner with wealthy donors or, even rarer, potential adoptive parents.

I start at the bottom, pulling out debris, brushing out the tangles. As I do, Lenore uses a towel to wash her face with slow, careful deliberation. She's even paler once the dirt is gone and, if I'm not mistaken, there's a fading bruise on her upper right cheek. She's been through a lot, I realize, with a pang in my chest. And she is my sister.

I pause, the hairbrush hovering between us.

"It was a good plan," I force myself to say.

Lenore's head bobs in a quick nod. "Thank you," she replies.

I run the brush through her shimmering curls. Her hair is darker than mine, curlier, and thicker.

"Are you okay?" I ask. "You need anything?"

She shakes her head. "No, thank you. That would be taking the handmaiden role a bit too far."

I shrug. In the mirror, Lenore's reflection raises a hand to trace the fading bruise on her right cheek.

"Do you have a family?" she asks, abruptly.

The brush freezes as I meet her eyes in the mirror. Blue on blue, both of us. Eyes the color of the winter sky.

"No," I say, slowly. "I'm an orphan."

She huffs something under her breath. It almost sounds like *lucky*.

"Excuse me?" I say.

I pull the brush out of her hair and set it down on the

table. Lenore sighs as her fingers trace the fading bruise on her cheek.

"I apologize," she says. "That was terribly rude."

"Oh, no," I snap. "I'm sure it's awful, being so rich and powerful."

And beautiful. And having Reznyk's heart.

"I did apologize," Lenore says, icily.

For a heartbeat, we both stare at her reflection in the mirror. She's very beautiful, the woman Reznyk loves.

"I'm sorry too," I finally say, with a sigh. "But why in the nine hells would you ever think an orphan is lucky?"

She frowns. Something in her expression shifts, like she's carefully considering her next move.

"My father wanted daughters for one reason," she says. "So we could marry rich."

"Oh," I reply, thinking of Reznyk. He's many things, but he's not rich.

Lenore lifts her gaze, until she's staring at her own reflection like she's meeting a rival on the battlefield.

"And my new husband knows it," she says. "I thought life with my father was bad. Life with my husband is worse."

"Oh," I say, picking up the hairbrush once more. I swallow hard as I pull the brush through her silky hair.

"It's quite all right," Lenore says, turning her face to examine the ghost of the bruise on her cheek. "When I return to Silver City, I'll make it known that he couldn't protect his own wife. Not even in his own house."

There's a gleam in her eyes that makes me feel cold. I've never once felt grateful for my childhood in the orphanage. That would be insane. Still, as I watch Lenore's reflection, I realize my childhood fantasies about being the long-lost daughter of someone rich and powerful left out a few details. Like arranged marriage and new husbands who leave bruises on your face.

And once she's out of her horrible marriage and he's broken free of the Towers, she'll go back to Reznyk, of course. Who wouldn't?

"Great," I say. "Good for you."

My hands are shaking. I set the brush down and step back. Lenore stands. Her beautiful hair tumbles over her shoulders. I help her into the velvet dress, then stand aside as the woman Reznyk loves walks through the door and into the role she was born to play.

CHAPTER 51

REZNYK

COWARDS

I'm aware of my aching body first and voices second. A woman is talking. I follow the cadence of her voice as her words slowly take shape.

"No reaction to the amulet," she mutters under her breath, as if she's talking to herself. This voice is familiar, in a distant sort of way, as if we've met in dreams. Not particularly pleasant dreams.

"Of course, that could be the nightmare steel," she continues. "But we should still see a reaction to this—"

Something heavy hits my leg. I ignore it, breathe in and out, slow and steady.

"No, not there either," she says.

There's a rustling sound. My mind fills with white robes and a dark scowl. That's Bethyl's voice, an Exemplar. I lived in the Towers for years and hardly ever saw her.

There's something heavy on my chest. I must be in Silver City, in the Towers. The taste of nightmare steel coats the back of my throat. My shoulder throbs, and my arms and legs are splayed out. I would guess I'm pinned like a rabbit in a trap, but I don't dare move to find out. Not with Bethyl muttering above me.

"So how do we get it out?" Bethyl continues.

There's a creaking sound from behind me, as if someone has just risen from a chair. Or perhaps opened a door.

"We have to take off the manacles," Bethyl announces.

The proclamation is so sudden that I almost flinch. Behind me, there's a gentle sigh, a sound of disappointment that might as well be burned into my soul.

"Oh, do we?" Fyrris asks.

I can almost see the expression on his face, one eyebrow raised, his lips pulled back in a smile that manages to look almost exactly like a snarl.

"It's the only way," Bethyl huffs from somewhere near my legs. "The magic won't come out of him with nightmare steel blocking the way. It's like trying to take a shit with a cork up your ass."

"You have such a way with words," Fyrris purrs.

Bethyl grunts. "I'm right. You know it."

Something cold taps the center of my chest, then trails downward. My skin trembles; magic skitters through my body like it's trying to run away. I force myself to breathe. Don't react. Don't think about Lenore, or Tholious and Matius, or Kira—

"How long has he been awake?" Fyrris asks.

Bethyl grunts again. As I remember, her conversational skills were always a bit limited.

"Open your eyes, Master Thorne," Fyrris says, in the gentle tone you'd use to speak to a child or a small animal. "Or I'll open them for you."

I do as he says. The world slowly swims into focus. I'm staring at rough stone, like the inside of a cave. A lantern flickers from somewhere behind me, but it's not enough to banish the shadows clinging to the ceiling. It's cold in here, and it smells like piss and desperation.

This has to be the Towers. There are more dank holes hidden beneath those white spires than even I managed to discover. They've stuck me in one of them and wrapped nightmare steel around my wrists and ankles. A shiver pulls my skin tight. The dim ember of pain in my shoulder turns into a flash of agony.

This is an awful place to die.

"Welcome home," Fyrris says, "Master Thorne."

I tilt my head enough to see Fyrris standing beside me. He looks quite proud of himself.

"You left her," I growl. My voice sounds worse than the squeaking rattle of the carriage that must have brought me here. "Lady Castinac. In the woods."

"Yes," Fyrris replies. "I don't like to ride in a crowded carriage."

"You pus-filled sack of shit," I spit.

Fyrris moves fast. I flinch, only realizing my hands are pinned to the ground when his palm hits my face. It's like running into a brick wall. White sparks explode across my vision. My skin burns as my head snaps back. My vision floods with hot, angry tears.

"Watch your filthy mouth," Fyrris snaps.

He pulls a white handkerchief from his pocket, then rubs it delicately across each one of his fingers, as if touching me has soiled him. The taste of blood spreads slowly over my lips and tongue.

"There's another way to get the magic out of him," Fyrris announces.

He's looking at Bethyl, looking directly over me, as if I'm not here at all. I swallow. Blood coats the inside of my throat.

"In fact, it would solve several of our problems at once," Fyrris continues.

Bethyl frowns. I'm not sure if she doesn't understand, or she doesn't like this idea, or she just thinks Fyrris is a prick in love with the sound of his own voice. Perhaps all three.

"This," Fyrris says, waving his hand over my body with a disgusted sneer, "is a problem. First him, then Pytr, then Tholious."

"They aren't supposed to leave," Bethyl says.

"They are not," Fyrris agrees. "But Reznyk, well, he inspired them."

His voice twists as he speaks, making it clear this inspiration is for fools and cowards. Bethyl grunts again, a perfectly noncommittal sound.

"Because of him, we had to rush with Aveus and Syrus," Fyrris continues. "And just look how that turned out with Aveus."

I try not to respond to the names of the men who'd become my closest friends over our shared years in the Towers. Nothing good would come from Fyrris knowing I still care for them. Just look at what my care did for Lady Lenore.

"We only need one," Bethyl says. She turns to me as she speaks, fixing me with a look I don't much care for.

"Yes," Fyrris replies. His head swivels toward me as well. "Thankfully, we still have Syrus. And we're keeping the chains on him."

I have to force myself to breathe. Does this mean Aveus escaped? Did Pytr make his way back to his wife? Or are all of my friends as dead as Lenore, with no one but wolves to mourn for them?

"So, how do you propose we get the magic out of him?"

Bethyl asks. She's frowning at me like I'm a problem she's considering solving with the application of brute force.

"Publicly," Fyrris purrs.

I shiver like something with cold, sharp legs just crawled across my chest.

"We'll make an example out of Master Reznyk Thorne," Fyrris continues. "In the main courtyard. Just before dinner."

Bethyl grunts, her main form of communication.

"And the magic?" she asks.

Fyrris grins at me. I feel like a gutted fish splayed on a market stall.

"Silver," Fyrris says.

My arms start trembling. I can't stop them.

"It worked once," Fyrris continues. "The hollow bolt captured the old god's magic, clearly. It just went to the wrong place."

"Inside Reznyk, instead of inside the amulet," Bethyl adds.

I turn my hands into fists. My pulse beats against the manacles of nightmare steel like a trapped bird thrashing against the invisible prison of a window. It doesn't stop the tremble in my arms.

"Yes. Maybe he was the weak spot all along," Fyrris continues, narrowing his eyes at me. "We'll have someone talented fire the bolt tomorrow. Someone we trust."

"Veloria?" Bethyl asks.

I close my eyes before they can betray my thoughts. Being publicly executed by Syrus's former lover is a particularly bad way to die.

"She won't do it," I whisper, almost to myself.

Fyrris makes a soft sound in the back of his throat, a polite little hum of disagreement.

"Just between the three of us," Fyrris says, "I don't think you know that much about women, Master Thorne."

I know enough to keep my mouth shut. There's a rustling sound as Fyrris walks toward the door and Bethyl follows.

"Very well," Fyrris announces. "We'll sort out the details in the morning. If this works, we won't need Syrus after all. And if not, we'll still have a fine example of what happens to those who disobey the Towers."

I crack my eyes open and twist my head. Fyrris and Bethyl stand before the closed door.

"Cowards," I whisper.

Both of them turn to stare at me. Fyrris's eyes widen into an expression that's so far from what I expected it's almost funny.

"Why didn't you kill the old god yourself?" I say, slurring the words around my swelling lips. "Why didn't you trap the magic in the amulet?"

Fyrris moves fast, closing the distance between us. But my tongue is faster.

"Because you're afraid," I say. "You're weak, hiding behind your Towers. You're scared, pathetic—"

This time, Fyrris hits me with his fist. Pain sets off feast day fireworks inside my skull and my neck snaps back.

I hear the slam of the door just before the world goes black.

CHAPTER 52

KIRA

THERE'S SOMETHING ELSE

"What about Reznyk?" I whisper under my breath.

Lenore nods demurely. We're sitting together on the shaded upper deck of the barge from Deep's Crossing, watching as it beats its way slowly up the Ever-Reaching River.

"What about him?" Lenore says, covering her hand with her mouth as she speaks. Her eyes never leave the river. She almost looks like she's expecting something to rise out of its murky brown surface.

What about him? My hands tremble in my lap, where they're folded over the perfectly serviceable gray dress one of the maids brought me this morning. She seemed rather put out when she handed it to me; maybe it was one of hers.

I close my eyes for a moment, trying to remember what it was like to bite my tongue in the Towers. To be calm, silent, and invisible.

"What are you going to do?" I whisper. "How are you going to rescue him?"

Lady Lenore barks a laugh that's quite unladylike. The coach driver escorting us turns to frown at me. Lenore huffs, then fans her face.

"Me?" she whispers. "Rescue him?"

I tuck my hand under my skirts, then ball it into a fist. My nails bite into the skin of my palm. I force myself to take another long breath.

"What's your plan?" I whisper.

Lenore is quiet for so long I start to worry she isn't going to respond. Then she sighs, fans her face, and turns to me.

"There are plenty of people in Silver City who oppose the Towers," she says, under her breath. "You don't think the Maganti family was happy to hand over Syrus, do you?"

I blink. I've never thought about it like that. Don't the Magantis get to do whatever they want?

"My plan," she continues, "is to tell my father exactly who kidnapped me, and exactly how my husband let it happen. Once I'm free of that marriage, my plan is to do everything in my considerable power to weaken the Towers' hold on my city."

She's scowling in a way that makes me think she's not expecting any objections. I swallow hard. My chest feels painfully empty, like I somehow managed to do what that stupid tavern song says and cut out my own heart.

"That's—great," I stammer. "But, Reznyk?"

Lenore stares at me like I've just hit my head and she's not sure if I'm going to recover.

"You do come from the Towers, don't you?" she asks.

I nod.

"And I assume you're going back there?" she continues. "Or at least, you're returning to Silver City?"

I'm not sure how to respond, so I nod again.

"So, what's your plan?" she says. "Out of the two of us, you're the only one who can walk into the Towers."

My mouth falls open. "I— I can't—"

Lenore frowns at me. "Do you not want to help him?"

"No," I say. "Gods, I mean, yes. I want to help him. It's just, what can I do? I'm— I'm nobody."

Lenore makes a prim little snort, then smooths down the skirt of her dress. It looks much softer than what I'm wearing.

"Nobody," she says, under her breath. "Reznyk hated the Towers, and yet here you are. A woman from the Towers. Trying to help him."

I open my mouth, but my throat is suddenly too tight to speak.

"He hid for years," Lenore continues, "yet somehow, you knew exactly where to find him."

"Well—" I begin, but my voice dies.

Explaining that I was sent by the Towers to find the Godkiller's amulet, which I found and brought back to Silver City, and then I paid off a mercenary to join a band of smugglers who dropped me in the middle of mountains, which I know for a fact hold a pack of direwolves, so I could travel alone at night until I returned to Reznyk's hidden outpost, suddenly doesn't seem like something a nobody would do. I look down at my feet. I'm still wearing my Guard's boots from the Towers.

"Ah," I finish.

"Like I said," Lenore whispers. "There are places not even an elven king can go. But servants go everywhere."

My teeth close over my bottom lip. Lenore shades her eyes and stares at the river as it spools past the bow of the barge. Something wild flutters inside my chest, the tiny, feathered start of a plan.

She's not wrong, this woman Reznyk loves. Guards go everywhere. Even into the hidden cells beneath the Towers.

"Oh!" Lenore cries. She jumps to her feet. "There it is!"

I follow her gaze. The barge moves slowly around a wide bend in the Ever-Reaching River, and suddenly, Silver City appears before us. The white spires of the Towers sparkle against the autumn sky. A great cloud of seagulls rises from the docks, crying and whirling over the water.

This is it, then. Our journey is almost over. I force myself to my feet, turn to Lenore, and say what I've been trying to work up the courage to say for days.

"There's something else," I whisper.

I can't quite bring myself to look at her as I speak, so I stare at her beautiful, polished boots instead. They're as dark as the underside of a stone.

"I think I'm your sister," I admit. "Or, your half sister. I mean, I think we have the same—"

Lenore sniffs again, that proper little huff, and I shut up.

"Yes," she says. "I thought so."

She stares at the walls and spires of Silver City, the light sparkling off its windows, the smoke rising from its chimneys. The barge shudders and turns as it approaches the docks.

"You what?" I finally manage to say.

Lenore bends her head and tucks a strand of hair behind her ear.

"My father isn't exactly subtle about his mistresses," she says. "And, when I was younger, my parents told me they'd replace me with a brat from the orphanage if I misbehaved." She glances at me, then back at the city spread before her. "No offense," she adds, like an afterthought.

"I— You knew?" I ask.

"I suspected," she says, her gaze tracing Fyher's Landing as it rises from Silver City with its glittering mansions and estates. "My parents don't make empty threats."

"Shit," I manage to stammer.

I spent my entire childhood wishing for a family like the Castinacs. I'm still turning over her words when the carriage driver walks up the steps to the raised dais where we're standing, offers Lenore his white-gloved hand, and walks her toward the dock and the waiting carriage.

CHAPTER 53

KIRA

HE CAN'T HURT YOU ANYMORE

"What the fuck was I thinking?" I whisper to the empty street.

The street doesn't respond. Ahead of me, the gates of the Towers open into the gathering dusk. Two Guards stand just outside, one of them scratching himself, the other yawning into the back of his hand. It's not the most intimidating sight, these two older men flanking a door that's wide open.

I swallow hard. I'm wearing the same bland brown clothes as the Guards with a stubby little Guard's dagger in my belt. I left the maid's dress with the Castinacs, and thank the gods. I should just walk through the gate, like I have for the last three years. As if I haven't been gone for almost two weeks, traveling on barges and carriages and my own aching feet.

But I feel like I've been gone a lifetime.

The carriage driver who met Lenore and me at the docks started talking about all the animals he's killed as soon as I climbed up next to him and did not stop until he dropped us off at the crest of Fyher's Landing, where the

Castinac's estate sparkles like a jewel in a diadem. A flurry of servants met us at the doors, because news apparently travels faster than carriages in Silver City. Lenore was swallowed whole by the crowd, while I stood in the doorway, twisting my fingers in the straps of the bag Zayne gave me until a large woman in a white apron pulled me aside, took me to a small room where I washed and took off the maid's dress, and then met me in the hallway to ask if I'd be staying on with them.

The look on my face must have given her enough of an answer, because she pulled back with a frown, pressed a bag into my hand, thanked me for all I've done, and summoned a young woman to lead me out through the back door.

I hesitated when she opened the door. My father was somewhere in that palatial estate, and some small, wounded part of me wanted to ask this woman to take me to him. But I remembered what Lenore said about her parents never making empty threats, and I thanked the woman politely before turning my back on the Castinac estate.

I counted the money in the bag the woman gave me once I was in the alley. There was less in there than I'd hoped, but hells, I wasn't going to go back and argue about it. The sounds of music and laughter drifted through the open windows of the Castinac estate as I walked past, heading down the hill and back to the heart of Silver City. The world of mansions and estates on Fyher's Landing was closed to me once more, as it always had been.

Reznyk, though. He wasn't born to it, but I could picture his dark eyes and sly half smile among the velvet and silk of Fyher's Landing. Lenore would bring him in once she was free of her horrible husband. And he would fit that world beautifully.

With a sigh, I tug my hood up over my head. I've had all day to come up with some sort of plan to rescue Reznyk from the Towers, and the more I think about it, the more impossible and stupid it sounds. Reznyk was one of the four Elites, the strongest and best students of the Towers. He was sent to hunt and kill an old god. He's the only human in the world who has magic, for fuck's sake.

But the Towers captured him. And why in the nine hells would I think I could succeed where he had failed?

A man leads a donkey pulling a clattering wooden cart past me. The Guards greet him as the cart enters the Towers.

Shit. If he can walk through the gate, so can I. Right?

I take a deep breath, square my shoulders, and walk back into the life I abandoned two weeks ago.

"Evening, Kira," one of the Guards says.

I nod. He's Mitrik, one of the oldest Guards in the Towers. His companion grunts something that's probably intended to be friendly, and I nod to him too. My feet cross the line of holes in the stone, anchors for the spikes of the Towers's portcullis.

And then I'm in. Trembling, I raise my head and look around the main courtyard. The man with the donkey unloads barrels from his creaky old cart. Two Guards stand by one of the training dummies with their hands on their hips. One of them laughs, a cloud of steam rising from his lips into the cold, heavy air.

"Feels like snow's on the way," Mitrik says, from behind me.

I'm not sure if he's talking to me or not, so I make a little cough of agreement and drift off in the direction of the dining hall. The doors are closed against the cold, but the clamor of voices pours through their wooden slats.

"Kira!"

I jump. By the time I recognize the man trotting toward me, my fingers are already locked around the hilt of my dagger and my heart is fluttering in the back of my throat. Benja stops just in front of me. Confusion ripples across his face.

"Shit," I say, before I can stop myself. "I mean, sorry."

I force my hand to relax and try my hardest to smile.

"Sorry," I say again. "It's been a long trip—"

My voice dies as I remember I was supposed to be visiting the orphanage to take a break from life in the Towers. And the orphanage is literally next door to the Towers.

"You know," I stammer, waving my hand in the air. "Long...stuff."

"Yeah," he replies. "Welcome back."

He gives me a hesitant smile, and I remember the way he looked at me when I asked for permission to leave. Like there was something between us, some spark he was desperate to fan.

"I guess you heard the news, huh?" Benja says.

I blink. "I'm sorry, what?"

Benja frowns. He looks like a man who's staring at his empty glass and wondering where his ale went. It baffles me that I ever found this man attractive.

"I didn't think you'd come back until you heard," he says. "We got him. You're safe."

I shiver beneath my brown Guard's cloak. "Safe?"

"Yeah," Benja continues. "You know, with your history, I get it. I'd want to leave too. But he's locked up now. You're safe here."

"He's—here?" I stammer. I try to swallow. My throat has gone completely dry.

Benja nods. The main courtyard suddenly feels very still, like the world is holding her breath, waiting for snow.

"Where?" I ask, as if it's the most natural question in the world.

Benja grins. "Come on," he says. "I'll show you."

Numbly, I follow Benja across the main courtyard, through an arched gateway, and across a smaller courtyard. He unlocks a door, and together we enter a room that's large enough to hold a carriage, although its wide gates are locked closed from the inside. Benja lights one of the torches on the wall while I stand next to the door, shivering.

"I'm not supposed to do this," Benja announces, like he's proud of that fact. "But, you know, after what you did, I figure you're entitled to see the bastard in chains."

I make a vague sort of murmur that's hopefully close enough to agreement. Benja pulls a ring of keys from his pocket.

"While you were gone," Benja says, "they appointed me to Keeper of the Watch."

"Great," I reply, my eyes tracing the walls.

There's a series of small doors set into the rough stone wall behind him. Ominous signs hang above each of them, filled with sketches of skulls and bright red X's. The air is cold in here, and it's oddly silent, as though it's not part of Silver City at all.

This room is where they keep the magic, the Guards say.

Gods, I feel like I'm going to be sick.

"It'd be a good position to support a family," Benja says.

I freeze. My mind shuffles through possible reactions as Benja stares at me with wide, dark eyes. Just like he stared at me in his office. His words come back to me, like a sliver of ice under my skin. *They're nothing like us.*

For a heartbeat, I feel like I'm staring into a dark mirror. Would I have come to believe that, had I never met Reznyk? How long would I have clung to the vain hope that there was, despite all evidence to the contrary, something special about me and my heritage? And how long would that promise have blinded me to the casual cruelty of the Towers?

"Oh," I finally stammer. "That's, um, something to think about, huh?"

Benja turns away. He picks a long, slender key from the chain, grabs the torch he just lit, and then walks to the door in the middle of the room. The lock opens quickly, with no resistance. It would probably open just as smoothly with a pair of hook picks. The lock isn't what keeps this place secure, after all. This door is protected by the Towers around it.

A long, dark hallway opens beyond the door. Fear traces a path down the back of my neck as I follow Benja through the hallway and down a set of roughly carved stairs. There's another door at the bottom, one which Benja opens with a skeleton key that's almost identical to the one in my kit.

"Don't go inside," he whispers, as he pushes the door open. "Just look from here."

I nod. It's dark in the room beyond the door, and it takes my eyes a moment to adjust. When they do, my breath catches in the back of my throat.

Reznyk lies flat on his back on the stone floor, pinned at the wrists and ankles by heavy chains, like an animal awaiting slaughter. The thin hiss of his breath breaks the cold, still air; steam rises gently from his lips. His shirt is torn open at the shoulder and stained with something dark. A streak of dried blood traces a path across his cheek.

He must be cold, lying on the ground covered with chains. The manacles must hurt his wrists and ankles.

I step back, away from the sudden mad impulse to rush forward, to claw at the chains, to shake Reznyk until he wakes and uses his terrible magic to burn this whole damned place to the ground.

Would I have ever accepted this? If the Towers kept lying to me, or if by some miracle I lived in a world where I did have magical potential, how would I feel about chaining a human being to a cold floor? About taking a traumatized child and turning him into a weapon?

Benja locks the door and tucks the key ring back into his shirt. He shakes his head as he turns toward me. It's a gesture that reminds me of Fyrris, and some distant part of my mind wonders if Benja knows who he's imitating.

"You're safe," Benja whispers. "See? He's knocked out, locked up. He can't hurt you anymore."

I take a gulp of air and wonder what exactly Benja was told about my mission to the Daggers.

"I know it doesn't look like much," Benja continues, with a glance over his shoulder, "but trust me, those chains are nightmare steel. And the Exemplars put so many wards on that door it almost burned down. If anyone with magic tries to cross it, they'll know right away."

"Th-thank you," I stammer.

Anyone with magic, huh? For the first time since the Exemplars arrived at the orphanage three years ago, I'm grateful for my complete lack of magical ability.

I force myself to smile and hope to all the gods that he doesn't notice how much I'm shaking. "I— I need to—to freshen up a little," I say.

It comes out as a whimper. My voice is trembling just like the rest of me.

Benja nods like he's granting me permission. I slip past him and practically run up the stairs and out of that cursed room and into the Guards' dormitory, where I lock the door and dump Zayne's pack out on the polished stone floor.

My lockpick kit is there. I unfold the leather flaps and run my fingers over the little picks and tension wrenches, the skeleton keys and rakes. I got damn good at picking locks in the orphanage, and the doors to Reznyk's cell look just like the doors to the Archives, which I could open in my sleep.

"Okay," I whisper under my breath. "Okay. I can do this."

As for the magical wards, or whatever other magical bullshit the Exemplars have in wait?

Well, that will have to be Reznyk's problem.

CHAPTER 54
REZNYK
TOO LATE

The dark comfort of sleep magic recedes, leaving me stranded on shoals of pain.

Every part of my body aches, from the bottom lip that Fyrris split with his fist to my ankles, where nightmare steel rubbed my skin raw. Hunger claws at the inside of my gut like a wild beast, and even the magic burns as it throws itself against the nightmare steel chains pinning me to the ground. I let my eyes close and try to find oblivion again.

But I find only flames. Did the forest really burn as I held the old god in my arms and sobbed into their silver blood, or am I remembering the fire that devoured Blackwater?

The faces of the dead rise to haunt me. My mother. Murus, my father, telling me he would raise me as his son just before I used the magic trapped in the silver chain to blow a hole through his chest. Lady Lenore with her hands bound and a gag around her mouth, yet another person who's dead because of me. Because I thought I loved her.

Kira's voice comes back to me, like a knife sliding

between my ribs. *I don't think that's love*, she said when I told her I wanted to lay the world at Lenore's feet. And then she showed me just how wrong I was by giving me something I never had with Lenore. Something that felt like home.

More than a lover, more than a friend. My mind tortures me with memories of her smile, her laugh, her body curled in my chair, the fire casting its soft light over her lips, one of the mugs I carved cupped between her palms. In my mind, it's snowing in the Daggers, soft white flakes drifting past the twin windows of my cabin, blanketing the mountains in fallen clouds while Kira and I sit together by the fire, loving and being loved.

I can even hear her voice, a soft whisper threading through this new torture that's more painful than any nightmare of flames and silver blood. She's chanting. No, she's muttering.

"Godsdamn it," Kira's voice whispers.

I frown. That's an odd thing for a fantasy to say. There's a sharp bite of pain in my wrist, and my eyes snap open. The darkness around me pulses, slowly resolving into shapes.

Someone is bending over my arm. There's the soft click of metal against metal, then a low, grinding noise. Magic flares against my skin, hot as an ember, and then there's a sharp snap.

"Fuck!" Kira growls.

Gods, she's beautiful. Her hair is swept back, and she's scowling at the chains holding me to the ground. For a heartbeat my body feels light, as if all the pain has vanished, and there's a burst of clarity.

I'm dying.

This is what my mind called forth to comfort me before

I leave this world for the Howling Plains. I stare at Kira as she frowns at my wrist, wanting to take it all in, to absorb every curve and shadow of this illusion. Metal clicks make a low tapping sound, followed by a slow grind. Pain shoots through my wrist again, sharper this time.

What the hells kind of vision is this?

There's a click so loud it sounds like a crossbow bolt loosed from its track. Magic flares in the air in front of me, a blinding golden flash. Kira gasps. My arm throbs. My mind slowly reassesses the situation.

I'm not dying.

I bend my elbow, raise my hand, and flex my fingers above the bloody wrist Kira just freed from the nightmare steel cuffs. There's a rustling sound, and a bolt of pain shoots through my leg as Kira leans over the manacles clamped around my ankles.

She's here. This is no vision. Somehow, Kira is here, and she's just opened the cuff on my wrist. I brace my arm against the stone and lift my head, a move that makes the room swim. There's another soft click, then a grind, and a loud snap.

A vicious grin flashes across Kira's face. She bends over my other ankle. Metal clicks and grinds. I stare. My breath makes clouds in the cold, heavy air as my mind struggles to acknowledge what my eyes are seeing.

Kira is not safe here.

I grunt as the third manacle falls, releasing another deep burn of pain and a flurry of golden sparks. There's a twist to that magic I don't like, something that sets off a great, tolling alarm bell buried deep inside my mind, but I can't think of what it is.

Kira crawls across the stone to my chained wrist. She grabs the cuff. There's a burn as nightmare steel rubs my raw skin, and then the deeper cut of magical energy searing my body as it flees the void of nightmare steel. Metal clicks against metal. I run my tongue over my lips.

"What—" I whisper.

Kira pauses. For the first time, she looks at me.

"What are you doing?" I say, in a sharp gasp.

She frowns, then looks down at the tiny metal pins in her hand.

"What the fuck does it look like?" she replies.

I open my mouth, then close it again. My throat feels like sandpaper. Kira turns back to my wrist. She mutters something under her breath that sounds like a string of curses. Pain sings through my arm, metal against blood, the low throb of magic and the sick, hungry tug of nightmare steel. I groan. The last manacle falls open. Another flash of magic bursts in the air, brighter and hotter than the first. It leaves spots dancing in my vision.

It means something, that burst of magic. Something I should recognize.

"Hey," Kira whispers. "You have to do something about the door."

I stare at her. I'm dizzy and I haven't even moved. When was the last time I ate? Or drank?

"You—" I stammer. "You shouldn't be here."

"Yeah?" Kira's face folds like she's about to cry. Then she shakes her head and glares at me. "Well, too bad. Get up. You have to do something about the wards on the door."

Wards. Panic bursts inside my skull like fire exploding from the tip of a match.

That's what I felt in the burst of magic when the manacles fell. It was the same feeling I got when the mirrors I used as anchors for my wards shattered.

"Wards," I mutter dumbly, staring at the black chains curled by my side.

"Yeah. Wards," Kira replies. Her hand clasps around my forearm. She tugs, like she's trying to drag me upright. "Come on!"

I turn from the chains to Kira's wide eyes.

"It's too late," I whisper.

The chains were warded. Hells, the wards probably broke the moment Kira touched them.

Now all the Towers know I'm free.

"Oh, for fuck's sake!" Kira snarls. "I didn't come all this way to watch you die!"

Kira yanks on my arm. Somehow, I rock forward onto my knees. Magic rolls inside me, pulsing through my body in time with my blood.

"Come on," Kira whispers. "Lenore's waiting for you."

I blink as the room twists around me. Why would Lenore be waiting for me? Lady Lenore is dead.

Kira grabs my hands and pulls. Magic burns inside my body. I stagger to my feet, and the floor lurches beneath me. My empty stomach rolls over itself.

Kira steps back. I stumble, then crash into her, pinning her against the wall. My forehead hits her shoulder as I collapse against her body, bracing myself on the rock behind her. She gasps. The soft heat of her breasts presses into my chest. For a moment, neither one of us moves. My cheek rests on her neck; her heartbeat flutters just beneath her skin. Her scent rises in the cold air between us, and something inside of me breaks.

She was supposed to be safe, damn it.

But she's here, and what's the point of any of it? What good is all the magic and power in all the worlds if I can't protect the woman I love?

"You have to go," I growl.

The words tumble out of my lips even as my mind howls their futility. Where could Kira go? Go to the front doors and sweet-talk her way out, at least until Fyrris realizes who must have set me free? Go through the gates and see how far she can run before the Towers catch her?

A door creaks open behind me. Kira gasps, and all the light and hope I'd managed to capture in this world bleed out of me.

It's already too late.

CHAPTER 55
REZNYK
YOU'RE AFRAID

Magic pulses inside me like a dying star. I push away from Kira, then spin to face the door, letting my tattered black cloak flare. Maybe, if the gods are merciful, it will hide the woman behind me.

Fyrris stands in the doorway, framed by the light of a torch in the wall behind him. His sparkling white robes gleam like a beacon as his lips pull back in a snarl. I step toward him, throwing myself between Kira and the monster.

His eyes widen.

It's only for a heartbeat, just a flash of white before his face settles back into its customary disapproving scowl. But I saw it, and I know what it means. I've held knives to people's throats, after all. I've hunted animals and humans, down narrow alleyways or between the knobby roots of half-submerged trees in the swamps.

I know fear.

Fyrris's hand darts into the folds of his robe and flashes back, a trembling silver chain in his fist. His mouth twists as he spits my name in the same voice that used to make me

352

jump. He's acting like the Exemplar of the Towers, the man who holds all the power.

But he's alone. And some part of him is starting to wonder if coming here by himself was such a good idea.

Magic boils inside my muscles. I leap before Fyrris can move. His eyes go wide once more, a second flash of white in the gloom. And then my knee hits his gut, and we both go down.

The silver chain flies from his hand. I feel it go, its trapped magic screaming and writhing when it hits the ground. There's a second chain in his robes, of course, but I grab both his hands and pin them to the ground. Blood drips down my wrists from the raw wounds the manacles left behind. Crimson drops land on the immaculate sleeves of his white robe.

He growls at me. I press my knee into the center of his chest. Magic sparks and hisses across his robes.

"More are coming," Fyrris sneers.

Of course they are. I suck in a breath; the hiss of captured magic burns along the edge of my awareness. More Exemplars, more silver chains. More nightmare steel.

I move my knee from his chest to his arm and let his hand go. Slowly, and close enough to his face that he can't possibly pull away, I drag magic from my body and force it to harden in my palm.

Fyrris gasps, a sharp inhale. We're so close I feel his breath draw across my skin. It's an intimate thing, to murder someone. It brings you almost as close as a lover.

"You taught me this," I whisper.

I grasp the solid blade of magic, then turn it over in my hand. There's a horrible familiarity to its heft and balance, as if this deadly weapon has always been a part of me.

Because this is what I am, something hard and sharp

held against the world's throat. I lower the blade toward Fyrris's neck. His skin ripples as he swallows.

"You can kill me," Fyrris whispers, low and thick. "But can you stop all of us?"

My hand trembles. The blade slips a hair's breadth. Blood pools against the magic, a gleaming red crack in his pale neck. Fyrris meets my gaze.

He smiles. My breath freezes in my throat. I'm going to kill him, and still, he looks like he's won.

Because this is what he expects, I realize with strange, numb certainty. He taught me how to make this blade, how to turn the magic trapped inside the Towers's silver into weapons. I raise my eyes for a heartbeat, glancing at the darkened doorway. I don't sense the magic yet, the silver chains and panic of the other Exemplars.

But Fyrris is right. They will come. And I will have to kill them too.

The scent of blood fills my nostrils and coats the back of my mouth. We'll have to pull their corpses from the doorway, Kira and I. We'll have to step over white robes slick with crimson, climb stairs sticky with blood, cross the courtyard filled with Guards and Novices and the man who comes to feed the donkeys, the women who come in the morning to bake the bread.

I'll have to kill them all.

Maybe they won't all try to stop us. Maybe some of them will survive, huddled under straw or overturned carriages, trying not to hear the screams or see the way blood glistens on the cobblestones. Maybe they'll live long enough to wish they could forget the way the smell of death coats the inside of your throat.

Kira and I will swim through an ocean of blood to escape this place.

And that's why Fyrris is smiling. That's what he expects, what he trained me to do. Even after I spill his blood across these stones, I'll still be the Godkiller. I'll still be his creation.

There's a low rustling behind me. It must be Kira, moving away from the wall. Maybe moving away from me. I don't dare turn back to look at her.

But something shifts inside my chest. Kira's face comes back to me, her scowl when she yelled that I don't have enough food. The tears caught in her lashes when she whispered that she doesn't want me to die.

Fyrris looks at me, and he sees a monster. Destruction, fear, and death; that's all the Towers have ever expected from me.

But Kira saw something else.

And maybe that's enough to free me, one person in all the world who doesn't think I'm a monster. Who thinks I'm worth saving.

My eyes catch on the glimmer of blood on Fyrris's neck, that single scarlet drop at the edge of my blade of magic. Red, silver, I've seen enough blood to last a thousand lifetimes.

I lean back, bringing the magical blade with me. Fyrris sneers at me. Blood leaks down his neck from the place where my magic bit into his skin, and his eyes are wide. I balance the blade of magic between my fingers.

"You're afraid," I say.

Fyrris makes a gagging sound, as though the thought disgusts him. But his pulse beats in his neck like a beast in a trap. I frown down at him as the truth slowly reveals herself.

"Not just to die," I say. "You're afraid that I'm going to escape."

Fyrris opens his mouth. I drop the blade, pressing the flat edge against his lips.

"Shhhh," I whisper. "I'm not finished."

His eyes grow even wider. One hand flutters against the stones, like he's going to try to reach for the silver chain hidden in his robes. I pull magic from my body and pin his wrists to the ground.

"The Towers are running out of magic," I continue. "Why else would you be desperate enough to murder an old god?"

Fyrris scowls at me.

"You need my magic," I say. "You need it so badly that you'd risk making enemies of the Castinacs."

I glance at the door to my cell. It's still wide open. I rock back, taking my blade with me. The hallway beyond the cell door still feels empty. There's no trapped magic in there, no silver chains. Perhaps the other Exemplars are coming. Perhaps not.

"You need it so badly that you risked coming here alone," I say. "Didn't you, Fyrris?"

"We'll kill you," Fyrris growls. "We'll kill you and everyone you've ever cared about."

I shake my head. That's the only language he understands, violence, threats, and death. That's all the Towers have to offer. There are no hidden wellsprings of magic, no stories come to life—

And suddenly, another answer appears. Something the Towers can't even imagine.

My next breath sounds almost like a laugh. Fyrris's eyes widen again, that flash of fear, because now I'm no longer speaking a language he can understand. Hope and love are as far beyond him as the bright shining stars in the sky.

I grin at Fyrris as I point the blade directly at the swell of his throat.

"I'm leaving," I declare. "And you cannot stop me. Nor will any of the other men or women from these Towers."

He frowns from behind my magical blade. I lean closer, until I'm almost whispering in his ear.

"You don't know who I love," I whisper. "You wouldn't even know where to begin."

I remember Lenore, standing with her hands bound, the Towers's attempt to find someone I love. They are desperate, just like I told Matius and Tholious. And it makes them weak.

"The Towers have made powerful enemies," I continue. "The Magantis. The Castinacs."

"Lenore is dead," Fyrris hisses. But he says it like a man whispering the words of a prayer he's never once believed.

"Lenore's not dead," I whisper. "She's in Fyher's Landing right now, telling her family everything."

That's what Kira implied, at least. I lean back, watching the white flash of fear in Fyrris's eyes.

"Chase me as long as you want," I say. "It took you years to find me, and it's taken me one day to break your gods-damned chains. I'm stronger than the Towers, Fyrris. Both of us know it."

He trembles. It's answer enough. I let my magical blade melt back into oblivion.

"I'm leaving the Towers," I declare. "I'm going to live. And whoever your enemies are, wherever they're hiding, I'll find them. I'll join them. And we will ruin you."

I step back, although I leave the magic pressing Fyrris's wrists to the ground.

"You'll never make it past the gates," he growls.

Blood from my wrists stains the sleeves of his white

robes. His fear is obvious now, naked and raw like the skinned rabbit on the grass outside my cabin. He was willing to die, some part of me realizes. He's afraid to live.

"What will you tell the other Exemplars?" I ask. "When they come in here to find you alone and the chains empty, and they want to know what deal you made with the Godkiller to save your own life?"

For the first time since I presented myself to the Exemplars of the Towers and begged them to teach me, Fyrris is completely silent. His eyes are wide; his face looks almost as pale as his dirt-smeared robes.

He's just a man, after all. Just a bitter old man, hiding behind stone walls, sending boys out to face the horrors he can't stomach and to bring the spoils back to him.

I turn away. Kira is standing behind me with Fyrris's silver chain in her hand. I shiver at the metal on her bare skin, imagining the scream and hiss of the angry magic trapped inside, but she can't feel any of it. It makes her powerful, able to do things I never could. I grab her hand, pressing the silver chain between us.

Travel magic is a myth, of course. Just like talking animals, old gods, and true love.

I pull on the magic in the silver chain and the magic trapped inside my body, the last remnants of an old god that I tried to free but that chose instead, for reasons I will never begin to understand, to stay with me.

And I all but hear the magic cry for joy as I release it.

CHAPTER 56

KIRA
WE CAN PAY

Breath leaves my lungs in a huge gust, like I've been punched in the gut. My feet slam into something hard. I gasp, blinking in the darkness as I bend over. The world swims around me. Something cold and wet lands on the back of my neck.

Reznyk sinks to his knees. I follow him down, our fingers intertwined, my vision pulsing with strange white dots. The ground is bitter cold and weirdly soft, like it's covered with frozen feathers.

I blink. Not feathers.

Snow.

It was snowing when I snuck from the Guards' dormitory to the horrible place where the Exemplars keep the magic just after the thirteenth bell rang. The snow was light then, enough to slick the cobblestones of the main courtyard but not enough to reveal my footprints in black against white.

But this is a storm. The veil of fat, white flakes falls like a beaded curtain, obscuring the edges of the buildings that surround us. I can tell we're on a street, or possibly an alley-way, but not much more.

"Reznyk?" I whisper. "Where are we?"

He groans, then falls face-first into the snow.

"Shit," I hiss.

I grab his shoulders and drag him back up to his knees, trying not to wince at the blood around his wrists. He looks very pale in the weak, snow-filtered light, and he's already starting to shiver.

Damn it. It doesn't matter where we are. We have to get out of the snow.

I shake my head, then stand up. It takes two attempts and a fair amount of stumbling around in the snow, but I finally get Reznyk upright with his arm wrapped around my shoulder. Together, we stagger down the sloping alley like a pair of drunks at the end of the night.

When we round the corner at the end of the alleyway, the wind throws snow directly into my eyes. I hiss as it stings my cheeks. Beneath the bite of the wind and snow, there's the low, muddy scent of the Ever-Reaching River. Squinting, I can just make out the narrow fingers of docks stretching into the river and snow-covered barges rocking heavily against their pylons.

We're still in Silver City, then. My mind races like the snow blasting past the end of the alley. This isn't my usual neighborhood. What do I know near the docks?

I peek out from the alley one more time, looking for the round sign with a goose's sharp, angry beak. And there it is, creaking as it rocks back and forth in the storm. The Next Best Gander. The pub's windows are dark, which isn't exactly promising, but it must be close to sunrise; even the heaviest drinkers are usually home by now.

I turn to Reznyk. He's shivering next to me. His black hair hangs loose in front of his face.

"We'll go to that pub," I declare. "Unless you have any better ideas?"

He moans something, then shakes his head. Or just shakes in general. It's hard to tell.

"Great," I mutter through clenched teeth.

We limp down the narrow street as the wind howls around us like it's trying to talk us out of a bad idea. By the time we reach the door beneath the round sign, I'm shivering as badly as Reznyk.

One storm a winter, that's what Dame Serena used to say. Silver City gets one massive storm every winter, just to keep us all on our toes. This close to the river, I can hear icy pellets of snow hitting the surface of the water as wind blasts my face and tugs at my cloak. You'd have to be desperate to be out in this.

And here we are. Desperate.

I give the tavern door's massive iron handle a half-hearted tug, and of course, it's locked. What kind of idiot would leave the door to their pub unlocked in this weather?

With a sigh, I grab the knocker, which is also shaped like a goose's head, and bang on the door. It's loud, the metallic smack of the brass goose head against its setting, but even so, the wind takes the banging and throws it into the river. I stare at the dark windows, curse under my breath, and bang the knocker again. Harder.

Nothing. Reznyk starts to say something, but all I can make out is the chatter of his teeth. I ball my hands into fists and wail on the door like it's to blame for the massive fucking mess I've made of my life.

And it opens.

I stagger forward as the door swings inward, revealing the dim glow of a candle in someone's hand.

"Get inside," a man says.

I hobble over the front step as the man grabs Reznyk's arm, pulls him in, and slams the door shut behind us. The candle gutters, then goes out, leaving us in a room filled with shadows.

"I'm s-sorry about this," I begin. "We n-need a room—"

There's a scrape, then a hiss as a match flares to life. The man brings the match to the candle. My voice fades.

It's Zayne. He stares at us, twisting his delicate features into something that's almost a smile.

"What are you doing here?" I blurt, before I can stop myself.

"This is my pub," Zayne says, with a shrug. "I live here."

I open my mouth. Close it. Swallow what I was going to say about him working for the Mercenary Guild and how I didn't think they were allowed to live anywhere but the Guild, then open it again.

"We can pay," I say.

Zayne nods. "Follow me."

He turns, the candle in his hand, and threads a path between the empty tables to a narrow door in the back of the room. Reznyk limps after him, and I follow, watching the shadows. Zayne unlocks the door with a click, then swings it open.

There's a hallway behind the door. The darkness inside swallows Zayne, then Reznyk, who makes his way with one hand pressed against the wall. My teeth sink into my lower lip as I contemplate the chances that Zayne is going to lock us away somewhere and sell us back to the Towers. But, hells, what choice do we have?

The hallway ends in a room. It's larger than I expected,

and far nicer than I'd have imagined, with a bank of windows that looks out over the dark curve of the Ever-Reaching River as snow swirls above it. Zayne bends down with the candle. It's only once he steps back, his delicate features illuminated by the soft glow of a fire, that I realize he's lit the hearth. Reznyk pulls off his cloak, hangs it on the wall, and then sinks onto the edge of the bed. He holds the mattress on either side of him like he's trying to keep himself upright.

"Give me a minute," Zayne says, with a strange shadowy expression.

Wind howls past the bank of windows on the far side of the room. The fire on the hearth crackles as it licks the dry wood, and a curl of smoke creeps around the corners of the room. Reznyk closes his eyes. He looks like he's fallen asleep sitting up.

I need to go.

I've done what I can for him. He's free, Lady Lenore Castinac is back in her city, and I'd rather choke to death than witness their happy fucking reunion. I stare at the windows, where the storm howls with all its fury just behind Reznyk's shadowed reflection.

The Towers will be coming for me. Whether Fyrris saw me standing behind Reznyk in that dank cell or not, they'll eventually put two and two together.

So, yes. I need to leave Silver City. Now.

The door creaks open once more, and Zayne returns. He's carrying a tray with two steaming bowls, half a loaf of bread, and a bottle of wine. Reznyk's eyes open as Zayne sets it down on the small table beside the bed.

"Just broth for you this morning, I think," Zayne says, looking at Reznyk.

Reznyk nods. Zayne stands up, then tosses something

to me. It glints in the firelight. I catch it, then open my hand. The golden butterfly necklace I found in the mud on Crown Day gleams in my palm.

"It's a fake, sweetheart," Zayne says, with a wink. "Real gold is heavier."

I blink, then stare down at the golden butterfly's delicate, lacquered wings. They're studded with tiny gemstones that shimmer in the firelight. Those stones must also be fake, but how in the nine hells would I know? This is the only piece of jewelry I've ever touched.

"I— I can pay," I choke out, again.

"I know," Zayne says. "Get some sleep."

He walks out of the room and closes the door behind him. I stare at the door, then at the snow dancing outside the window.

I need to go, damn it.

Reznyk picks up one of the bowls, drinks from it with slow, measured sips, and then kicks his boots off and lies back on the bed. His eyes close. Heat swells inside the room as the fire crackles and spits on its hearth. I stare at the bed with a longing so deep I feel its ache inside my bones. When was the last time I slept on an actual mattress?

I turn toward the window once more, where the wind whips ghosts of snow across the dark waters of the Ever-Reaching River. Yes, I need to go. But I can't leave tonight. No barges will be moving in this storm, no carriages traveling on the roads.

I turn back to the bed, and a different kind of ache spreads through my chest. I can't sleep that close to Reznyk. My heart already feels like a bleeding open wound. Closing my eyes and pretending we're back in the cabin together is only going to make everything worse.

With a sigh, I grab a blanket from the foot of the bed,

spread it out on the floor, and lie down on the cold tiles below the window while the wind howls above me. Give me an hour, I tell myself as my eyes close. I'll leave in an hour.

Maybe two.

CHAPTER 57
REZNYK
THE ONE

Wherever I am, it's warm.

I hold my breath and listen before opening my eyes. The dull murmur of distant conversation washes over me. It could almost be the clatter of a river tumbling over stones, if it wasn't for the occasional clink of glass or barking laugh. Am I in a pub?

My eyes open, and I take in the room around me. A low fire flickers on the hearth. There's a tray on a table with a bit of bread, a wine bottle, and two empty glasses. The windows along the far wall glow with dull gray light that makes me think the day is coming to a close. Gods, I must have been asleep all day.

I roll over in the empty bed. Kira was here with me, wasn't she? My memory is like fog, thin and impossible to grasp. I remember Kira standing against the wall of this room, don't I? But perhaps that was a dream.

I sit up, then let my head fall to my hands. My body aches, and my stomach voices its discontent with a long, slow rumble. My cloak hangs by the door, still and solemn and utterly alone. Wasn't there another cloak there? I come to my feet, then chew the bit of bread slowly as I turn over my thin scraps of memory, prodding each one until they fall apart in my hands.

Fine. I'm not going to figure it out here.

I hesitate before the door and run my fingers over the empty hook where I might have imagined I saw Kira's cloak. Magic purrs softly inside my body. It's weak and distant, just like it was the first time I used it to rip Kira out of one place and bring her to another, but it's still a part of me, for whatever inscrutable reason.

The door leads to a narrow hallway. I wait in the dark hall as my heart thuds inside my chest, listening to what sounds like ordinary pub chatter drift in from the other end. There's no sign of the one voice I want to hear. Disappointment burns low in my gut. Did she leave already? Have I been out that long?

Or perhaps she didn't want to stay. I wasn't kind to her when we last parted in the Daggers. What reason would she have to linger? For that matter, what reason did she have to free me from the nightmare steel chains in the first place?

I swallow hard, then leave the hallway and enter the pub. A few heads raise at my sudden appearance, then just as quickly drop back into their varied conversations. It's a small pub, with a polished wooden bar at one end and a fire crackling on the hearth at the other. The clientele look a bit scruffy; this doesn't appear to be the kind of place Lady Lenore or anyone from the Towers would visit. Thank the gods.

I run my eyes over the crowd. There are several older men playing cards, two women by the door deep in conversation, and a woman behind the bar. There's a young boy sitting at one of the tables frowning down at a scrap of paper. Two people stand by the pub's door, deep in whispered conversation. The man is tall, with dark hair and a face so delicate it's almost out of place.

Zayne. And next to him, with a cloak pulled up over her fiery hair and a scowl on her face, is Kira.

I can't breathe. Kira is dressed for traveling with a bag slung over her shoulder, and she's standing beside the door, arguing in hushed, low whispers with Zayne.

She's leaving. Without saying anything to me.

Magic flickers dully beneath my skin. My heart chokes, coughs, and decides to keep on beating. Kira shakes her head. She frowns, turns away from Zayne, and then sees me. Her back stiffens. A strange expression flashes across her features. Is it fear? Gods, have I given her reason to fear me?

She shoves the front door with her shoulder. It's halfway open by the time I reach her. Swirls of snow dance across the threshold, and I can't stop thinking about all the times I imagined Kira in my cabin, sitting at a window while the snow fell outside.

"Kira," I say. "Wait."

My voice sounds like a rusty hinge. Kira freezes. The door closes, leaving her inside. She doesn't quite turn to me, not exactly, but her eyes trace a path across my chest before settling back on Zayne.

I feel like I'm trying to breathe through mud. There are so many things I have to say to this woman, and I don't want any of them to be witnessed by an entire room full of people I don't know. Zayne breaks the silence.

"Welcome back to the land of the living," Zayne says as he claps me on the shoulder.

"Thanks," I stammer.

Kira's hand is still wrapped around the door handle.

"Kira," I say, in a voice that's almost a whisper. "You left something in the room."

Her eyes widen, then close in a heavy scowl. She turns away from the door and sweeps through the room, vanishing down the hallway.

"Good luck with that," Zayne mutters.

For one desperate moment, I actually consider asking Zayne for advice. But I come to my senses and turn back to him with my arms crossed over my chest. A suspicion I've had since Matius and Tholious turned up on my doorstep resurfaces.

"You broke her ankle," I say.

Zayne doesn't deny it, which is answer enough.

"You piece of shit," I hiss. "I should break yours."

"I'd like to see you try, magic man," Zayne replies.

I stare at him. Gods, it's been a long time since I've talked to someone who's not afraid of me. I'd almost forgotten what it was like. I rub my hand across my mouth to destroy the curve of my lips before it can become a smile.

"You're an asshole," I announce.

"You're just now figuring that out?" Zayne replies, with a grin. "How's Matius? Did they make it to you?"

"They both did," I answer. "They're safe. They're together."

"Well, that's disgustingly heartwarming," Zayne replies. He runs his hand over the back of his neck, then looks down the hallway once more. "You know, if it makes you feel any better, she's been talking about leaving all day. But that was the first time she actually opened the door."

I stare at the hallway, wondering if that does, in fact, make me feel any better.

"But," Zayne continues, "I don't think she's going to send you an invitation, if that's what you're waiting for."

"Right," I say, sucking in a breath. "Right."

I cross the room, which feels much larger going in this direction. The hallway is dark and silent, and the door to the room with the windows and the wide bed is closed. By the time I reach it, I have the first, pathetic fragments of a plan.

I pull the door open. Kira stands in the middle of the room, her arms crossed over her chest, the low firelight licking the curves of her body as she scowls at me.

"I didn't forget anything," she snaps.

I smile at her. Her eyes widen as I step forward, moving so close that I can almost smell her.

"You forgot to say goodbye," I say.

Kira steps back. Her eyes drop, and she turns toward the door.

"Wait," I say.

She glances at me, raising an eyebrow. I turn away from her, pick up the wine bottle, and pull my knife from my belt. The cork comes free with a soft pop. The scent of red wine swirls around the room, mixing with wood smoke.

"Before you go," I say, reaching for one of the two glasses.

I fill it, then hold it out to her. She makes no move to take it. I shrug, set it on the table, then fill the second glass.

"One last round?" I ask.

"You're kidding me."

"Not at all."

"Questions?" she asks.

"Questions," I answer. "Do you want to go first?"

She makes a sound that's part laugh and part frustrated bark, then waves her hand in the air between us like she's trying to swat down my stupid idea.

"I don't have any questions," she snaps.

"Very well," I say. "I'll go first."

She frowns but doesn't disagree. I bring the wineglass to my lips and take a sip. This wine is far better than it has any right to be, given the surroundings. I turn to Kira.

"Why did you free me?" I ask.

She makes that sound again, part laugh and part whimper of defeat, then sinks onto the chair opposite me and shakes her head.

"Right for the jugular," she mutters.

I shrug. Kira grabs her wineglass and takes a massive gulp, clearly avoiding my question. I try to swallow my disappointment.

"I suppose that makes it your turn," I say.

Kira shakes her head. "I don't have any questions," she says. "Really. It's not like I'm going to want to know the wedding date."

"Wedding date?" I reply.

She takes another drink from her wineglass, then frowns at the fire. She looks like she's in pain, like just being in the same room with me is some kind of torture. My chest aches; I have no idea how to cross the gulf between us.

"Are you getting married?" I ask, as gently as I can.

"Gods, no," she replies.

I try not to look as relieved as I feel. She shakes her head again as her teeth close over her lower lip. Wind rattles the windows behind me.

"I met Lenore," she finally says. "That's how I know she's here. That she's waiting for you."

"Lenore Castinac?"

Kira nods. "She's, um, lovely. I think you're—"

Something ripples across her face. For just a moment, Kira looks like she's going to cry. Then she frowns, and the moment passes.

"You'll be very happy together," she says, in a way that makes *happy together* sound almost like a curse.

My mouth opens, but it takes me a moment to find the words. Something cracks in the fire, releasing a cloud of sparks. Wind throws snow against the windows behind me. It sounds like something scratching to get out.

"How did you meet Lenore?" I say, voicing one of the many, many questions swirling inside my skull.

"In the Daggers," Kira replies.

"What?"

Kira crosses her arms back over her chest and meets my gaze. There's something defiant about her expression, like she's daring me to disagree with her.

"You went back to the Daggers?" I ask.

"Oh, you know, it's such a lovely place," she mutters. "I just wanted to have a little holiday there."

Kira grabs her wineglass, drains it, and puts it back down. I refill it. My heart slams against the inside of my rib cage like it's trying to escape. I take a long, slow sip of wine in the hopes that I can drown it.

"You saved Lenore's life," I say, as my mind slowly pieces the story together. How else would Lenore have made it back to Silver City?

Kira snorts. "I don't think that's how she would see it."

"Of course not," I say. "You went back to the Daggers alone?"

Kira shrugs, like traveling through the wilderness by herself is nothing. My throat feels tight; the room suddenly feels far too warm.

"Why?" I ask.

"I— I wanted to warn you," she replies, in a voice so low it's almost a whisper. "About the Towers. I figured I owed you that much." She blinks, then wipes at her eyes. "But I was too late. By the time I made it past the hunting lodge, there was nothing left but carriage tracks. And, you know, Lady Lenore."

"Gods," I mutter. That black carriage must have gone right past Kira. If Fyrris had known—

A shiver trembles down my back. I try to smother it with more wine. Kira glances up at me. Our eyes meet. Magic sings under my skin, and for a moment it almost slips free to dance in the air between us. Kira's lips part.

Then she slams her hands down on the table, pushes her chair back, and jumps to her feet.

"Okay," she stammers, her eyes darting toward the door. "Great. So, uh, good luck."

Kira puts her hand on the door. Something cracks inside my chest.

"Wait," I say, pushing back from the table. The room swims slightly when I come to my feet. "Where are you going?"

Kira shakes her head. Her eyes shine in the firelight.

"Lenore's waiting for you," she says, in a voice that's almost angry.

"Why do you keep saying that?"

Kira blinks at me. "Because she's The One."

My breath catches in the back of my throat. I walk to Kira, then place my hand gently beside hers on the door.

"Kira," I say. "Lenore doesn't love me. She never loved me."

Kira's mouth opens. A tear traces a path down her cheek. I can't stop myself. I raise my hand, press my fingers to her cheek, and catch it.

"But—" Kira says. "She was the trap."

"That's because Fyrris didn't know," I say. "Lenore loves her city and the Castinac family's position. Even if she cared about me, she'd never marry me. A match like that would cost much more than she'd be willing to pay."

I smile as I say it. Years ago, that truth hurt me far more than any of the injuries I'd received in my very colorful career. But now it's just a fact, like snow in winter or the foolishness of youth.

"Do you remember what you told me your first night in the cabin?" I ask.

Kira's breath hitches. She turns away.

"You said you didn't think it was love," I continue, "trying to win the whole world just to place it at her feet."

"I don't remember that," Kira whispers.

"I haven't stopped thinking about it," I continue. "Maybe I never loved Lenore. Because maybe love isn't feeling like you need to prove yourself. Maybe it's someone who feels like a friend. Or more than a friend. Maybe it's someone who wants you to live, even when the world expects nothing but death."

"Great," Kira mutters under her breath. "That's why you let the Towers take you in exchange for Lenore."

Gods, I'm terrible at this. I remind myself to never try writing love poems.

"No," I say.

I meet her eyes. Something flashes in the air between us, an older and wilder form of magic than what's trapped inside my body. I let my fingers drop from her cheek to her chin.

"I let the Towers take me," I whisper, "because I was afraid they would come for you."

CHAPTER 58

KIRA

SOMEONE WHO MATTERS

T close my eyes. I can't stop the tears that slip down my cheek and onto Reznyk's fingers. His hand pulls away. My cheek is still warm where he touched me, and I have to stop myself before I bring my own hand to my face and press it there, trying to capture the warmth of his body.

Of course Reznyk surrendered to the Towers. He was ready to spend the rest of his life alone, in the middle of nowhere, to protect a bunch of wolves and an old god who were clearly getting on just fine by themselves. Of course he sacrificed himself for humans.

"Then it's a good thing I released you," I say, in a voice that sounds like it's being pinched tight in a vise. "I saved you. You saved me. I guess we're even now."

"No," Reznyk whispers. "We're not even close."

I open my mouth to tell him to stop being so stupidly heroic, but he speaks first.

"Why did you rescue me?" he asks again.

Because I love you, you idiot.

The words simmer in my throat; I step away from the

door, then grab my glass and take another gulp of wine to drown them.

"No," I say.

Reznyk glances up at me, surprise widening those gorgeous, dark eyes. "No?" he echoes.

"No," I say. "It's my turn to ask a question. That's how the game works."

He gives me a very weak smile, and my heart cracks in a dozen new places. Why didn't anyone ever tell me how painful it was to be in love? I never would have wished for it.

"Ask away," Reznyk says, waving his hand across the table like he's granting me something.

I swallow hard. My mouth tastes like wine and unanswered questions. Some part of me is screaming to leave this room, to leave Silver City and to never even think about Reznyk again. But I still need his help, don't I?

"Where should I go?" I ask.

Reznyk stares at me in a way that makes the shattered remains of my heart grind up against one another inside my chest. Gods, is this ever going to stop hurting?

"What do you mean?" he asks.

"Zayne thought you could help, and I can't stay here," I say, waving my hand at the window with its delicate swirls of frost. "Sooner or later, the Towers are going to figure out what I did. And, even if they don't—"

My throat feels tight. I stare at the fire until I can breathe again.

"I can't serve the Towers," I say. "Not anymore. Not after what they did to you."

Reznyk stares at me for so long that I take a step back, even though it puts me further from the door.

"Kira," he finally says. "I am so sorry."

I blink. "Excuse me?"

He runs his hand through his hair, then collapses onto his chair and drains his wineglass. He still looks pale and exhausted, not at all like the fearsome Godkiller we were sent to hunt in the Daggers. Hells, he doesn't even look that much like the confident stranger who wandered into the Golden Peaks Hunting Lodge during an autumn storm. He stares at the window, as if the next words he's about to speak are out there somewhere, getting tossed around by the wind and snow.

I stand up a bit straighter. Try to relax when you're about to take a hit, Mitrik told me when he was training me how to fight. Tensing up just makes it worse.

Yeah. That never once worked for me. I clench my jaw and try to force my shoulders to relax as Reznyk looks at everything but me. Until finally, his dark eyes find mine.

"The Towers lied to you," Reznyk says, softly. "I don't think your parents were Exemplars. And I don't think you have any magical potential. That's not why they wanted you, and I should have told you much earlier."

"Oh," I say. My voice sounds like wind over ice.

Reznyk's expression looks like something's hurting him. I have to strangle the part of me that wants to reach for him.

"They wanted you because of me, I think," he continues. "And what I felt for Lenore."

"Oh."

"You know I said you look like her?" Reznyk continues. "You must have seen that for yourself, right?"

I nod.

"The Towers must have thought they could use you," he says, "to, well, to make me behave. To make me do what they wanted."

I look down at the wineglass in my hand, which is almost empty a second time. What he's saying makes sense, in a sick sort of way. Why else would the Towers want the bastard daughter of Lord Castinac? Why send someone with no magical ability into the Daggers to hunt for the Godkiller? Why offer me as a trade for the amulet?

Gods. My gut lurches around the stew I had for dinner. I don't know what's worse, that I was sent to the Daggers to be some sort of knock-off replacement for Lady Castinac, or that it worked.

"I see," I say, in a whisper.

Reznyk tugs his hand through his hair again. "I'm sorry I didn't tell you earlier," he says. "I'm sorry they lied to you. And—" He pauses. His neck bobs as he swallows. "I'm so sorry I'm the reason the Towers took you," he finishes.

"Ugh, gods," I groan as I collapse into the chair across from him. "Reznyk, do you blame yourself for every single thing that goes wrong in this world?"

He stares at me.

"Did you give them my name?" I snap. "Or say, hey, there's this girl who looks like The One living in the orphanage next door?"

"Stop calling her that," Reznyk says.

I ignore him. "Were you the one who decided I should go to the Daggers? Or who said they should offer me up as a trade for some stupid piece of jewelry?"

My voice fades. Shame curdles inside my gut, hot and bitter. I turn away from Reznyk's face and stare at my hands as they clench into fists.

"If anyone should be sorry, it's me," I admit. "I never should have taken your amulet. I never should have even touched the damn thing."

I risk a glance in his direction. He's staring at the table. I feel like I'm about to choke, but gods, if this is my last chance to tell him the truth, I'd better fucking take it.

"When I saw it," I begin. "I— I thought maybe it could help me. Since nothing else had. Maybe the amulet you stole from the Towers could finally unlock my magical potential."

I fall silent. It sounds so pathetic now that it's out in the open. Outside, wind howls down the river, making the window rattle. It's going to be a miserable walk along the docks, and there's no way I'll find a barge leaving tonight.

"I am sorry," I admit. "I know you have no reason to believe me, but I am. I never wanted to take the amulet from you. I never wanted to hurt you."

Reznyk meets my gaze. "I believe you," he says.

He reaches across the table slowly. His fingers wrap around mine.

"Maybe I shouldn't blame myself for what the Towers did," he says. His dark eyes are watching me like I'm the only thing in the entire world worth watching. "But I do blame myself for what happened with the amulet."

I try to breathe. My chest is tight; the room suddenly feels too small.

"I was an idiot and an ass," Reznyk says. "I didn't even give you a chance to explain. And I regret it. Deeply."

"I understand," I say. "I would have done the same thing."

He laughs softly, then shakes his head. "No," he says. "I very much doubt that."

There's an explosion of laughter from the pub on the other side of the door, that other world where people are going about their business as if my heart wasn't collapsing in on itself.

I take a deep breath. I hate the questions that's coming,

but I need to ask it if I'm going to have any chance at all of moving on with my life. Otherwise, I'll dream about those dark eyes for the rest of my stupid life.

"So, what now?" I ask, even though my voice trembles. "Are you going to win her back?"

He thinks Lenore doesn't love him, that she won't marry him. But, by all the many names of the gods, how could any woman refuse him? She'd have to be insane to let Reznyk go.

Reznyk smiles at me in a way that makes me feel like the room is spinning.

"I'd like that," he says.

His thumb traces a circle on the back of my hand, and my gods, that does things to my insides that no man should be able to do with one finger. My eyes sting. I try to blink back the hot rush of tears, because I'm not going to humiliate myself any further in front of this man.

"What would it take to win you back?" Reznyk asks.

My mouth falls open. Feast day fireworks go off inside my skull, drowning out the sudden rush of blood from my exploding heart.

He could not possibly have said that.

He could not possibly have meant that.

"That counts as my question, by the way," Reznyk finishes. "It is my turn."

He takes his hand off mine to pick up the wine bottle and refill both of our glasses. He lifts mine and offers it to me.

"But I am going to be quite disappointed if you drink instead of answering me," he adds.

He's still smiling, although there's a strange look in his dark eyes that I haven't seen before. If I didn't know better, if this wasn't a completely ridiculous way to describe the

Godkiller who bested the Towers of Silver City, I would say he looks afraid.

"But—" I stammer. "I'm not her."

"Yes," he says. "I am aware of that fact."

My mouth falls open again. Reznyk watches me with that wary look, like we're in the training courtyard and I'm circling him with one of the Guards' wooden swords.

I want to laugh. I would laugh, if I could breathe.

"But," I begin again. "You said it yourself. I don't have any magical ability. I don't—"

He frowns, and my voice dies in my throat.

"Kira," he says. "You are the strongest and bravest woman I've ever met, magic or not."

This time I do laugh. It's a panicky sort of noise, like an animal caught in a trap. Reznyk isn't smiling anymore. Now he's staring at me like—

Like I'm someone who matters.

"None of the mercenaries came back after I chased Tholious away," he says. "Only you were brave enough to stay."

"Well, I had a broken ankle—" I begin.

"You just told me you came back to the Daggers, by yourself, to warn me about the Towers," he continues. "The gods only know how you managed to get there, but you did. And then, not only did you make it out, you also rescued Lady Castinac and brought her back to Silver City."

I grab my wineglass and shut my mouth. My heart is still beating like it's trying to run away.

"You broke into my cell," Reznyk continues. "I don't know if you were pushed into it or if you felt somehow indebted to me, but you helped me when no one else would. And—"

He hesitates. His eyes drop to the floor, then come back to me.

"We had something, I think," he says in a voice that's hardly more than a whisper. "The two of us. We had something real. Or the start of it, at least. And, if there's any chance at all that you can forgive me for being such a stupid bastard, maybe we can try again. We could leave Silver City together, at least. As friends, or—"

Reznyk's voice fades. He stares at me with a wild, naked look on his face, something so raw and hungry it makes me feel like I'm coming apart in all the places I've tried so hard to hold myself together. It's the way he looked at me in the meadow, I realize, with a shiver. When he was naked and between my legs, and tiny golden sparks of magic danced in the air between us.

When everything in my life felt right.

"I love you," I blurt.

Tears spill down my cheeks, making the firelight wink as it fills the room.

"That's why I rescued you," I say. "Even if you don't feel the same way, I couldn't leave you. I couldn't live with myself if I did."

"Kira," Reznyk whispers. "Beautiful, brave, brilliant Kira."

He leans across the table slowly, giving me plenty of time to pull away. I don't.

"I do love you," he says.

And all the magic in the world couldn't make the kiss he gives me any better.

CHAPTER 59
REZNYK
COMING HOME

I t's not sweet, the kiss I give Kira across the table. It's not hesitant, or innocent, or gentle.

No, it's hungry. I press into her like I've been starving, like I've been waiting for her for my entire life. Like she needs to break my curse with her lips.

And then, suddenly, it's not enough. I pull away. Our eyes lock, and then Kira is pushing back from the table without speaking, staring at me with fire in her eyes. I grab her shoulders as she comes to her feet, pull her to me, and devour that sweet mouth.

The bed is too far away. I shove her into the wall, some part of me wincing at my urgency, my own frantic, pulsing need, but the rest of me is drowning without her, dying to get her out of her clothes. She moans into my mouth, and suddenly I'm back in the Golden Peaks, under the moonlight on that massive bed, and my gods, I should have fucked her then. I should have fucked her hard, over and over.

I'm going to spend the rest of my life making up for that mistake.

Kira's hips tilt up to meet mine. Her leg wraps around my waist, and her hand tugs at the waistband of my pants. She's panting against my lips, gasping and moaning, and how did I ever think I could survive without her? How did I ever think I could stop loving her?

"Gods," I gasp. "Gods, Kira—"

She wins the battle against my belt. I pull one hand out of the tangled mess of her hair and help her shove my pants down over my hips, and I remember how she looked standing in front of the door, one hand on the handle, my heart shattering as she pushed open the door and snow curled over the lintel.

I shove her pants down to her ankles, and my hand dives between her legs. She's gasping, her hips rising and falling against the wall, her head thrown back and her hair a wild, messy wreath against the wall. I press my lips against her neck, kissing and biting, as my fingers sink inside of her, and the heat of her sex coats my hand.

"Fuck," she mumbles. "Fuck, please—"

I curl my fingers. Her breath cuts off as she moans something that's not even close to words. Still, I understand. I understand her just fine. I pull back, trailing my wet fingers across the soft skin of her inner thigh.

She whimpers. I bring my hand to my lips, licking the taste of her from my fingers. Her eyes are wide, her pupils huge in the dim light of the fire, and the room is hot, and my gods, nothing has ever been so beautiful. My cock aches; I feel the heat of her even through my clothes.

Soldier coming home. That's what the women in the Blackwater brothel called this position, some part of me remembers. I never understood. Wouldn't a soldier returning from some foreign war take his time, reacquaint himself with his wife, spread roses over the sheets and make slow love all night long?

No. Fuck that. I press my hips between her legs. Her ankle digs into my waist; her hands form fists around the back of my shirt. Her breath is hot against my lips. The head of my cock throbs against the wet heat of her sex as I stare into her wide, wild eyes.

"You're the only one," I gasp, although my breath is as ragged as steam hissing from a teakettle, "who knows what —what this means to me."

"I know," she whispers.

And she waits for me.

I drive into her as slowly as I can, pleasure climbing my spine as I enter her, one hand around her waist, the other braced against the wall, our bodies joining as our lips meet, drowning in each other.

Coming home.

The frantic hunger that reared as soon as our lips touched comes back with a vengeance, and I pull my hips back and sink into her again, harder and faster. She rises to meet me, gasping, crying. I drop my hand between our bodies, finding the hard, hot nub at the crest of her sex, driving into her with everything I have.

She knows. She knows. She knows. Everything I am, everything I have to offer, everything this act means to me. She takes me in, all of me.

Kira's leg tightens around my waist, and she cries out something that might be my name or might be some frantic, forgotten prayer. I close my eyes and thrust blindly into her, losing everything, giving it all to her. Her body tightens around me, pulling me forward, and when I finally spill my seed, I make a sound that's ripped out of somewhere deep, somewhere hidden. Somewhere just for her.

The room spins around us. I drop my head to Kira's shoulder and breathe her in, the salt and sweat of her body, the thick, rich scent of her sex. When I bring my lips to trace the curve of her neck, my cock trembles back to life inside the warmth of her body. Coming home.

Kira laughs, low and soft. I blink open my eyes, but the room still swims with golden sparks, the afterglow of my last orgasm.

Or. No—

"Shit," I whisper.

I stagger back, our bodies coming apart with a noise that sounds almost like a kiss. Magic swirls in the room around us, golden stars dancing against the wall and shining in the darkened windows.

"So that does happen every time," Kira says, with a grin.

The sparks are already starting to fade, the magic returning to purr contentedly beneath my skin. Kira's cheeks are flushed, her shirt is a wrinkled mess around her shoulders, and she's smiling at me like I'm the answer to something important.

"Does it?" I say. "I don't know."

I reach forward and pull her into my arms. She giggles as I claim her mouth for another deep, bruising kiss, a kiss that makes my cock stiffen once again. I wrap my arms around her waist, spin her across the room, and then collapse onto the bed, dragging her with me. At some point we're going to have to get rid of that shirt she's wearing. But not yet.

"Let's find out," I whisper as I pull her lips back to mine.

EPILOUGE - REZNYK
A PLACE TO STAY

"Are you fishing or just wasting my time?" Dreures asks without looking at me.

I glance down at the thin and inconveniently long fishing rod in my hands. A few dim flickers of awareness drift up from the murky water below the boat, but I haven't spent enough time around deep water to know if the magic is rubbing up against fish or some other aquatic creature. Either way, I don't particularly want to impale anything with the brutal metal hook Dreures gave me.

I force my lips to curve into a smile, then flick my wrist and send the thin fishing line out across the muddy water that slinks through Labrinth Swamp on its way to the sheltered harbor that holds the Port of Good Fortune.

"That's more like it," Dreures grunts. "What were you thinking, letting your rod sit that long?"

I know the head of the Port's major crime syndicate well enough to know that he's not expecting an answer. I glance at the muscular, silent man rowing the boat beneath a wide-brimmed hat. He hasn't looked at me once. I assume he's either one of Dreures's most trusted men, or he's had his tongue ripped out to keep from talking about the things he's seen. Possibly both.

There's a small splash as Dreures pulls his hook out of the water, then grunts at it. He holds the rod out to the man rowing, who puts a sliver of rancid meat on the end, and then he casts it long and low over the water. It lands near a nest of tangled roots along the far bank.

I feel for the magic linking me to Kira. We found a necklace with a massive glass gemstone in the market, and I turned it into a ward.

"If anything happens," I told her, after setting the ward, "break the glass, and I'll be there."

Travel magic has worked for us twice. There's no reason to think it won't work a third time to bring me back to her.

"Break the glass?" Kira asked. "What, step on it?"

"Whatever works," I said.

"You said this Dreures guy is your friend?" she replied, raising an eyebrow.

"A very close friend," I replied.

She smiled. I didn't.

I assumed Dreures wouldn't allow Kira into our negotiations, and I was right. I also assumed those negotiations would take place in his office or his parlor, the two parts of his vast estate that I'd seen before. When he told me he'd rather talk and fish, I realized there was a good chance he'd decided it would be easier to kill me than to repay the favor he owes me. That wouldn't end well for him, and it'd be a mess for me.

But we've been on the water for hours now, and he hasn't tried to murder me yet. Also, I haven't felt so much as a tremble of magic from Kira's ward. Perhaps she really is playing cards with his wife, like Dreures suggested.

Dreures makes a different sort of grunt. The man sitting

at the oars comes to his feet as Dreures's fishing line snaps taut. Magic prickles the back of my neck as whatever is on the other end of that line sends a low flicker of alarm through the water.

Dreures pulls on the line. The dark water churns along the far bank. Our boat rocks as the silent man at the oars steps closer to the edge.

Then the water breaks, and something impossibly big and impossibly silver leaps toward the sky. Dreures's hook flashes in the corner of its mouth. The man at the oars gasps; Dreures curses.

The fish rejoins its aquatic world with a massive splash. Dreures hauls on the line. The churn of muddy water comes closer to the boat. The man at the oars grabs a net I assumed was comically large, a nod to the massive egos of the men who thought they'd catch something big enough to warrant that kind of net.

There's a flash of silver under the water, close to the boat. My magic simmers with the rage and fear of the monster beneath the waves. Dreures's line vibrates in the hot air, humming like an insect. The man at the oars plunges the net into the water.

It comes back in a riot of foam and muddy water, and now I see the net's almost too small for the massive fish. Ragged edges of silver tail hang over the handle of the net, which is shaking in the man's hand. Dreures makes a sound I've never heard him make before; it's almost childlike, his victorious whoop.

"That beats last week," Dreures cries.

The man holding the net nods. Dreures grabs a long, thin board from the side of the boat, then lies it along the edge of the net. The silver fish's eyes roll in its head. Its gills flap, revealing bloody red edges. I open my mouth, then close it. Magic hisses inside me, almost like it's urging me to make an argument for this piscine bastard's life. One battle at a time, I tell the magic.

Dreures takes a stick of charcoal and makes a mark on the long board, right at the ragged edge of the fish's massive tail. Then he reaches into the net and tugs the hook from the fish's mouth. When the man holding the net drops it into the water, I freeze, expecting Dreures to explode at what must have been a dire miscalculation.

Instead, Dreures shakes the man's hand. The man mutters congratulations. He must still have his tongue after all.

"You let it go," I say, staring at the silent brown river that just swallowed the monster fish.

Dreures turns to me with his intense black eyes.

"Sometimes you get tired of killing," he replies. "That's why you're here, isn't it? That favor I owe you?"

I swallow hard. I've turned the words I'm about to say over and over in my head, polishing them until they shine. But now they feel thin and insubstantial, a weak hope to pin my entire life on.

No, not just my life. Our lives.

"I want a place to stay," I tell him. Then I correct myself. "A place to live, I mean. Somewhere safe, for both Kira and me."

I pause, remembering what Tholious and Matius said about meeting me in the Port this spring.

"And some friends," I add. "With, uh, a cat."

Dreures doesn't respond. My throat tightens, as though invisible hands are closing around it. It's best if I don't mention what I'm really after, and I know it. I need a safe place first, before I start searching for the enemies of the Towers.

"I'll work for you," I continue. "You know what I can do. But I won't do anything that might threaten Kira."

Dreures grunts, then sits down on the padded bench in the center of the boat.

"You came back from Silver City," he says. "Had a spot of trouble with your last employer, no?"

"Perhaps," I reply. "Maybe I just wanted a change of scenery."

Dreures makes a low sound in the back of his throat. I'm sure he knows exactly what happened to me in Silver City. This man knows everything.

"This employer," he continues. "I heard they taught you some new tricks. Might be useful."

"It might," I answer.

Dreures spits over the side of the boat, then turns back to me. His eyes narrow.

"What do you think of the Towers?" he asks.

He's watching me closely, but I can't get a read on him. I have no idea how Dreures feels about the Towers or what kind of answer he's expecting. He's wise enough to treat his personal opinions like precious currency.

I wasn't expecting this. I consider my next words carefully.

"The Towers wanted a weapon," I say. "I thought that's what I wanted too. That's why I joined them."

As usual, Dreures doesn't respond. He rests his hands on his knees and leans forward, like he's trying to make sure he catches my next words. The sun beats down on the swirling, murky surface of the river. Somewhere far below, the massive silver fish rests in the cool water, its panic and fear dissipating as the river washes into the ocean.

"You know what I did after that," I say. Fear closes my throat, making my voice sound high and thin.

"I'd like to hear you say it," Dreures responds.

I swallow again. My heart trembles like a line pulled tight between a fist and the bony lip of a monster fish.

"I did what they trained me to do," I tell him. "I killed the old god, and I captured their magic. But I didn't do it the way the Towers wanted me to. I captured the magic inside myself."

I sigh, then drop my head and stare at the fishing rod dangling loosely in my hand. There's no sound but the hum of insects in the woods and the soft gurgle of the river as it bends around the bow of our boat. I admitted my guilt, shared my terrible secret, and the world purrs along just like it always has.

"You do it on purpose?" Dreures asks. "Capture the magic the wrong way, that is?"

For one trembling moment, I hesitate. If Dreures is wondering whether or not he can trust me, what I say next could tip the balance. But what choice do I have?

"Yes," I admit, meeting his gaze. "I never planned to return to the Towers."

"Why?" Dreures asks.

Somewhere in the forest, a bird cries. It's a long, mournful sound, like the creature is trying to announce the end of something.

There are so many ways I could answer that question. I could tell him about Kira and how the Towers ripped her life away from her. I could tell him about the ways they tortured the four of us, even while they called us their precious Elites. Hells, I could tell him where the Towers find their magic.

But in the end, I stick with the what's simplest.

"Because I hate the Towers," I reply. "They shouldn't have this magic. Hells, they shouldn't have any magic."

Dreures leans back. The boat rocks slowly as he shakes his head, then crosses his arms over his chest.

"Reznyk Thorne," he begins. "I'll be damned. You know, there are three people in this world who have saved my life."

I keep my mouth shut.

"I married one of them," Dreures continues, "and the other two are in this boat."

I glance at the man sitting by the oars. He stares back at me with no change in his stony expression.

"A place to stay," Dreures says. "Hells, Reznyk. I thought you'd come asking for barrels full of money. But, since you're being so damned modest and reasonable, I'll do you one better."

I lean forward. My pulse shivers in the back of my throat.

"How about I give you a place to stay and a shot at vengeance?" he asks, lifting an eyebrow.

My mouth opens, but I can't quite force words through the sandpaper of my throat.

"The Towers are powerful," Dreures continues. "Powerful people have a tendency to make powerful enemies. There's quite a few out there who'd like to see the Towers burn. When it's time, I could put you in touch with them."

I swallow. I know too much about vengeance for my next words to come easily.

"I won't kill anyone," I say. "Not again. Not anymore."

It feels like an admission of guilt. Dreures just shrugs.

"Figured you wouldn't," Dreures says. "You never were a killer, Reznyk."

I open my mouth to argue, but he cuts me off.

"Oh, sure, you'd do the work," he continues. "But you're not a killer. That's why I trust you."

He pauses, glancing out over the water as though he's looking for the silver fish to reappear.

"You mentioned working for me," he says. "Turns out, I am one of the bastards who'd like to see the Towers burn, and not just for what they did to you. They've got ships running out of the Port now, those sons of bitches. And they think no one can touch them. How about I set you up with a nice place by the water, big enough for you and your friends, and you can use that training you've got to keep an eye on their operation? Maybe you can find out what's going on with those ships. Without killing anyone."

His eyes narrow, and I almost think he might be making a joke. I open my mouth. Close it. Open it again.

"I— I don't know what to say," I stammer.

Dreures laughs. "Start with thank you," he says. "Maybe later on, you can invite me to the wedding."

He makes a spinning gesture with his fingers. The man at the oars takes the fishing rod from my open hand and winds the line around the reel, and it's only after he's guided the boat back to the dock that juts into the swamp from behind Dreures's massive estate and Kira runs down the soft emerald lawn to meet us, that I realize what wedding he's talking about.

"Wedding invitation," I mutter, glancing at Dreures.

He grins. "You two make a cute couple," he says.

"Don't worry," I tell him. "You'll get the first one."

With that, I jump from the boat to the dock and wrap my arms around the woman who saved my life. My partner, my best friend, my lover.

And, someday soon, my wife.

WHAT ABOUT THE CAT?

Would you like to know what happened to Tholious and Marius? Or to that damn cat?

Join Meredith Hart's newsletter at https://dl.bookfunnel.com/4fc9v8w20m for a free bonus scene involving jewelry, wine, and an angry cat in a basket!

SNEAK PEEK AT MONSTER OF THE SILVER CITY

"WHAT DO YOU WANT FROM ME?" I GROWL.

Fyrris blinks, as if the question surprises him. "I would have thought that was obvious," he replies.

I stare at him with what I dearly hope is a ferocious sneer. He sniffs.

"You, Syrus Maganti, are now a reservoir of magic," he says, staring once again at the amulet melted across my chest. "All the magical energy of the old god you murdered is now trapped inside your body. Wondrous, is it not?"

I feel like I've been punched in the gut. I know this, of course, but somehow knowing it and hearing it are two different things. My shoulders curl forward, but I keep my gaze on Fyrris. That bastard.

"The magic inside your body will power the Towers," Fyrris continues. "It's a great honor, really."

Oh. Oh, gods. I try to breathe, but my throat seems to have shrunk. Magic hums inside my neck, and suddenly air forces its way into my lungs. I blink to clear my vision.

Magic is making me breathe. Just like the magic healed the infection that sent red ribbons across my chest, bleeding out of the metal as I, in chains, huddled with the rats in the bilgewater of the Towers's great ship.

The godsdamn magic is keeping me alive. I just wish I knew why.

"A great honor for how long?" I manage to stammer.

Fyrris blinks again. "Why, for the rest of your life, of course."

I drop my head. My vision swims, making the manacles around my wrists float and spin.

For the rest of my life. Fyrris means to keep me prisoner inside the Towers of Silver City forever, to bleed this magic out of me until either the magic or the process of draining it kills me.

So this really is my last chance.

Fyrris and the other Exemplars have to get me from the barge to the Towers, after all. A lot of things could go wrong during that process. Especially now that I know I have nothing left to live for.

"Now, Syrus," Fyrris begins, in what's probably supposed to be a conciliatory tone but sounds instead like he's talking to a small animal. "I want you to understand something."

I blink against the rush of tears, then lift my head. Fyrris's white robe swims before me.

"You will spend the rest of your life inside the Towers," Fyrris continues. "That's not up for debate. But the quality of that life still depends on you."

He leans back in his chair and smiles like he's caught me in another one of his logic puzzles.

"You will serve a very important purpose for the Towers. And, in gratitude, the rest of your life could be quite comfortable."

Comfortable. Magic flares under my skin; I wince at the

burn. Yeah, I'm sure getting this magic drained out of me will be comfortable as fuck. Fyrris nods at the guards holding my chains.

"Bring him to the window, please," Fyrris says. "And bring the spyglass. There's something I want this man to see."

Rough hands wrap around my shoulders, pulling me to my feet. My gut seizes. For a moment, I'm almost glad I have someone holding me up. I stumble, and suddenly I'm bracing myself against the gently rocking wall of the barge and staring out the window at my beloved Silver City.

There are so many ways to die out there. Crushed under a carriage. Drowned in the Ever-Reaching River. My eyes trace the ramparts of the Towers, where a white-clad Exemplar is standing next to a Disciple in gray. Easy to fall from those ramparts, too, and I'd bet there's not a damn thing the magic could do to keep me alive under those circumstances.

Someone presses a cold, smooth cylinder into my hand. I look down to find a rather nice spyglass in my palm.

"Use it," Fyrris says, in a tone that raises the hair on the back of my neck. "See who's in the Towers."

He gives me a smile that is absolutely a trap. The meal I just ate makes another valiant attempt to escape, and my whole body seizes up with the effort of containing it. I choke spiced meat and flatbread back down, force myself to stand up straight, and slowly raise the spyglass to my eye. It's not like I have much of a choice.

My hand is trembling so fiercely that, at first, all I see is a ragged jumble of images. Slate rooftops and open windows and seagulls wheeling against the sky.

But the magic purrs inside me, calming me down, and slowly my city takes shape. I follow the edge of the harbor first, watching sailors and harbor men as they unload crates off barges that I'd never even once considered might hold a chained human being. Or a chained whatever I am now.

Then I turn to the rough edges of the brick buildings along the wharves, to the glinting windows of the dangerous inns and sad little apartments near the water. There's a woman brushing her hair in one of the windows, and I watch her until Fyrris clears his throat impatiently.

Fine. My hands tremble as I raise the spyglass to trace the whitewashed wall that surrounds the Towers. The lower ramparts are empty, but that's not where I'd seen the robed Exemplar, now is it?

I trace the stone walls with the spyglass until a flash of white flutters inside the circle of my vision. I follow it. Robes dance behind the stone of the highest ramparts, billowing in the wind. I turn to the face.

It's Randyll.

I hiss; the metal embedded in my chest suddenly feels hot. Randyll made this damned amulet, the one that shattered and then melted into my flesh and failed to kill me. I turn the spyglass away from him, toward the gray-robed Disciple beside him.

My heart stops.

The spyglass slips from my fingers. Its lens catches the light as it falls, sending a burst of refracted sun through the window like a silver crossbow bolt fired through the heart of an old god, and then it crashes against the floor.

My legs collapse. Magic hisses under my skin as my mind howls and the rough wood of the river barge fills my vision.

"Ah, yes," Fyrris purrs. "Veloria Averyaseth. She was your favorite, wasn't she?"

I don't respond. I can't respond; my heart is trying to

run away from my body, and I'm sucking in my breath as if I'm drowning. Memories burn through me like magic, like the first curls of lightning illuminating a thunderhead as it sails across the Sea of Grass.

A smile in the courtyard, a scrap of parchment folded into a triangle. Her golden hair is longer now, her expression darker, and her robes gray, but by all the stars above, that's her. Veloria is standing on the Towers's ramparts right now.

Her voice comes back to me, carried across the years that have piled up between us. *Are you sure you want this?* she whispered as candlelight traced the lines of her lips, the swell of her breasts.

I've never been more certain about anything in my life, I replied.

How many hours passed between the kiss that followed and my life shattering like a crystal goblet dropped from the highest ramparts? Five? Maybe six?

"Like I said," Fyrris continues, dragging me away from the memory of lips and kisses and whispered promises I never imagined I wouldn't be able to keep. "The quality of your life is up to you. And, incidentally, so is the quality of whatever remains of Ms. Averyaseth's life. Veloria's done quite well within the Towers, you know. She could continue to do well here. If you cooperate."

Monster of the Silver City comes out in May of 2025!

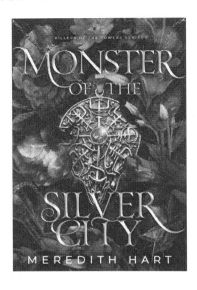

THANK YOU FOR READING!

I'm so glad you decided to join Kira and Reznyk in the Dagger Mountains!

The next book in the series, *Monster of the Silver City*, will follow Syrus and Veloria through the Towers. If you're still wondering where the Towers gets their magic, *Monster of the Silver City* answers that question! It comes out in April of 2025, and you'll find a sneak peek on the next pages.

If you'd like to spend more time in Kira and Reznyk's reality, the *Fallen Hearts* series and the *Deceptions and Dragons* series both take place in this same world.

Finally, if you enjoyed this book, please consider leaving a review. Heck, please consider leaving a review even if you didn't enjoy this book. I'm not picky when it comes to reviews!

Reviews make or break the careers of independent authors like me, and I'll be forever grateful.

ALSO BY MEREDITH HART

ROWAN UNDERVALE IS NOBODY'S HERO.

With dark magic that's made him an outcast, Rowan cares for one person and one person only: his brother Phaedron. When a monster from the Worlds Above attacks his brother, Rowan manages to save Phaedron's life. But when that first monster is followed by a second, this time a woman looking for her prince, Rowan is ready to hand the lady over to the king and be done with monsters forever.

But his brother asks for a favor... so Rowan promises to look after the woman, at least until he can get her back to the Worlds Above. Rowan is certain he'll be able to find a hole in the barrier between their worlds.

But will he be able to let her go?

LADY ARRYN CAME TO THE LAND OF MONSTERS TO RESCUE HER PRINCE.

It's what any lady would do for the man she'd been raised to marry. Besides, rescuing the prince might finally be enough to force the king to agree to the marriage her parents have been trying to arrange for her entire life.

But the frozen Lands Below are nothing like Arryn expected. And Rowan, the brilliant and bitter sentry who is now her only hope of finding her prince or returning to the Worlds Above, possesses strange, horrific magic. What's worse, he treats her far more like an equal than like a lady.

And the most terrifying part is, she's starting to like him.

*Snarky and steamy, **Heart's Rescue** is an enemies-to-lovers adventure with dual point-of-view (his and hers). The first in a complete series of connected stand-alone novels, this sweeping tale of love, survival, and discovery ends with a hard-won Happily Ever After and is perfect for readers looking for a sprinkle of spice in their next swoon-worthy, passionate romantasy.*

∼

LORD VETHE SCARVIAN KNOWS HE ISN'T ONE OF THE GOOD GUYS.

Ever since he was old enough to control his illegal wild-mage talents, Vethe has done horrible things to support his once-noble family. When his aunt hires a guard to help Vethe retrieve a long-lost contract bring in some extra coin, Vethe expects the journey to be short and painful. He's not expecting the guard to be a beautiful woman who looks at him like she wants to strangle him.

And, if she discovers the secrets hiding in his family's past, she just might want to kill him.

LYRIA GUARDIA LET HER FAMILY DOWN AND GOT HER HEART BROKEN.

After she discovers her boyfriend in bed with another woman, Lyria limps back to the family and Guild she'd abandoned three years ago. Desperate to prove herself, she accepts a lowly escort mission: Drag a spoiled nobleman through the abandoned and supposedly harmless Demon Forest. But Lord Vethe, the nobleman she's guiding, is far more infuriating and intriguing than she was expecting. Lyria doesn't know if she can get through this entire mission without slapping him.

Or kissing him.

Sexy, snarky, and fast-paced, **Flame and Blade** *is an enemies-to-lovers fantasy romance with multiple points-of-view and characters who think, act, and curse like adults. A complete, binge-worthy series, this epic adventure of forbidden magic, dangerous monsters, and a love that just might change the world is perfect for readers looking for sword, sorcery, and spice.*

$\sim$

RAYNE CAME TO CAIRNCLIFF TO KILL A DRAGON. NOT TO KISS ONE.

This secret mission is Rayne's chance to finally prove that, despite her gender and her childhood in the orphanage, she can serve the Valgros Royal Army. When she enters a dusty antiquities shop looking for information about the dragon she's been sent to kill, Rayne isn't expecting the gorgeous man behind the counter to take her breath away. And she certainly isn't expecting him to invite her out for wine.

Doshir moved to the sleepy village of Cairncliff to

escape the constant drama of dragon politics, not to mention his cheating ex-girlfriend. When a beautiful woman from the mysterious kingdom of Valgros arrives on his doorstep, Doshir is delighted to be mistaken for a human, and he's even happier to have the chance to seduce a woman who isn't only interested in him because he's a dragon.

But secrets have a way of coming to light, and one night will tie Rayne and Doshir's destinies together in ways neither of them can imagine. In a city where dragons take human form and forbidden magic runs wild, betrayal waits for both the dragons and the dragon hunters.

*Steamy and fast-paced, **A Matter of Dragons** is the first book in a romantic fantasy trilogy with dual point-of-views (his and hers) and characters who think, act, and curse like adults. This sweeping tale of seduction, adventure, found family, and the power of love is perfect for readers who want both high fantasy and high romance in their next read!*

Made in the USA
Columbia, SC
16 April 2025